BARON OF EMBERLY

Louisburg Library
Bringing People and Information Together

BARON OF EMBERLY

The Feud: Book Two

TAMARA LEIGH

The characters and events portrayed in this book are fictitious. Any similarity to real persons, living or dead, is coincidental and not intended by the author.

ISBN: 1942326165
ISBN 13: 9781942326168

TAMARA LEIGH NOVELS

CLEAN READ HISTORICAL ROMANCE
The Feud: A Medieval Romance Series
Baron Of Godsmere: **Book One** 02/15
Baron Of Emberly: **Book Two** 12/15
Baron of Blackwood: **Book Three** 2016

Medieval Romance Series
Lady At Arms: **Book One** 01/14 (1994 Bantam Books
bestseller *Warrior Bride* clean read rewrite)
Lady Of Eve: **Book Two** 06/14 (1994 Bantam Books
bestseller *Virgin Bride* clean read rewrite)

Stand-Alone Medieval Romance Novels
Lady Of Fire 11/14 (1995 Bantam Books best-
seller *Pagan Bride* clean read rewrite)
Lady Of Conquest 06/15 (1996 Bantam Books best-
seller *Saxon Bride* clean read rewrite)
Lady Undaunted Late Winter 2016 (1996 HarperCollins
bestseller *Misbegotten* clean read rewrite)
Dreamspell: **A Medieval Time Travel Romance** 03/12

INSPIRATIONAL HISTORICAL ROMANCE
Age of Faith: A Medieval Romance Series
The Unveiling: **Book One** 08/12
The Yielding: **Book Two** 12/12
The Redeeming: **Book Three** 05/13
The Kindling: **Book Four** 11/13
The Longing: **Book Five** 05/14

INSPIRATIONAL CONTEMPORARY ROMANCE
Head Over Heels: Stand-Alone Romance Novels
Stealing Adda 05/12 (ebook); 2006 (print) NavPress
Perfecting Kate 03/15 (ebook); 2007 (print)
RandomHouse/Multnomah
Splitting Harriet 06/15 (ebook); 2007
(print) RandomHouse/Multnomah
Faking Grace 2015 (ebook); 2008 (print edi-
tion) RandomHouse/Multnomah

Southern Discomfort: A Contemporary Romance Series
Leaving Carolina: **Book One** 11/15 (ebook);
2009 (print) RandomHouse/Multnomah
Nowhere, Carolina: **Book Two** 12/15 (ebook);
2010 (print) RandomHouse/Multnomah
Restless in Carolina: **Book Three** Mid-Winter 2016
(ebook); 2011 (print) RandomHouse/Multnomah

OUT-OF-PRINT GENERAL MARKET TITLES
Warrior Bride 1994 Bantam Books
*Virgin Bride 1994 Bantam Books
Pagan Bride 1995 Bantam Books
Saxon Bride 1995 Bantam Books
Misbegotten 1996 HarperCollins
Unforgotten 1997 HarperCollins
Blackheart 2001 Dorchester Leisure

*Virgin Bride is the sequel to *Warrior Bride*
Pagan Pride and *Saxon Bride* are stand-alone novels

www.tamaraleigh.com

1

Barony of Blackwood, Northern England
Mid-Spring, 1334

SHE LIKED TO imagine she entered the lair of a beast. It excited her, though not as it had in years past. But then, she *had* tamed this particular beast—clipped its claws and dulled its teeth. Somewhat.

Hand on the door, Thomasin listened for voices on the other side. It was quiet but for an occasional muttering. Either something so bedeviled the beast that he could not contain his irritation, or his dreams were of such weight he spoke aloud his hauntings. Regardless, he was alone, meaning she was welcome—rather, tolerated, which was as near as one could come who was as disliked as the misbegotten Thomasin de Arell.

Disliked, but no longer hated, she mused with satisfaction that would have warranted a smile were it not best to enter without even the suggestion of happiness upon her lips.

She gave a quick rap, counted to twenty as further required, and opened the door.

The chamber was dully lit, evidencing some of the shuttered windows had been latched back and the one who more often dwelt amid the glow of candles was better of body and milder of mind than usual. Though such a mood presented less of a challenge, on this day and with these tidings, she did not mind. Were she bored, she might feel different.

She stepped inside, closed the door, and leaned against it. The room was second in size only to the great hall belowstairs. Extravagant, some would say—those whose lives had few boundaries—but in this instance, it was more a necessity for one who had once known the depth and breadth of these lands and enjoyed sufficient wealth to exploit their every corner. Now, as he was wont to grumble, his life was lived on the point of a great mountain. This chamber. In Castle Mathe. Upon the barony of Blackwood. In the vastness of England. In a world through which he would never again swing a sword.

"My father—your son—is displeased," she said of the brooding man she had left belowstairs, the same who had unwittingly fathered her while a squire of ten and six years of age.

The silence that followed was expectant. Somewhere beyond the floor-to-ceiling hangings that rippled and fluttered in the breeze that dared enter this place, was the one she had once thrillingly feared.

"Fiend?" she called.

Still he gave no answer, though what she named him ought to arouse some anger—mock, of course, for the expression born of mutual dislike had long ago become nearly an affection. Nearly, for who could truly care for one such as he?

I do, she silently admitted what she could not speak lest he wielded it against her.

"What say ye, fiend?" she tried again, deliberately slipping into the commoner's speech he detested.

"I have a name," he rebuked.

Ulric de Arell, reviled by the neighboring barons who, for twenty and more years, had been his adversaries. Soon, marriage would make them his family's allies.

Moving in the direction of his voice that sounded from beyond the curtained bed, Thomasin gave the usual response. "For me, that name is *Grandfather,* but since ye deny me its use just as ye deny me *my* proper name, fiend it be."

The hanging that partitioned off the far end of the chamber rustled, indicating he stood before the window affording him the best view of all that was no longer his to command. Well before her existence had been made known to the De Arells four years past and she had come to Castle Mathe, Ulric had been forced to relinquish the barony to her father, Griffin. And that loss remained a heavy one.

With slow, considered steps, he came around the hanging. Between the edges of the embroidered shawl draped over his head, she could just make sense of his shadowed features, evidence he did not wear the carved mask that put an eerie, though relatively comely, face on the ravaged one he allowed none but the physician to gaze upon.

"Is this to be a tediously long or blessedly short visit?" he asked.

She lowered her gaze to where his tunic swept the floor. The garment was longer than most, but there was purpose to it—to conceal legs either misshapen or emaciated. Of added benefit, the tunic provided cover for the small creature who often traveled beneath it. It did not do so out of fear, well capable of being as bold as the wolfhounds in the hall below. Rather, affection and mischief caused it to so closely seek its master's side.

"Well?" her grandfather demanded. "Tedious or blessed?"

"No need to get all twitched," she snapped. "I can tell what ye wish told in but a few minutes."

"But you will not."

She *did* have an abundance of words about her, though they were not beyond her control as most believed. She knew when to leash and when to loose them. Mostly.

She made an exaggerated *tsk*. "If ye be content with bein' the last to know what I know, I can leave."

"Cease with that vulgar tongue, girl. Speak proper!"

There. Now that he had exerted his superiority, they could proceed more civilly. "I shall do me—er, *my*—best."

— 3 —

With a hand whose glove could not entirely hide its bunched affliction, he motioned toward the stool she was made to perch upon when she visited. As uncomfortable as it was, it was a better arrangement than when she had initially ventured to the uppermost floor her father had forbidden her. That first year, her grandfather had taken no such precautions, drawing near enough that she could smell and feel his breath. Only later had she realized it had been done in the hope she would be struck down by the disease that isolated him.

"Sit, Sin," he commanded.

Sin, what most would think an abomination of *Thomasin,* and which he had named her for the wrong her father had committed in begetting a child on a commoner—more, for claiming her as a De Arell. Not that she minded the name. It made her feel naughty, something it would be interesting to explore beyond her penchant for improprieties that others—nobles, mostly—deemed sinful.

But she gave her grandfather his due, making a show of irritation by flicking her eyes heavenward as she lowered to the hard seat. "Should I begin, or would you first seek your own comfort?" She nodded at the overstuffed armchair that ensured him as much ease as possible.

"As I have been sitting much of the day, I shall stand." He took another step forward, so labored her eyes were drawn to a tall, elaborately carved wardrobe against which her latest offering was propped—one of dozens of walking sticks she had foraged from the wood and pared down. Wonderfully gnarled and twisted through with light and dark grains, it was much like the man for whom it had been fashioned. As with its predecessors, it would be tested by fire. And fail. However, providing he did not toss it on the flames in her presence as he had done with the first, she could bear it.

"Now, tell—" His voice cracked, and with much effort, he cleared his throat. "For what is my son displeased?"

The hem of his tunic ruffled, and the creature's front paws peeked out from beneath, evidencing it had settled in where its master had halted ten feet distant from her.

Thomasin drew up her legs, wrapped her arms around her knees, and tilted back until she balanced on her rear. Terribly unlike a lady. "A missive has come from King Edward."

"Its contents?"

Telling herself she was not disturbed by the tidings, that she would make the best of what was asked of her to keep the king's displeasure from falling on her father and his people, she said, "It speaks of the next marriage to be made." Three in total that would see the De Arells, Boursiers, and Verduns wed into one another's families in the expectation such alliances would end their feuding.

The Boursier—as that baron was better known, a name in which Thomasin delighted—had wed Lady Elianor of the Verduns nearly six months past. Therefore, the next marriage was to be between Thomasin's father, Baron De Arell, and Quintin Boursier. The final marriage, several months from now, was to have been her own with Baron Verdun. But the king's missive set all on its head.

Ulric de Arell's growl was echoed by a growl from the one whose paws quivered. "Then the time has come for the house of De Arell to unite with the Boursiers," he spat. "My blood ever fouled."

"Further fouled," she reminded him of what he had oft said of her, and would have been secretly pleased it was no longer fast off his lips if not for what the missive told.

She breathed deep. "But first it shall be Verdun blood that offends."

His startle was so large, it caused the shawl to slip off his brow. In the moment before he snatched the material forward, she saw the pale and dark patches on his face. The last time she had been afforded a glimpse, the disfigurement had featured on his cheeks and nose, but now also his brow and chin. And she secretly hurt for him, for he would not tolerate pity, especially from one who was more to be pitied for the noble blood infected by the common blood scuttling through her veins.

Using the least deformed hand she had not seen out of a glove these past two years, he jerked one trailing end of the shawl across the lower half of his face and settled it over the opposite shoulder to prevent it from slipping again.

If not that she listened for his breath of relief, she would not have heard it. Once more as formidable as it was possible for a perishing man to be, he crossed his arms over his chest. "So the Boursier termagant is granted another delay in wedding your father." It was said with rancor so keen, it reminded her of when he had truly hated her.

She released her knees, set her feet to the middle rung, and leaned forward. "'Tis said Lady Quintin continues to mourn her mother."

His snort became a cough so wracking, she tensed to keep from bounding off the stool and pounding him between the shoulders. When he recovered, he seemed a smaller man, a bow to his back and slump to his shoulders that caused the tunic to puddle over the paws.

"The time for mourning is months past," he said. "Nay, what that woman does is roll the dice well."

There could be truth in that, but during Lady Quintin's captivity at Castle Mathe last Christmas, Thomasin had been afforded many occasions to observe the slightly older woman and several to converse with her, and the lady had not seemed one to feign weakness—she who had drawn a dagger on Thomasin's formidable father.

"'Tis told her mother was murdered," Thomasin said, though still it was hard to accept, for the woman who had befriended Thomasin years past had played a large part in that wickedness. "That can be no easy thing." *Especially,* Thomasin silently added, *had Maeve Boursier been a devoted mother. Unlike mine.*

"Regardless," her grandfather snarled, "you shall pay the price for the king's indulgence of that heathen woman."

Despite what this day's tidings portended, a smile so determinedly tugged at Thomasin that she dropped her chin lest he catch sight of it.

"Something amuses you?" he demanded.

Letting a bit of the smile move her mouth, she looked up. "Careful, else I will think you are concerned for my wellbeing—indeed, more than you are concerned for that of your most noble son who, by the theft of my last months of freedom, has been granted a stay of marriage to that *heathen*."

She could not see his glower, but she felt it.

"Or perhaps you truly are concerned," she dared, "meaning you no longer consider me throw away." It *was* as he had named her the first time she had stolen into his chamber.

He shifted his weight, and she heard his groan of discomfort, saw the stagger in the step he took to remain upright, and caught the patter of paws.

Once more suppressing the longing to force the walking stick on him, she curled her toes in her slippers.

"As you now carry my name," he said, "and I am without recourse, I have reason to be offended by the game the king plays against the De Arells."

"But surely you have greater cause to be gladdened that all the sooner I will no longer carry your name."

He lowered his arms to his sides, and she saw his gloved hands curl into fists that could no longer return a person to a place beneath him. "Though you wed a Verdun, still all will know you for a De Arell."

And for that, her father was to blame, though the widest portion of the chasm between Griffin and Ulric had been dug by the revelation the latter was responsible for the disappearance of Thomasin's mother when it was discovered the chambermaid was with child.

Feeling a pang, Thomasin thrust aside thoughts of the one who had birthed her and stood. "Ere you further weary of me, I shall bid you good day."

"When is your marriage to take place?"

"The king wishes it done within a fortnight. But since the delivery of the missive was delayed, only a sennight remains ere I wed."

He slowly nodded. "Then I will see you no more."

Was that regret? If so, did it go beyond the diversion she provided in the midst of a painful, monotonous existence?

Telling herself it was useless to ponder, she said, "You are wrong. With or without my husband's consent, I shall return to Castle Mathe on occasion."

That said, she wondered if it was only wishful. She had believed herself adept at slipping unseen outside the castle, but months past had learned her father merely pretended he did not know of her excursions. To ease his concern, he ever had a knight follow at a distance—so discreetly that, until her eventful meeting in the wood with *The Boursier* last winter, she had not suspected the presence of Sir Otto, who had been forced to reveal himself to defend her. Now, she was ever aware of being followed, though she did not reveal it lest a better means of escaping her notice was devised. As for her betrothed, if Magnus Verdun tried to cage her within Castle Kelling's walls, she would seek a way out.

"So I am not to be entirely rid of you," her grandfather said. "Pity."

Deciding to swing the sword back at him, she said, "As I am the only one who seems to enjoy visiting you, I would think you grateful."

Her words roused another startle, but this time the shawl did not betray him. "You would have me believe you enjoy my company?"

"Oh, have mercy! For what else would I subject myself to your unkindnesses? Like it or nay, I am more of you than my father is." She pointed to her face. "And methinks you do not mind peering into this mirror as much as you would have me believe."

Though she had never had the opportunity to fully explore his chamber, there was one thing of which she was fairly certain—the absence of mirrors in the face of his disease.

When he did not respond, she turned away. "Good noon, fiend."

"Thomasin!"

She came back around so fast it shamed her. Like a dog eager to be pardoned for disappointing its master, there she stood, breathlessly awaiting further confirmation of the acceptance he denied her.

Fool that I am, she silently rebuked and forced a laugh. "Thomasin? Surely I did not hear right."

His hands at his sides opened as if still capable of splaying, then slowly returned to their huddled selves. "Beware the Verduns. They are like molten metal, recasting their shapes one pour to the next."

Then Thomasin the dog was not to be pardoned—at least, not fully. "You speak of my betrothed's father."

"A man I was well enough acquainted with to know the son is as treacherously changeable."

Ever switching sides between the De Arells and the Boursiers, it was said of the deceased Rand Verdun.

Thomasin crossed to the door.

"And their minds are not right," he called with what seemed desperation.

She looked around. "I shall take your warning into account... *Grandfather*."

Beneath the cover of his shawl, he was not vulnerable to expression, but she felt something in the air. And it was not antagonism. Not even dislike.

But this time he let her go, and she quietly closed the door. Telling herself that what he had given her was enough and she had too much with which to occupy herself to spend more time upon their peculiar relationship, she traversed the corridor. And with none the wiser she had yet again penetrated the forbidden chamber, she slipped belowstairs.

The once and nevermore Baron of Blackwood stared at the door, on the other side of which stood life. Winding corridors down which to walk. Wide spaces through which to ride. Worthy men with whom to war. Welcoming women over whom to linger. And family who did not understand him and rejected him for it—above all, his heir.

His son and he had never been close, but there was a time it had been better between them—before Griffin learned the truth of the pretty chambermaid whom Ulric had sent away upon learning she sought to capture a besotted young nobleman with a babe.

The fool girl had not realized that were it even a possibility, the Baron of Blackwood would have, instead, named his second son heir. Not that Serle had shown better judgment. Perhaps worse, for his downfall had been a Verdun woman.

Ulric ground his teeth. This was not how he had envisioned the outcome of the betrayal of his liege twenty-five years past when Verdun and Boursier had stood with him and all three were awarded lands of their own. His allies-turned-enemies were now dead, but their sons kept the feud burning. A feud King Edward was determined to end by entwining the families through marriage. And not even the common blood tainting the noble could save Thomasin.

Aye, *Thomasin*, as Ulric had somehow come to think of her. He had not wished to feel anything but disgust for the young woman, but over the course of her many visits, something had made him aware of this thing that yet beat in his breast.

Only men weak of mind gave otherworldly attributes to an organ whose sole purpose was to push blood from one part of the body to another and, when a man's life was done, stop pushing, but he had come to feel something for one who was undeserving of it. Fortunately, he could be forgiven, for this disease was responsible, leaving him almost as weak of mind as of body. And more and more making him long for one thing.

"Quietus," he said—rather, mouthed. Repulsed, he loudly cleared his throat and gained enough voice to speak unto his ears, "Quietus." An exquisite word for death, a release from life that, for those hale of body, was a terrible thing. But not so for one mortally ill of body.

He growled, and the small dog beneath his hem nudged its nose forward and emerged with a long, stretching crawl punctuated by a yawn that revealed tiny, sharp teeth.

"Ah, Diot." Ulric started to bend down, but a wave of darkness swept him, and he braced his legs apart and drew full breaths. When the black receded and his vision was restored, he looked to the wardrobe containing the bulk of his earthly goods.

The walking stick propped there called to him, as did every one of those relics of fallen trees Thomasin had delivered over the years. Unbeknownst to her, only the first was absent from his hoard. Also unknown to her was that he used them, though only when none were near to witness the humiliation.

Movement drew his gaze to Diot who rocked back and forth on his haunches as he prepared to scale the bed. Astute as always, the dog sensed its master would not long remain upright.

"A moment," Ulric muttered and shuffled forward, each drag of his feet making him once more question God for sentencing him to this misery.

For what do I deserve this? he spoke heavenward. *I have done no worse than most—only what was needed to survive. Aye, to survive well, but am I not noble? Are not great things required of me that are not required of my lessers? Great things do not come without cost. Your Son knew that. I know that. What has so offended Thee that I deserve this wide-awake death?*

No reply, and no longer was one expected.

Once he had in hand a stronger appendage than his arms and legs combined, he leaned heavily on Thomasin's gift and opened the door of the wardrobe. Pushing aside floor-skimming tunics hung from hooks, he eyed the walking sticks stacked upright in the back corner. Most were crude and simple, but a few were handsome.

Not that he thought them precious, these things fashioned by and for a commoner, but they had been given to him without asking for anything in return—except, perhaps, the company Thomasin professed to enjoy.

Why did she continue to seek him out? Though he no longer put forth an effort to be cruel to her, neither was he kind. And yet, ever she returned, satisfying his appetite for tidings of what went belowstairs and in the villages beyond, revealing more than Griffin who less often ascended to this chamber.

Telling himself it did not matter what lured her to the tomb of a leper, Ulric started to close the wardrobe's door. And paused. He stared at the light running up a silver wedge behind the walking sticks, told himself to ignore it, then retrieved that vile thing.

As he raised it before his face, bile surged. Choking it down, grateful to keep its burn clear of his lungs, he pushed the shawl off his brow.

The mirror revealed him in all his leprous glory. And there was Thomasin in the spaces between decay, sores, and swellings. Though he had been fiercely opposed to declaring her a De Arell, arguing it was impossible to be certain she was of their blood, Griffin had been determined to claim her—even before setting eyes on her. As the recently titled Baron of Blackwood, he had prevailed.

Though Thomasin bore several of her father and grandfather's features, it was the unnaturally blue De Arell eyes that convinced Ulric she would not live had he never lived. And quite fortunate she was to have been born with those eyes, for they were her only exceptional feature. Had they been the muddy brown of her harlot of a mother, she would be so plain of face she would sit on the fence between pretty and not pretty. Entirely unremarkable.

Woe to Magnus Verdun, Ulric silently feigned lament for one who was even more cursed with a handsome face and frame than the father had been. But if there was a way to ensure future Verduns were better known for their prowess at arms than mastery of a mirror, Thomasin's union with the Baron of Emberly ought to make it so.

Had any told Verdun what to expect when his betrothed was presented? Ulric hoped not—wished he could witness his enemy's reaction upon discovering he would be bound to a woman who was not only far from his equal in blood but in beauty. However, the pleasure Ulric took in such imaginings dissolved when it occurred to him that the greater Verdun's displeasure, the more strongly Thomasin would see and feel it. If Verdun humiliated her—

"What?" he rasped low. "You will what, you feeble excuse for a man?"

He thrust the mirror into the wardrobe, slammed the door, and jabbed the point of his walking stick to the floor to more quickly propel himself toward the bed where Diot had made himself comfortable. As

Ulric stretched out on the coverlet, he caught sight of his leper's mask on the bedside table and fought the longing to fling it across the chamber.

Clasping the stick to his chest, he fixed his gaze on the gathered canopy that seemed a wall between heaven and him.

"You are not going to let me in, are You, Lord?" he mostly mouthed, and Diot, sensing the distress Ulric did not wish to acknowledge, rolled up against his master's side.

Setting a gloved hand on the creature's belly, Ulric returned his thoughts to his granddaughter.

After a time, his sluggish, aching mind conceived. The knight most often entrusted to follow Thomasin when she ventured outside these walls must accompany her to Castle Kelling and remain with her. Thus, Sir Otto could keep those of Castle Mathe apprised of how she fared. And Griffin, who liked to gainsay his father, would not refuse the old baron this one thing—providing he believed the idea was his, for it would not do for him to know how soft his father had gone where Thomasin was concerned.

A good plan. Now to see it done.

2

⸺◦◦◦⸺

THOMASIN CONSIDERED THE great edifice rising above the town laid out
before it. There she was expected to live out her days titled Lady of
Emberly, she who was to have aspired to no higher than a chambermaid.
Or so the steward of Waring Castle had believed, just as he had thought it
his right to pursue the girl she had been four years past. But she had possessed something his other prey had not. Beyond the temerity to defend
herself, she knew how to use the glistening ink at the tip of a quill—a
skill hidden from those who would not have approved, and known only
by the one who had made it possible. She who was no more.

Swallowing sorrow, Thomasin glanced over her shoulder to confirm
no others had happened upon this portion of the wood. All was still. Too
still?

When she had shed Castle Mathe this morn, she had not intended
to venture this far, but impulse had struck as she moved through the village of Cross distributing bread. Prompted by the knowledge she would
leave her father's lands five days hence, and the galling presence of the
one who kept watch over her, she had borrowed a horse from the miller
and put heels to it.

She did not doubt that the one who followed her, likely Sir Otto, had
also obtained a mount, but not before she had gained a league or more
on him. Had he known her destination, he could have overtaken her due
to her fair horsemanship, but she had bested him. As he deserved to be.

Aye, he who skulked after her outside the castle walls, who had little to do with her inside them, who had looked too long and often upon her father's betrothed, Quintin Boursier—

"Fie on ye, Thomasin," she rebuked. Jealousy benefitted her naught. Had she the beauty of Lady Quintin, therefore a chance to catch the handsome knight's attention, perhaps it would be worth churning up her insides and risking disdain. But as her mother had oft said—one of few remembrances of that woman Thomasin had not abandoned as she had been abandoned—one ought not wish where wishes were prey.

She caught back a laugh. She *had* wished, as well as prayed, though not for a man to look well upon her. A better life was what she had longed for, away from orders she resented, given by those who pinched and prodded her as if she were freshly baked bread to be granted no more thought beyond satisfying a man's immediate hunger.

Miraculously, her wishes and prayers had been answered, and chafe though she sometimes did over her father's control, a far better life he had given her. Rather than dirtying her hands amid the foul things others left behind, she was a lady whose hands were to be kept busy with the offices of sewing and weaving and resting prettily in her lap. And now…

She returned Castle Kelling to focus. Now her half-noble blood would become intimate with the full-noble blood of a baron—of handsome note, she understood. More handsome than Sir Otto?

Though she told herself she did not care what her husband thought of her and that marriage to her was more than a traitorous Verdun deserved, she felt a nervous flutter. Regardless of what his face revealed and what words he spoke when first they met, she would not flinch. She would clasp to her the blessing in being bereft of beauty—that one did not have to struggle to match what was inside to what was outside. And if he ill-treated her, he would discover she was noble enough of mind to retaliate.

"I shall not be afeared," she whispered and looked to the sky in the spaces between the canopy of brilliant leaves. From the village of Cross, it had taken two hours to reach the home of her betrothed. Thus, two hours back to return the horse, and another hour on foot, would see her at Castle Mathe by late afternoon. Though it was possible she would not be missed, her father confident she was in the care of his knight, it was also possible the knight had returned home to report she had evaded him.

Averse to starting back, she pondered what Griffin de Arell would do if he learned she was missing. It had been quiet of late upon the three baronies, almost as if the threat of last Christmas had never been.

Almost, for murder had come. It was not known for certain who had killed Lady Maeve Boursier, but the woman Thomasin had thought was her friend—Aude to her, Agatha to others—had been involved. And though Aude was now dead herself, it was believed there were others who wanted what the woman had failed to deliver—revenge against the De Arells, Verduns, and Boursiers whose betrayal had caused the once immense barony of Kilbourne to be divided into lesser baronies to reward the three vassals who had exposed their lord's treachery.

Aye, all was quiet, so perhaps the threat no longer existed. Perhaps any left behind to stir the longstanding feud between the three families was forever gone.

She wanted to believe it, especially in that moment, for it would mean the difference between starting back now or later.

Later, she decided. She had come this far and been this long missing, so what were a few more hours that could be spent exploring the demesne she would eventually traverse as she did Blackwood? Even if her sire responded by increasing her guard such that she could go nowhere unescorted, she would not suffer it long.

"Five days, Magnus Verdun," she said, imagining him somewhere inside those walls. "Then you will be my problem. As I may prove yours."

The *lady* could not have made it much easier, mused the one who had watched her since this morn when she had stolen out of the castle.

The plan had been to take her to ground after she departed the village of Cross, but she had borrowed a horse and headed opposite—here, to the home of the one she was to wed. *Was.*

Throughout her ride, there had been opportunities to bring her to ground when she veered off the road into the wood to avoid travelers, and he had been tempted to give the signal. But a need to scratch his months-long boredom had made him linger over her fate. Thus, he had allowed her to draw near Castle Kelling, though only because the one who lorded it had two days past gone to the village over the eastern border of the barony of Kilbourne—this portion of which the grasping Verduns had named Emberly.

Bile surged, and he let it bathe his teeth before spitting it out.

Emberly. Blackwood. Godsmere. By those names and the actions of the three who had betrayed Baron Denis Foucault, Kilbourne was debased. But it would rise again once he dealt with those who did not know they were dead men—and women.

Singing returned his attention to the lady, and he tensed in recognition of the pastorela that told of a nobleman who pursued a shepherdess with flattery and deception to convince her to lie down with him—a not uncommon pursuit, though it was sometimes the shepherdess who convinced the nobleman to lie with her.

This was not the first time he had heard the song from Griffin de Arell's misbegotten brat, it having been taught her by the woman who had befriended her years past.

Fear not, Aude, he silently assured the presence that had fastened itself to his back after her passing. *Her end will be as cruel as yours.*

Seeing his prey turn her horse aside to follow the road from the cover of the bordering trees, he signaled the others to hold. They would assist the *lady* in dismounting once she went deeper into the wood where none but judge and jury would hear her cries—of which there would be a goodly amount since he was not the only one bored with waiting.

Soon, he told himself, for she had not yet watered her mount and it must be done. But as they trailed her, she did not stay the road that led back the way she had come. She took the one branching left toward the village just over the border, the same Magnus Verdun visited once and twice a month.

Pleased to know that baron's secret, the watcher narrowed his eyes on Thomasin de Arell. He did not think she had lost her way, having observed her often enough to know she had a good sense of the land and made use of the sun's position to guide her. Thus, she was not done with her venture—else she had no intention of returning to Castle Mathe, this being her escape from marriage.

That gave him pause, but he shook it off. To her detriment, he would have to insist she accept his aid to ensure no marriage was made between the houses of Verdun and De Arell, for he could not risk failing as Aude had done in the marriage between the Boursiers and Verduns. Too, he could not resist the possibility that suspicion for the death of the low-born woman would fall on Magnus Verdun. Not necessary, but it would be a pretty boon—of which Aude would approve.

He sighed over memories of the woman who had sung the pastorela and had once tempted him to intimacy, that same dead thing he had fished from the frozen lake following her failure. Ah well, she had served her purpose. Mostly.

3

A VILLAGE LIKELY lay in this direction, as evidenced by the occasional footprint in moist earth, a partially-hidden trap awaiting a creature destined for the pot, and scraps and threads that thorns and rough bark had snatched from the garments of those who passed too near.

Thomasin once more looked around and decided to venture farther east another league. If the village did not come into view, she would begin the journey home.

She stepped to her mount and patted its neck bent low over the stream it had been necessary to venture deep into the wood to find. "Enough?" she said.

It continued to drink, and she rebuked herself for not sooner leading it to water. Just as she had much to learn of handling horses, she must become better versed in their care.

Her own thirst satisfied, she swept her gaze over the ground. She should not bother, and yet she began searching for a walking stick worthy enough that her grandfather would give his weight unto it.

A dozen paces from the stream, she found one whose lower reaches were sunk in the loam. Of good size, she determined as she freed it. She brushed the soil away and was pleased with its character—of a golden color from its bulbous hilt that would fit well the palm, to its thick tip that required little shortening and would not skitter out from beneath one who leaned on it.

Smiling, she swung around. And the breath went out of her.

Two men, wearing the garb and arms of warriors, stood before her mount. And beyond them, on the other side of the stream, another was seated on a great stallion between two riderless horses. Had she time to look nearer at one who was likely of the nobility with such a mount beneath him, she did not think she could have made out his features owing to the distance and the tree's immense shadow falling over him. But that could not be tested, for the two men this side of the stream advanced.

Though she longed to flee, on foot it would be a token resistance. "What do you want?" she demanded.

Neither gave an ugly, knowing smile like that which the steward had often slanted at her, but she was not so fool to think they were different. She was a woman alone in a wood, and this time, unlike when she had come face-to-face with *The Boursier*, Sir Otto was not here to protect her.

"I am..." She swallowed. "...Lady Thomasin of Blackwood. My father is Baron de Arell." She hated vaunting her status, but other than teeth, fingernails, and a stick that would prove a pitiful defense, it seemed her only weapon.

"Aye, you are," the bearded one rasped.

He knew? Or was this mockery? She jerked her head in the direction from which she had come. "I am betrothed to Baron Verdun of Castle Kellin'."

"Kellin', eh?" said the bald, stubble-faced one, exaggerating the commoner's turn of word into which she had lapsed.

Was that her heart in her throat, so large it felt as if she would choke?

Quiet thyself, she silently counseled. *Watch your words and behave the lady, else this could go worse than wrong.*

She set the stick's tip to the ground. "Five days hence, I am to wed the Baron of Emberly upon whose lands ye stand."

They halted ten feet distant, and she felt a flush of relief.

"Wed?" one said. "We think not. Now all you must do is decide how unpleasant you wish this."

Dear God, she silently beseeched, *help me.*

"What say you?" the bearded one asked.

Thomasin shot her gaze to the one who watched from afar. "Sir Knight," she called, "if ye see me safely returned to my father, ye will be rewarded."

He remained unmoving.

She looked back at his companions. "All of ye will be rewarded."

"Alas"—the bald one jerked his head toward the one who remained astride—"I answer to another." Then he and his companion strode forward.

She had just enough time to jump aside and raise the stick. Gripping it with both hands, she used it to stir the air between them. "Come no nearer!"

"Pity this must be so unpleasant," the bearded one said and lunged, ducked beneath her next swing, and came up in front of her.

She stumbled back, gaining enough space to swing again. This time, she landed a blow, but not to the one at whom she aimed. The stick caught the bald one alongside the head, and she glimpsed a slash of crimson near his left eye as he wrenched the weapon from her.

The rough wood tore across her palms as it left them, and she knew there would be blood and stinging pain, but before either was seen or felt, her assailant turned the stick on her. The first strike caught her on the shoulder and finished its arc against her ear.

She screamed—or tried to, for if she had voice, she could not hear it above the ringing in her head.

Then she was dealt a hit to the ribs.

She loosed another scream, and as all began to blur, doubled over. Or was she already down? Curled on her side? All she knew for certain was that hands were on her, and no matter how she struggled, her only gain was more strikes and punches to the face and ribs.

Then weight fell upon her, and in the breaths drawn between screams, she inhaled the odor of a long-unwashed body.

As she continued to bite, claw, and kick, the men began shouting, and there was distant satisfaction in knowing that even in defeat, she could mark them for their sins—their flesh bruised, blood beneath her fingernails, soft places pained.

Amid a pounding of hooves, their shouts rose, and she became aware of the weight lifting from her and removal of the hands that had touched where they should not. But as her senses struggled to right themselves, she felt warm air upon her legs before the yank of her skirts that surely preceded the first sensation.

Dear Lord, preserve me, and by my words and actions I shall aspire higher, she silently vowed, and opened her eyes.

"Cur!" she shrieked at the one who loomed over her, though not as near as when she had last looked upon him. "Miscreant!"

His words were harsh and forceful, but the only one she made sense of was, "Cease!"

Attempting to keep her consciousness above dark waters, she saw enough of his wavering face to realize the one reaching for her was neither of the two who had beaten her to the ground.

This, then, the one who had watched from astride his horse. Now he would take what his men had gained for him. But she was not done fighting. And suddenly she had an abundance of means to defend herself.

No longer pinned, her arms were free to reach and rake, legs to kick. Though her head was too pained to allow her to look clearly on her assailant, when her knee struck hard muscle and she sank nails into stubbled flesh, there was no mistaking the baring of his teeth and tightening of a face too handsome to be fastened on a devil.

"Fie on ye!" she spat, and again reached with hooked hands.

He caught her wrists together and lowered his face near enough for the steel gray of his eyes to be told and the strangely pleasant scent of his body to be breathed.

"Me father'll kill ye!" she shrieked over whatever threats he made. "Gut ye like the pig ye are!"

As the spit of his angry response flecked her face, she strained her back upward, then dropped to the ground and thrust her head toward his descending one.

There was a crack as of lightning near enough to burst one's ears, and like the clouds through which it sounded, it dimmed her world.

"Pray, do not," she whimpered as she was swept deeper and darker. "I am to…wed."

Magnus Verdun knew it was possible to be angrier than he was in that moment, but not outwardly so—at least, not easily.

As he filled his lungs and slowly exhaled to bring his mind and body under control, he watched the woman's lashes flutter and lips part on a sigh.

She had been beaten, this one who appeared to have ventured alone to the wood, her sullied and torn garments the least of her worries. The greater concern was the injury to her head, and not just the one he had shared with her when she believed him a party to her attack. Beneath scratches and smears of dirt were swellings and bright spots likely to present as bruises. Of further concern was whether or not her assailants had wrested from her what she had obviously refused them.

The one holding her to the ground had been the first against whom Magnus struck when, having followed her screams, he thundered his mount onto the scene. It had been no easy thing to allow to flee the one who watched his companions seek to ravish the young woman. But Magnus had granted it all the sooner to stop the one who had her skirts up.

The thrown dagger had served, though only just, for his mark had not been the shoulder into which the blade stuck. His horse's movement had denied him the center of the back that would have laid down the bald man and allowed Magnus to give his full attention to the second one drawing a sword.

Guiding his horse with the press of his thighs, Magnus had veered away, those extra moments giving him time to bring his own sword to hand and counter the bearded one's thrust. Thrice he had come around, and twice his blade let crimson that also marked him. But death was not to be for that one any more than the other. The bald man had made it astride and spurred toward the woman as if to trample her.

Magnus had sent his own mount into that one's path, saving her, but gifting the bearded one with time in which to gain his own saddle. Then he and the other had set off after their companion who had first fled.

Now Magnus had an injured and unconscious woman on his hands. And the sooner she was tended, the better. But he could not convey her to Castle Kelling, not because it was more distant than the village he had departed this morn, but because of the one he had hidden in the undergrowth before answering this woman's cries.

He gathered up the seemingly slight woman and found her firmly built. Not that she was weighty. Rather, she lacked the fragile, fine-boned frame he expected. Whatever work she did, it put muscle on strong bones.

He lifted her onto his horse, draped her over its neck, and swung up behind her. As he drew her limp form back into his arms, his gaze fell on the flecks of blood staining his tunic. They were not his own, and it took effort to move his senses elsewhere, but he did and frowned over the scent of violets wafting from hair of lightest brown. She was no common laborer, as further evidenced by garments that, though simple and now near ruin, were far from worn. Too, whatever her destination, she had not come on foot. A merchant's daughter or wife, he guessed.

He nudged his mount toward the horse by the stream—an animal far from fine—caught up its reins, and setting it to a gallop, guided it back the way he had come.

Minutes later, the one he called forth poked his head above a tall shrub. "Who is that?" asked the wide-eyed boy of seven and some.

"I know not, but the sooner you show me you know how to mount a horse"—Magnus jerked his head toward the riderless one—"the sooner your mother can tend this woman's injuries."

As the boy emerged, he raised his strung bow over his head and settled it diagonally shoulder to hip. "Who did that to her?"

"Again, I know not, Eamon. I but stopped them from doing worse." It was true he could not name her attackers, but the boy need not be told of the suspicion that the months-long respite following the death of the woman he now knew to be named Aude as well as Agatha, could be at an end. He prayed not, but that lone figure watching his lessers from astride a fine horse boded ill.

"Did you kill them?" Eamon asked, flushing with excitement as his gaze took in the blood upon Magnus.

"I did not, but they are done for—will surely seek other lands upon which to work their ill. Now make haste. We shall continue our hunt another day."

It proved a challenge for the boy to mount the woman's horse, for what the animal lacked in beauty and youth, it made up for in height. But shortly, Eamon accepted the reins. "May I lead the way?"

Magnus might have allowed it if not for those who were yet somewhere in this wood. "Another day. This day, stay near."

Nanne straightened and turned her back on the woman Magnus had laid upon her pallet. "She will come out of the black, but she will be one great ache and unsightly fer a time."

Magnus finished fastening his sword belt around the clean tunic he had donned while her back was turned. "You can care for her?"

"As well as anyone, I suppose."

"Then I will leave you to it." He nearly disregarded the blood-stained tunic he had dropped on a stool, but swept it to hand and started to turn away.

Nanne's sharply indrawn breath halted him.

"Forgive me," he said. "I know I said I would remain through the morrow, but I must return to Castle Kelling to ensure the brigands who did this can work no more ill upon Emberly."

"But Eamon so looked forward to—"

"As did I. He says he understands."

Her mouth tightened. "As ye will, then."

Magnus set a hand on her shoulder, lowered his head, and touched his lips to her brow.

She quickly lifted her chin, but he did not give her mouth the consideration she sought.

Stepping back, he shifted his regard to the bruised and abraded face of the woman who would live, though it was questionable whether or not she would still wed. Much depended on the extent of the attack. And the man to whom she was promised.

"I shall try to return within a fortnight."

Nanne's smile was not quite bitter. She knew the way of things.

"And this woman?" She nodded at her pallet.

"I ask only that you provide the care she requires so she might return whence she came."

"What should I say if she asks after the one who saved her?"

"That you know him not, but she ought to thank the Almighty her cries for help were answered and she was brought to you for healing."

And that would more than suffice, he thought, for he would not chance revealing who once and twice a month crossed his border to visit this cottage set apart from others.

"As ever," Nanne said, "I am glad ye came. It gets lonely."

Guilt never far, especially when he departed, he said, "As I am glad," then draped the soiled tunic over an arm, opened the purse on his belt, and drew out a coin pouch that he set in her palm.

He looked one last time at the woman who would never know that the one who had aided her was a man who hid secrets in this village, and turned on his heel.

Eamon was outside on his belly in the dirt, using a stick to scratch out the letters Magnus had taught him this visit. If the boy applied himself and learned the sums to which he was resistant, a good life could be his when he grew to manhood—whether as a merchant or a man of God should his heart lead him that way.

Eamon scrambled to his feet. "I wish you did not have to leave."

"As do I, but ere you know it, I shall return."

The boy groaned. "Always ye say that, and ever 'tis longer than I know it."

Magnus ruffled his hair. "Forgive me?"

"If you promise I shall shoot more than two arrows when next you come."

"It will be done."

"A fortnight, aye?"

"I shall try."

The boy hugged Magnus about the legs before bounding into the cottage and calling, "He will take me hunting again in a fortnight, Mother."

Magnus pulled a hand down his face. A fortnight should be attainable. By then, he would be wed over a sennight and, doubtless, eager to escape his disagreeable De Arell wife.

He grunted. He had not told Nanne he was to wed sooner than expected, but if not for the necessity of returning to Kelling, he would have this eve. Thus, it would be as a married man when next he visited, and though Nanne knew what was required of him, she would be hurt that he had given no warning.

But again, she knew the way of things, and without being cruel, he could not make it clearer they were also his way of things. Even were it not necessary to form an alliance with the De Arells, he would not take Nanne to wife and Eamon to son. He cared for them, especially the lad, and accepted responsibility for his role in the boy's birth, but he did not feel for Nanne beyond friendship, and no matter how longingly she looked at him, he could not make more of their relationship than he had done since moving her upon the barony of Orlinde to birth Eamon and make a life for the two away from Emberly.

Just as he knew he could not make more of his relationship with Thomasin de Arell than as a grudging husband to her grudging wife. The best they could hope for was to make an heir—though even that was uncertain—and spend as little time as possible in each other's company.

4

—∞∞—

Rɪsɪɴɢ ᴜᴘ ᴛʜʀᴏᴜɢʜ painless sleep into painful awareness, Thomasin did not expect to see out of both eyes. And she certainly did not expect to find a woman bending near.

Focusing on brown eyes wide with questioning, she whispered, "Where am I?"

"Upon the barony of Orlinde."

"I...know it not."

"'Tis small and poor, hardly worth mention."

The dim glow of the room in which she found herself evidencing it was night, Thomasin glanced left, right, and quickly left again, returning to the one who sat before a cooking fire at the center of the cottage.

He was not a handsome boy, his features a bit uneven and head a size too large for his slender body, but though much of her was jumbled amid the struggle to hold back sharp-edged memories, the smile in his eyes and the one at his mouth soothed her.

I am safe, she told herself. *I escaped. Or was I rescued? Perhaps found?*

"How do ye feel?" the woman asked.

"I hurt all over." Thomasin tried to moisten her lips, but her tongue was too dry. "How did I get here?"

It was the boy who answered. "Me and my—"

"A passing traveler heard your cries and frightened off yer attackers," the woman spoke over his small voice. "As he needed to continue on, he left you in my care that I might see ye well again."

Like the Good Samaritan of the Bible? Thomasin considered, and frowned. This was different. One man, likely a commoner more comfortable with plow than sword, had sent three men trained in arms running? It made no sense, but her head ached to think on it. And after what had been done to her—

Across her mind flashed images of the two who had beaten her, then a wavering image of the one for whom they had done it. She shuddered. That such a handsome face should mask so evil a heart!

Dear Lord, she silently called, *am I no longer virtuous?*

She squeezed her eyes closed, determinedly returned her thoughts to this moment, and raised her lids. "I thank him. And ye."

"We did what we could." The woman's smile was sympathetic. "Now we must see ye well enough to return to your home."

Thomasin gasped. Doubtless, she was now missed. And her father would be angered by the worry her waywardness caused. "I must go." She pushed the blanket off and started to rise, but her body protested so vehemently she did not resist when she was pressed back down.

"Too soon," the woman said. "Ye were beaten as I have only seen men beaten."

Thomasin lifted a hand to her face and touched the tender bruises and scrapes.

"I am called Nanne, and my son is Eamon."

Thomasin nodded. "My horse?"

"Outside. Watered and fed."

"I must get home. My father will be anxious."

"But grateful when ye are returned whole, and that cannot happen until you are sufficiently healed to make the journey. But perhaps I could send word to him?"

Thomasin bobbed her chin, but the movement sent such pain slamming through her that her mind began to slip.

"Later, then," Nanne said in a voice so muffled Thomasin knew the sleep to which she succumbed would long hold her under.

The room shifted one direction, then the other, and she closed her eyes.

The sunlight pressing its face against her lids was so warm and beautifully bright, she longed to believe the memories raking across her mind were of terrible imaginings, that when she came up out of them she would be in her chamber at Castle Mathe.

How could it not be? After all, she hardly hurt.

Nay, that was not true. The pain was at bay providing she did not move and she choked down the bitter drink given her by—

Who was it?

Regardless, if she could drink that which had been pressed upon her some time back, there need be no more pain of the sort that urged her to cry out.

"Sin?"

She inhaled sharply, coughed to expel the saliva seeking her lungs.

The one who called to her, though not in her grandfather's voice, pulled her up and slapped her on the back.

Lifting her lids, she saw she was in the cottage of the day past. And this was Nanne.

"Sin? How do ye know me by that name?" Thomasin rasped, not caring that she slipped into the woman's rustic speech.

A frown briefly marred Nanne's pretty face. "Though 'tis hard to believe ye are called that, you told it to me last eve. Do ye not remember?"

Thomasin shook her head, winced at the pain.

"Ye were worried about a stick, though mayhap I misunderstood."

She had not. But what would have been a beautiful walking stick was gone. And there was another thing she feared might be gone. However, too much of her ached to know if it was so.

"How badly am I hurt?"

"As already told, quite badly."

"But do ye know...can you tell if...?"

"Ah." Nanne's mouth turned down. "I am sorry, but I know not. Does yer body not tell ye?"

Heat rushing into her face, Thomasin murmured, "All of me feels violated."

Nanne nodded and carried a cup toward her. "Drink."

As the bitterness went down, the warmth of it once more tempted Thomasin toward sleep.

Nanne said something about her son...the market...that she would return...

When next Thomasin awakened, the heat in the cottage was so thick, it had to be past middle day.

"Nanne?" she called, and twice more before accepting she was alone—and drawing nearer the end of another day in which she was absent from the barony of Blackwood.

She levered onto her elbows, next her palms. Drawing deep breaths to counter dizziness and divert her attention from her aching places, she lowered her chin. And saw the state of her front-laced gown. In addition to stains and rips, it was spotted with perspiration.

She turned on the pallet and dragged her legs beneath her. Then she was on her knees, next her feet. She stood unmoving until certain she was well enough not to go into darkness again, then she took small steps through the still, warm air. Upon reaching the open doorway, she leaned against its frame and looked out at a land set aglow by early afternoon.

There were no other cottages in sight. The fields in the distance were grooved by plows, and there was enough of a green cast to the darkly rich soil to evidence this was not the season they lay fallow. The scene reminded her of the fields alongside the village where she had grown up before her mother had given her as a help and companion to their lord's ill-fated daughter, Joss.

Suffering too much physical pain to add sorrow to it, Thomasin pushed down memories of the little girl. It was then she saw the shadow stretching long from behind the right corner of the cottage.

"Oh, have mercy," she breathed and tensed to flee from those who had come to finish what they had begun in the wood. But then a nicker sounded and she realized the shadow belonged to a horse.

Grateful for the support of the door frame, she held to it until her knees agreed to bear her weight, then crossed the threshold. With each step, she became more sure of foot, and when she came around the corner of the cottage and confirmed it was the miller's horse tethered there, its crude saddle yet upon its back, she did not stop.

She loosed the lead attached to a post, and with much effort, made it astride.

Though she regretted being unable to thank Nanne for aiding her, the sun was on the descent side of day, and she had to make it back to Castle Mathe before nightfall. But she would not forget the woman and her son. When she was Lady of Emberly, she would find her way back here and properly thank them. And if ever she chanced upon her Good Samaritan, she would thank him as well.

5

⟨⟨⟩⟩

IF RUMOR WAS true, she had fled, just as Magnus had believed his niece had done to avoid wedding the enemy last Christmas. *Believed.* Rather than flee, Elianor had accepted the aid of the now departed Agatha of Mawbry—also known as Aude—and rendered Baron Boursier unconscious in an attempt to imprison him past the day required to ally with his enemy. The women had failed, and now Elianor was contentedly wed to that same man. And expecting their first child.

Magnus was pleased for them. But he would be a dullard to think his own marriage would have the same outcome, and not only because he had received word his betrothed had run—word surely not meant for his ears nor the king's. Even were it only rumor and four days hence he was presented with an eager bride, still he had his demons. And they did not like company.

Returning his thoughts to Lady Thomasin, he almost pitied her father who must make this alliance with the house of Verdun before he could himself ally with the house of Boursier by wedding the inscrutable Lady Quintin.

Grateful Lady Thomasin was yet Griffin de Arell's problem and the king could not fault the Verduns if vows were not spoken between the two families, Magnus opened eyes he had only meant to rest for a moment and considered the old leather map that represented the entirety of the barony of Kilbourne before it was carved into three smaller demesnes.

He moved his gaze over the lines later dug into the leather, one painted blue, one green, and one red to denote the borders of the lands awarded to the Verduns, De Arells, and Boursiers. Primarily concerned with that of Emberly, he considered the impressions that rendered its villages.

Upon his return to Castle Kelling on the day past, he and two contingents had ridden in search of the brigands and to warn the villagers to be vigilant. Then, as now, there were no sightings. But worry, that thing which could be more curse than blessing for its ability to eat at him until his ordered life strained even its sturdiest threads, urged him to ride again.

Fighting the temptation, he studied his easternmost border beyond which lay the barony of Orlinde where Nanne and Eamon dwelt, and considered sending word of the brigands to that one's lord, just as he had sent word to De Arell and Boursier.

A rustle of skirts brought his head up, and he saw his sister before her gaze landed on him. Color high, steps brisk, she crossed the hall and halted near him where he stood at the table before the hearth.

"I have just spoken to the wine merchant," she said, clasping her hands at her waist. "He tells that Lady Thomasin has fled marriage. Is it true?"

As she did not need to voice the cause of her excitement, he said wearily, "It is yet rumor. Thus, no more true to me than it is to you."

"But if you are not to wed a De Arell—"

"Constance," he said sharply, this being one of many times talk of family alliances had led them to this place. "The king knows what he wants, and 'twould be folly to try to move him."

"But what choice has he if Lady Thomasin was, indeed, gone from her bed this morn?"

"A choice most dire for those who play King Edward's game, Constance. Griffin de Arell will forfeit his lands, the same as the Verduns and Boursiers do we not honor the decree."

She raked her teeth so hard across her lower lip, he was surprised the return of color to the pinched flesh was not of blood.
"But surely the king is all threat. To unland a noble for not allying
through marriage—a sacrament that requires the consent of both
parties—could cause an uprising among the nobility lest it set a
precedent."

Magnus sighed. "It is the feud between our families that gives him
cause to threaten us. Marriage is but a solution to our warring." And
though it was now known Agatha had been behind many of the inci-
dents that had caused the families to retaliate against one another over
the years, the king's position remained the same.

"Regardless," he continued, "if Lady Thomasin has fled, I doubt it
will be long ere she is dragged out of whatever hole she has gone down
and convinced to do her duty."

"But if still she refuses—"

"Constance."

"Do you not see? It could fall to me and—"

"Cease!" Though glad she was no longer subject to the self-imposed
vow of silence that had held her tongue for years, he almost wished she
would return to that state.

"You know not how hard it has been for me," she said in a quavering
voice.

"You are right, and I am sorry, but I would waste no more talk on
what could be when we will soon know what is."

She slowly nodded. "Four days. I suppose that is not long."

Considering the hollow years behind and, perhaps, ahead of her, it
was true. Determined to ensure the conversation had turned the corner,
he said, "Is the chamber ready?"

She blinked, and a glint he did not like entered her eyes. "That it may
receive your bride who may not be?"

"Is it ready?"

She shrugged. "There is progress."

Magnus felt a jerk at the corner of his mouth, and it angered him, for she surely saw it and knew she caused it. "You recall, do you not, that I brought you out of the convent not only to bear witness to my marriage but so you might aid in readying Castle Kelling to welcome its new lady?"

"Aye, and I have applied myself to that end. But you know not how much doing must be done."

So she would not further witness the twitching muscle he struggled to bring under control, he bent his head to the map and began rolling it. "You have four days, more than enough to see it completed."

He heard her breath of frustration, and as he began to fasten the map with its leather thong, saw her move toward the stairs.

When she went from sight, he shoved a hand back through his short, dark hair and dug fingers into his nape. He kneaded the muscles, and gradually his tension eased—as did enough of his worry so it could not eat holes in him.

The brigands who had attacked the young woman were only that, he assured himself—miscreants who had naught to do with Agatha of Mawbry and the Foucaults. As for the rebellious Lady Thomasin, until they exchanged vows, he need not concern himself with her. That honor belonged to her father.

A half hour later, he learned Griffin de Arell had another problem, but this one he disclosed, for it was not his alone. In answer to the missives Magnus had sent on the day past informing the Baron of Blackwood and the Baron of Godsmere that a commoner had been attacked upon Emberly, word arrived from Castle Mathe. Masked brigands, a half dozen strong, had this day attacked men laboring in the fields upon Blackwood, killing four and injuring three.

"Foucault," Magnus rasped, and in that moment pitied De Arell whose daughter was likely missing amid such chaos. That rebellious streak of hers, of which he had heard, could see her dead, not unlike the woman of the day past had Magnus not aided her.

He frowned. Was it possible she and——?

Nay, the wine merchant who had also poured the rumor upon Constance had said Lady Thomasin had fled *this* morn. They could not be the same.

Recognition of the colors of the house of De Arell remedied the fear threatening to unhorse Thomasin.

The riders thundering toward her with green and black pennons raised high atop lances were her father's, as further evidenced by those colors upon their tunics.

"Home," she breathed and relaxed legs she had been about to press into the horse's sides. Easing her grip on the reins, she let her back bend as she had denied it since regaining the saddle, and by the time the Blackwood knights surrounded her, she lay over the horse's neck.

"Almighty, she has been beaten!" exclaimed one whose voice she recognized above the others, then she was plucked off the horse.

Dropping her head back against a broad shoulder, she considered the face of the one she had likely eluded on the day past. It was blurred, but she could not have said if her eyes were responsible or the lowering sun at his back. Regardless, he presented as fine as ever, brown eyes set on either side of a nose that was a bit too long, bottom lip fuller than the upper, jaw square, and golden skin a nice contrast to his black hair.

"I am to fault for this, Sir Otto," she murmured. "I should not have run from ye."

"'Twas not me you bettered, my lady. I would not have been as easily duped."

She nearly argued he could, indeed, be as deceived as whoever her father had set to follow her on the day past, but she was too fatigued and grateful it was into this knight's hands she had fallen. "My father?"

"Most anxious." He firmly settled her between his thighs. "As he also searches for you, we will send word you are returned."

Thinking she should not so like his arm around her, she lowered her lids. When next she lifted them, the place in which she found herself lacked harsh light, hard edges, and the jostle of being astride. It was coolly dim, soft all over, and still.

A calloused hand cupped her cheek, and she smiled. But it was not Sir Otto's voice that said, "You are safe, Thomasin."

She blinked up at the face that moved into her line of vision. Set with eyes as blue as her own, it was fairly handsome despite a short, coarse beard and grooved skin that made her father appear older than his thirty and five years.

Recapturing her weak smile, she said. "I am a mess, aye?"

His mouth tightened. "The physician tells there is no damage that will not heal. You should be out of bed in a few days."

In time to wed, and to a man who would surely require proof that any babe presented nine months hence was his. For a moment, she wished her mother were here. In the next, she berated herself. That woman's presence would make all worse.

She pulled a long breath. "Everything went dark, so I know not if I am yet a..."

The muscles in his jaw convulsed. "The physician asked if he should examine you for such. Thinking you would know, I did not want you further—" He growled, and she mused how like her grandfather he sounded. "I told him nay."

Feeling the heat of tears, she swallowed. "So much of me aches I can hardly separate one hurt from another." Especially of a sort she had never experienced. Still, if that had happened, she would know it in some part of her, would she not?

Her father laid a hand on hers that she only then realized gripped the coverlet. "Ere you rest, Thomasin, can you tell me who did this?"

She shook her head. "Three whom I have never seen."

"Brigands?"

"Possibly. Certes, men of the sword."

"Think you they were of Agatha whom you knew as Aude?" he pressed, his anger slipping through the tight spaces between his words.

"I know not."

"Where did they set upon you?"

Though she did not wish to lie, she could not bear him to know the depth and breadth of her foolishness. Thus, she told him she had ridden to within a few leagues of Blackwood's easternmost boundary that gave unto Emberly's westernmost boundary, and had been attacked while watering her horse. Too tattered to anticipate her father's question of how she had escaped, she told the truth of awakening in the cottage of a woman to whom she had been delivered by a passing traveler who had sent the attackers running.

Though most of Griffin de Arell's anger seemed directed beyond Thomasin, she was done with the telling. "I would like to sleep now."

"Answer one thing more. Were you running from marriage?" Resentment, as of one not in control of something he believed he ought to be, darkened his voice. Did he love her, this father who had long ago dispelled her belief he could never care for her? Or did such depth of emotion have more to do with the king wresting her fate from him?

"Were you running from marriage, Thomasin?"

"As already told, I am content to wed Baron Verdun."

After a long moment, he said, "We will speak more of this later."

She started to lower her lids, forced them up. "Rhys?" she whispered, certain the eight-year-old would be as curious as he was concerned over his half sister.

"I have set him to tilting at the quintain, but he is less enthusiastic than usual."

"I do not..." Fighting the tug of sleep, she blinked. "...wish him to see me like this."

"The morrow or the day after will be soon enough. Now gain your rest."

Ulric saw the hand in this, as he had fearfully and less clearly seen that hand in the attempt upon the life of Bayard Boursier's wife, Elianor, months past. But though he had not wished to believe it then, he believed it now that it had raked its claws over one of his own, bleeding her before settling down to a feast that ought to have seen Thomasin more quickly taken than leprosy took her grandfather.

But something—mayhap God?—had snatched her from the avengers of the deceased Baron Foucault who had once held the barony of Kilbourne. Thus, as Ulric had earlier looked down upon Sir Otto carrying his granddaughter up the keep's steps, he had decided that the game he had meant to play with his son would not be played.

"Aye, in this you are right," Griffin said. "As her attackers stink of Foucault and are likely among those who slaughtered and injured the laborers in the fields, Verdun shall accept Sir Otto into his household the better to protect Thomasin."

Ulric lowered his goblet to hide his struggle to keep his misshapen fingers turned around it and slid his gaze to his son who stood at the hearth with hands clasped behind his back.

Griffin's smile was slow and one-sided, that sardonic, in-between place that had offended Ulric until the boy he had been learned respect for his sire. Respect he no longer showed—

Nay, not true, Ulric sought to cool his ire. During his son's rare visits, Griffin mostly showed respect, though it was often steeped in tolerance. And now he was quick to agree, no argument upon his tongue.

"Neither do I wish to play today, Father," he said.

As further evidenced by addressing him in that blessed manner rather than by his Christian name.

Griffin sighed. "Your concern for my daughter tempts me to forgiveness." He gave an annoying shrug. "Temptation only."

Ulric grunted. "Of course." But acknowledge it or nay, his son had extended forgiveness of a sort three years past upon discovering Thomasin visited her grandfather. Griffin had stipulated he would permit it providing Ulric kept his distance and allowed her to continue to believe her sire remained oblivious to her trespasses. It had amused Ulric, for by then he had become familiar enough with his granddaughter to know she would find a way in regardless of her father's wishes. And one day, perhaps Griffin's son by his deceased wife would find a way in. Not that Ulric would risk visits from his grandson, Rhys being the only De Arell heir. Though Thomasin, she of sturdy stock, might be resistant to this disease, an eight-year-old boy...

It did not bear thinking upon. Thus, Ulric would continue to watch from afar as Rhys grew into a man worthy to bear the De Arell name.

"I take my leave," Griffin said, and Ulric startled to find his son had crossed to the door.

"What of Godsmere?" Ulric called.

Griffin peered over his shoulder. "No attacks reported upon that barony."

Then having failed to prevent the alliance between Boursier and Verdun, the Foucault supporters concentrated their efforts on obstructing the alliance between De Arell and Verdun.

"Sir Otto, aye?" Ulric prompted.

"It will be done."

As the door closed behind Griffin, Ulric's companion emerged from beneath his tunic. Diot circled once and again, sat, and looked up.

"Bored, eh?" Ulric murmured. Unlike other visits from Griffin, this one had provided the little dog with few opportunities to feel useful.

Setting his head to the side, Diot lifted a paw.

"Worry not." Ulric opened a pouch on his belt. "He shall test me again as I shall test him." He tossed a piece of dried meat to the dog who barely applied teeth to it before swallowing. "You earned that."

It was true. Diot had performed well the important task of providing adequate warning that someone ventured abovestairs, allowing Ulric time to present himself in whatever state he wished. Of less importance, though also appreciated, was Diot's reaction to specific sensations. When Griffin came, the little dog growled low, indicative of the strain between father and son. Thomasin's advance called for wet-nosed bumps to Ulric's ankles that bespoke an eagerness to receive her tidings. Regular servants warranted a yawn as befitting Ulric's indifference. The physician was heralded by a deep growl for the indignity suffered by the man's prodding. And the rare unknown visitor was presaged by a bark so savage it was hard to believe it sounded from something that tucked beneath an arm. Such a creature would serve Thomasin well at Castle Kelling.

"Indeed," Ulric rasped, but shook off the thought. Assuring himself Sir Otto was sufficient, he moved slowly to the armchair and lowered to it.

Diot followed, curled up on his master's lap, and sighed.

6

———◦◦◦———

GRIFFIN DE ARELL had wished to petition the king for a stay of marriage on two fronts—it would be weeks before his daughter fully recovered, and the danger of travel now there was evidence the Foucault uprising had not died with Aude.

Though Thomasin had longed to agree with her sire, she had disagreed, though not as ardently as she had done in the past. She would keep her word to the Lord that if He preserved her through the attack, she would aspire to do better in all things. And accepting what could not be changed was one of those things.

There had been improvement in her health and appearance these past days, but she needed none to tell her she would not present well when she wed. However, she reasoned that not only was she sufficiently healed to be out of bed, but her betrothed must be well-enough informed to know not to expect a beauty.

Her father had frowned over her argument. Hoping to shake him out of his dark mood, in which direction memories of her attack sought to move her, she had teasingly submitted that once she was fully healed, it was possible her husband would think her passing pretty—relative to their wedding day.

Amidst Griffin de Arell's glowering, she had addressed his concern about travel and convinced him there was no honor in allowing brigands to dictate when and where and how far to move upon his own lands—and that no good could come of angering the king with a request to delay the marriage.

Thus, Castle Mathe was left well garrisoned to protect Thomasin's brother, Rhys, whom their father would not risk upon the road to Emberly, and her grandfather, whom she had visited this morn for the first time since her attack. Though denied the old man's facial expression, she had felt his anger and heard it in his words. If not for the disease that made impossible his vow that he would cut out the eyes, tongues, and hearts of those who worked such ill on his family, she would have believed him.

The sizable entourage that departed for Emberly was heavily armed. Throughout the ride, there were no brigand sightings, though Thomasin's flesh pricked with the sensation of being watched. But at last, they reached Castle Kelling with none the wiser it was not the first time she had looked upon its walls.

Now as she stepped into the hall, she let the great space fill her eyes. Great in size only, for it was as simple as it was clean and orderly, and she liked that, especially if it was a reflection of a lord who did not overly burden his people the better to display wealth gained from their toil.

"My lord, De Arell!" called one whose voice was infused with what sounded like genuine welcome—an improvement over how they had been received by the peevish steward in the inner bailey who had told that brigands near the most distant Emberly village had taken Baron Verdun from the castle.

"Lady Constance," Thomasin's father acknowledged the lovely woman gliding toward them.

That I shall never do, Thomasin thought as she peered past her sire. She had been raised to walk sure-footed and at such a pace that the tasks set her were more quickly accomplished. Not that she had neglected to learn how better to carry herself, but it took effort to make something unnatural appear natural.

Magnus Verdun's sister halted with such grace, her skirts settled as gently as a leaf drifting to the ground.

"It has been many years," Griffin de Arell said as he looked down upon the woman.

"Too many," the lady said brightly, as if she did not hear the disapproval in his voice.

"I did not expect to find you at Kelling, Lady Constance."

Understandable, for it was well known her sins of years past had led to an annulment of her marriage to Baron Boursier and her confinement within a convent. Her accomplice—Griffin's younger brother, Serle—had also paid a price. And still he paid it, though King Edward had the matter under consideration, and it was possible he would pardon the two who had made a cuckold of the Baron of Godsmere.

"I am sorry you were not warned of my visit." The warmth in Lady Constance's voice wavered. "Be assured, that is all it is. I have returned only to witness my brother's marriage." She looked beyond the Baron of Blackwood to Thomasin, and her eyes widened. "Th-this is your daughter?"

Griffin reached a hand to Thomasin and drew her forward. "Lady Constance, I present Lady Thomasin."

When he offered no explanation for the state of his daughter's face, Lady Constance curtsied. "Well met, Lady Thomasin." Once answered in kind, she returned her attention to Griffin. "I apologize for my brother's absence. Should he return this eve, it will be late, but do not doubt he will be present to wed on the morrow."

And resigned to it, she did not say, though Thomasin felt the words.

"Allow me to show you to your chambers."

As they departed the hall, Thomasin glanced over her shoulder at her father's men and caught the eye of Sir Otto who was to remain at Castle Kelling in service to the wife of Baron Verdun.

The comfort of knowing she would not be completely alone put a smile on her lips, and he returned the gesture.

Abovestairs, Lady Constance led them past one door and opened the next. "Your chamber, Lady Thomasin."

That which she entered was smaller than hers at Mathe, and just as simply furnished as the hall belowstairs. Its far wall was set with a single shuttered window, to the right before an unlit brazier were a table and chairs, to the left a bed draped in a russet coverlet, and beside the bed a door that must let into the chamber they had passed—likely the solar, meaning this was where the children of the Baron of Emberly would sleep.

Our children. Thomasin touched her belly that even now might hold a babe. *Pray not,* she silently entreated and turned to Lady Constance. "I thank you."

The woman inclined her head. "I will order your belongings delivered and send a servant to rouse you for supper." Without awaiting a response, she turned to Thomasin's father who stood behind, and as she pulled the door closed, said, "Your chamber is two doors down, my lord."

Thomasin considered the bed. She had thought herself well aware of the toll the ride had taken, but in that moment, she felt other aches and pains.

Despite the temptation to fall across the mattress, she forced herself to properly gain the bed so that when the servant came for her, Emberly's new mistress would not be more ill-spoken of than already she was with the blood of commoners in her veins and bruises on her face.

Once she was clad only in her chemise, she slipped beneath the coverlet, drew it up to her chin, and gave herself to sleep.

Someone had sought to awaken her, she recalled upon finding her chamber draped in night but for a candle on the bedside table. As she focused on the flame, she remembered how grateful she had earlier been upon hearing her father order the one whose hand was on her shoulder to leave her be.

But now she was hungry. Unfortunately, she would have to sleep away the gnawing in her belly. As tempted as she was to search out the kitchen, were she discovered creeping about in the middle of night, such unseemliness would reflect poorly on her sire. Thomasin de Arell, the lowborn, could shrug it off. Griffin de Arell, noble father of the lowborn, could not. And as promised the Lord, she would do better in all things.

She turned onto her side, and with a gasp, returned to her back.

She fingered the ear the brigand had struck with the walking stick. Much of the swelling was gone, but it remained tender—as did her face, ribs, and hip that had known the fist and boot.

"Sleep," she whispered. But the minutes dragged into what felt like an hour—felt, for she knew better than to allow impatience to count the passing of time.

"Oh, have mercy," she grumbled and slowly sat up so she would not be surprised by her aches, then lowered her feet to the floor. As she moved about, the only thing the candle revealed that daylight had not was that her chest had been delivered. There was nothing of interest—except the door to the solar.

Thrice now, it had drawn her eye, and twice she had turned aside temptation. But now...

Has Baron Verdun returned? she wondered. If so, surely she would have been awakened by the commotion a returning lord caused—at least have heard him and his attending squire move about on the other side of the wall against which her bed was positioned.

She set her teeth in her lower lip. Was it truly wrong to trespass upon a chamber that this time on the morrow would be as rightfully hers as it was her husband's? It did not seem wrong, but if so, none need know she had better prepared herself for her new role. And surely God would not begrudge her something that would make her a better wife.

She stepped forward and pressed her uninjured ear to the door. Silence. She curled her fingers around the handle and pulled. Immovable.

However, the key projecting from this side of the door was movable, and she thrilled when it clicked beneath her turning. Still, the door resisted, and she guessed the key on the other side must also be turned.

Though it made sense that a stranger occupying this chamber would not have such easy access to the lord of the castle, it annoyed.

Seek your rest, she told herself, but retrieved the candle and crossed to the other door. Finding the corridor empty save for the light of two torches in sconces at either end, she stepped forward and eased the door closed.

As hoped, the first chamber off the stairs was not locked, but it was dim inside. Lit only by moonlight come through an unshuttered window, whose slant fell to the right of the bed, it could not have been known if the Baron of Emberly had returned. Fortunately, her candle revealed he had not.

Closing the door behind her, she swept her gaze around the solar into which three chambers the size of the one she had been given might fit, and noted the furnishings were nearly as elaborate as those of her father's solar.

Though reluctant to look near upon the immense bed after what she prayed had not happened to her in the wood, she forced herself to consider it. Set between two windows, it was hung around with curtains gathered back to reveal pillows that stretched the length of the head-board, a coverlet fashioned of dark blue cloth, and a folded fur at the foot of the mattress.

There she would lie with her husband and one day birth babes.

She studied the left side of the solar. In its far corner was a narrow door behind which the garderobe surely lay. Farther down that wall was a large fireplace with a raised hearth that extended well into the room, and upon which two armchairs sat.

There she would recline with her husband, hopefully with a measure of civility.

Directly to her left, on this side of the corridor wall, was a long table surrounded by chairs. There business of a more private nature would be conducted, just as in her father's solar.

The last place to which she applied herself was the right wall. On one side of the door that accessed her chamber was a tall wardrobe, on the other side a chest. And jutting from the door was the key that must be turned to make a private way between the rooms.

Thomasin knew she ought to be satisfied with such short acquaintance, but she lingered over the three rugs butted one against the other, so expansive they covered the entire floor except for a hand's width around the edges.

In this place, not upon a lumpy pallet in a crowded hall of a lord whose every whim she must obey, she would be wife and mother until her end days.

She raised the candle high and lifted her other hand to examine its palm and fingertips. They were not as soft as a lady's, but neither were they cracked or calloused as they had been when first her father had claimed her. She was almost ashamed of the relief to be had in no longer toiling her life away. Such relief others did not enjoy. Had any commoner ever dreamed a dream so fantastic?

Her swallow in the silence was loud, and for a heart-tripping moment, she feared it was of another. Dropping her arm, she slowly moved around the room. She smoothed the bed's coverlet that needed no smoothing, trailed fingers over a pillow she would soon rest her head upon—providing her husband would have her in his bed once told of the uncertainty of the state of her virtue.

As much as she disliked falsehoods, whether formed by words or the absence thereof, and strive as she did to be more pleasing to the Lord for preserving her, shame had made her protest when her father had said Baron Verdun must be informed of the possibility she had been ravished. As naive as she was over what went between husband and wife, she had not known it was possible for a man to detect that a woman had been with another. With high color that evidenced his discomfort, Griffin de Arell had assured her it was so and her husband might insist she be examined.

Insist he could, but resist she would, and if her refusal proved a poor start to their marriage, the fault would be Baron Verdun's.

Determined not to think further on it, she crossed to the chest. It was locked, likely containing valuables. However, the wardrobe's door opened to her pull. She peered in at a modest, well-ordered collection of hanging tunics and mantles, and neat stacks of folded chausses and undergarments. As neither did she possess garments in excess, though not for lack of her father's generosity, there would be room for her clothing.

She closed the wardrobe and caught a sound from the corridor that made her heart faint against her breastbone—the booted tread of a man on the stairs.

Pray, not Baron Verdun, she sent heavenward, then snuffed the candle, stepped to the door adjoining the two chambers, and reached for the key that moonlight ventured only near enough to reveal its shape to one who knew where to look.

But as she gripped its iron head, the corridor door opened.

7

~⚬⚬⚬~

Magnus blamed a day lost to the elusive brigands for languid senses that had him halfway across the solar before he caught the scent of a recently extinguished candle—one his squire might have lit had his lord not sent him to his rest after a relentless day in the saddle.

Sliding back into the warrior he had let slip after traversing the hall where De Arell's men slept, he smoothly altered his course to avoid the wedge of moonlight that would render him more vulnerable. As he advanced on the chest and wardrobe whence the scent wafted, he began unbuckling his sword belt as though to make ready for bed.

And there his intruder huddled on the far side of the wardrobe—a lighter shadow amongst darker. Was it a brigand come to hunt him as he had been hunted this day? A De Arell retainer who aspired to remain an enemy?

Either was possible, though the latter would surprise. Despite the Baron of Blackwood's treachery, should he attempt to prevent his daughter's marriage by way of murder, he would have little hope of retaining his lands.

No matter, Magnus told himself as he laid his sword belt atop the chest to the right of the door. Regardless of who trespassed, the man would learn the consequences of such a mistake.

Magnus's sword, having waited all day to prove itself worthy, slid from its sheath with a sharp whisper of excitement. And two running strides saw its point pressed to the chest of the intruder who recoiled back against the wall.

"Rise! Slowly, if you care to see another day."

The intruder complied, confirming he was foolishly garbed in white as he inched up the wall with the sword keeping pace. Though he presented a slight figure, Magnus knew that one who possessed not the strength of a large man could prove all the more deadly when underestimated. "Reach your arms to the sides and spread your palms flat to the wall," he ordered.

The intruder drew a sharp breath, and in a voice as surprising as his size said, "Ye need not fear me."

That this one spoke with the tongue of a commoner barely registered past the realization that tongue belonged to a woman.

Yet more easily underestimated, he silently cautioned. "Do as I say!"

"I be not armed. I am——"

"Do it!"

She swept her arms to the sides and splayed hands bereft of weapons.

Magnus lowered his sword and grasped her arm. As he pulled her out of the shadows, he caught a scent that had been hidden beneath that of the extinguished candle—violets, the same that had wafted from the woman he had denied the brigands days past.

Surely it was not her.

But as he dragged her toward moonlight that showed she was clothed in a fine white chemise, over the shoulders of which tumbled hair of the length and color of that young woman's, he prepared himself for the face denied him as she struggled to keep her feet beneath her.

He halted, and she fell against him, whipped her head up, and glared at him through bed-tangled hair.

It *was* her, just as he had too briefly considered days past upon learning Griffin de Arell's daughter had fled. Though her face was not as unsightly as it had been when he had left her with Nanne, evidence remained aplenty of her beating.

"I am La—" She gasped, and in her wide eyes he saw recognition of the one she had believed to be among her assailants.

Pray, do not, she had pleaded before losing consciousness. *I am to wed.*

He sensed the gathering scream he could not allow to pass her lips with Griffin de Arell in a chamber just down the corridor and Blackwood men in the hall below. Releasing his sword to the rug, he swept his hand up and clapped it over her mouth.

She cried into it and began to writhe with a fierceness that might have bent him over had he not anticipated her kicking and flailing and taken her to the floor.

The pitch of her muffled scream rose when they landed on the rug, and he knew she was pained by the impact of a body recently abused. But there was nothing for it until she calmed sufficiently to be set right about his role in her attack.

Pinning her, he met her desperate eyes that not even the muted moonlight could deny were the most beautiful blue. Strange, he thought, that he had not noted the color during their first meeting. But then, all his thoughts had been for putting distance between her and the brigands.

Feeling her chest expand with the breath she dragged through her nose, he said, "Quiet now, and I will explain."

She continued to struggle, and he captured her scream in his hand.

"Lady Thomasin! Cease, else you will see your father and me at swords, blood spilled, and De Arell lands forfeited alongside Verdun."

Her rising chest stilled, as did the rest of her.

He did not lift his hand, nor his weight, certain she could as easily seek to catch him unawares as concede the fight. "You know me to be Magnus Verdun, aye?"

She did not know that—at least not entirely, for there was questioning in the eyes she searched over his face, and he guessed she sought to reconcile her supposed assailant clothed as a commoner with her betrothed clothed as a nobleman.

"Thomasin, I vow *you* need not fear *me*."

He saw her throat convulse, heard her swallow.

"Hmm?" he prompted.

She jerked her chin.

"I shall remove my hand, and 'twill be upon you should De Arells set themselves against Verduns."

She hesitated, nodded again.

He released her mouth, and she drew a sharp breath as his hand hovered above her lips lest she deceived. But when she exhaled, it was on the hissed words, "Get off me, swine!"

She had named him a pig—among other things—when she had thought him a ravisher of maidens, but on that day as this, she had cause to think ill of him.

"Off!" she huffed.

Holding her gaze to all the sooner catch her intent, he moved his hand to the side and considered the face he was to look upon all the days of his life. Plain, he had been told, and it was—except for eyes that, were they passed to a son or daughter, would make for a more beautiful child.

Pity the son, he thought, just as his own father must have thought, he who had begrudged no scar upon his countenance and had wed a woman whose lack of great beauty ought to have produced a son better known for his skill in battle than an ability to fill a woman's eyes so full she saw no other. *The Verdun Curse,* Magnus's father had called that which had diminished him in the eyes of fellow warriors.

"Still we are in agreement?" Magnus asked.

"I shall not scream," she said in a less common voice than when fear and surprise had unfurled the one beneath the lady. "Unless you give me cause to."

He slowly rose and reached to her.

Ignoring his hand, she scrambled upright, and as she swatted at her mess of hair, demanded, "Now you will explain."

He considered retrieving a torch from the corridor, but until he was more certain she and he were of a similar mind, he could not leave her untended. He gestured to the chairs before the hearth. "Shall we sit?"

She crossed her arms over her chest. "Not I."

Though his saddle-weary body longed for the comfort of the chair denied it, he remained standing.

"I also require answers," he said, "but since I am certain you will deny me until you are satisfied with yours, let us begin there."

Jaws clenched to counter the chattering of her teeth, Thomasin stared at the man she had prayed never to see again. But here he stood, claiming to be her betrothed. Now, as she rose from the shock of finding herself face-to-face with the uncommonly handsome one who had set his men—and himself—upon her, the only motive she could find for his attack was opposition to wedding a woman who was no match for him in breeding and appearance.

Was it chance he had happened upon her when she had ventured to Castle Kelling? Or had he followed her from the castle that day and rejoiced when his plans were more easily realized? Likely the latter, for though it was mostly his face she recalled from that day, she was fairly certain he had worn the clothes of a commoner as if to disguise the nobleman. Too, how else would he have known who she was? And been ready to kill her for it?

Feeling another scream rise, she pressed it down with the reminder of his threat to meet at swords with her father.

When next he spoke, his voice was so soothing that only the distance between them proved he did not actually touch her. "From your reaction in the wood, I know you believe I was one of your attackers, but I merely answered your cry for help."

There was no humor in her laughter, but there was shame aplenty in the chattering of her teeth. "You? Alone against three? That does not bear believing."

Though his back was to the moonlight falling upon her, she saw his dark eyebrows rise. "Three is not beyond me, especially against men of that ilk, but when the one astride fled, I had only to turn my sword against two."

She shook her head. "You were the one astride, watching whilst they…" Had they? The question remained. And this man knew the answer.

"'Twas not me, my lady. My word I give."

"The word of a ravisher?"

He sighed, and she saw his gaze flick to the sword he had dropped to take her to the floor. It was as near to her as it was to him, but had she a chance to retrieve it, his threat of spilled blood would be as potent. Too, she was not certain she could heft such a weapon. And if she could, what to do with it?

"Think on it, Lady Thomasin. If it was not me who aided in your escape, who?"

"A passing traveler," she snapped and regretted not thinking on her answer as advised.

The space between them strained further, making her wish she could clearly see his face, but finally he said, "You believe a mere traveler capable of fending off three armed men, yet refuse to believe the same of a warrior?"

It was true her Good Samaritan made no more sense this day than he had the times she had thought on him since her attack. Some piece was missing. But surely it was not Magnus Verdun.

"Aye, lady. I sent the brigands running. If they are the same who aided Agatha of Mawbry in seeking vengeance in the name of Foucault, 'tis likely their attack on you was an attempt to prevent our marriage."

Thomasin's father also thought it possible, as had she until this eve when she had looked upon her betrothed's face for what should have been the first in a thousand upon a thousand times.

"Dressed as you were," he said, "I assumed you were a commoner foolishly traveling the wood alone."

Thomasin started to argue her foolishness, but pressed her lips tight to hold back words that, spoken out of a bruised face, would make her appear more the fool.

"As I had intended to spend the day hunting," he continued, "I did not take care with my appearance. Thus, I am not surprised the woman into whose care I gave you so I might sooner alert my people to the brigands mistook me for a traveler."

Thomasin caught her breath. "What know you of her?"

"Hers was the nearest cottage, she was called Nanne, and..." He paused as if searching for something. "...she had a son whose name I do not recall."

Relief made Thomasin's knees shake and hands convulse with the need to hold onto something. Magnus Verdun had to have been the one who saved her. Had he sought her ravishment and death, he would not have given her unto Nanne. "The boy's name is Eamon," she supplied.

He inclined his head. "Are you satisfied with my innocence?"

She drew a deep breath. "It seems I have wronged you where gratitude is owed. I pray you will forgive me."

"Naught to forgive. Now let us sit and settle these other matters."

She glanced at the chairs. Though certain she no longer had cause to fear him—at least not as one who ravished and murdered—she shied away from the answers he would require of her. "'Tis late. I would return to my chamber."

"Not yet." The tone with which he had minutes earlier soothed her fear was gone. "As the first of the morrow will be taken with wedding preparations, the latter with celebration, that leaves the nuptial night, which is hardly the time to answer me as I have answered you."

He was right. The next time they were alone together would be when they became husband and wife in deed. And more for that than any other reason, she did not wish to sit with him.

"Come, Lady Thomasin, this hour cannot be much later than when you first trespassed upon my chamber."

She winced. "I know I should not have entered, but I awoke and could not return to sleep, and…" She shrugged, causing her shifting chemise to make her all the more aware of her state of undress and her hair tumbling about her shoulders. A proper lady would have donned a robe and confined her tresses to a braid. But then, she would also have kept to her chamber.

"I apologize. As my sire oft notes, I am overly curious."

"On that one thing, he and I agree. A pity he did no more than *note* your bent toward such behavior."

And now she was scolded. Though she knew it was his due, resentment threatened to test the promise she had made the Lord. Deciding to distance herself as she had mostly learned to do her first year at Castle Mathe when attempts to shape her into something she was not had tested her patience alongside her father's, she said, "I think it best we speak further on our nuptial night," and swung toward the door.

His hand closed over her arm. "Nay, my lady, we speak now."

She considered wrenching free and lunging for the door, but reason prevailed again. To move their argument into the corridor would draw her father from his chamber. With sword in hand.

Magnus Verdun drew her to the raised hearth and handed her into one of two chairs. "Stay."

His command once more tempted her to the door, but she set her chattering teeth and remained perched on the chair's edge while he retrieved his sword, sheathed it on the belt left atop the chest, and strode to the door and into the corridor. Upon his return, he carried a torch that he fit into a wall sconce alongside the door.

What the pale flicker of Thomasin's candle had left to her imagination came to light, and she became distantly aware of the cold that caused her to hold her body close as she took in the vivid images and colors of the tapestry covering the upper portion of the wall behind the large table set with chairs. Three knights upon steeds were woven into its center, their colors flown from raised lances. The pennon of the first was deep blue and silver, the second red and gold, the third green and black.

House of Verdun, House of Boursier, House of De Arell, for whom the barony of Kilbourne had been carved into three pieces. Further evidence was seen in the upper left corner that showed a bearded nobleman fallen upon crimson ground, over which two women clasped their hands in prayer—the defeated Baron Foucault and his surviving wife and daughter. In the lower right corner was another fallen nobleman, this one clean shaven. Simon Foucault, who had died in France before he could return to England and avenge his father's death.

"My father commissioned the tapestry," Magnus said, and she startled to find him alongside her, settling a fur around her shaking shoulders. "He called it *The Betrayal*."

As she stared up at him, torchlight clearly revealed his face, and her heart sank. He was as handsome as was told. Were all men fine of face, still he would stand ahead of most, even with the bruise upon his brow and scratches beneath a stubbled jaw. Recalling when she had thought he meant to ravish her, she guessed she was responsible for those fleeting imperfections.

"My lady?"

Shamed at being caught staring like a besotted girl, she returned her gaze to the tapestry. "*The Betrayal*, referring to Baron Foucault's betrayal of his earl and people, aye?"

Her betrothed gave a sharp laugh and dropped into the chair opposite. "I see your father taught you as he was taught."

"What mean you?"

"There was betrayal on both sides. Baron Foucault against his liege, the earl. Verdun, De Arell, and Boursier against their liege, Foucault. But it is the latter the tapestry renders." He jutted his chin toward the hanging. "Notice only the sword hilts of the baron's vassals are visible."

It was true. Jutting from their sides, they indicated the blades were hidden behind the knights as if belonging to ones who nodded and smiled while waiting for an unsuspecting victim to show his back.

"I do not understand." Thomasin pulled the fur nearer. "Surely it was for the good of all that the traitorous baron met his end."

He raised his eyebrows. "You think it good that a feud born of jealousy has made enemies of our three families for more than twenty-five years?"

Perhaps born of jealousy, Thomasin reflected, but if Aude had done all of what was told, much of the discord was due to her attempts to set the families at one another's throats.

"More," he continued, "you think it good our people, who look to us for protection and a peaceful life, have enjoyed little of either?"

Once more, she gazed near upon him. Was it possible this man who her grandfather had warned was treacherously changeable and not right of mind, had a care for the common folk? That he was truly burdened by what they endured amidst the feud? She had learned the history of the barony that had been Kilbourne, but if her father suffered guilt as it seemed the Baron of Emberly did, it was not in such abundance one would know. And her grandfather certainly did not bother with guilt.

Magnus sighed. "Let us speak of other things, beginning with your purpose upon Emberly. When you were set upon, were you fleeing the king's decree to wed?"

She preferred to own to that, to be viewed as strong-minded rather than foolishly daring, especially considering her eight and ten years to his nine and twenty, but it would be a lie. "It was curiosity and the wish to prepare myself to become Lady of Emberly that bade me ride upon Castle Kelling."

"You are telling me your father allows you, a lady, to leave Castle Mathe unescorted?"

Resenting his censure, she said sharply, "I tell you not. When I leave the castle, ever he has me followed by one of his men."

"Ever? Where was this protector when the brigands sought to ravish you?"

Had they ravished her? "I escaped his watch by borrowing a horse from one of the villagers."

Magnus narrowed his gaze. "You are not much more than a girl, are you, Thomasin de Arell?"

She jumped up, causing the fur to fall to her feet, but as she summoned words to cast back at him, he ran his eyes down her and up again. "In a woman's body," he added.

She longed to look where he looked so she would know how much the torchlight revealed of her curves beneath the chemise, but she kept her chin up. And hated the heat in her cheeks that had no right to reflect the color of shame. After all, as if to compensate her for so unremarkable a visage, God had been generous with her figure—as well she had come to know during her last year as a servant.

"Sit, Lady Thomasin. We are not finished."

She snatched up the fur, dragged it around her, and dropped into the chair with an absence of grace she refused to regret. "What else would you have me tell?"

"Did you recognize the brigands who attacked you?"

"Nay, the two who dismounted were unknown to me."

"Would you recognize them if you saw them again?"

Dread memories thrust their faces at her. "I would. Would you not?"

He inclined his head. "Did they speak to you?"

"Aye. When I gave my name in the hope they would prefer to be rewarded for aiding me rather than by my ruin, they seemed unsurprised and told I would not be wedding. I believe they sought my death, but first they…wished to make sport of me."

"Did they?"

She gasped. Had he not seen what she could not recall? Regardless, he must suspect the worst, for now that she knew he was no ravisher, she understood what had not made sense when she had seen him in the wood—the sensation of her skirts being yanked down rather than tossed up, his attempt to undo what had been done to her. At least, in some small measure.

"Believe me or nay," she said, "I do not remember. But though what was muddled by the blows dealt me has not come right, methinks had I been violated I would know it."

His silence was heavy with something she hoped was not disbelief, but it became so evident on his face she said, "You think I lie."

"The day after I aided you, I heard rumor you had fled our marriage. And that is all I heard—rumor. Since your father neglected to inform me you had gone missing and it was upon Emberly you were attacked, I have good cause to suspect deception."

"You believe his silence to be an attempt to have you think that if I am with child, it is yours?"

"It occurs."

Calm, she counseled. *Of course a man would fear that, especially one with lands to pass to a child of his own blood.*

"I vow deception was not intended. I returned to Castle Mathe the day following the attack—"

"The day following?" He sat forward. "The woman, Nanne, allowed you to leave so soon?"

She frowned over the implication she ought to have sought permission. "Though I would have liked to thank her, when I awoke the last time and found myself alone, I knew the passing of another day would see my father more anxious. Thus, so I might make Castle Mathe before nightfall, I took my horse and departed. As for the reason you did not receive word of my attack upon Emberly, my father assumed it happened on Blackwood, and I did not correct him."

"For what reason?"

"That he would not be more disappointed in my wayward ways. Too, when I learned you were hunting the brigands upon Emberly as my father did upon Blackwood, it seemed not to matter." She resisted sinking her teeth into her lower lip. "And still I think there is no gain in revealing it was upon Emberly I was attacked."

"If the Foucault uprising is to be put down, all must be known, even what seems insignificant. Thus, Griffin de Arell will be told."

Struggling against further argument, she clasped her hands hard. "Regarding what was done to me in the wood, I would have you know my father insisted you be made aware of the possibility that I am no longer chaste."

"Did he, indeed?"

Offended by his doubt, she snapped, "Had you been here to receive us, all the sooner you would have been told." Holding the fur closed at her chest, she stood. "Now if we are done, I shall return to my chamber."

After a long moment, he said, "We are done."

She turned and stepped from the hearth toward the door by which she had breached the solar.

"This way." He overtook her and moved instead toward the door between wardrobe and chest.

She followed, and when he turned the key and pushed the door inward, she stepped past him.

"I pray you sleep well," he said. "The morrow will test us both."

With those last words, she realized they had veered away from what should have followed her admission that she did not know if she might be with child.

She swung around. "I will not consent to an examination to determine the state of my virtue."

He paused in closing the door.

"That I will not suffer," she asserted.

Some emotion akin to regret softened his eyes and mouth. "As I would not have you do, Thomasin."

Glimpsing again the man who had sought to ease her fear of him and, once that was accomplished, had turned cool, she felt a flutter of hope. "I thank you."

His lids momentarily lowered, and when his eyes beheld hers again, they were once more emotionless. "As there is no reason to subject you to something so repugnant, gratitude is unnecessary."

She frowned. "No reason?"

"Unlike those more in control of their lives than we, regardless of your state of virtue, still we will wed to preserve our lands."

It was true. But were she to find herself pregnant a month hence, he would question—

Nay, he would not. If there was to be no examination, she would not be touched until her menses evidenced an empty womb. "Aye," she said, "no choice have we, so no cause to get all twitched over it."

The tension he exuded surged, and she saw a muscle at his mouth jerk, but just when she thought he might speak again, he stepped back and closed the door.

Doused in dark, she gripped the key to turn it. And paused. The sound would speak of her fear. But what would his turning of the key speak of him? Not fear, but a means of ensuring his privacy in the wake of the woman soon to be his wife.

She listened for the turning, but heard only his tread as he moved away, likely toward the bed she would not share for a month. And far longer if her menses did not flow.

"Pray, do," she whispered and dropped to the bed, huddled into the fur with which Magnus had relieved her chill, and sighed when sleep tugged at her.

8

NEVER HAD HE been so near this enemy. Though as a young man, Magnus had been held captive by the Boursiers for a time, always there had been a battlefield, a castle wall, or armed men between De Arell and him. Now there were little more than words spoken across a short expanse of table in the great hall, and most of them Magnus's.

De Arell responded curtly to the tidings it was at Emberly his daughter had been attacked and that not until last eve, upon finding her in the solar, had Magnus known whom he had saved from the brigands.

The Baron of Blackwood's displeasure was more deeply felt when Magnus asked the purpose of not informing the lady's betrothed she had gone missing—more, that she had been attacked and possibly ravished.

The color darkening the man's bearded face deepened. "Let us be clear on one thing, Verdun. Regardless that we are to be joined through marriage, I answer to you no more than I did whilst our families were divided by twenty and more years of conflict."

Magnus raised his eyebrows. "I am of the same mind."

De Arell, only six years older than the one who would become his son-in-law, leaned back in his chair. "Then content yourself with this—my word that had you and I talked when first Lady Thomasin and I arrived, you would sooner have known of the assault and the question of its extent."

Just as the lady had told on the night past.

Her father settled his elbows on the chair arms and linked his hands atop his chest, but despite the appearance of relaxation, Magnus knew he was likely more alert to trouble and more prepared to pull a blade than his host. Not only were his surroundings unfamiliar, therefore commanding greater study and caution, but like the one who had sired him, he was foremost a warrior.

"I am grateful you aided my daughter," he said, "and curious."

Curiosity, Magnus mused, further proof beyond the intense blue eyes that the man had fathered Thomasin.

"Why was my daughter's injuries not tended here?"

Dangerous curiosity. "As I did not know how severely she was hurt and the hunt had distanced me from Castle Kelling, I delivered her to the nearest village."

"Upon the barony of Orlinde, you say."

"Aye."

De Arell frowned. "Strange that."

Magnus feigned ignorance. "Strange?"

"That you hunt alone and so far from Kelling. It strikes me as irresponsible, especially whilst our lands are under threat by those seeking to avenge Foucault."

Inwardly, Magnus tensed. Outwardly, he shrugged. "I grant that, though 'tis less irresponsible than a father who allows his daughter to slip outside castle walls and believes that setting one man to follow her offers sufficient protection."

De Arell blinked, and the seam of his mouth that had stitched itself closed split into something near a smile, albeit sardonic. "You have me there, though still I am curious."

And would remain so, Magnus determined, resentful of prying that tempted the muscles at eye and mouth to jerk—and returned him to the night past when Thomasin had said there was no cause to get *twitched* over the state of her virtue. That word had drawn him up short, making him suspect it was used to shame him for the means by which his body expressed what prowled beneath his skin, the same as it had his father.

But Magnus had sensed no maliciousness about Thomasin and concluded it was a phrase from her commoner days.

"Regardless," De Arell said, "were there a means of preventing the marriage between my daughter and a Verdun, I would embrace it."

As if Magnus's family, rather than the De Arells, were the primary instigators of the ill that had ravaged these lands. True, it was now known Agatha and whoever aided her were more to blame, but next in line were the De Arells.

"There is a way," Magnus said, "as the king has made abundantly clear. Forfeit all."

De Arell narrowed his lids.

Magnus smiled, a fairly effective means of disguising twitching muscles that threatened to be as seen as they were felt. "I thought not," he said. "Hence, as I am just as averse to losing my family's ill-gotten gain, it appears this day you shall become my father-in-law."

Once more, the Baron of Blackwood's piercing eyes sought to cow Magnus. Once more, they failed.

De Arell settled more deeply into the chair. "That is also strange, but stranger yet will be when I am grandfather to your sons and daughters."

If there were sons and daughters, Magnus silently qualified. "Most strange, though you ought not expect that for at least a ten-month."

Showing no surprise that consummation would be delayed until it was proved his daughter was not with child, De Arell said, "I am sure Lady Thomasin will appreciate the reprieve."

Magnus continued to hold his gaze, and when the other man conceded with a nod, retrieved the missives delivered to him before he had sat down with De Arell. The first was from Baron Boursier, expressing regret that he and his wife could not attend the wedding due to sickness brought on by Elianor's pregnancy. The parchment had been placed in Magnus's hand by Father Crispin, Boursier's priest sent to perform the ceremony between Magnus and Thomasin since Kelling's priest had passed a year ago. The second missive was from King Edward, instructing the Baron of Emberly to receive his man who would this day deliver a royal gift to the newly wed couple.

Certain the latter was thinly veiled cover for the true purpose of witnessing the wedding, Magnus disliked it all the more knowing that the one who would serve as the king's eyes and ears was Sir Francis Cartier. Last Christmas, the mercenary had been sent to the barony of Godsmere to ensure The Boursier and Magnus's niece wed as decreed. Magnus had not liked the man then, doubtless would like him less now.

He stood. "There are other matters to which I must attend ere the ceremony."

De Arell did not rise. "Of course," he said.

Mere hours, Magnus thought as he strode across the hall, *then this suitably solitary life is lost to me. Ever will there be a De Arell underfoot, and what I hold close shall be that much harder to control.*

But there was nothing for it other than to aggressively pursue an end to the Foucault threat, thereby allowing him to more frequently absent himself from Kelling without risk to his people. And that he would do, he assured himself as he stepped out into sunshine that seemed out of place on such a day as this.

Castle Kelling's great hall might be unremarkable, but it did not lack for shadowed alcoves and recesses that allowed one to observe and listen in on private conversations.

So concluded the one who detested doing just that, who had already known what the Baron of Blackwood had not of how Lady Thomasin had survived to breathe another day. And now to wed.

Regrettably, the opportunity to ensure no marriage was made between the houses of Verdun and De Arell was lost.

Mercifully, others were to blame.

Regrettably, the game that had seemed nearer its end could stretch another year.

Mercifully, one could not be better placed to effect the same result—providing impatience was not allowed to show its face.

It would not be permitted, determined the one in shadow. No matter the push, no matter the anger, patience would reign, just as those who sought justice for the Foucaults would reign. But first, more shedding of blood. Unfortunately for Lady Thomasin, hers would be easier to let than that of the man she wed.

Repulsed by remorse, that one sank deeper into the dark and watched Griffin de Arell who remained unmoving as if his mind turned over things that might never be overheard or spied upon.

Until that false baron quit the hall, it would be dangerous to slip away, for Ulric de Arell's heir sensed much. And for it, he could prove difficult to put down—even more so than Baron Boursier and the man's wife whose blood Aude had failed to let. But then, Aude had been a woman, and though she had possessed the heart of a man and some of the strength, it had not been enough to see the task to its end.

But here at Emberly, what needed doing would be done. Then the one who exercised patience would be named worthy. And all would come right after years of waiting and watching and warring. And berating and cutting. Aye, those things, too.

"You are a plain little thing."

Yanked up out of her swirling thoughts, Thomasin brought the mirror into focus and upon its silvered surface sought the gaze of Constance Verdun who stood behind her.

"And you are unkind," Thomasin said when their eyes engaged.

The comb tugging through her hair stilled, and the lady gasped. "You were not meant to take offense. I but spoke to break the silence I believe to be as uncomfortable for you as 'tis for me."

"I am to think that generous?" Thomasin raised her eyebrows. "I need none to note I possess not your beauty, just as you need none to bear witness you possess not a plain face."

As if wary of wrinkles upon that visage, Lady Constance's frown quickly came and went. "Forgive me for ill choosing my words. Sadly, conversation does not come as easily to me as it once did. Not only have I been long deprived of the world outside the convent, but until recently, I kept a vow of silence."

Though nettled by this woman who presented as being much too privileged and disposed toward the rights thereby granted her over her lessers, Thomasin's promise to be more careful in word and deed urged her to say with as little grudging as possible, "I understand. And I thank you for attending me."

The lady returned to the hair she had loosely pulled back from Thomasin's brow to work into a cap of interlaced strands. It was beautiful, making more of her hair than she had thought was possible.

Unfortunately, the taming of tresses that usually fell about her face did little to soften the appearance of injuries she had told Lady Constance were a result of a fall. But though vanity had urged Thomasin to reject the style, she had quieted the enemy of common sense with a reminder of the night past. Even if Magnus Verdun was surprised by what daylight revealed that torchlight had not, he knew what to expect. Too, being prepared, he would not react in any way that would offend her father.

Sliding back into her thoughts, Thomasin found little relief from the anxiety that had beset her upon awakening to the knock of a servant bearing viands. Surely by now, her betrothed had revealed the truth of where she had been attacked and who had been her savior. And once again, Thomasin's father would be disappointed with her.

Lady Constance sighed heavily. "I am surprised you have not a lady's maid."

Griffin de Arell had gifted his daughter with one despite her discomfort at being closely waited on, and she would have liked to have one with whom she was familiar accompany her to Emberly, but the woman of middling years had in recent months found a prospective husband in a nearby village. Thus, Thomasin had refused to deny her a long-awaited chance at happiness.

"Worry not," Lady Constance said, "I am sure my brother will provide you with one."

The mirror revealing the tangled ends of Thomasin's hair had been smoothed to softly cape her shoulders, she asked, "Are you near finished?" Not that she was anxious for Magnus Verdun's ring upon her hand. Though grateful for help in ensuring she was made as presentable as possible, she wearied of what was required to see her to the church door.

"Such impatience," Lady Constance said. "I would have thought by now you were accustomed to all that a life of privilege entails."

As opposed to a more fitting life of servitude? Thomasin darkly mused.

Do not take offense, she reminded herself, but when she answered, she did so with resentment. "Though privilege offers more control over certain aspects of one's life, I find it offers less control over others, such as marriages made not for love but alliance."

The woman's hands ceased their plaiting, and her stricken eyes sought Thomasin's in the mirror. "Aye, to which I can attest."

Beware curiosity, Thomasin once more silently counseled, then ventured, "I have not met my Uncle Serle. Do you think he shall ever return to England?"

The lady blinked, and once more applying herself to Thomasin's hair, said, "If the king pardons him."

"You are sure?"

"As sure as I am of his love."

"And of yours? Do you feel for him that which made you..." Thomasin trailed off.

"...made me make of Bayard Boursier a cuckold?" Lady Constance finished the question. "I do, and I would make it of The Boursier again."

In response to Thomasin's gasp, the lady laughed. "Of course, the next time I would be more wise in the undertaking."

"But what you did was wrong."

Her mouth flattened. "No more wrong than what The Boursier did in seeking my hand in marriage though I was promised to Serle. Your uncle and I but set matters aright."

And paid the price, Thomasin thought.

Lady Constance retrieved a jeweled fastener from the dressing table, secured her handiwork, and said. "At least you have good hair."

"At least," Thomasin muttered and stood.

"One more thing." Lady Constance crossed to the bed. "For fear the powder would not sufficiently cover your bruises—as it did not—I brought a veil." She held up one of a weave so dense Thomasin's features would also be hidden.

"I thank you, but nay."

"But you will shock my poor brother."

Having no reason to reveal she had already done so, Thomasin said, "I shall have to trust he is of stronger constitution than you believe him to be."

The lady huffed. "As you will." She lowered to the mattress edge, laid the veil beside her, and folded her hands in her lap.

Though Thomasin remained standing in anticipation of being summoned to the chapel, it was a long half hour—filled with further worry over what went between her father and Magnus Verdun—before a knock sounded.

"'Tis time, Daughter," Griffin de Arell called from the corridor.

"You are certain you will not wear the veil?" Lady Constance said as she rose from the bed.

"Most certain." Thomasin crossed to the door and paused to smooth the skirt of the gown her maid had fashioned out of green samite and embroidered through with black thread to represent the colors of the house of De Arell. By the end of this day, her colors would be the blue and silver of the Verduns.

With a deep breath, she opened the door.

Clothed in a tunic of a slightly darker green, with a mantle of black draped over one shoulder, her father offered a smile that evidenced none of the disappointment he must surely feel—unless her betrothed had not revealed her lie.

He laid a hand to her cheek. "You are lovely, Daughter."

Tears sprang to her eyes. "I thank you," she said, then more softly lest Lady Constance listened, "Have you spoken with Magnus Verdun?"

"All is known." One side of his smile edged higher. "And understood. Worry not on it."

Then he was not angered that she had allowed him to believe the attack had happened upon Blackwood, nor that she had stolen into Magnus's chamber in the night. Relieved, she said, "Can you forgive me?"

"'Tis done."

She stepped close, wrapped her arms around him, and pressed her head to his broad chest. "I love you, Father."

He touched his mouth to her hair. "You are also loved."

As thought—at least hoped.

He let her be the one to pull back, and when she did, his teeth were visible in his bearded smile. "Take my arm, Daughter."

She did, and when he looked to Lady Constance, his smile lowered. "I thank you for assisting my daughter."

"I advised a veil, but she refused."

"It is not needed," he said and turned Thomasin down the corridor.

She heard Lady Constance's sigh, next her slippers sweep the floor as she followed.

Toward the church.

Toward Magnus Verdun.

Toward lasting peace—providing the Foucault uprising could be kept from these walls, these lands, these lives.

9

—∞∞∞—

The ring fit, though it had been fashioned for the hand of Magnus's mother who had died when he was old enough to remember her well. Too well.

When he had slid it on Thomasin's finger after vows exchanged at the church door and before the wedding party moved inside for mass, his wife had lifted her gaze to his and he had been struck by how closely her eyes matched the sapphire set in latticed gold. And further struck by the face so near his.

Though not stunning like Quintin Boursier, whom he would have wed had Elianor not upset the order of things with Bayard Boursier, Thomasin had been made quite presentable for her wedding day.

When Magnus had sent Constance to her, he had not expected his sister would be generous with her ministrations, especially as she would have little time for her own. But despite Thomasin's refusal to don a veil—the crime of which had been fiercely whispered to Magnus before Constance took her place near the church door—his bride was passing pretty.

The gown of De Arell green was well-laced to emphasize the womanly figure that had surprised him on the night past, the powder dusting her face belied the severity of her bruises, and her mess of hair was woven back off her brow—tresses so smooth and gleaming, he envisioned drawing fingers through them, loosening their weave, and wrapping his hand around them as they sought to revert to their unruliness. And he sought to aid them.

Now, kneeling beside Thomasin, the canopy stretched over them held on her side by her father, on the other by Magnus's senior household knight, Sir George, the priest intoning the mass overhead, Magnus berated himself for allowing his thoughts to drift. Not that he tormented himself over God's displeasure as he had done as a boy, but it was disrespectful, and more so that his thoughts had turned carnal. And that they should move in that direction further unsettled him, for he was not attracted to his wife.

The mass ended, the canopy was removed, and Father Crispin raised man and wife to standing. After the kiss of peace was given to the groom, ceremony dictated it be transferred to the bride. Thus, Magnus tipped up Thomasin's chin, and avoiding her gaze, touched his mouth to hers. And was pleased he was mostly unmoved.

As he drew back, the priest called out, "Let this woman be as amiable to her husband as Rachel, as wise as Rebecca, as long-lived and faithful as Sara. Let not the father of lies gain advantage over her through her doings. Let her remain united to one man and flee all unlawful unions. Let her be reverential and modest and fruitful in child-bearing. Let her attain a good old age to see her children's children unto the third and fourth generation, and thereafter attain the rest of the blessed."

Following a murmur of agreement, Father Crispin said, "Go with the blessing of God."

Magnus turned Thomasin from the altar. As they progressed down the aisle, the first one to draw his regard was the least welcome.

The late arrival of the king's man had delayed the wedding a half hour. Accompanied by two of his mercenaries, men who preferred the title of knight errant, Sir Francis Cartier had strode from beneath the raised portcullis. Leaving his men just inside the inner bailey, he had advanced on the church and set himself among a score of others gathered to witness the fulfillment of the king's decree.

Now that it was done, Cartier parted from the gathering and placed himself before the church doors.

Magnus knew the moment Thomasin looked close upon the man. Though her feet did not falter, she caught her breath at sight of the lower half of Cartier's face upon which fire had once feasted. And again when the man made a show of removing his gloves and revealed hands more intimately familiar with that cruel hunger.

Gaze upon Emberly's new lady, Cartier moved his mouth into an approximation of a smile, an expression Magnus suspected would be nearly as unsightly even had it not been lapped by fire.

As sensed upon first meeting the king's man upon the barony of Godsmere, Cartier was as skilled in the use of his disfigurement as he was with a sword, and it sat ill with Magnus. He had not wished to wed, but until death parted the two made one this day, he would protect the woman at his side.

He halted before Cartier—as did Griffin de Arell on the other side of his daughter, still acting her protector though she was now her husband's to defend.

Telling himself to leave it be, that sending the mercenary from Kelling was of greater concern, Magnus said, "Sir Francis Cartier, my wife, Lady Thomasin Verdun."

The eyes Cartier moved over her bruised face lit as if with private amusement, and Magnus felt her tense. "Lady Thomasin," he said and took her pale, smooth hand in his livid, puckered one and raised it to his ruined mouth.

She submitted to the gesture without visible distaste, and when he released her, said, "You are the king's man sent to witness the uniting of our families?"

Cartier's distorted smile returned. "Indeed." He bent his head near hers, and in a conspiratorial whisper, said, "Of course, there are those outside King Edward's favor who would title me a lowly mercenary of monstrous countenance—just as some would name you an all too common nobleman's indiscretion."

Magnus's hand did not often yearn for the hilt, his use of a blade one of necessity, but in that moment he very much wanted the furrows and ridges to press hard into his palm. Feeling a kinship with the tension coming off the man on the other side of Thomasin, he glanced at Griffin de Arell. Face hard, the jerking of a muscle beneath his beard evidenced his sword hand suffered longings of its own.

But it was Thomasin who acted. Foiling Sir Francis's attempt to shame her into the silence of downcast eyes, she stepped nearer him and said, "Methinks you mock me, Sir Knight, and yet you must know I can no more control the circumstances of my birth than you can control the effects of the fire to which you succumbed."

Magnus was intrigued. The king's man was not.

It was Sir Francis who sucked a breath, whose throat bobbed—and so quickly recovered one might think his response imagined.

"And for which I am ages sorry," she continued with seemingly genuine concern.

He raised an eyebrow. "Are you, my lady?"

"Indeed. I cannot imagine how one survives such agony."

His lids flickered—again, almost imagined. What was far from imagined was the chill in his voice when he said, "Nay, you cannot, for whatever ill befell your face, my lady, the damage shall fade. Never will mine." He dipped his chin and looked to those on either side of her. "The king will be pleased Verdun and De Arell are united—providing you can keep your swords sheathed and daggers from one another's backs, aye?"

Both men denied him a response.

Cartier chuckled. "A pity neither of you is pleased." He returned his gaze to Thomasin. "Nor you, my lady. Ah, the price of dirt."

Thomasin did not look away, instinct that had served her well as a servant warning her to hold steady. Though moved by his plight and imaginings of how altered his life must be since being blackened by fire, compassion had given way to wariness and pique when she discovered he played a baiting game—and not only with her. It had not been easy to maintain a semblance of civility, but as best she could, she had kept her promise to the Lord to be more pleasing in His sight. And surely He approved of her veiled verbal sparring as opposed to the slinging of insults. A good effort.

At last, Sir Francis said, "Methinks my lady will prove a challenge to her lord husband." Then he pivoted so sharply, the tail of gray hair bound at his nape swung in an arc. "Come, Verdun, I have a wedding gift for you and your bride—two, in fact. Though I believe the better one is mine, you may judge for yourself."

"I do not like this," Griffin de Arell grumbled as he kept pace with his daughter and her husband into the sunlight of mid-afternoon.

"Agreed," Magnus rasped, his grip on Thomasin's arm strangely comforting.

Sir Francis strode toward the two soldiers who had earlier caught her eye for how watchful her father and those patrolling Kelling's walls were of them. "Bring forth the gifts!" he commanded.

While his men hastened beneath the portcullis, he halted and clasped his hands behind his back.

Magnus drew alongside him, and Thomasin was pleased her husband was taller by two hands and broader of shoulders. Not that worry gave her cause to be satisfied, for the contest between them was not physical. At least, not yet.

Hearing the murmurings of those who had witnessed the marriage, doubtless as curious as Thomasin over the wedding gifts, she looked behind. The men of Emberly and Blackwood were as much distinguished from one another by their parting of ways as they came off the church steps as the colors of their tunics. And leading her father's men was Sir Otto who offered a sympathetic smile that both offended and warmed her.

She hated being pitied, and yet there was something to be savored in knowing he was enough aware of her to feel for her. Heat moving up her neck, she looked forward again and saw Sir Francis's men reappear beneath the raised portcullis. Each led a horse, a massive silver-gray and one of smaller proportion whose coat was deepest black.

She gasped, but before her smile was fully formed, she saw it was not saddles with which the great animals were fit. Bodies were bent over their backs—face down, arms swaying, the blood upon their garments crimson enough to evidence it was recently shed.

"What is this, Cartier?" Magnus demanded.

"I would also know, *king's man*," Thomasin's father growled.

Sir Francis raised his eyebrows. "As told, wedding gifts, the destrier and palfrey given by King Edward, the brigands given by me."

"Brigands," Thomasin whispered, the chill going through her as vast as last eve's when she had recognized Magnus as the one she had seen above her in the wood.

"They attacked as we crossed from the barony of Godsmere into Emberly," Sir Francis said, "and paid with as much pain as could be carved from their flesh ere they forswore this world." He laughed. "A worthy excuse for being late to your wedding. Eh, Verdun?"

Bile stirring, Thomasin sealed her lips lest her stomach rejected its meager contents.

"Where were you attacked?" Magnus asked.

"Near a small, heavily wooded lake."

Thomasin frowned. That place where it was said Aude had tried to kill her husband's niece, Elianor, and met her own end when she fell through the ice?

"The lake that lies at the center of the three baronies?" Magnus pressed.

"I think that one." The mercenary jutted his chin toward the horses. "Come see."

Magnus released Thomasin. "Remain with your father," he said and strode forward.

As Griffin pulled his daughter against his side, she glanced up. "Do you think they are the brigands who...?" She sank her teeth into her lower lip, swept her gaze back to the burdened horses Sir Francis's men halted twenty feet distant.

"I almost wish it were not those knaves," her father said, "for I would myself bring them to ground."

While they watched, Sir Francis snatched hold of the hair of the corpse draped over the palfrey and jerked the head up and to the side to show its bearded face to Magnus.

"Do not look," Thomasin's father said.

But she clasped her arms over her chest and watched as Sir Francis released the dead man's hair and stepped alongside the destrier.

That one's corpse being bald, the king's man gripped an ear to turn the face toward Magnus.

"They are known to you?" Sir Francis asked.

"I recently encountered them working ill upon Emberly and sent them running."

Do not, Thomasin silently begged her husband not to elaborate on what had nearly seen her murdered, her aversion to revealing the source of her bruising not only because she wished to preserve her privacy over so delicate a matter, but she did not want it known to a man like Sir Francis.

He released the dead man's ear. "How disappointing they eluded you, but that makes my wedding gift all the sweeter—at least, for me."

Magnus's face being turned from Thomasin, she wondered if dislike shone as clearly from his as it sounded from him when he said, "My thanks to you and the king."

Sir Francis attempted another smile, moving it from Thomasin's husband to her. "I speak for Edward in saying we are pleased to have made this day more memorable for you and your bride."

Magnus inclined his head.

"The Verduns," Griffin de Arell murmured, "ever in control."

She looked up at her father.

"Rather, the men," he clarified, with those few words exempting Lady Constance who had lost control with his brother, Serle.

"You have searched these men to determine whence they came?" Magnus asked.

"Thoroughly," Sir Francis said, "and gave them chances aplenty to spill their secrets ere we spilled their innards. But they proved uncooperative."

"Thus, you have naught to give me but silent bodies."

"Far more than you had ere I gifted them."

"Indeed." Magnus motioned two of his men forward. After speaking low to them, the horses were passed into their care and the burdened beasts led out of the inner bailey.

"Sir Francis, if not that you are too occupied with the king's business to tarry," Magnus said, "I would invite you and your men to partake of the wedding feast. But I am certain King Edward would rather you further his interests than mine. Thus, I bid you Godspeed."

Sir Francis chuckled. "Surely you can be less obvious with your dislike of the king's man, Verdun."

"Surely I cannot."

The mercenary clapped Magnus on the back. "We are much the same. Thus, for the sake of our kinship, I leave you and your wife to celebrate the alliance of your families."

When Magnus gave no further response, the man looked to Thomasin. "Dear lady, mount that mare with caution. A palfrey she may be, but she is spirited." Then he motioned to his men and all three strode beneath the portcullis.

"The tales told of Sir Francis are not exaggerated," Thomasin's father said. "Indeed, they may be too kind. There is something black in that mercenary's breast."

She would not argue that, so deeply felt was her relief at his departure.

Magnus strode forward, and she saw the strain in his face and spasms at mouth and eye. Clearly, she was not the only one to exercise control over emotions roused by Sir Francis. And if she had to wager as to who had paid the highest price, she would guess it was her husband.

Halting before her, he offered his hand. "Now we feast."

As she slid her fingers over his palm, she was struck that what should not fit for the discrepancy in sizes fit well.

Or mayhap 'tis relative, she considered as he led her toward the keep and the great meal that would have been laid out while their vows were spoken. Far better Magnus's hand than Sir Francis's—not because of the burns upon the latter, but because she sensed no cruelty in her husband's. Nor welcome.

I am well with that, she told herself, and several times more as bellies brimmed with food and drink, and night slew day.

She laughed too much, a behavior all the more disconcerting alongside a lack of self-consciousness over her bruised face. And yet Magnus was divided, equally disapproving of and fascinated by this creature who was now his wife.

He had thought to ignore her, but when he was not engaged in strained conversation with her father, she proved a good distraction from bloody imaginings of Sir Francis's *gift.*

Though bride and groom occasionally exchanged words, most of Thomasin's conversation was with Father Crispin at her side and Kelling's senior household knight, Sir George, beside the priest.

"Get on with ye!" she exclaimed, and Magnus winced over the rim of his goblet. It bothered that she sounded a commoner on a voice that carried well, but not because he found it offensive. Castle Kelling was no manor house. It was of grand size, the town outside its walls boasting a good population. Thus, more would be expected of the Lady of Emberly than Thomasin seemed capable of giving. If she did not soon learn to conduct herself as one of the nobility, it would not only be difficult for her to gain the respect due her, but might prove impossible.

"You appear ill at ease, Baron Verdun," Griffin de Arell said.

Magnus lowered his goblet. "Do I?"

The man's smile was stiff. "You will make my daughter a good husband."

It was a command, and as with commands given by such men, carried a threat of what would happen to one who did not take it seriously.

It would be easy to return the threat, but Magnus was only mildly tempted. Not because he feared this enemy-turned-ally. Because now having met the son of the despicable Ulric de Arell, he was even more impressed Griffin had claimed his illegitimate daughter. More, that he seemed to genuinely care for her. He was not the man their long-standing feud had prepared Magnus for—just as Baron Boursier had shown himself to be of a different character. Further proof of the extent of Foucault involvement in the quarter-century-long feud.

"I shall be a good husband," Magnus said, "as I am certain your daughter will be a good wife."

The Baron of Blackwood stared, then grumbled, "Those behind the Foucault uprising have much to answer for."

Magnus was not surprised their thoughts ran the same dark alley. After all, this day was owed to those who had set the families at one another's throats. "Indeed, they do." He inclined his head. "And shall."

Thomasin laughed, a clear, sparkling sound that turned other heads besides Magnus's. It ended on a long sigh and a patter of slender fingers atop the table that caused light to glance off her sapphire wedding ring.

Though her face was angled toward the priest, as if feeling her husband's gaze, she looked around. And her wide open smile closed into one with softly rounded corners.

Another sigh, and she leaned in and whispered on a breath of sweet wine, "I know. Too loud. And too much." She shrugged. "'Tis my wedding day—*our* wedding day."

Surprised by the urge to put his mouth to lips lightly stained by wine, he murmured, "And now our wedding night."

Her lashes fluttered, and she swept her gaze over the hall that evidenced it was fast approaching a new day. Though many guests remained engaged in conversations and alcohol-induced laughter that carried as well as Thomasin's, several were slumped on upturned hands. And the snores of one could be heard.

"I believe the time has come for us to climb the stairs," Magnus said.

Thomasin straightened in her chair, and lacking even the slip of a smile, said, "So it has."

10

————— ⚬⚬⚬ —————

Rose petals. Cast across propped pillows and white sheets, their crimson curves gave Thomasin pause. But greater pause was given by the men gathered to the right of the open corridor door where torchlight fell full upon them.

Lady Constance, who had accompanied Thomasin to her chamber to aid in undressing her down to the fine chemise embroidered neck to hem, had told that a number of wedding guests would witness the bride and groom being put to bed. Though not unaware of the tradition, Thomasin had been unsettled by imaginings, but they did not compare to reality that tempted her to dart back into her chamber and turn the key so hard it broke off and nevermore opened the door between the rooms.

But then you would prove you are yet the girl you vowed not to be, she reminded herself. *And shame your father.*

"'Tis for you to first lie down," Lady Constance whispered where she stood behind.

As Thomasin gazed upon the wedding guests, all of whom were of Emberly, except her father and Sir Otto, she tried to swallow, but her mouth was dry. And her mind frantically submitted that it might not be so bad to be the girl on her wedding night. After all, was not a bride, by merit of her chastity, more a girl than a woman?

Providing her body *was* chaste…

"Thomasin."

Her father's voice a comfort, she brought him to focus where he stood before *The Betrayal* tapestry and summoned the courage to move her feet forward.

By the time she came around the left side of the bed where stood Father Crispin, the priest beside whom she had dined this eve and with whom she had first become acquainted when he had wed Bayard Boursier to Elianor of Emberly at Castle Mathe, she felt as if she had crossed the whole of the barony.

"Take your place, Lady of Emberly," he said kindly.

Feeling her chemise cling, alarmed that she perspired in the relative cool of the solar, she lowered to the mattress and sat back against the pillows.

"Lord of Emberly," Father Crispin called.

There was movement to the right, and she looked around to see Magnus rise from the chair in which he had sat on the night past after discovering her in his chamber. White tunic falling to his knees, revealing muscular calves and bare feet, he met her gaze as he descended the raised hearth. And she nearly choked over how darkly handsome her husband was.

Averting her eyes, she tried to calm herself with the reminder there would be no consummation this night. Still, her heart refused to shorten its stride and her chemise more firmly fixed itself to her figure.

If not for her circumstances, she would have laughed at the realization that the last time she had perspired enough to so dampen her clothing was when she had been on her hands and knees scrubbing a floor for the lady of the castle who was a stranger to grime beneath her fingernails.

As now I am, Thomasin reflected—and caught her breath when her husband lowered beside her.

"Lady Constance," the priest said, and the woman aided in drawing the top sheet up from the foot of the bed and over husband and wife. "Now the blessing."

While Father Crispin entreated the Lord to favor the couple with children, Thomasin closed her eyes and tried not to feel the heat of the body whose arm and leg brushed hers. Though she tried to make herself smaller by squeezing her arms nearer her sides, still she felt Magnus— until the priest asked the Lord to remove any taint of premarital relations from the bride. Then she felt discomfort. And when it became evident the prayer applied to her alone, she resented that a man could have such relations and not be considered tainted.

Once the blessing was given, the priest turned aside. As he moved toward the wedding guests, Thomasin looked to her father. She tried to return his reassuring smile, then moved her gaze to Sir Otto whose figure before the tapestry blotted out that of the fallen Baron Foucault. As he regarded her with an apologetic slant to his mouth, she once more experienced aversion for his pity and gratitude for being worthy of his notice.

Then he joined the others in exiting the solar ahead of Lady Constance and Father Crispin, the latter taking the single torch with him and closing the door.

Bathed in the flickering light of candles set about the solar, Thomasin wondered what she was to do. Simply ignore the man beside her? Try to sleep away her wedding night? Or was it possible now that the ritual to ensure consummation was completed, she would be allowed to return to her own chamber?

"Your father's knight has a care for you," Magnus said. "Have you a care for him?"

She turned her eyes upon him. "What say you?"

His dark eyebrows rose. "The question is simple, and I would have the answer be as well. Do you care for Sir Otto as he cares for you?"

She frowned. "He does not care for me—not as you imply. Pity me, aye, but that is all."

He raised himself on an elbow above her. "That is not all, Wife, and still I have not my answer. What do you feel for him?"

Is this jealousy? she pondered, but in the next instant rejected the possibility. Even the least of a man's chattel, of which marriage had made her, was defended for whatever worth could be squeezed from it. Her own worth would be measured by how smoothly she ran his household, how well she reflected on him before his peers and his betters, and how abundantly she birthed heirs. Thus, he but wished to make clear he would not tolerate any feelings that interfered with what was expected of the Lady of Emberly.

Of course, the same did not apply to him, just as it had not been necessary to cleanse him of premarital relations.

Deciding she need not answer with apology, she said, "I have long been attracted to Sir Otto. Not only is he handsome and genial, but he is attentive, ever keeping me from harm."

Magnus's lids narrowed. "Ever? 'Twas not he whom your father set to follow you the day you were attacked?"

"Though oft 'tis him, that day it was another."

"Then it is well he was not tasked with your safety, else your claim that ever he keeps you from harm would be invalid."

"But had he followed—" She closed her mouth. She longed to argue the knight would have prevented her from reaching Emberly, but even had he followed her that day, he would have been as open to failure in light of her advantage in securing a horse. And still her betrothed would have been the one who delivered her from brigands.

She sighed. "I fear you are right." Hoping the discussion was at an end, she turned her face opposite.

His hand closed over her jaw and brought her head back around. "We may neither of us like this, but our lives are entwined. And God willing, they shall be for many years to come. So though I need not concern myself much longer with Sir Otto, I would know if you will be faithful to your wedding vows."

He spoke as if he expected the knight to depart with her father. Either he had not been told Sir Otto was to remain, or he refused to allow it. She started to ask for clarification, but his next words moved her worries back to that other place.

"Will you put away longings for other men, Thomasin?"

It seemed an exaggeration to name her feelings that, and yet she supposed they were. She *had* wanted Sir Otto's gaze to fall upon her as it had upon Quintin Boursier.

"Tell."

"You fear I will make a cuckold of you as your sister and my uncle made of The Boursier?"

His nostrils flared. "Again, my question is simple, as should be your answer."

She pushed down resentment, but it resisted, likely for how often she had to suppress it of recent. Determining that in this her husband ought to be as accountable as he would hold her, she said, "Will *you* be faithful to your vows?"

"I shall."

No hesitation. A good portent—unless lies came easily to him as indicated by her grandfather's warning of Verdun treachery. But he had also said their minds were not right, and thus far, she saw no evidence of that.

"The simple answer is that I shall keep my vows," she said. "And should I long for a man, I shall do my best to long for you."

Something like amusement flickered in his eyes, only to be snuffed. "I am glad," he said, though he did not sound it. But then, she was not the bride he would have chosen. And he had no high regard for one he believed was mostly a girl.

He released her. "Sleep now."

"My lord!"

"My lady?"

"I know I am years younger than you, but I am more than a girl, and not only—" She moistened her lips and shivered when his gaze lowered to them. "Not only in body."

Clouds moved across his eyes, but the longer he looked upon her mouth, the more quickly they cleared, and he said low, "Are you?"

"I am."

He shifted his regard to her hair. And where his eyes went, his hand followed.

Gently, he tugged at the tresses plaited off her brow, loosening them and drawing them forward and down around her face and over her breasts.

Touch by touch, shiver by shiver, scalp to toes, he raised awareness across her limbs. And when the order Lady Constance had made of her hair was returned to disorder, he set his gaze to hers and what she saw there made a mess of the beat of her heart.

She knew what desire looked like—the perverse as she had experienced as a servant, and the wondrous as glimpsed when her father and Sir Otto looked upon Lady Quintin. And what shone from her husband was the latter.

A woman was in his bed, dressed only in her hair and a thin chemise, and it was well within his rights—and expected by those belowstairs— to do with her what men liked to do with women.

Would he? Might he seek to make heirs on her this night, risking that she carried another man's child? And if he did...

What am I to do? she wondered. *Rather, what will my body do? Welcome him? Or will it remember what it forgot of the attack? Prove me untouched or defiled?*

Magnus's sigh moved the tendrils on her face, and she opened eyes she had not realized she had closed.

"Certes, you are a woman in body, Thomasin Verdun." He started to draw back.

"And in mind," she said.

He stared at her, then lowered his head.

If he meant to kiss her, it could only mean he would also—

His lips brushed hers, stilled upon them, then fit to hers with a passion that caused something sweet to shoot down her spine. And that was all.

"We wait," he said and turned away.

Staring at the ceiling, she wondered where her breath had gone, if it would come again, and if the sensations running through her body as his fingers had done in her hair were normal. For certain, they were kin to desire. But it seemed wrong that they should be so keenly felt, especially as it had only been one mouth upon another.

Only...She tried to make sense of that word in the context of a kiss, and failing that, wished she had someone who could assure her she was not feeling things a respectable woman should not.

Am I wanton the same as my mother? she wondered. *Unworthy of the De Arell name? What if I shame my father? What if I long for what I told Magnus I would not and Lady Constance's sins become my own?*

Nipping the inside of her lip so hard she tasted blood, she turned her back on the one who would ever share this bed with her.

Ever, she assured herself. *Time aplenty to cross the divide between us.*

Two hours? Three? It seemed never would she sleep, but when all but one of the candles had guttered out and her breathing told she was no longer conscious of him, Magnus rose from the bed to which he would return before dawn.

He lingered alongside it, staring at Thomasin where she hugged the edge of the mattress as near as was possible without the floor rising up to meet her.

His De Arell bride surprised him. Last eve, when he had discovered her in the solar, he had seen benefit in wedding one whose foolish actions had made him believe she was too much of a girl to tempt him. But in the hours spent in her presence since, it was a woman—albeit a young one—he had most often encountered.

True, during the wedding feast she had time and again revealed the commoner beneath the noble, abandoning reserve in favor of enjoyment, but it was as a woman she had done so. And when Cartier had attempted to belittle her for her common blood, she had coolly and sympathetically pointed out the mercenary's own flaws that he could control no more than she could control the circumstances of her birth. Thus, it was the mercenary who had been unsettled, even if evident only for a moment.

Remembering the exchange, Magnus reflected on the discipline required not to act upon the man's trespass, but had any looked near upon him, his facial muscles would have betrayed him. As they would betray him now.

"Sleep," he muttered. The dark of him was always at its worst in the absence of rest, but he had not dared yield to sleep with Thomasin beside him lest she witnessed what he permitted none to see—not even his squire who, rather than make his bed on a pallet in the chamber or in the corridor should his lord require him, slept in the hall.

He might have chanced this one night had he not looked upon the brigands whose lives Sir Francis had severed, the violent sight of which he had done his best to shield from his bride. Had her father not kept her distant, she would have beheld men torn in the most unholy manner, and the defiling of the exquisite horses whose coats had been matted with gore where the corpses stiffened over them.

Those crimson images mostly suppressed throughout the wedding feast had visited him when he had ascended the stairs to the solar, when he had awaited Thomasin's entrance, and when he had closed his eyes to receive Father Crispin's blessing. And again when Sir Otto had come to Magnus's notice.

The knight had regarded Thomasin with familiarity, and not as if she were a girl in need of protection. And when she had admitted to being attracted to him, anger had buzzed around Magnus like a fly seeking the damp stench of perspiration. For that—to prove to himself and Thomasin he need not concern himself over Sir Otto—he had yielded to the impulse to explore his wife.

He had liked the order Constance had given Thomasin's hair, and yet been moved to undo it, making her look more the lover than the lady.

He should have stopped there—*had* stopped, but she had been determined he would acknowledge she was a woman beyond what her body told, and the desire he had struggled to subdue had concurred.

Fortunately, though her sweet trembling amid the scent of violets had further tempted him, it had alerted him to a loss of control, something he could not allow.

Magnus drew a deep breath, and as he released it, strode to the door connecting the chambers. Once inside the room where his wife would spend her nights henceforth, he turned the key in its lock, stepped to the bed, and laid down.

Muscles that had been tense for hours relaxed into the mattress, burning eyes he had dared not close too long lowered their lids.

First prayer, he told himself. Though he knew there would be little relief from what awaited him in sleep, he asked the Lord to give him strength in the absence of a sword to carry into his night travels, and rest of sufficient duration to sustain him throughout the morrow.

But much depended on the crimson flashes and their disturbances to which he knew better than to subject his wife—regardless that she was more woman than girl.

11

———✦———

HE HAD GONE from her. And returned to her.

She had discovered his absence during the night when a dream whose darkness she could not recall had awakened her. Remembering where she ought to be, and seeking reassurance she was there, she had turned onto her back. When her searching hand confirmed her husband had stolen away, it had occurred to her he was with another—that the passion with which he had kissed her had sought ease in the favors of one with whom it did not matter were she with child.

Now as she looked at Magnus where he sat on the end of the bed, the creak of leather and click of buckle evidenced he donned boots—or removed them.

Having finally slept following her night awakening, she did not know when he had returned to the solar. But it made no difference. As expected, he had not known her on their wedding night. As might be expected, he may have known another. And meekly accepting the latter in spite of his assurance he would keep his wedding vows was surely what a girl, rather than a woman, would do. But even as a woman, what recourse had she?

Magnus lifted his sword belt from the mattress beside him and stood. As morning's light reached through the unshuttered window and touched his short black hair, he said, "Good morn, Wife."

Though she muffled her yelp, her swallow was embarrassingly loud.

He fastened the belt and turned. "You slept well?"

Certainly better than he whose eyes were deeply shadowed, the whites shot with red. She pushed to sitting, letting the sheet settle down around her waist. "I slept fair enough. Did you sleep at all?"

He dragged a hand down his face. When it came off his chin, there was a smile about his mouth. "It shows, hmm?"

Despite her suspicion over where he had been, her resentment lightened over his show of teeth and teasing tone. "Surely 'tis right that a wife notices such things—things others might not."

The curve about his mouth eased. "It is right, providing she does not overly concern herself."

And wish him to account for his whereabouts. Resentment once more bearing down upon her, she reminded herself of her vow to God and said evenly, "That would be the same as asking you not to concern yourself with my wellbeing, and did not our vows call for such devotion?"

Fully garbed down to his boots, he came around the bed. "So our vows did, but I would not have you needlessly worry."

Or pry. "I assure you, I am no frail thing."

He lifted her chin and studied her face. "Indeed, you are not, Thomasin Verdun." He moved his hand to her shoulder that she did not realize was bare until his fingers skimmed it. "Methinks you may yet convince me you are more woman than girl."

Before the sensations his touch roused betrayed her, he pulled the chemise over her shoulder and stepped back.

"Once you have clothed yourself, join me in the hall. We shall assure your father of your wellbeing and break our fast with him ere he departs."

She caught her breath. "He leaves this day?"

"Though I would permit him and his men to remain longer, with the forces of Foucault afoot, your sire has determined he shall return to Blackwood this morn."

He must have done so whilst seated on the other side of Magnus during the feast, the din of celebration having made it difficult for her to follow their exchange.

Though she knew she should not begrudge her father the precaution, especially since his journey to Emberly had necessitated leaving his young heir behind, she longed to beg one day more before being left alone among strangers—rather, mostly alone. Reminded that Magnus would soon learn Sir Otto was to remain at Kelling, she could not be more grateful, no matter that it would surely sit ill with her husband.

"I understand," she said.

As he turned toward the door, a knock lengthened his stride and more quickly delivered him there.

Without invitation, Lady Constance swept inside, followed by a servant bearing a tray. She halted at the end of the bed, glanced at Thomasin, and motioned the servant to the bedside table. "You should be abed with your bride, Magnus," she said over her shoulder.

"There are matters that need attending."

She looked around. "Surely on this day, they can wait."

"They cannot. As I have informed my wife, Baron de Arell departs this morn."

"Aye, and I have assured his comfort so your presence is not required. While the horses are being readied, he and his men break their fast in the hall."

Feeling a curious regard, Thomasin looked to the servant who positioned the tray on the table.

The woman averted her gaze, snatched linen napkins from atop the viands, and hastened to Lady Constance. "My lady?"

Magnus's sister flicked a hand toward the door. "Be gone."

As the servant scurried from the chamber, Thomasin clenched her hands. She knew impulse met with anger did not serve a lady well, but how she longed to protest such treatment of a servant as she had done at Castle Mathe to the betterment of relations between nobility and those who served them—the exception, of course, being her grandfather. And as Lady of Emberly, she would effect such changes here. But now was not the time.

"Come, Magnus," Lady Constance said. "Join your bride."

His gaze flicked to Thomasin. "I have spoken, Constance. Now leave."

She sighed. "Very well, attend to your business. I will see to matters here."

"Constance!"

She stepped alongside the bed and tossed back the sheet. "Where is it?" Her gaze pounced upon Thomasin. "Do you sit upon it?"

Knowing she referred to proof of consummation with a previously virtuous woman, Thomasin felt heat rise in her face.

Magnus strode to his sister, took her arm, and pulled her toward the door.

"But, Magnus, is she not——?"

"'Tis not your concern."

She jerked free, and regaining her balance, said, "Pray, tell me 'tis simply a matter of consummation. *That* can be remedied."

Resenting that he must reveal the brigands' attack, Thomasin looked between the two.

"As already told," her husband said, "'tis not yours to question."

Lady Constance *tsked*. "You may think it does not concern your silly sister, but what reflects ill upon one Verdun reflects ill upon all."

He grasped her arm again, and as he drew her to the doorway amid spluttering, glanced back at Thomasin. "Join me in the hall when you are clothed."

She stared at the door he slammed closed, and moments later caught the rasp of voices that evidenced their conversation was not done.

Telling herself she should not, countering that she could be forgiven since it concerned her, she sprang from the bed. Grateful the rugs muffled her footsteps as rushes would not have, she ran to the door and pressed an ear to it.

"Even if your bride knew another before you," Constance hissed, "still you must give proof of consummation."

"As you gave proof to Bayard Boursier you were untouched, though 'twas a lie?"

After a long silence, Constance said, "Displaying the sheet serves two purposes—the marriage is sealed in the eyes of all, and the bride declared pure such that any child born thereafter is known to be her husband's."

"Of which I am not unaware, but I do not believe in displaying blood as if 'tis something to be glorified. Enough I have shed to know it is not."

"But this is different. No violence—"

"'Tis barbaric, even more offensive than admitting wedding guests to the nuptial chamber that they might look upon a barely clothed bride and feed their imaginings. That I yielded to. This I will not."

Then neither had he liked that invasion of privacy, Thomasin silently approved.

"Offensive it may be, Magnus, but necessary. Regardless of whether or not your wife came to you a maiden, regardless of whether or not there was consummation, for all concerned, there must be a show of blood."

"All concerned? The only ones who should be concerned are my wife and I."

"You think she will not be when she is looked upon with greater ill than that which already afflicts her for not only being a De Arell, but one tainted by common blood? When 'tis further believed she is either a harlot or too undesirable to tempt the man in her bed?"

Thomasin's breath stopped.

"What of Baron de Arell? Surely you do not believe he will gladly suffer his daughter being publicly dishonored? His name sullied?"

Though Thomasin also found the sheet's display distasteful, Lady Constance spoke true. False or not, unless a bride was previously wed, proof was to be given that she had been virtuous on her wedding day— the ceremony performed by the priest likened to words written on parchment, consummation likened to the wax seal upon those words to assure the recipient that what was inside was true.

She glanced at the bed, and when no more was spoken on the other side of the door as if the two had gone elsewhere, crossed to the viands. The knife on the tray was meant for the apple, but it would serve another purpose.

She set its point to the tip of a finger and hesitated. How much blood was required? A prick would not suffice, for it must be sufficient to be seen when the sheet was flown from the keep's walls. She moved the blade to her palm.

"Thomasin!"

"Oh, have mercy!" She snapped her head around and saw Magnus stride past the door she had not heard open, his sister coming behind.

"What do you?" he demanded.

"I like it no more than you, but Lady Constance is right. There must be blood."

He halted before her. "As she has convinced me." He took the knife, thrust up his sleeve, and sliced his forearm.

Thomasin flew her gaze from the welling cut to his face, noted the flare of his nostrils and spasming muscle at his mouth. How deeply had he cut himself?

As she snatched up a napkin to press to the wound, he tossed the knife on the platter, wrenched the bottom sheet from the bed, and pressed it to the cut. Then he turned to his sister and thrust the crimson-on-white evidence at her. "See it done."

She hastened forward and accepted the ruined sheet.

Thomasin stepped near her husband and reached the napkin toward his arm, but he took it from her and pressed it to his injury. "Make haste, Wife," he said and strode from the chamber.

"I am very right in this," Constance said as the door slammed. "Now dress while I hang this out the window."

Thomasin could not leave the solar fast enough. But once in her chamber, she lingered over choosing a gown in which to see her father away. Not that there was any question as to the one she would don, for she loved dark red—so vibrant, especially compared to the drab clothes she had worn before being claimed as a De Arell.

Next, she deliberated over how to wear her hair. Outside of leaving it loose and free to make of itself what it would, braids were easiest. But rather than one on either side of her face that would make her appear younger, she fashioned a single braid and let it drape her right shoulder. Then all that was left to do was descend to the hall and brave the knowing looks that would be sharper if it was known the sheet had been hung out. Blessedly, not sharp with condemnation.

12

⁃⊶⊶⊷⊷⁃

THE TABLES HAD emptied by the time Thomasin stepped off the stairs, and she almost wished she had eaten from the tray delivered to the solar, but the roil of her belly was surely more disquiet than hunger.

She found her father's gaze first where he stood at the center of the hall with a half dozen others, and she knew he had watched for her. But it was her husband who broke from the gathering. As he crossed to her as was now his duty ahead of her father's, his eyes swept her and a frown lined his brow.

Thinking she had not properly tied her front laces to permit only a glimpse of the white chemise beneath—else they had loosened as happened when she was careless with bowing—she glanced down. All was as it should be. Perhaps he thought the gown reflected poorly on him. Though of fine material, its design was simple as she preferred over the one she had donned for her marriage.

Magnus halted and leaned near, but before he could speak, she said, "Something is amiss? My gown is too simple? Too common?"

He drew slightly back, and she realized how sharp and defensive her words were, having fled her mouth before she could think them through as she strove to do to please the Lord. But before she could apologize, he said, "I prefer simple. 'Tis just that I am not fond of red, especially that shade."

"Oh." She peered down her front. "But I am."

"Hence, you ought to wear it." Then, as if done with the matter, he said, "I had begun to think I might have to collect you. Are you well?"

She nodded. "Your arm?"

"Bandaged." He took her elbow, turned, and led her back the way he had come. "My lady wife," he said as he drew her into the space he had vacated alongside her father.

Reminding herself of the proper way of things, Thomasin smiled and dipped her chin at each of the men—Kelling's glowering steward, the somber Sir George who had come around some during the wedding feast, Sir Otto, Father Crispin, and the immense man-at-arms who had escorted the priest to Emberly. Rollo, was it?

She saved her true smile for her father, who put his mouth near her ear and rasped, "Your husband's blood marks the sheet?"

"Aye."

He straightened, and though the turn of his mouth was tight, it was a smile. "Regrettably, Daughter, I must leave this day," he said for all to hear. "But my one consolation, as I would have it be yours, is I do not leave alone one so dear to me."

Then he meant to do this here.

"What say you, De Arell?" Was that warning in Magnus's tone? Likely, for Sir George moved his hand from the pommel of his sword to the hilt.

Her father nodded at his knight who had also put a hand to the hilt. "Sir Otto shall remain at Kelling for a time."

Thomasin looked sidelong at her husband and caught what was becoming a familiar twitch at his eye.

"What makes you think I would be good with this, De Arell? That a man I know not is extended hospitality not offered nor due him?"

Movement drew Thomasin's gaze to Father Crispin. Pressing an arm to his midriff as if to settle a tossing belly, he looked between the two men. Beside him, the Godsmere man-at-arms picked his narrowed gaze over each of them, likely determining where first to act should it be necessary to more than knead his hilt.

At last, with an edge of disbelief as of one compelled to explain something too obvious to warrant discussion, Thomasin's father said, "I think it because of our shared concern for the wellbeing of my daughter. In light of the brigands' attacks upon the baronies, most particularly that which transpired near a sennight past, I would provide her with the added protection of one with whom she is familiar and who has many times kept her from harm."

Teeth met, Magnus said, "You think *I*, who am more intimate with that attack than you or your man here—neither being present to prevent it—cannot adequately protect my wife?"

Surely aware of what he roused in one who should no longer be counted an enemy, Thomasin's father raised his eyebrows. "I vow, Verdun, no offense is intended. I am but concerned that you do not yet know my daughter well enough to make provisions for her...restlessness."

Were the situation not threatening to erupt, Thomasin would have more appreciated that he did not name it what he often did—wildness.

"And that is something with which Sir Otto is well acquainted," he continued. Then the smile that had often offended Lady Quintin—lopsided and rife with private humor—appeared. "Thomasin is, after all, a De Arell."

Magnus was too blessed of looks for anger to turn his countenance unsightly, but it detracted from his appeal, and Thomasin thought it due to the control he exercised, its vastness more felt than seen—like a gust of heat or blast of cold.

"A De Arell, indeed." His pleasantly deep voice was no longer pleasant. "Hence, methinks what your callow, impetuous daughter requires is a firmer hand rather than a warrior to play handmaid to her."

Callow. Impetuous. Anger gave Thomasin's disquiet a shove. As that powerful emotion tried to slip free of the promise she had made, she heard her father's low growl.

You gave your word, she told herself, *vowed that if the Lord preserved you through the attack, you would be more the lady in word and action. Be worthy!*

She looked between the two men who faced one another on either side of her. And could hardly breathe for how much the air seethed. If the day was not to be spoilt by sharp edges—now of tongue, next of blades—the air must be cleared.

She drew a deep breath to calm her own roiling, then laid a hand on her father's chest, the other on Magnus's, and in a voice whose teasing sounded false, said, "'Twould appear the king knew well what he did in brokering peace through marriage, making bridges of us hapless women so we might stand between your swords and cause you to think again before swinging them."

Feeling no easing of the muscles beneath her palms, she continued, "Father, this is my husband. Husband, this is my father. Both shall ever be, united through me." She looked to the priest who continued to brace an arm across his abdomen. "Aye, Father Crispin?"

"Wise you are, my lady."

That she had never been named.

Griffin de Arell gave a sharp laugh. "So speaks my callow, impetuous daughter, eh, Verdun?" He caught up the hand upon his chest and kissed her knuckles.

Was the worst past? She looked to Magnus. "Husband?"

It seemed with effort he removed his regard from her father. "So speaks my wife."

"Then you will grant me this boon?" she said, all proper. "Sir Otto at Kelling until I am well enough known to you and my *restlessness* sufficiently curbed to ensure I do not endanger myself?"

"So you do not endanger yourself *again*, I will grant it—for a time."

"I thank you."

He looked to her father. "Now to see you away, Baron de Arell." He strode toward the great doors with Sir George following.

Thomasin's father summoned his men who had surely witnessed the exchange and been prepared to defend their lord if necessary. As he led his daughter across the hall, he said, "You dealt well with that, though methinks you were tempted to handle it differently."

She smiled. "I reminded myself I am not only Thomasin, but a De Arell, a name I do not alone own."

"You shared it well this day."

Warmed by his praise, she stepped out of the keep into sunshine dimmed by clouds that, for all their lazy drifting, were taking on a gray cast.

"Do you think you will reach Castle Mathe ere the sky spills?" she asked.

Her father eyed the heavens. "Only God knows."

"Then I shall pray that if His mind must be changed, I can change it."

When they came off the steps, he peered over his shoulder. "For that, I can forgive Verdun much."

She followed his gaze upward and paused on one who appeared in the keep's doorway. Their eyes briefly met before the heavy woman turned back inside.

Hoping she did not fear being seen absent from her duties, Thomasin looked higher to the sheet hung from the solar's window. "I meant to use my own blood, but he would not allow it."

"As he should not have," her father growled, then sighed. "Though I would not have chosen Magnus Verdun for you to spend your life with, I believe he will be an acceptable husband."

"Only acceptable?"

"He is a Verdun. But he will be all the better for it with you as his wife." He pulled her against his side and kissed the top of her head. "Now, about Sir Otto. I would have your word you will heed his counsel."

She tilted her face up. "Even if I do not agree with it?"

Displeasure plowed his brow.

"Very well. I shall heed his counsel."

He inclined his head. "Certes, my mind will be less weighted knowing he watches over you."

A quarter hour later, atop the outer wall she had ascended to watch her father go from sight after Magnus and she had seen him over the drawbridge, Thomasin let the tears fall. She counted each that wended to her chin, allowed herself ten, then dashed away the moisture and turned toward the stairs.

Sir Otto stood there, face solemn, hands clasped behind him.

"There is something you require, Sir Knight?"

"Only what my lord requires of me—that I assure your safety."

She almost laughed. "I am within Kelling's walls, not without, and 'tis full daylight."

"Of limited comfort, my lady, for these walls are not Mathe's, and evil does not lurk only in the night."

She halted before him. "I fear you are too cautious, but until we are both accustomed to Kelling, I suppose you must be."

He smiled, and though he was not as handsome as Magnus, she flushed with pleasure at being so kindly looked upon.

He held out an arm. "May I assist?"

He had never offered before, always letting her fly up and down steps ahead of him. Further pleased, she set a hand on his forearm.

"I was impressed with your handling of the difficulty between your father and husband," he said as they descended to the bailey. "And a bit addled."

"Why addled?"

"'Tis hard to believe you are the same girl who, for nigh on four years, has led me quite the chase with your exploits beyond the walls."

"My *exploits*," she said as he drew her off the last step, "were so I might not only find relief from the tediousness of being a lady, but become acquainted with my father's demesne."

"The latter after thieving viands from the kitchen." He released her arm.

"Since I am my father's daughter, it can hardly be called thieving. Too, it has been to his benefit that I distribute foodstuffs to his people who have suffered greatly from the feuding between the families. As for your difficulty in believing I am the same *girl*, that must be because I am now a woman."

He swept his gaze over her, and though it did not linger long on any part of her, warmth tickled her cheeks.

"Do you not agree?" she asked, longing for his acknowledgement.

"Of course I see the woman, Lady Thomasin. 'Tis simply hard to forget the girl."

She sighed. "I pray I shall give you plenty of opportunities to become better acquainted with the woman as I assume my role as Baron Verdun's wife."

Something flickered in his eyes that made her wonder if her words had sounded inappropriate, but before she could clarify, he said, "As do I, my lady. Now, unless you would have me escort you to the keep, I shall leave you to your privacy."

"I can see to myself."

He strode opposite and disappeared around the smithy's shop.

Certain he would serve as her escort regardless of her wishes, though he would do so out of sight, she raised her skirts—and more heavily felt the regard of those in the bailey and upon the walls. Knowing she showed too much leg to people who would not make allowances for her as her father's had done, she lowered the hem to within a hand's width of the ground.

And watch your stride, she told herself as she headed for the chapel to pray for her father's safe travels. *Rather, watch your step. Men stride, ladies step.* And for it, they had to stretch their legs twice as often.

"Oh, have mercy," she muttered.

"Be gone," Magnus growled as he brushed his destrier's coat, the rhythmic motion slowly loosening his knotted insides. *Too* slowly, and it was the fault of the crimson flashes, a violation not limited to what his eyes had beheld.

TAMARA LEIGH

He saw again the king's gift, so fouled and desecrated the air tasted of iron.

Next, the glint of blade, sting of sliced flesh, sullied sheet.

Then Thomasin's gown of a color that birthed imaginings of being imparted by her life's blood.

Lastly, he heard again the tidings that Sir Otto would remain at Kelling, which had given rise to emotions that stank of slaughter.

"Lord, what other ills await me?" he grumbled, and tossed aside the brush, dropped his forehead to his destrier's back, and breathed deep the scent of horse. He held it in until his lunged ached, eased it out until his lungs ached anew.

It was then he heard the rain he had hoped would fall, regardless that it would slow De Arell's return to Blackwood.

Soon the air would be awash in the scent of wet foliage and earth, and so might be his thoughts and, this eve, sleep.

He lifted his head and, hardly seeing the stall over which the gloom of a heavily clouded day settled, mulled the disruptions Thomasin had—and would—work upon his life. How was he to settle into this new normal?

Eamon, he thought. *Nanne.* It was too soon to visit that place of peace and rest where he had only to be Magnus, but once the brigand threat was dispelled...

Of course, it might be over now that the men whose corpses had been delivered to Kelling could no longer work their ill upon Emberly. And only for that did Magnus regard the king's man with something slightly better than loathing.

He strode from the stall, secured its three-quarter door, and stepped out into gentle, cleansing rain. "Thank you, Lord," he rasped.

By the time he ascended the keep's steps, it was with no mere spotting of his garments, but he did not mind the skin-deep wet that made his hair cling to his scalp with the same enthusiasm his tunic and chausses gripped his body. He did not mind at all.

— 108 —

Nor did his wife who had exited the chapel as he strode past, who began to smile as she stared after the man who seemed in no hurry to escape the rain.

But the one who looked between the two did mind. And not just the rain.

13

⎯⎯∞⎯⎯

IF IT COULD be said one area of her education was lacking, it would be that of running a household. Thomasin's father had pressed her to take more interest in directing the servants, but she had balked. It was not that she minded the effort, but that it unsettled her to command others—people the same as she, whose blood none would ever convince her was different from that which bled as mortally from a noble's veins. Directing servants to do her bidding made her feel pompous, just as she had once regarded those who had sent her scurrying hither and thither, begrimed and aching from hours of striving to undo their messes.

Now here she stood before the heavy woman who had hastily retreated from the keep's doorway prior to Griffin de Arell's departure. Following a supper over which the lord of Castle Kelling had spoken little and his lady had responded in kind, the woman had intercepted Thomasin and introduced herself as the cook.

Thomasin glanced at the stairs denied her, wished for a way out of discussing matters of the kitchen as had twice been requested of her— once upon her return to the keep following her prayers this morn, and again following the nooning meal. Could the cook, whose short, heavy figure was likely a result of the superb culinary skills that produced dishes tastier than those from Castle Mathe's kitchen, be put off a third time?

Raising her voice to be heard above those readying the hall for the many who slept here, Thomasin prompted, "Aye?"

The woman raised brown eyes that had lingeringly traveled Thomasin head to toe as if to assess the value of one to whom she must answer. "I would discuss the menu with you, my lady." Her speech was another deception. Though not refined, it was more proper than most commoners'—and confident, as if she did not bow and scrape to any, nor fear the hand of displeasure.

"I am satisfied with your menu," Thomasin said. "Thus, I leave it to you."

The woman's mouth pinched. "Whilst Lady Elianor ran the household, she saw the importance of applying herself to ensure a variety of viands that pleased our lord."

Then Thomasin was to be compared to one born to privilege who likely felt no twinge at ordering others' lives. "As you can see, I am not Lady Elianor. I am—"

"Lady of Emberly in truth, second in esteem only to your lord husband. Know you what that entails?"

Thomasin closed her mouth against a retort.

Strange, she mused, *I balk at ordering servants, and yet take offense at being addressed in so familiar a manner to indicate we stand shoulder to shoulder.*

"I am aware of my duties," she said, "and I shall assume them ere long—"

"You would do well to assume them now."

Thomasin drew a sharp breath. "I have been at Kelling little more than two days."

"Time aplenty to assert yourself."

She turned her fingers into her palms. "What is your name?"

The woman raised her eyebrows. "Mathilde."

"I thank you for your concern, Mattie—"

"Mathilde, my lady. Only my friends know me so intimately, and then 'tis *Maddie* with a hard center."

Thomasin warred between the temptation to take further offense and apologizing. She yielded to the latter. "I did not mean to be so forward, Mathilde. Forgive me."

The cook made a sound of disgust, gripped her lady's arm, and pulled her into an alcove. "You err in allowing me to speak thus to you!"

Thomasin stared into eyes in line with her own, and to which shadows were kind, revealing cheekbones in Mathilde's round face. She knew the woman was right—though only insofar as it was acceptable for a servant to address her mistress—but it confused that she now took her lady to task for allowing a servant to be offended at being trespassed upon.

Before Thomasin could request an explanation, Mathilde snorted again. "You do not make it difficult to determine the truth of talk you are of common stock."

Thomasin was not surprised she was the subject of speculation. Lengthening her small frame as much as was possible, she said, "I do not hide that my mother was a commoner, of which I am neither proud nor ashamed. 'Tis simply who I am."

"Then you are also, *simply*, daughter to the Baron of Blackwood, now wife to the Baron of Emberly?"

That was not so simple, but she inclined her head.

"Then simply you shall be treated, my lady, and a burden you will be to your husband."

"A burden?" It came out as a yelp. "If treatin' well those who serve the baron makes me a burden, then a burden he deserves. I will not behave ill toward those who ensure me life is more comfortable."

"Oh, have mercy!" Mathilde hissed. "Stir up your anger and the commoner slides right off your tongue."

Thomasin startled at hearing her own expression of frustration pass the woman's lips, startled again at having her speech corrected.

"I am not saying you should treat your servants ill, Lady Thomasin. I am saying you must present as one in authority."

"Such was not necessary with me father's—*my* father's servants—and they served me well."

The woman leaned nearer, and Thomasin was relieved her gusty breath was not offensive. "Did you oversee your father's household, my lady?"

"I——" She stifled the argument that was no argument considering where she was being led. "I did not."

"Ah! And does *he* exercise authority in his dealings with servants?"

"He does."

"There is order in his household?"

Thomasin sighed. "There is."

"Then you were served well out of respect for him. Here at Kelling, you are no mere daughter, and Baron Verdun will not thank you for the added responsibility of seeing you served well here."

Thomasin frowned. "Why do you, a servant, counsel me?"

"Ah, so you *can* be reached!" Mathilde gave a quick smile that revealed decent, albeit discolored, teeth. "I had feared you might not have enough wit about you."

Thomasin's temper flared anew. "Not enough wit?"

The woman backhanded the space between them. "Listen well, for I've tasks that need tending. An ordered household is as good for the servants as it is for the lord and his lady. When all know their place and what is expected of them, there is well-being. Without fear, they answer to their lord, his lady, and others placed in authority over them."

Mathilde pressed a hand to her chest. "The kitchen is mine. There my bidding is done quickly and efficiently. Why? Because I am respected by those who answer to me and those to whom I answer. Hence, my orders are all the more powerful for having the blessings of my lord. And I would have it be so with you, my lady. Gain the respect of those who serve you, and there will be no disruption in this household. Show you are weak with indecision and unwarranted apologies, and you will be twisted around the interests of those happy to take advantage of you. And 'twill not only be you who suffers, but all in authority, including your husband."

These were the things Thomasin's father had expressed, but never as forcefully. Because his daughter too closely related to his servants and too vehemently defended them even when one was clearly in the wrong?

"You understand?" Mathilde asked.

"I believe so."

"That is near enough—for now." She smoothed her aproned gown. "After you break your fast on the morrow, come to the kitchen, aye?"

"I will be there."

"Good, we shall make the menu together." The cook stepped past. Thomasin followed. "Mathilde?"

"My lady?"

"I thank you, but what do I not know about you that I ought to?"

Mathilde narrowed her eyes. "We share circumstances of birth, the difference being I was not claimed. Of course"—she snorted—"most are not. Good eve, my lady."

Thomasin watched her until she went from sight, then once more pointed herself toward the stairs. Feeling eyes upon her, she paused and looked to the right.

Sir Otto smiled with enough crookedness to appear apologetic.

Trying not to be offended at being under close watch, she nodded and continued to the stairs. Halfway up, she heard the tread of one descending, and the big Godsmere man-at-arms appeared.

"Pardon, milady, I be in a hurry. May I pass?"

"All is well, Sir Rollo?"

He grunted. "I be a man-at-arms, not a knight."

"Of course. I am sorry." In the next instant, her encounter with Mathilde had her questioning if the apology was warranted.

"I am not sorry," Rollo said with indignation. "I be a God soldier."

Did he mean *good*? As noted several times since she had first seen this man of formidable size and weaponry—an immense sword at his side, four daggers upon his belt—he was different in a way that made her think he might be a simpleton. If so, he could not be much of one, for he was regarded well enough to escort his lord's priest to Emberly.

"I am certain you are," she said. "All is well?"

He shook his head. "Father Crispin be ailin'."

She was not surprised, having earlier seen him press an arm to his abdomen. Too, he had been absent from the evening meal. "Can I help?"

His brow became a mess of furrows. "I am to fetch honey milk for the God priest to settle his gut. I be needin' no help with that."

"Then I will not keep you from it."

When he lumbered past, she continued up the stairs. Upon the landing, she paused to consider the solar's door, then that of the chamber she had been given upon her arrival. Though tempted toward the latter, she knew her place was with her husband. Did she not spend her nights there, speculation would abound, and some might even question if there had, indeed, been relations between lord and lady.

Feeling remiss for not arranging to have her chest moved to the solar, she stepped to its door and opened it.

Magnus looked up from where he sat at the far end of the large table, ledgers at his elbow, one open in front of him, a quill in hand. "Thomasin?" he said with what seemed surprise.

Thinking she must have interrupted business with his steward, she looked around, but no other was within.

Might Magnus have expected her later? Were there tasks to which the Lady of Emberly ought to attend before seeking her rest? In that moment, she almost wished the disagreeable Mathilde were here to steer her.

Lord, she silently beseeched, *I liked not the life of a servant, but this is also difficult.*

She stepped inside and closed the door. "I have come from the cook. We have arranged for me to discuss the menu with her in the morn."

Rolling the quill between thumb and forefinger—quickly, as if impatient—he said, "I am glad you take an interest in the workings of your new home."

Silence followed, as if there was more she ought to tell and he waited for it.

"Oh!" She advanced and halted before the table opposite where he sat. "I met Godsmere's man-at-arms upon the stairs. He says Father Crispin has fallen ill."

"His stomach?"

So Magnus had also noted the man's discomfort. "Aye."

"Then their departure on the morrow may be delayed."

More silence. Thomasin shifted her weight. "If you do not mind, I shall ready myself for bed."

"I do not mind."

As she moved toward the door that joined the two chambers, she said, "I am sorry I did not think to have my chest moved here. I shall see to it on the morrow."

"You need not."

Something in his tone indicating he did not mean he would arrange it himself, she drew back the hand she reached to the door. "What say you, my lord?"

"The chest shall remain where it is."

"But 'tis not where I sleep."

He set the quill in the ink pot. As it settled at an angle, he pushed his chair back and stood. "I have decided you shall keep your own chamber."

She frowned. "There will be talk if lord and lady do not share the solar."

"The household will settle in to it."

She stared at him, mind awhirl with the proper things expected of a lady, and sharing a bed with her husband was among them. Then of a sudden, she understood. What he proposed was temporary. On the night past, he had touched and kissed her without reluctance. Indeed, his absence from their bed indicated he had been moved enough to seek another woman. Thus, he must fear she would tempt him before it could be proved she was not with child.

"I see. You would have it so until my womb proves empty."

His mouth compressed, nearly subduing the spasm at its corner. "I speak of a permanent arrangement, Thomasin."

Pain pushed a sliver through her heart. She was no beauty, was only as refined as she strove to be, and struggled against impulsivity, but did she truly warrant such disregard? She had wanted this marriage no more than he, but she was the one in a strange place among people she did not know. She was the one believed to be unworthy. She was the one who would be faulted for the keeping of separate chambers.

Something inside her flipping, she tried to turn back words she would regret, but they too much longed to be spat—to be as fists to this man's ears. "I am told to rise above me breeding, not to shame the noble Magnus Verdun forced to take this lowly woman to wife. I am warned I shall prove a burden to ye if I do not command servants I know to be no less deservin' of respect."

His eyebrows drew close.

"And so I must prove meself a lady"—her voice rose, and she heard her speech go all the way to the other side of her—"one ye would shut out of the lord *and* lady's solar that all might think her more unseemly than already they do."

"That is enough."

"And for what?"

Magnus strode forward, but she did not retreat.

"So ye might take women into yer fine bed and not sneak off in the night as ye had to last eve, eh?"

He reached for her. "You speak nonsense!"

She lurched back, and when he caught her left arm, she swung the right. But she did not land a blow to his nose, which had once proved an effective means of freeing herself from the lord's steward.

Magnus deflected her fist with his forearm, gripped the offending wrist, and pressed her back against the door. "Hear me, Thomasin!"

What she wanted was to spit in his face, the urge so powerful she drew breath to do so.

He must have realized what she intended, for he released her wrist, cupped her chin, and settled his body against hers to hold her to the door. "Do not!"

When the first hot tear spilled, she thought she would be sick. Trembling with the effort to keep more from falling, she said between her teeth, "Loose me, knave!"

"*After* you have heard me."

"I do not wish to hear ye!"

"But you shall—like this, if needs be."

She strained to the side.

"Then it needs be." He more tightly fit himself to her.

Though she loathed being in another's control, Magnus was not repugnant as the steward had been—so vile she had struggled until she caught the man unawares between the legs. But even if she wished to do that now, she could not, her husband giving her too little space.

"I was not with another woman last eve." His eyes were hard. "I told I would keep my marriage vows, and I shall."

Knowing her disbelief swam to the surface of her tears, she said, "Where were ye?"

At his hesitation, she almost laughed that he did not have a lie ready. "I was restless and could not sleep," he said. "Not wishing to disturb you, I availed myself of your chamber."

Now she laughed. "I am to believe that? Ye think me so simple? So gullible?"

"I think you frightened and feeling very alone, mayhap even abandoned with your father so soon gone."

"I am not a child."

"Then do not behave one."

"Ah! So only a child would imagine her husband with another woman when she awakens in the middle of night and finds herself alone?"

"Nay, 'tis one set on believing what she wishes to believe, though given an explanation she refuses to consider, who I think a child."

"And I think ye a liar!"

With a sigh that moved the hair on her brow, he loosed her chin. But rather than release her, he slid his hand to the back of her head and pressed her face to his neck. "Breathe me."

"What?" she gasped against his skin.

"What is my scent?"

"Loose me!"

"When you have told me what I would have you know."

Hating that his strength far surpassed hers, she snapped, "Yer scent is that of a man."

"Which man?"

She was tempted to use the nails of her free hand against him. And she might have were it not ridiculous to think a warrior, whose every jagged scar a wife ought to know, could be bettered by scratches.

She pulled a long breath through her nose that carried the scent of…Was it sage? It was and not unpleasant. "I smell Magnus Verdun." And if he wanted more than that, he could smell himself.

He released her head, and when she whipped it back, he said, "That scent you will find in your bed."

Upon her sheets? In the pillow?

"Just as yours is now in my bed."

"My scent?"

"Of Thomasin Verdun clothed in violets."

She blinked. Had that scent yet been upon her on the night past— more than a dozen hours after she had touched the oil to her throat in remembrance of little Joss who had loved violets?

"As for keeping separate chambers," Magnus continued, "I vow 'twas not you that decided me. Had I wed Quintin Boursier, still I would wish it so."

That gave her pause. But again, she determined he lied. Though Lady Quintin was not as beautiful as Lady Elianor, she was becoming despite hair that barely skimmed her shoulders.

"Tell," Thomasin said, "if 'twas not me that decided you, what?"

"Selfish it may be, but I covet privacy."

She nearly pointed out privacy was not needed in sleep, but a lord's chamber was more than a place to pass the darkest hours. Here meetings were held, granting greater privacy than that found in the hall with its alcoves and dark corners. Here a lord might relax, pray, sit, and read. Here a lady might do the same and sew and weave and make conversation with her attendants and other ladies.

"Forsooth," Magnus continued, "so much I value it that I eschew the convenience of my squire sleeping within my chamber or outside its door."

He did? She stared at the man she had wed.

"Now you understand, Thomasin?"

Only just, for there seemed more to his need for privacy—had to be were he willing for his own ears to burn with gossip over the lord and lady sleeping separate, though their rooms were joined by a door.

She drew a deep breath. "The woman has listened, and if ye wish to call the one who does not concur a child, so be it. Now, I am tired and would leave ye to wallow in your privacy."

He muttered something with such vehemence, she was certain it was a curse, then he once more gripped her chin. But this time it was not to keep her from spitting on him.

He brushed a thumb down the bow of her upper lip and onto her lower lip. "When the time is right, you will be in my bed."

She narrowed her eyes, and when her lack of response returned his gaze to hers, said, "Only if 'tis *our* bed. I will not steal in and out of yours like a harlot, nor will ye steal in and out of mine. So turn yer key, and I will turn mine, have who ye wish in your chamber, and I shall have who I wish in mine." She forced a smile. "And if King Edward gets all twitched over that, I care not."

His steel gray eyes wavered, then gave unto the black of his pupils. "You will keep your wedding vows, Thomasin."

She longed to further the argument, but it was then she recalled the promise made the Lord for delivering her from the brigands. Swallowing hard, she raised her eyebrows. "Providing *both* our actions are in accord with our vows."

"They will be." He lowered his head, touched his lips to hers. "Thus, this shall be the only lover's mouth you know." Then he kissed her as he had done last eve, as if he truly wished to, but more lingeringly.

What was cold and hard inside Thomasin going warm and soft, she longed to do more than receive his kiss—to see if she could do to him what he did to her. If she could somehow make him deeply desire her, surely they would not require separate chambers, there being no need for her husband to wish privacy apart from her.

His mouth moved off hers, and when she opened her eyes on his handsome face, he said, "The only one," and released her.

Feeling as if her mind had returned to this place absent her body, she stared.

"Sleep well," he said and strode toward the table.

Commanding legs she could barely feel, she turned, opened the door, and hastened into the chamber that fell dark as she shut herself in.

She gripped the key, the child urging her to twist it hard so its scrape and rattle would be heard on the other side, the woman prying back her fingers and lowering her arm to her side.

She took the few steps to the bed. As in years past when she had mostly spent her waking and sleeping hours in the same garment, and bone deep fatigue made a straw-stuffed pallet seem the finest feather-stuffed mattress, she stepped out of her shoes, tossed the covers aside, and dropped upon the bed.

While her body slowly returned to her, she stared into the black overhead. Hearing the words she had flung at Magnus—pitted, scored, cracked sounds that ought to have been softly rounded; snarled and near shouted when they ought to have been firm and resolute, she felt tears run from the corners of her eyes into her ears.

I have no cause to be ashamed, she told herself. *He deserved that and more. What care I if the one who rejects me further regrets he was made to wed one whose first language is that of a commoner?*

"Fie on ye, Magnus Verdun!" she hissed. And the child's words spoken aloud made her cringe. She did have cause to be ashamed, and not only for lapsing into speech far distant from a noble. Rather than express the feelings of a wronged woman, she had expressed the feelings of a disgruntled girl. And what man would take such to heart?

She rolled onto her side. Tucking into herself, she turned her face into the pillow and detected scents she was fairly certain had not been present her first night at Kelling. The most easily identifiable was sage, and faintly beneath that was what a man exuded when his skin grew moist and salted with heat. It was the same she had breathed when her husband had pressed her face between neck and shoulder, was it not?

"Oh, Thomasin," she whispered, and moved onto her belly, buried her face in the pillow, and yielded to her misery.

And the scent of Magnus Verdun.

He detested blood on his hands. It was the worst sort of fouling, the hardest to remove from the pores and creases of one's skin—more, from one's mind.

Magnus moved his gaze from the crimson-stained hand he had gripped over his forearm, to his tunic's sleeve. Blood bloomed through the white weave, evidence Thomasin's fist had reopened the cut that had this morn provided proof of consummation.

Straightening from the table, he closed his fingers into his bloodied palm, and with his unsullied hand, dragged the tunic off over his head. The bandage around his forearm being cut of gray cloth, it was not as noticeably discolored by blood, but it was darker and glistened where it clung to his skin.

He strode to the sideboard, dropped the garment beside the basin, and plunged his hands into tepid water scented with sage and rosemary as his squire knew to prepare it.

He rubbed and scraped at his skin until it was only the flush beneath it that turned them red, then dropped the tunic in the basin. Providing the water soaked away the stain, the garment could be salvaged. Otherwise, a less fortunate man would think naught—as Magnus wished to do—of the discoloration and be glad to wear such a fine tunic.

As he dried his hands on a towel, he once more considered the bandage. Though tempted to replace it in its entirety, he determined it would suffice to bind another over it to ensure he did not foul the bedclothes. He set the towel aside, lifted his hands, and turned them front to back. Satisfied, he lowered his lids.

Just as there had been no crimson flashes before his open eyes, there were none in the dark, the cut on his arm of little consequence compared to the abomination Sir Francis had made of the king's gift. Such a bloody mess.

Knowing it best not to linger there lest it sowed seeds from which crimson memories would spread anew, he opened his eyes.

It was his burden, as it had once been his greatest shame, that blood affected him so. Fortunately, with determination and repeated exposure, he had taken control of what had been out of his control when he was a boy aspiring to become a man of the sword.

Now, spurred by the urgent need to survive, he could spill blood in battle—profusely, if need be—just as he had learned to do while hunting game and slaughtering pigs for the winter stores. And all the more easily he could spill it by using the full reach of his blade in what some derisively called *The Verdun Dance*. His father had danced it as well and taught it to his son as a means of keeping an opponent's blood off the skin and garments as much as possible. If not that the technique was so unexpected, it could place one who utilized it at greater risk of injury or death than those who adopted more familiar techniques for engaging a foe. But even those who knew what to expect from a Verdun were rarely practiced enough with the dance to triumph. Rarely...

Years past, when the De Arells had convinced the Verduns to make siege upon the Boursiers, Magnus's father had lost an arm to Archard Boursier. And last Christmas, there again upon the barony of Godsmere, Archard's son had adapted to Magnus's far-reaching jabs, swings, and swipes. And prevailed. Blessedly, it had only been practice combat in the bleak of winter when snow had forced Magnus and his men to accept Bayard Boursier's hospitality.

Blood had been shed, but without the enthusiasm that, following mortal combat, always bred crimson flashes while Magnus gave thanks that life yet coursed beneath his skin. Flashes that made him detest the dreams of wakefulness nearly as much as those of sleep.

He glanced at his bed, next the door behind which Thomasin had gone. Had she lain down? Happened upon his scent? Might she now believe what he told?

It gave him no pleasure to hurt her by insisting on separate chambers, but it was that or alarm her—possibly even harm her in other ways. Given time, talk of the wall between husband and wife would fade and she would accept the arrangement. And, perhaps, be glad of it. Thus, the two impelled to spend their lives together would settle into their new roles.

God—and Thomasin—willing.

14

⎯∞⎯

FATHER CRISPIN WOULD not depart Kelling this day. The big man-at-arms, who had requested a draught of peppermint and dandelions from the cook a half hour past, had told that the priest's stomach was no better disposed toward travel, then returned abovestairs with the slopping goblet and Thomasin's well wishes for a quick recovery.

"Surely I have not asked the impossible of you?" Mathilde returned the Lady of Emberly to her task.

Thomasin frowned over the rebuke. She was not ignorant of the workings of the castle kitchen, a great room often uncomfortably hot, loud, and humid with the scent of perspiration met with food. Nor was she uninformed as to the making of a menu. While she had held relative favor as a servant—before little Joss had gone from her—she had closely observed the particulars of being noble, especially those of the lady of the castle.

Telling herself not to mind Mathilde's rebuke, for she had kept the woman waiting on an answer, Thomasin cleared her brow. "Aye, roast fowl in ginger sauce will make a good meal."

"I am glad you agree. Set it down."

Thomasin dipped the quill. In the small, tight script she had years ago mastered to make the best use of parchment scraps upon which to practice her writing, she carefully drew the lines and curves that ever held her in awe of their ability to convey what one's mind and senses beheld.

"Now that we know the morrow's dinner," the cook said, "what say you of supper?"

Thomasin returned the quill to the ink pot. Since the final meal of the day was usually a simple repast compared to the hearty dinner served near noon, she said, "A stew."

"'Twill serve. Of what would you have it made?"

"The leavings of dinner and..." She shrugged. "...more vegetables, mayhap another meat."

"Certes another meat, my lady, lest there be insufficient fowl remaining of dinner. What meat, think you?"

"Venison."

Mathilde winced. "Mutton is more fitting."

"Why?"

"Did I not tell you we have much that needs cooking ere it goes foul?"

Inwardly, Thomasin groaned. "You did."

"And the venison is too fine and fresh to chop to bits and toss into a pot of twice-cooked food. Better to save it for a nooning meal when thickly sliced and sauced, it will make the most favorable impression on your lord husband who, you ought to know, likes well his venison."

She ought to know? A lump rose in Thomasin's throat. Though she tried to turn back remembrance of Magnus's refusal to share the solar that proved he less respected her as his wife than previously thought, it swept through her. True, her sage-scented bed evidenced he had slept there, but as concluded on the night past during her struggle to gain sleep, it did not mean he had not been with another woman before or after.

A chuckle brought her chin around. Having forgotten Sir Otto had followed her from the hall, she was surprised to find him seated at a table on the far side of the kitchen.

"What so humors you, Sir Otto?" Mathilde asked.

"Do not all men like well their venison?"

She snorted. "Such a fine specimen as you would know."

The knight raised an eyebrow. "And such a fine cook as you knows how to satisfy a man's appetite for the best of meats."

Once more, Thomasin frowned. Sometime between her arrival at Kelling and coming belowstairs this morn, the knight had become well enough acquainted with the cook that the two seemed easier in each other's company than their lady was in either of theirs. Too, this side of the knight she had only glimpsed when he was among other men of the sword. As for the cook, her behavior seemed a strange fit for what Thomasin knew of the woman thus far. Might she be attracted to the knight? If so, it could not go the other way. Thomasin was certain it was with longing for the youth and beauty of Lady Quintin that Sir Otto had looked at the one out of his reach. In contrast, Mathilde was at least a dozen years older, and though she had good features that evidenced she could be quite pretty, one had to look close to find them beneath so much weight.

When Thomasin returned her gaze to the knight, he said. "Forgive my interruption, my lady. I shall content myself with my own company so you may proceed." He lifted the tankard of ale Mathilde had poured for him after clearing the kitchen of those who answered to her, eyed Thomasin over the rim, and winked.

At me, she marveled. Never had he done that. Why now?

She pushed aside the question. As drawn to him as she was, and as much as she would have previously welcomed the flirtation—if it was that—she was wed.

Returning her attention to the menu with its too few entries, she said, "Mutton, then," and once more put quill to parchment. Then she rose from the stool.

"What do you?" Mathilde asked.

"We have made good progress. I will work more on it later."

"It must be done now." Annoyance raised the woman's pitch. "I must know which ingredients we require in the days ahead."

Restlessness uncoiled in Thomasin as it had earlier when she had learned her husband had already broken his fast and departed Kelling. She ached to be out of doors—walking the wood, visiting villages, distributing food to the hungry. "I have need of fresh air."

Mathilde stepped near. "My lady, just as I have duties, so have you. Just as I raised myself from chambermaid to kitchen servant when I came to Kelling over a dozen years past, then to cook by keeping the trust given me at each advancement and putting forth work that exceeded others', so must you be second to none."

Thomasin opened her mouth to continue the argument, but the one who perched at the back of her mind flew to the fore and she said, "You must have known Aude—er, Agatha—whilst she served Lady Elianor."

The woman's lashes fluttered, and she took a step back. "Of course I did."

"You were friends?"

Mathilde snorted. "One does not pet a snake." She frowned. "You knew her?"

It was Sir Otto who answered. "The one known to you as Agatha befriended Lady Thomasin. Though she surely did so out of ill intent, it was my lady who provided Baron Boursier with the information that led to that woman's downfall."

The cook swung her gaze back to Thomasin. "There is more to you than there looks, my lady," she said, then jerked her head at the table. "Now then, let us be done with this."

At Thomasin's hesitation, Sir Otto said, "Methinks you ought to heed her, Lady Thomasin. Then the rest of the day is yours to command."

She looked to him.

He turned his mouth down in a shrug nearly as pronounced as that of his shoulders. "A bargain. Give yourself over to Mathilde, and afterward I shall escort you to the stables so you may make the acquaintance of the horse King Edward gifted you."

She nearly pointed out she need not bargain since, if she wished to venture to the stables, still he would escort her—albeit at a distance—but she reminded herself to be gracious and looked to Mathilde. "Let us continue."

"She is beautiful." Thomasin drew a hand down the horse's jaw. "Is she not, Sir Otto?"

He grinned where he stood on the other side of the horse, and again she was intrigued by the boyish slant to his usually solemn face. "As one would expect of a gift from the king, my lady. And, certes, this mare has spirit."

That gave Thomasin pause as it had when Sir Francis had warned her of it. Since being acknowledged as the daughter of Baron de Arell, she had become passably comfortable in the saddle. But she had no experience with a horse of this breeding.

"Aye, spirited," Sir Otto said, and added low as if to himself, "not unlike its lady."

It seemed a compliment, and it pleased her so much she felt a pang of guilt. *Why,* she longed to ask, *do you only now show me such kind regard?*

In the next instant, it struck her this might be akin to what nobles called courtly love—a longing for and devotion to a lady already spoken for. The sweet forbidden. Was that what had so captured him about Lady Quintin? That, destined for Thomasin's father, she could never be his beyond imaginings?

"Something is amiss, my lady?"

She smiled. "I am thinking you are right, that the mare is quite spirited." She considered the immense eye regarding her. "We shall be friends, aye? And I will give you a name as beguiling as the one who shall be known by it."

The mare nickered as if in agreement.

"What think you, Sir Otto? Should I name her for a flower? Or is that too—?"

The eyes he fixed on her mouth reminding her of when he had observed Lady Quintin, she told herself to feign ignorance. But his expression made her too wondrously uncomfortable. "Sir Otto?"

With a grimace, he said, "My lady?"

She struggled over how to ask what he meant by regarding her in that way, but said instead, "You seem changed."

His eyebrows peaked. "Do I?"

"The knight I have known these past years is more serious than that who so readily converses with Mathilde. And now me."

"Am I?"

"You *were*."

He smiled apologetically. "I mean no disrespect, but your father has powerful expectations of those who serve him. If I am changed, 'tis because I am more at ease here than at Castle Mathe."

"Out from under your lord's thumb."

"You say it, not I. As for the cook, I am also surprised to be at my leisure in the company of one so common."

That made her tense. "If you judge Mathilde by her birth, then surely you judge me by mine."

His brow grooved. "Pray, believe me, my lady. I did not mean to insult either of you. 'Tis but a matter of not thinking through my thoughts. As for Mathilde, I am drawn to her for how much she reminds me of my mother."

It seemed ages since Thomasin had pondered his past. Did the one from whose breast he had been weaned yet live? What of his father? Had he siblings? Easing out her resentment, she said, "Tell me of your mother."

He sighed. "Naught to tell other than that though she could be a hard woman, I saw enough of the soft in her that I yet mourn her passing."

Thomasin ceased stroking the mare's jaw. "Has she been gone long?"

"Indeed—such that my thoughts should not go to her so often." He gave a grunt of laughter. "That I should not admit lest I be thought less a man."

"I think nothing of the sort. Truly, I am sorry for your loss."

"I thank you." He slid his gaze down her. "There is one whom you also call to mind. Until recent, you much resembled my sister."

She was equal parts disappointment and intrigue, the latter owing to those two words—*until recent*. Did he regard her differently now than before she had wed? How so? Before she could think of a way to ask without sounding pitiful, his eyes returned to her mouth.

Such warmth flooded her she said in a rush, "I do not understand why you look at me that way when you never did before, especially now that I am not only wed but unsightly with all my scrapes and bruises."

He dropped his chin. "Once again, I beg your forgiveness, and before I make more of a fool of myself, I will take my leave." He strode past her.

Thomasin stared after him, and when he exited the stall, wished she did not feel all the more alone. As his footsteps were swept beneath other sounds within the stables, she murmured to the mare, "Most curious," and sighed. "I will think on a name for you, and soon you and I will explore Emberly, eh?"

Upon stepping outside into a day clear of clouds, she paused to savor the sun on her face. When she lifted her lids, her gaze fell on Sir Otto where he conversed with a bulky man-at-arms alongside the fenced training yard.

Guessing he sought one with whom to practice weaponry, she was tempted to linger and enjoy the clash of blades and thrust of bodies moving between positions of offense and defense. However, as Mathilde had impressed upon her, she was Lady of Emberly, and with noon approaching, she must oversee the meal of middle day. But first, a visit to Father Crispin to inquire if she could make his stay more comfortable.

Minutes later, the big man hunkering alongside the door to the priest's chamber straightened. As Thomasin halted before him, he smiled broadly, revealing yellowed teeth and missing incisors. "The God priest is at his rest," he rasped.

"Is he improved, Rollo?"

His eyebrows shot high. "Ye remembered me name. I thank ye."

Wondering at his surprise, she said, "But of course."

He frowned. "Still Father Crispin's belly bothers him terrible."

"Has he been seen by——?"

A door opened at the far end of the corridor, and Thomasin looked across her shoulder to see Magnus's sister exit her chamber.

The lady closed the door and glided forward.

Returning her regard to Rollo, Thomasin noted the pucker of his brow and flare of his nostrils. Though curious over his reaction to Lady Constance, she put the question to him again. "Has Father Crispin been seen by a physician?"

The big man jumped his gaze back to her. "Your lord husband did offer to send one, but Father Crispin told him nay."

"Why?"

He flicked his eyes to Lady Constance. "When the priest be laid down like this—and it do worry Baron Boursier—naught can be done but treat his aching belly with rest, calming draughts, and prayer."

"This ill befalls him often?"

He looked again at Magnus's sister, following her progress the remainder of the way to Thomasin's side. In a gruffer voice, he said, "It does not befall him often, but it do come around again."

"Poor Father Crispin," Constance drawled. "Does he suffer the same as he did last Christmas when he had to absent himself from the feast?"

The man-at-arms narrowed his eyes at her.

She made a sound of disgust. "Why do you glower at me, old friend?"

"Where once I liked ye, Lady Constance, I do not now."

Thomasin nearly stumbled where she stood. It was confusion enough that Lady Constance was familiar with the man, but that he spoke so boldly to one of the nobility...

"Nay," he said forcefully, "no matter if me lord do forgive ye, I like you not."

More confusion, this time over The Boursier pardoning his first wife for cuckolding him. Though Thomasin knew she ought to put her expression in order, she left it agape as she looked to Lady Constance and caught a flash of what seemed hurt on the woman's face.

Magnus's sister jutted her chin at the door. "Then you and Father Crispin remain in accord."

"I speak only for meself."

She snorted. Then loudly, as if to be heard beyond the door, she said, "I have eyes to see how that self-righteous priest regards me, he who hides his own sins behind holy vows."

As Rollo's face mottled, Thomasin was moved to keep the argument from escalating and disturbing the priest's rest. And surely it was her right, this being her household.

"Enough!" Startled by the strength and depth of that one word, and that it had not flown from her own mouth, she turned to see Magnus striding from the stairway. His gaze moved from her to Rollo to his sister.

Halting, he turned a hand around Constance's arm. "Have you not packing with which to occupy yourself?"

She fluttered her lashes. "Of that, I would speak to you."

"I see no purpose in such a discussion. As promised the abbess, you return to the convent come the morrow."

"But—"

"The morrow." As he drew her down the corridor, her fiercely whispered protests carried, but if he responded, it was in no way seen or heard.

"Cur!" Lady Constance cried when he handed her into her chamber. "I do not—"

He closed the door, and when he started back, Thomasin was one moment dismayed, the next offended by the reproach he shone upon her.

He shifted his regard to Rollo. "The priest?"

"No better, milord."

Magnus came alongside Thomasin. "And still he will not be seen by the physician?"

"He says prayer better serves than the lettin' of blood."

"Jakes is less partial to bloodletting than most. Mayhap I ought to speak with Father Crispin."

The man moved his bulk in front of the door. "When he stirs, I shall tell him ye would like an audience."

Magnus slowly nodded. "Do, and inform him I have sent word to your lord that illness prevents the good priest from returning to Godsmere."

"Aye, milord."

Magnus looked to Thomasin. "We must needs speak."

In what else does he find me lacking? she wondered, then asked, "Your bedchamber or mine?"

There—a twitch at his eye. Because she had referenced their peculiar arrangement in Rollo's presence?

Oh bitter me, she mused and wished she were grateful Magnus slighted her so. But no matter what he told, no matter the truth of why he denied his lady her place in the solar—and she did not believe he would have done the same to Lady Quintin—it hurt.

"Your chamber will serve." He stepped past her.

Thomasin followed her husband inside, closed the door, and leaned back against it. Looking to Magnus where he turned to face her at the center of the room, she said, "I am listening."

"I know you have much to learn of running a household, but the time to start is now."

She folded her fingers into her palms. First Mathilde, now Magnus. But at least the cook had shown her how. "So I have done. Not only was my morn spent with the cook planning a sennight's menu, but she has arranged a gathering of the household servants this afternoon so I may make known what their mistress expects. Tedious exercises, I vow."

"I appreciate that, but is it so wearying you have only enough strength to stand by as my sister and Baron Boursier's man work themselves into a state that threatens to disrupt the household? Surely even you must know more is expected of Emberly's lady."

"Even *I* must know? What mean you by——?" She thrust off the door. "Ah! Ye refer to the dullard. The commoner. The one now speakin' outta this mouth."

"Thomasin, I did not mean—" He groaned, pushed a hand back through his hair. "'Twas your few years to which I referred."

"Another of yer excuses, and a convenient one, eh?"

"I will not argue this."

"Fine. Let us return, then, to yer sister and Rollo. I was not just standin' by. I was thinkin' what to say and how to say it when ye interrupted. As for bein' mistress of all, why should I know better how to behave than your most noble sister who set herself to baitin' a man-at-arms?"

Magnus's brow took on the weight of thought, and she was pleased to give him pause. "Unlike Constance, you are the wife of the Baron of Emberly."

"Ha!" She pointed at the bed. "Lest ye forget, there I slept on the night past the same as I did the night whilst I was yet yer betrothed."

His shoulders lowered with a sigh. "I have explained that."

"Explained—nay. Excused—aye." She turned and wrenched open the door, but there was not enough space to slip into the corridor before he hooked an arm around her. Pulling her back against him, he landed a hand to the door and slammed it closed.

Then his breath was in her ear. "Did you find my scent in your bed, Thomasin?"

A thrill sped her spine, and though she tightened every muscle, she could not contain her shudder. "It may have been you."

"It was."

She brought her chin around and blinked at how near her face came to his. Indeed, their mouths might have met if not for their noses. Of course, if he angled his head...

"And will be again," he murmured, his breath on her lips like the softest kiss.

"Only if you take what I will not give. As told, I am either evermore in *our* bed or not at all." She curled her hand over his that gripped her waist and pried at his fingers. "Now, as you have reminded me of what I need not be reminded, release me so the Lady of Emberly may perform her duties."

He so soon complied that when her back was no longer pressed to his front, she stumbled forward. Regaining her balance, she swung around and jerked at skirts that required little straightening.

"I apologize," Magnus said.

She considered his face and found nothing there to give her cause to question his sincerity. "For?"

"My penchant for offending you, not only by questioning your commitment to the role into which you have been dropped, but expecting more of you than you have been prepared for and ere you are fully recovered from your attack."

The eyes he moved over her face that yet evidenced the beating tempting her to touch those tender places, she drew herself up to her full height. "That is a beginning."

His mouth flexed toward a smile. "Only a beginning?"

She shrugged. "Better I could accept your apology if you explained some curiosities."

He raised his eyebrows.

"Why does Rollo so dislike your sister?"

Magnus considered her several moments, then crossed to the window and peered into the bailey. "As you have surely noted, for all Rollo lacks in being quick of mind, he is gifted with being quick enough in body to make a formidable warrior. Bayard Boursier's father saw that, and though few would have given Rollo a chance beyond toil of the land, 'tis believed guilt caused Archard to take the boy into his home and train him up in arms."

"Guilt?"

As he turned to her, his gaze narrowed on the chest splashed with the red of the topmost gown she had draped over it.

Though he had said he did not like that shade of red, doubtless he more disliked that she laid out her garments—perhaps thought her lowly for doing so—but how else was she to keep them free of wrinkles?

Magnus moved his gaze to her, and the disapproval there eased when he said, "Rollo is believed to be the misbegotten son of Baron Denis

Foucault, who was content to leave the boy and his common mother to their sorry fate. Archard Boursier was not content. Thus, Rollo is fiercely loyal to all things Boursier."

A liking for the one who had first been titled *The Boursier,* the same as his son was now known, further eased Thomasin's anger. "'Tis said guilt was also the reason Archard Boursier wed Baron Foucault's daughter," she ventured, and in that moment realized Lady Maeve would have been Rollo's half sister.

"Aye, but whilst I was a prisoner at Castle Adderstone as a youth, I witnessed great affection between Archard and his Foucault wife. I believe there was love there."

Though the woman's demise this past Christmas was tragic, especially if it was true that murder by a Foucault supporter had been her end, Thomasin was pleased Lady Maeve had known happiness while her husband lived.

"As for the division between Rollo and Constance, he blames my sister for the ills that befell the Boursiers when she and your uncle cuckolded Bayard Boursier—an act witnessed by Father Crispin whose testimony saw the marriage annulled, Constance committed to the convent, and Serle sent on pilgrimage."

Thus, his sister did not look any kinder on the two men than they looked on her. But what of that which Constance had called through the door? "When you came abovestairs, did you hear your sister accuse the priest of hiding his own sins?"

"I did." Magnus folded his arms over his chest. "When Baron Foucault suspected his vassals moved against him, among those he set to spy on our three families was Crispin, one easily overlooked for being a stableboy. He was caught out and, given the choice of death or allegiance to our families, came to our side. After Foucault was ousted, Archard Boursier sent Crispin to be trained for the church. Thus, 'tis surely his betrayal of Foucault all those years ago of which Constance spoke."

Thomasin frowned. "I do not see that he had any choice. And is it not hypocrisy to judge others for crimes in which one also engages—as well as one's family? That is, after all, the tale told by *The Betrayal* tapestry in the solar."

A tight smile moved Magnus's mouth. "I can offer no excuse for Constance. I love my sister, but she is difficult, and these past years of confinement have made her more so."

Especially since she had forsaken her vow of silence, Thomasin imagined.

"If your curiosity is satisfied, I have a question I would put to you, Thomasin."

"Aye?"

"I rode the demesne this morn, and just as I have received no further reports of brigand activity upon Godsmere and Blackwood, all is quiet on Emberly. Though 'tis possible the corpses of which Sir Francis made wedding gifts ended the threat, I am not convinced. Thus, I would speak to you of Agatha, the name by which I knew that woman—Aude, the name by which you knew her."

Doubtless, he was aware of her connection to Aude from when Thomasin had months past revealed to Baron Boursier the location of the hovel where the woman had taken Elianor Boursier to question her ere attempting to end her life. As much as it had hurt to learn of Aude's true nature that likely meant she had never had a care for the misbegotten daughter of Griffin de Arell, there was consolation in knowing Lady Elianor's life had been saved because of the information Thomasin had imparted.

"I shall speak with you of Aude," she said, "but lest I frustrate the cook by delaying the nooning meal, may we discuss it later?"

He inclined his head. "After dinner, then."

"Or over dinner."

"I would speak in private."

"Your chamber or mine?" She raised her eyebrows.

He lowered his. "Mine." He stepped from the window, and once again his gaze fell on the gowns draped over the chest.

"If I am given a wardrobe, such disorder can be contained," she said.

"Disorder?"

"I know 'tis unseemly for a lady to leave her garments about, but my gowns become a mess of wrinkles in the chest."

He halted before her. "Hang them in my wardrobe."

She blinked. "That would require I trespass on the privacy you so value, and I would not wish to see you all twitched over that."

His lids narrowed. "Twitched?"

Inwardly, she groaned, not only for how common she sounded, but the realization he might think she chose that word to mock the facial spasms that evidenced his dark emotions. "You know...distressed."

He smiled tightly. "As each morn I am early out of bed and below-stairs, it should not present a problem."

"Your wife is grateful."

"Too, I should have had Constance secure you a maid. I shall——"

"Nay. I am well without one."

"A lady ought to have a woman to aid her."

"Perhaps later."

He inclined his head, and speaking no further word, departed.

When Thomasin heard his tread on the stairs, she followed and, after meeting Rollo's gaze where he stood at attention outside Father Crispin's chamber, made her way to the kitchen.

15

---eaae---

FATHER CRISPIN'S APPEARANCE in the hall surprised. Drooping flesh beneath his eyes, a bow to his shoulders, a drag to his stride, he approached the dais at the Baron of Emberly's beckoning. By the time the priest and Rollo reached Magnus, the chair beside the lord's high place was vacated by the knight who had enjoyed the honor of being esteemed only second to the Lady of Emberly who occupied the chair on the other side of her husband.

"I am please you are of sufficient health to join us at meal," Magnus said as Father Crispin lowered onto the seat and the man-at-arms positioned himself behind and over his shoulder.

The priest smiled weakly. "I almost regret the undertaking, but restlessness is a weakness of mine, and I could no longer bear the still and solitude."

Magnus motioned a servant forward, and she set a goblet before the priest. But as she reached her pitcher toward it, he laid a hand over it. "I thank you, but warm milk better serves me."

"Of course, milord." She descended the dais and hastened toward the kitchen.

"Your man told I wished to converse?" Magnus asked low.

Father Crispin eased back in the chair. "Rollo is Baron Boursier's man, but aye, he told me."

"I would put my physician at your disposal. Jakes is accomplished at rooting out and treating difficulties, usually with little bloodletting."

"I thank you. However, the difficulty is known to me and is best treated as I have done since it took hold."

Magnus waited for him to elaborate, curious if what ailed him was the same that had caused him to absent himself from Baron Boursier's hall when Magnus had last visited Castle Adderstone.

When the silence stretched, Magnus said, "As you will," and looked to the meat and sauced vegetables placed between him and Thomasin.

A platter was also set between Father Crispin and the steward, but the priest pushed the meal toward the other man. "I but require bread," he told the servant.

The man bobbed his head and soon returned with a small loaf.

As the priest picked at it while awaiting his milk, Magnus looked to his wife. Her goblet was at her mouth, and when he followed her gaze, he saw Sir Otto held her attention. And she held his, as evidenced by the half smile directed at her.

Magnus leaned near Thomasin. "Is there a confidence you and your father's knight share of which I ought to be aware, Wife?"

Cheeks brightening, she lowered her goblet. "No confidence. Mere kindness."

"Of what measure this *kindness?*"

What might have been guilt yielded to indignation. "Of greater measure than you have shown me, *Husband*, but not as you imply."

The muscle at his eye beginning to spasm, he said, "I heard tale he was with you in the stables this morn."

Her eyes flashed. "I am watched?"

"Not by my order—not yet."

She drew a sharp breath, but before she could empty it on words, he continued, "As my wife, you are more visible than as the daughter of De Arell. Whether you do not know it or you disregard it, people talk.

Thus, whatever privacy was granted you at Castle Mathe you will find in less abundance at Kelling."

Blue eyes flashing, she put her face nearer his. "You think I did you an ill turn with Sir Otto? That I have not only taken the Verdun name, but now behave as a Verdun?"

Constance and her cuckolding…

The eye muscle quickening, Magnus said, "I do not, but these are deep waters into which you venture, currents so strong they could drag you under, so I urge you to think like a woman, not a child."

She especially did not like that last, dropping her hands into her lap and gripping her skirts.

He sighed. "Thomasin, I know I offend, but these are things you must learn."

"And you must learn how to treat a wife so she is eager to do your bidding."

He frowned.

"Had you shown me enough regard to escort me to the stables that I might look upon my wedding gift, I would not have accepted another's offer."

"You had but to ask—"

"Did I?"

Magnus did not like how often this young woman gave him pause, but she did, and it was true he had mostly neglected her—a blow on top of being told she would not take her place in the solar.

He breathed deep. "I had duties to attend to this morn. But tell, what would you ask of me?"

Her eyebrows rose. "You would do *my* bidding?"

"Within reason."

"How unreasonable would it be to ask you to take me riding that I might become familiar with Emberly?"

Beginning to relax, he said, "I shall take you."

"When?"

"Providing the affairs of the demesne are in order on the morrow, we shall ride to the nearest village."

A smile rose on her face, drawing his gaze to her mouth—and his imaginings to kissing her again.

"I thank you," she said. "You know not how much."

"I am glad to give you cause to be eager to do my bidding."

A laugh parted her lips. "Not eager—yet—but certainly more resolved."

He returned to the platter between them, speared a piece of meat, and offered it to her.

She leaned in, and with white teeth past promising lips, took the meat from his dagger's point. Though nowhere near beautiful, approaching lovely only when her eyes joined her smile, his young wife had appeal.

Enchantingly peculiar, he mused. And wished it were not so.

"'Tis a beginning," Thomasin murmured as she fingered the gowns she had hung alongside Magnus's garments.

She closed the wardrobe door and eyed the corner where she had pressed herself the night she had been caught trespassing. The night she had believed would be the only time she trespassed. The night shadows had parted to grant her a first look at her betrothed. The night her heart had one moment fluttered over proof he was as handsome as told, and sank the next. The night she had questioned how she could expect constancy from such a man when the lovely wife of the lord she had once served could not keep her husband out of the beds of other women.

Distracting herself with humming, Thomasin crossed to the table before the immense tapestry. A ledger lay there, a quill and ink pot alongside.

Wondering how long Magnus would make her wait, twitched over the possibility he had forgotten they were to speak following the nooning meal, she opened the ledger. As she ran a finger down the entries, she noted monies paid for household items, including linens and foodstuffs. Most figures seemed similar to what her father paid, but the latter—

"I am thinking you learned that song from Agatha."

She ceased her humming and swung her gaze to Magnus. Just as unprepared for his words as she was for his entrance, she straightened and watched him stride forward. Her examination of the ledger—surely another trespass—was worthier of notice than a pastorela that told of a nobleman's attempt to seduce a shepherdess with flattery and deception. But then, since they met to discuss Aude, the deceased woman must be uppermost in his mind. And as Aude, calling herself Agatha, had served Constance and his niece, he would have had occasion to hear the pastorela of which the woman had been fond.

"I did learn the song from her whilst I believed her to be a friend, not the foe I am told she was."

He halted. "It sounds as if you are uncertain there is sufficient evidence to prove all Agatha did to avenge the Foucaults."

She frowned. "There is proof enough, especially as she tried to kill your niece, but still I struggle to reconcile that the woman who was kind to me—indeed, my first friend when I came to Blackwood—did such."

"She did."

Thomasin sighed. "Aye."

The tension at his mouth eased, though she had expected it to spasm as it did when he was more stiff than usual.

"I am glad we are in agreement." He pulled out a chair and motioned to it.

As she lowered herself, he claimed the one alongside. "What can you tell me about the Aude you knew?"

"No more than I told Baron Boursier and my father. Except for the one time shortly ere Lady Elianor was abducted, I only saw Aude—and then on rare occasion—when I visited Blackwood's villages. Since she ventured upon Emberly and Godsmere as well, she did me good turns by distributing foodstuffs to those distant from Blackwood."

"Or so you believe. She may have taken the food for herself and those who aided her—the same who set our families against one another with burning and pillaging. Thus, 'tis more possible you fed the enemy."

Thomasin tensed. She did not wish to think on that any more than already she had done since learning the circumstances of Aude's death.

Magnus covered her hand with his. "I do not blame you. I but give you something to consider so you can better protect yourself and the people of Emberly."

She nearly pulled free, but it would be childish. Relaxing her fingers and liking even better his touch, she said, "I have considered it, and regret my part in whatever game Aude played."

"A deadly game."

She inclined her head. "Be assured, in future I will not rely on others to do what I myself can do."

"Which will not be what you did upon Blackwood, Thomasin. I will not have my wife wandering the demesne, content to set Sir Otto to steal around behind her—even were the baronies not under threat of brigands."

She raised an eyebrow. "You will serve as my escort when I wish to visit the villages?"

He shifted his jaw. "Mayhap at times, but my duties—"

"Then a proper escort you will have to arrange for other times."

"I will see what can be done. Now let us return to your Aude. You told Baron Boursier and your father that you saw her within Castle Mathe's walls shortly before my niece was abducted and delivered to the woman's hovel."

Stuffing down frustration, she said, "When I was passing into the outer bailey. But she went from sight ere I could reach her and ask her purpose."

"As she did not seek you out, 'tis likely she had one or more allies within your father's walls."

"He believes the same, but has not been able to root out such a person."

"What of when you saw her in and around the villages? With whom did she converse?"

"I rarely saw her with others, but when I did, I cannot say there was anything suspicious about their interactions. Mostly, when I happened on Aude, she stayed my side."

"Then there is no one who made you look nearer upon him—or her?"

"As I told my father, the day I followed Aude to her hovel, I saw a rider who moved in the saddle as does a man. But he remained astride and beneath his hood whilst they spoke too low for me to hear. Dressed well and upon so fine a horse as he was, I thought it peculiar, especially for how long they conversed, but I saw no evidence of wrongdoing."

Magnus nodded.

"You think me a fool for allowing Aude to befriend me."

He lifted his hand from hers. "If you are a fool, Thomasin, bigger fools Baron Boursier and I are for allowing that woman to dwell amongst us."

Thomasin was almost ashamed at how grateful she was for his understanding, that though he might view her more as a child than a woman, in this he did not condemn her.

"What is it?" he asked.

She flattened her smile and shifted her regard to the ledger. Recalling the discrepancies, she pulled the book between them and tapped a figure. "This one is summed wrong."

Silence, and when she looked up, Magnus's face reflected the question that next left his lips. "You can sum?"

Laughter escaped her. Now she understood the reason he had paid no heed to her trespass with the ledger. "Aye, and read and write, lord husband, just as I did ere my father claimed me as a De Arell. But since such is beyond many a commoner—mind, only for lack of education—I shall try my best not to be offended that you are surprised."

His smile showed more teeth than previously seen. They were not as straight as expected, and it struck her he was more handsome while brooding. But how she wished he would smile more!

"Too," she continued, "I am observant and capable of reason." She nodded at the ledger. "Methinks you pay too much for foodstuffs, and the candles would have to be of grand size to warrant as much coin as you render."

Though his smile lightened, the beat of her heart seemed not to notice. Indeed, the one side of his mouth that remained raised made him look a bit like a boy. Charming.

But then he said, "You will have to tell me of your life before Blackwood."

That life, the door to which she had thrown open. Not that there were any great secrets beyond the threshold, but as her grandfather had warned and himself proved, the less told of it, the sooner she would be accepted by the nobility.

Seeing his regard had turned curious, she said, "I am sure it would be of no interest to you."

"It is."

"Why?"

"You are my wife."

Here they were again, in the bedchamber he would not share with her. And once more resentment rolled off her tongue. "In name only."

As his face and posture returned to a state of brooding, she stood. "If we are finished, I will be about my duties as I am sure you wish to be about yours."

"We are finished."

She started past him, paused. "With your permission, I hung my gowns in your wardrobe."

After a hesitation, he said, "Of course."

What is it about you? she wondered. *Certes, it is not all me that stands between us.* In face and body, her husband presented well—so much it was easy to overlook that which seemed to coil within him, surfacing only long enough to be seen at the edges of his eye and mouth, the pulse at his throat, and the clench of his hands. Such one expected from a man faced with danger or amid great distress, but small things seemed to elicit such a reaction—as if those small things added fuel to a long-burning fire.

Their minds are not right, her grandfather had warned. Was this to what he had referred? Evidence of madness lurking beneath Magnus's fine face and figure?

"Good day, Wife," he unseated her musing.

She crossed the solar and shut the door behind her. Noting the corridor was absent Rollo, she murmured, "And what is it about you, my fellow misbegotten offspring of a nobleman?"

He felt a cur. He had no reason to resent that Thomasin had placed her gowns in his wardrobe, yet here he was with a hand on the knob, mere imaginings of her garments alongside his causing him to tense anew. He did not understand why he had offered the wardrobe, rather than assurance he would have one delivered to her chamber as Constance should have seen to. But without his usual precaution of thinking through what to say, he had violated his own privacy, giving his wife good cause to enter the solar whenever it pleased her.

He closed his eyes. "Lord, scatter these demons that scratch at me... beneath whose nails my bloody flesh can be found." Imagining the words drifting heavenward, he opened the wardrobe door.

Simple of design and gentle of color—excepting the one of crimson cloth—her gowns hung to the right. But though they did not crowd his garments, there was little order to them. And he liked order.

Determinedly, he closed the door and turned his back on it.

And you are only at the beginning of the disorder Thomasin Verdun will make of your life, he told himself. *So how are you to keep clear the path between your two lives?*

16

⎯⎯∞⎯⎯

A FORTNIGHT. AND still no further reports of brigands upon the baronies. And still talk over the lord and lady keeping separate chambers. And still she longed for her father and his people. And still she missed visits with her grandfather. And still Godsmere's priest lingered at Kelling.

But some things had changed. Thomasin's injuries were mostly healed, and though there were murmurs she was not as unattractive as originally thought—*Somewhat pretty, were I generous,* one knight said—she could not help being pleased. She had also become more adept and confident in her duties, made all the more possible with Mathilde's prodding and Constance's departure. Too, she had named her horse, though she had yet to ride Arundel since Magnus had not honored his agreement to acquaint her with Emberly.

"I shall remedy that," she murmured. "This day, this hour, and with none the wiser." Not even Sir Otto whose guard was down in the absence of earlier attempts to slip outside Kelling's walls. She had not schemed to catch him unawares, having several times come near to setting off on her own, but each time memories of the brigands' attack had discouraged her from taking a bite of that particular apple. But now...

Her heart beat so fast it felt as if it scaled her throat. Even as she told herself it was more excitement than fear, visions of the brigands flashed before her, drying her mouth and moistening her palms.

"Magnus," she whispered, summoning the vision of him bending near—saving her, though she had not known it then. But how soon had he saved her?

Beneath the homespun mantle she had borrowed from a servant to whom she hoped to return it before it was missed, she touched her belly. It remained flat, but still no menses to disprove she was with child. Soon, she prayed, and wished her monthly flux was just that so it might sooner be upon her. But since first she had crossed into womanhood, she was without regularity. It could be three weeks between menses as easily as six.

Lowering her hand, she peered up from beneath her hood. The sky did not portend well, its blue largely blotted by clouds that had begun gathering shortly after she had determined this was the day. Still, what was a little rain—even much—when it was so warm that perspiration dampened the hair about her face? Indeed, her venturing might be all the better if the skies opened up.

She looked to the raised portcullis beneath which visitors and the townspeople outside the walls passed, minimal heed paid to those exiting compared to those entering whose persons were as closely scrutinized as their baskets, bags, and carts. Thus, she need only concern herself with her return. Though the wife of Baron Verdun would be easily admitted, the longer she was able to hide that she stole outside the walls, the longer she would avoid reproach and opposition. For that, upon her return she would eschew the drawbridge and use the postern gate Sir Otto had pointed out on the day past when he had accompanied her to the stables to visit Arundel. The knight had teased that it was not as well hidden as the one at Castle Mathe, and that once her courage was up, he did not doubt she would make good use of it. And so she would, and without his knowledge. Although, were she to tell him—

I am not afeared, she assured herself. The brigands were gone, most certainly the two who had thought to undo her body and soul, and now she would meet her people.

Adjusting the basket on her arm in which she had nested hard cheeses, dried fish, and loaves of day-old bread that were to have been scooped out to hold pepper-sauced boar at supper, Thomasin stepped forward.

Trailing a lanky, loose-legged commoner who pulled a hand cart upon which a lad of ten or so perched, she passed beneath the portcullis with but a nod from one of two men-at-arms. Then she was on the drawbridge, next the well-maintained road that wound down the center of the town outside the castle, finally the rock-strewn dirt road that led to the wood through which she would pass to reach the village.

As she hurried forward, meadow on either side of her, she glanced around to ensure she was not followed. Several others came behind her, but all looked to be about the business of commoners.

"I have done it," she whispered. This day, the nearest village. Another day, one farther out. And eventually the home of Nanne and Eamon to thank them for caring for her following the attack.

Heart slowly returning to her chest, she hurried her steps to keep up with the one pulling the hand cart, comforted by the safety to be found in the company of others.

The lad placed in the cook's service to alert his lord to peculiarities had earned his coin. His tale that Thomasin had filled a basket with food had sent Magnus in search of his wife. Finding her absent from the keep, he had gone to the outer bailey. Had he not known to look for her, he would not have guessed she was beneath the homespun mantle, a basket on her arm where she lingered beside the stables. But it was Thomasin, further evidenced by the appearance of Sir Otto. Also beneath a hooded mantle—one of finer cloth than that worn by the Lady of Emberly, the hilt of his sword jutting beneath the fabric—he had stood out from others departing Kelling as he followed Thomasin at a distance.

Magnus had, in turn, followed the knight. He did not believe his wife and De Arell's man were intimate, but with Thomasin's admission of attraction and the lingering looks and smiles cast between them, Magnus would be a fool not to watch for the moment that thoughts and feelings became actions as they had done with his sister and Serle de Arell. And even had Thomasin and Sir Otto not arranged a meeting outside Kelling's walls, this could be the day they yielded to the forbidden.

Observing the knight who had yet to reveal himself to Thomasin as he watched her move among the villagers to distribute the contents of her basket, children hovering about the red skirts revealed upon the removal of her mantle, Magnus felt a stab of guilt. He had said he would escort her around Emberly, but had immersed himself in tasks of greater import—and not entirely unwelcome compared to the risk of allowing his wife to affect him more than she already did with her loose laughter, mischievous bent, and too generous honesty with nobles and commoners alike. All of which ought to offend, but over which he was less inclined to correct her.

Though unseemly for the wife of a baron to be so open and at ease, he found himself excusing her behavior with reminders of the past about which she did not wish to speak and assurances she would grow into her new role. Surprisingly, he almost regretted that day—almost, for logic dictated his life would remain disordered until she was in control of her person. And in this moment, she was not in control, squealing delightedly when a boy demonstrated his mangy dog's ability to walk on its hind legs and jump in time with the clapping of hands.

A rumble of thunder returned the dog to its forelegs, sweeping the smile of wonderment from Thomasin's mouth as she glanced at clouds that appeared to have been dragged through soot. With the breeze beginning to whip into a wind, there would be rain, likely before she made it back to Kelling.

Grateful he had donned a mantle before following her to the outer bailey, Magnus returned his regard to Sir Otto. Attention fixed on

Thomasin, the knight adjusted his hood as his lady bid farewell to the villagers who regarded her more kindly than they had done when first she had appeared. Then, taking the wide way around the wood bordering the village, the grip on his sword evidenced by the displacement of his mantle, De Arell's man once more trailed her as she moved toward the road.

Though Sir Otto would pass near the one who watched *him*, Magnus remained unmoving. It was time to relieve the knight of his duty—and take Thomasin in hand.

If Sir Otto was surprised to discover he was stalked by the Baron of Emberly, he did not show it when Magnus stepped from behind a large oak. He halted, inclined his head. "Baron Verdun."

"Sir Otto."

The knight's mouth curved. "And so I have proved capable of my duty to keep watch over Lady Thomasin."

At what point had he realized he was also observed? Magnus pondered and glanced at Thomasin who remained in sight as she traversed the road to Kelling. "'Twould seem, but better had you not allowed my wife to leave the castle."

"Ah, but this is Thomasin de Arell."

"Verdun."

The knight's eyebrows rose. "She has the name, but not yet—and perhaps never—the inclination to fit herself inside it. As her father learned, she chafes at confinement. Thus, the only surprise of this day is that she did not sooner steal outside your walls. And be assured, she will do so again if you do not yourself acquaint her with the barony."

Had Thomasin taken the knight in her confidence, expressing displeasure over a promise not kept?

"Forgive me," Sir Otto said, "I do not mean to interfere. 'Tis simply that I have long known your lady and her ways and have grown fond enough to be concerned for her happiness."

Was it concern only behind his smiles? Magnus wished it so, but he did not believe it. "I thank you for your dedication to my wife's wellbeing, but she is now my responsibility. Thus, your services are no longer required."

The man splayed his hands. "Until my lord grants me leave to pass his daughter's safety into your care, I shall perform my duty to Baron de Arell."

Magnus warred over the temptation to this day send the knight back to Castle Mathe. In the end, reason prevailed. Not only must peace be kept with Griffin de Arell, but until Thomasin's restlessness was contained, it benefitted all that another watch over her since Magnus could not always do so. Providing Sir Otto did not trespass beyond distant flirtation, he must be tolerated.

"I shall allow you to remain at Kelling a while longer, though I will require you to keep me informed of my wife's wanderings—in advance."

Sir Otto's hesitation was of sufficient length to be noted. "I will send word, Baron Verdun."

Magnus glanced across his shoulder at Thomasin's retreating back. "I shall ensure my wife's return to Kelling. You may leave us."

Another hesitation, then Sir Otto set off through the wood in a direction that paralleled the road but would be too distant to keep Thomasin in sight.

Magnus considered the clouds that had quickened their advance. In the wood all around, trees had begun to bend like soldiers leaning into war—planting their back feet to maintain their positions as they awaited the signal to charge.

"Now, Wife," he murmured, "'tis just you and me."

And the storm.

Out of sight of Verdun, Otto halted and dropped his head back. Narrowing his gaze on the dark sky, he growled.

It was long since he had been so disappointed in himself, though certainly not as disappointed as his lord would be if he learned it was not until moments before the Baron of Emberly stepped into his path that Otto's senses had alerted him to the other man's presence. Until then, he had been as oblivious to being tracked as the one he tracked, perhaps more since Thomasin was not always as unaware as she had him believe.

Standing before the predator to his prey, it had taken the full stretch of Otto's control to keep surprise from his face and his sword arm from drawing upon Verdun. Fortunately, had the one who stalked him proved other than the baron, Otto could have defended himself, having learned well the lesson of keeping a hand on his hilt in the midst of so many edges, corners, and shadows.

"Too well," he muttered and gripped his sword hand. He slid his fingers up beneath his sleeve and paused on the first scar above his wrist that was but one of many forming a ladder that scaled his inner forearm. Each horizontal mark the width of his thumb represented a lesson, though not all had been learned at the time they were sliced into his flesh by the one to whom he answered. This scar, and four more up, and seven up from there, had required repetition. And the disappointment heaped on him each time a lesson was repeated had made him vomit as a boy and gulp bile as a young man. Then there was the condemnation that had alternately made him wish for his own death and the death of the one whose words flayed him. But there was nothing for it. Even his mother, who had fed him at her breast until his fourth winter, had said there was no other means to ensure he proved worthy.

Silently recounting each scar's lesson as if a bead on a rosary, he dragged his fingers up over them all the way to the last one at the crook of his elbow, then recounted them back down to the hand gripping the hilt so hard it felt as if on fire.

He had been prepared to wield his sword against Verdun, but that he had not sooner known he was watched would see him rebuked for being too confident, careless, irresponsible—

If it was learned.

Assuring himself it would not be, that Verdun could not be certain and the wood would not tell, Otto turned his thoughts to the confrontation awaiting Thomasin. From what he had been told of the Baron of Emberly prior to accompanying De Arell's daughter to Kelling and had himself gleaned these past weeks, he did not believe she was in need of protection, but he was tempted to witness their meeting.

However, he dared not. Since Verdun moved too well through the wood to be detected, it followed that his senses were as finely honed to perceive the moment he was made prey.

Certes, Thomasin would know her husband's displeasure over her wandering ways, but she would likely suffer little more than sharp words. At worst, the back of a hand.

Otto grunted. Though these past years she had annoyed him so near the edge of patience his toes had curled over it, a plunge down its side threatening to earn him De Arell's wrath, he had somehow grown fond of the misbegotten creature. And strangely and most dangerously, of late he was attracted to her. He who was not drawn to the plain and rough-hewn watched her more closely than was required of him and smiled more often than was prudent. Yet another thing to keep from his lord.

"Quintin Boursier," he reminded himself of one worthy of such regard. Though betrothed to De Arell, such a prize he would do better to think on. And so he did as he resumed his trek to Castle Kelling.

17

IT HAD BEEN futile to try to outrun it. Why had she? She did not fear rain, even the less amiable sort. And though this one might turn chill and stinging, at the moment it fell warm and soft, inviting her to let it anoint her crown to sole.

Imagining God at His leisure, tenderly laundering His creation, Thomasin halted, released the hood she had held to her head in defense of the stirred air that sought to drop it to her shoulders, and lifted her face heavenward.

The rain pressed gentle kisses on her hair and face, trailed them down her jaw and throat, slipped them beneath the neck of her mantle, rewarmed them between her breasts.

With a laugh so joyous she knew she would offend those much too important were they present, she lowered lids that also longed to be kissed—and not only by rain.

She smiled in remembrance of Magnus's mouth on hers, imagined it kissing her eyes closed. Would it ever? If so, would he see her or imagine another?

"Oh, have mercy, Thomasin," she muttered and told herself to be grateful for all she had that once she had not.

Hair growing weighted with rain, moisture seeping down her back against which the fat braid lay, she dropped her basket. With another laugh, she raised her arms out to her sides.

She felt a girl again, stealing to the garden while little Joss slept, whirling amid rain, breathing in sweetly moist air, sipping from cupped hands.

Whenever possible, she had indulged in those rare snatches of time, imagining it was she who was given a servant to carry her wherever she wished and do her every bidding.

Having allowed her thoughts to push her in a direction she should not have wandered, Thomasin dropped her arms, opened her eyes, and blinked against rain none would know was as distant from her tears as water was oil.

"Forgive me, Joss," she whispered. "If only I had not done it." Lowering her head, she assured herself she was not entirely at fault. Had the girl not been so terribly persuasive, never would Thomasin have risked it.

Or would she have? It had seemed harmless—unless they were seen and it was reported to the lady—and good for Joss.

Her shoulders quivered. A pained conscience would not bring back the girl. And even if it could, Joss would surely wish to remain above all where she could carry herself where she wished, feel no pain, and suffer no whispers and pitying glances.

A sob escaped.

"Thomasin."

She told herself it was thunder that sounded like Magnus, not Magnus who sounded like thunder. But then a hand was on her shoulder, reminding her of the attack she had tried not to dwell on when she had slipped outside the castle walls, certain the memories would send her scampering back to suffocating safety.

She pulled her meat dagger from her girdle, but the gentleness with which she was turned made her falter. Thus, had the one belonging to the unhooded face above hers—who smelled of sage, and was it rose-mary?—meant her ill, she would have failed to defend herself.

"Magnus!" she gasped as his hand captured her wrist between their chests, keeping the blade from his neck.

Rain slowly coursing his face as if it would be too distressing to quickly pass over such agreeable features, he said, "You are unwell?"

Relieved he was not a brigand, and his tone was concerned rather than angered, her knees weakened, and she leaned into him. "Not at all."

He took the dagger from her, returned it to the sheath on her girdle, and drew her off the road and beneath a tree whose leaves blunted the rain beginning to fall more heavily. Setting both their backs against the expansive trunk, he said, "You defied me, Wife."

She looked sidelong at him. "And you did not keep your word to show me Emberly, though I have reminded you."

"I concede that, but it does not justify you wandering the demesne and exposing yourself to another attack."

"There has been no further brigand activity." She swept a hand down her front. "As you can see, I am unharmed—and happier than I have been in weeks."

His brow creased. "Such happiness would have come at great cost had another overtaken you."

"But it was you."

"And could as easily have been one who intended you ill. Though you had much to fear, foolishly you did not."

As she turned toward him and put a shoulder to the trunk, the wind snatched open her mantle and flew it back off her shoulder. "But I did fear." She wiped rain from her face. "Thus, I watched and listened well lest I be surprised again."

"As you were surprised," he growled. "'Tis not happenstance I am here. I followed you from Kelling."

"Oh." She sucked breath through her teeth. "Then you are very good. Much better than Sir Otto—"

"Who also followed you. Ahead of me."

She snapped her head around and searched the road and bordering wood.

"I ordered him to return to the castle."

"Ah. So I *am* a bit foolish."

"More than a bit."

"But not so much I am once more in need of rescue."

"Either because no brigands are near, else they saw what you did not and dared not challenge two warriors bent on keeping you safe."

She raised her eyebrows. "I am grateful for your concern, but you must admit I would likely have returned to Kelling without a mark upon me."

He turned his own shoulder to the trunk and peered down his fine nose at her. "I will not admit to what may not be true."

Lord, he is most pleasant to look upon, she noted, though surely the Almighty need not be told, having Himself formed Magnus Verdun—from the black hair that rain fit smooth to his head, to broad shoulders her hands longed to grip, down long, muscular legs, to feet encased in rain- and dirt-spattered boots.

And I can be passing pretty when I smile and do not resemble a near-drowned cat as I surely look in this moment, she mused.

"Is what distresses you now what distressed you when I called to you upon the road?" Magnus asked.

Her smile felt stiff. "I am not distressed, only very damp and beginning to take a chill."

It was more of an excuse than the truth—certainly not intended to move him to action—but he stepped nearer, with his body pressed her back against the tree, and braced a forearm on the trunk above her head. "Better?"

Sheltered from the wind and rain, she breathed, "Aye." And it was true, but only in terms of the heat coming off him, and only until she became more aware of all the places their bodies touched—and the scent of sage that should not waft more pleasantly from a person than viands. And just beneath it, rosemary did, indeed, travel.

Attempting to distract her awareness of him, as well as keep him from returning to her distress, she said, "I am pleased you are well regarded by the villagers, especially that even the poorest among them do not want for adequate food and shelter."

"A commoner's life is difficult enough without denying them basic needs," Magnus said. "As the feud between our families has often made those hard to attain, I intervene when necessary so my people do not pay a debt not their own."

Thinking this must be the reason Castle Kelling mostly lacked extravagance, Thomasin warmed further toward this man whose vanity she had believed would be at the expense of his lessers. Her father was also a good lord, but if what was true of the village visited this day was true of all of Emberly, Magnus's people fared better.

"Now," he said, "I would know what distressed you."

She sighed. "The past."

"Of which you will not speak."

"Perhaps I shall once we are more than landlord and lodger." She nearly groaned. She had determined she would speak no further about their sleeping arrangements, but there it was.

"We are far more than that, Thomasin."

She shrugged. "Our separate chambers say otherwise—as do the castle folk."

He crooked a finger beneath her chin and raised her face toward his lowering one. "A landlord would not—certainly should not—do this." His thumb traced the curve of her lower lip. "Or this." Now her upper lip. "Or this." He drew his moist hand down her neck to the hollow of her throat. "And, certes, this would be unforgivable." He touched his mouth to hers. "Would it not?"

Thomasin did not know how her hands came to be on his shoulders, but they were. She did not know how they could with such abandon push up into his hair, but they did. She did not know whose hunger turned a near innocent kiss feverish, but mayhap they were both to blame.

What she did know was what pulled them apart—bright, stuttering light followed by thunder, then wind so fervent and rain so hard she felt it reverberate through Magnus.

"Come!" He hastened her into the wood, firmly holding her arm as her feet sank into wet earth that aspired to snatch her body out from under her.

All a blur, she ran beside him until it was exertion that stole her breath and the rain and wind suddenly stopped beating on her and the ground turned firm.

As Magnus drew her into near darkness, she swept her gaze over what appeared to be a stone wall. "Where are we?"

He released her. "An old quarry—a cluster of caves from which blocks were cut for the construction of Castle Kelling."

A wall of stone, indeed. She dropped her head back and squinted at the high, jagged ceiling, then turned. They stood in what resembled a room, so expansive several of Kelling's great halls could fit into it. Bounded on three sides by stone, the fourth was open to the wood where rain fell so solidly it appeared they stood behind a waterfall.

"Is it safe?" she asked.

"At the moment, safer than remaining outside, and too open to tempt bears and boars to long linger here."

It was too dim to see more than Magnus's figure and the bit of light reflected in his eyes, meaning she was no more easily seen. And that assurance increased her daring.

Longing to return to what he had made her feel beneath the tree, she stepped close, slid a hand up his chest, and set it on his cheek.

"Thomasin?" he said so warily she nearly reconsidered.

She leaned her body into his. "Out there, it felt as if you truly wished to kiss me. That you...liked it."

When he finally responded, the two words were sweet. "I did."

"True? You like kissing me?"

His chuckle fanned her moist face. "Did I not, I would have stopped long ere the storm parted us. Indeed, I would not have kissed you at all."

Rising to her toes, she slid her arms around his neck. "Then continue. And this time, do not stop."

Had she been able to see the struggle on his face, she did not think it could be better known than what she felt between them. But he yielded to her whatever battle he fought and once more claimed her lips.

It was no sweet kiss that might progress to something more. Already it was more—well beyond where they had ventured beneath the tree.

She liked it.

And his arms winding so tight around her she could hardly breathe.

His hands spanning her back and exploring her curves.

His fingers loosening her braid, pushing through wet tresses, cupping the back of her head.

The urgency with which he broke from her to remove his mantle and lower her upon it.

The rattle of his sword belt as he unfastened it.

The shedding of her slippers and removal of her hose.

The skim of his fingers over her calves, knees, thighs, and waist.

Her name spoken in her hair, ear, and against her lips.

His answer to his name when she beseeched him not to stop.

All these things she liked—and all that followed.

It should not have happened. Not that he had been so gripped by passion he did not know what he did. Not that he could not have stopped what he had begun and for which Thomasin had called him to account. He could have. He should have. But he had answered the longing that had gripped him upon seeing his bride lose herself in the rain—before whatever she would not tell had scattered her joy. He had been impulsive, behavior in which he rarely indulged for how vulnerable it made him—and the price to be paid for it.

Now the long-denied consummation was had—and in advance of his wife's menses. Blessedly, on one side it mattered not. On the other...

"Regret?" Thomasin asked where she curled against his side with a knee drawn up his thigh, what she whispered easily heard now that the storm had passed, how she appeared easily seen by sunlight filtering into the stone room.

Head propped on the arm crooked beneath it, Magnus peered into her upturned face.

"Regret?" he said, though he knew to what she referred.

She shifted her regard to her hand on his chest, with the tip of a finger traced a muscle. "You fear that if I soon prove to be with child, you will not know 'tis yours."

Worse, he thought, but said, "We need no longer fear you carry another man's child, Thomasin. I am fairly certain you were untouched until this day."

Her eyes jumped back to his. "True?"

Contrary to what many believed of one who oft stole the regard of women from others, Magnus was not exceptionally versed in matters of the flesh. "I believe so."

With laughter so musical he nearly closed his eyes the better to feel it smooth the sharp places within him, she rose up over him, lowered her head, and dropped her smile onto his mouth.

Though tempted to return her kiss, he remained unmoving.

She lifted her head. "But still you regret being with me like this?"

How to answer? "Why would I regret it?"

She gave a huff of frustration. "I am not blind, Magnus, nor do I delude myself by believing I am even half as fair as Lady Quintin or Lady Elianor. Do I take care with my appearance and smile often, some say I am passing pretty, but one cannot always be so attentive to one's grooming—especially amidst a storm—and there is not always something over which to smile."

Magnus did not pity her, nor did he believe she wished him to. It was true that one's eyes upon her would elicit no gasps of delight or great stirrings among men, nor would most women feel threatened by her—at least, not from a distance. Up close, near enough to be warmed by the light in her eyes, moved by the true of her smile, and intimate with the sweet of her body, one had only to be honest with one's self to be drawn to and envy one of such unpretentious spirit.

And in that moment, jealousy moved through Magnus at the thought of another man being as near her as he was.

Turning with her onto his side, he pushed up on an elbow and peered down into her wide-eyed face. "Had I been given a choice in whom to take to wife and been wise in my choice, a woman of true beauty I would have sought."

Her slight smile lowered, and he berated himself for being too loose with his words—as he was wont to do since she had burst upon his life. In that regard, she was a poor influence.

"I do not speak of outward beauty, Thomasin. Such is shallow, covering more sins that it has cause to." As the form into which God had poured him covered the ugly things he struggled to control in lieu of ridding himself of them. "Regardless of how long outward beauty lingers, it will abandon even those most gifted with it, and its loss will be all the more cruel does one depend upon its currency. But beauty within…" He laid a hand to her cheek. "That is true beauty—able to be seen in the dark, allowing one soul to touch another's. As did ours this day."

A curve returned to her mouth. "Is my husband a poet?"

"Hardly. He would but have you think better of yourself and never again question if he likes your kisses."

Her smile opened, showing pretty teeth. "Or question if he wishes me in his bed? Or would have me give him an heir, a son as dark and handsome as he?"

Though there seemed no challenge or goading in her words—being more teasing than anything else—Magnus dropped back into himself, so forcefully he did not doubt she saw his answer.

Her own body tensing, hurt displacing her smile, she said, "So still we are there, even after ye profess to value what is within me by naming it true beauty. But 'tis not enough, is it, this *beauty* that can be seen in the dark. Still ye would not awaken beside it with morn's light cast over it."

"Thomasin, I have told you. 'Tis not you."

Her nostrils flared. "Then ye hide something."

What she could not know—and that was for the best. He released her and thrust to his feet. "We should return."

"What do ye hide?"

He swept up their garments, dropped hers beside her, and dragged on his tunic.

"Is it true the Verduns are not right of mind?"

Chausses in hand, he narrowed his eyes at her. "Who told you that?"

Sitting up, she tugged her chemise down her legs. "My grandfather, Ulric, warned me."

Anger diluted by foreboding rose through him. Just as his father had done his utmost to keep from prying eyes and off loose tongues the ills with which he had been afflicted, so had Magnus. Had one or both failed in Ulric de Arell's sight? Or did the man but add fuel to what ought to appear to be no more than nervous spasms and distaste for staining one's fine clothes with blood?

Calm, he counseled and donned his chausses. "Ulric de Arell, the instigator," he grumbled. "Ever setting fires amongst our families, and when they are reduced to embers, quick to return them to flame." He jerked at the ties of his chausses. "Methinks he is as much—perhaps more—to blame for our feud as your friend, Aude."

Indeed, he considered, it was possible that woman had been in De Arell's employ. After all, as Agatha, the witch had moved among the Verduns and Boursiers. It was only among the De Arells she had named herself Aude—at least, to Thomasin. If Griffin de Arell's assertion he had not known her was true, his father might well have. And Thomasin, whom there seemed no cause to disbelieve since she had exposed the witch's lair, had said she had seen the woman once within Castle Mathe's walls. With whom had Aude met? Griffin? Ulric? Another?

"Perhaps my grandfather is as much to blame," she said as she stood to don the red gown, "but did he speak true about the Verduns?"

Jerking leather through his sword belt's buckle, he snapped, "We are as right of mind as you, Thomasin." A lie, but better that...

"Then what do you hide?" She bent her head to address her gown's laces.

Magnus retrieved his wet mantle and snatched up hers.

She secured her laces with a sloppy bow, and ignoring the mantle thrust at her, dragged her hair over her shoulder and began plaiting it. "'Twould not do to look as if the husband who bars me from our bedchamber has just made love to me," she said and met his gaze.

He drew breaths of patience, and when she secured the braid with a knot in its tail, dropped her mantle over her shoulders. "We will be fortunate to reach Kelling ere dusk." He stepped past her.

Though no further word did Thomasin speak, he felt her thoughts and questions throughout the walk to Kelling. During the evening meal. Through the wall between their bedchambers. And amidst his dreams.

18

⸺⧉⸺

ANOTHER SENNIGHT. THAT was what it took to confirm Thomasin's womb was empty, not only of a brigand's child of which she had been fairly certain, but of her husband's child that she hoped one day to give him.

Guessing her long-awaited menses had made ruin of not only her chemise but the coverlet she wished she had not slept atop, Thomasin sprang to her hands and knees, crawled off the bed, and whipped around.

Fortunately, the coverlet was of a russet color. Thus, the damage was not as obvious as it was upon her cream-colored chemise, the front of which bloomed red.

In that moment, she wished she had accepted Magnus's offer to secure a maid for her, the thought of delivering evidence of her menses belowstairs for laundering making her cheeks warm. She could leave it to the woman who straightened and freshened her room along with the other chambers abovestairs, but if it was possible to salvage the two items, it could not wait.

The sun outside her window having ascended high enough to ensure Magnus had departed the solar as he did early each morn, Thomasin crossed to the door between the two chambers and halted as pain lanced her lower abdomen, this cramp sharper and of greater duration than the one that had awakened her.

When it passed, and with it the faintness that made her press a hand to the wall to support herself, she slipped into the chamber Magnus denied her, and of which neither had spoken again since she had become Lady of Emberly in full.

She swung open the wardrobe door, chose a gown of dark blue that would best disguise her flux if it could not be contained by the abundance of folded cloths she required the first few days of her menses, and dropped the garment over her arm.

As she closed the door, she heard another settle into its frame.

"Almighty! What has happened, Thomasin?"

A shriek escaped her, and she spun to see Magnus striding from the garderobe—with urgency, as if for fear the blood was a result of injury rather than what she usually thought of as a woman's nature, but in that moment seemed more the curse other women named it.

"N-naught has happened!" Awash in shame that he bore witness to the mess she had made of herself, she convulsively bunched the skirt of her chemise in a sorry attempt to hide what was already seen. "Naught but prove I carry not a child, misbegotten or legitimate."

Though his stride did not shorten, relief swept his face, whether a result of tidings she was not pregnant or that she was not hurt, she could not know. And told herself she did not care. Following consummation of their marriage, they ought to have become more comfortable with each other. Instead, they were more distant.

He halted before her. "I feared you were injured."

"Only by humiliation." She turned toward the door she had left open between their chambers, but he pulled her around.

"Thomasin—"

"Oh, have mercy!" She strained against his hold. "I bleed, and soon upon your rug."

He muttered what sounded like a curse and drew her into her chamber. "I would speak with you."

"Now?" She wrenched free, released the handful of stained chemise, and gestured at the bed. "This moment?" And with another cramp twisting her insides?

His gaze moved to the stained coverlet, then back to her ruined chemise. As he stared at the latter, the spasms at his eye and mouth sprang to life and she felt his tension swell.

"Forgive me," he said. "After you have seen to your ablutions will be soon enough for us to speak. Join me in the solar." He pivoted, strode into his chamber, and closed the door.

Gripping an arm across her abdomen, Thomasin stared at the wall between husband and wife as she waited for the pain to recede. When finally it did, she lowered her shoulders with a sigh and set about removing all evidence she bled.

"Three days," Thomasin said, wishing his pending absence did not trouble her.

"Aye, there are matters to which I must attend."

She stared at him where he sat beside her at the head of the table in the solar. "What matters?"

"Of the demesne," he said curtly.

Having kept him waiting a half hour while she set herself aright and delivered the coverlet and chemise to the laundress—to her further discomfort, happening upon Father Crispin and Rollo on her descent of the stairs—she supposed it was impatience that made him less civil.

"You will be visiting the villages?" she asked.

"Aye."

"Surely a good time to introduce me to the people of Emberly."

A muscle in his jaw convulsed. "But for your menses."

It was true, but even in the absence of her flux, she did not think he would have asked her to join him. Just as he refused to share the privacy of the solar, he would not share his ride upon Emberly.

Moved toward anger that was more precarious amid the discomfort of her menses, and determined to keep her promise to the Lord, she laid a palm to the table and began to push upright. "We are finished here?"

He closed a hand over hers. "We are not."

Grudgingly, she resettled in the chair.

"I want your word, Thomasin, you will not leave Kelling in my absence."

She put her head to the side. "How is that different from not leaving while you are present?"

"'Tis of greater import, for I would not rely upon Sir Otto to keep you safe should you venture outside the walls."

"And if I do not give my word?" She nearly groaned. How she wished she had half the control he had—and he half her abandon!

"Then I shall set a guard on you day and night, and well within your sight so he need not be discreet and risk being evaded."

Thomasin held up the hand she longed to press to her abdomen. "Forgive me. The difficult start to my day makes me all twitch—" She snapped her teeth, but too late, as told by his raised eyebrows. "It makes me ill tempered," she corrected. "I would not argue with you."

"We are agreed, then? You will not leave Castle Kelling?"

"While you are gone these three days, I will find some way to while away my time so I will not be tempted to venture beyond the outer bailey."

He nodded. "Hence, there is another thing I would ask of you."

"Another condition to avoid being leashed like a dog?" Again, regret. But her woman's time was playing such foul games with her that she wanted nothing more than to burrow beneath her covers and find relief in sleep.

"Something that, I hope, will make the passing of days less tedious." He nodded at the ledgers, the great number of which she had noted upon her return to the solar. "I confirmed the discrepancies you noted, and as you seem to know well your numbers, with which I am versed with some effort, I would have you search out other errors."

She nearly startled. Such might be the duty of a well-educated and esteemed wife, but one fairly educated and of such disregard she slept separate from her husband? "I am surprised you would entrust me with so important a task."

"My niece oversaw the books ere she wed. Now, whom better to entrust with the task than my wife whose interest in the wellbeing of Emberly ought to be as great as mine?"

And could be if he would show the depth of his own acceptance by taking her around the barony and welcoming her in his bed. This time, though, Thomasin kept her thoughts to herself.

"What of your steward?" she asked. "Do you suspect——?"

"He is aged, having long served my father before me. Whatever errors you find—and I do not expect them to be numerous—will likely be a result of his advanced years."

Likely. Meaning there was doubt. That pleased her, though not because she would see his disagreeable steward exposed as incompetent or a thief. It meant the task set her was not merely a means of keeping her out of mischief, that in some measure, Magnus trusted her.

"I will see to it."

His hand on hers relaxed, and he drew a thumb over her wrist. "I thank you."

Remembering more sensual caresses that, despite her menses, she longed to feel again, she pulled free. "Are you opposed to me examining the ledgers here?"

He leaned back. "As you see, 'tis where I delivered them."

"Of course. When do you depart?"

"Come the morn."

"You would have me begin then?"

"Or now if you feel well enough." He searched her face. "You are quite pale."

Hands tempted to her cheeks, she stood. "I shall rest for a while, though perhaps when I arise..." She nodded at the ledgers.

Magnus stood and reached to her.

"I do not require assistance," she said and crossed to the door she had left ajar. As she stepped into her own chamber, she put over her shoulder, "I wish you well with preparations for your departure."

"Thomasin!"

She paused in easing the door closed.

"I will keep my word to take you around the demesne, but at a better time than this."

"Then I will keep my word to remain within these walls." She closed the door.

Settling his wife against his chest, Magnus mused that her face was as innocent as a girl's. But not her body whose curves were all woman, nor her kisses and the hands with which she had held to him that day in the rain—a day that returned to him each night, making rest all the harder to attain. But strangely, once he slept, his dreams were less troubled. And often he was tempted to accede to the condition she would share a bed with him only if they shared a chamber. But his dreams would not always be so mild. Indeed, this night did not portend well.

Thomasin sighed and opened her eyes just enough to reveal their blue in the candlelit solar. "I but meant to rest a moment," she murmured and reached ink-stained fingers to his jaw.

Distantly acknowledging it was a fool thing to act first, Magnus turned his mouth into her hand and kissed her palm. "I expected you would be abed, Wife."

"It seems I was—upon your table."

He glanced at the ledgers that made him long to correct their disarray. Three were splayed open, and nearby lay a parchment upon which she had jotted notes and worked numbers in a hand so small he would have to bring them much nearer his eyes to make sense of them.

He started to ask if she had found more errors, but she so lightly drew her fingers across his lips that his body intercepted his thoughts and flung them behind him.

'Tis her time, he reminded himself.

Even so, he turned toward the bed with the promise he would merely hold her. But as he lowered her toward the mattress, she grabbed a fistful of his tunic and asked, "Am I to share the solar with you henceforth?"

He slowly straightened. "Thomasin, I—"

"Then deliver me to my own bed."

Reason stepped forward again, and he was grateful she refused him, especially considering the number of times crimson flashes had given him pause since his mind—not right according to her grandfather—insisted on dragging forth memories of her blood-stained chemise and bed.

Never would he have guessed a woman paid such a price that she might bear children. And now he better understood his mother's mutterings of years past when she had named her monthly time a curse—as did his sister.

"You are right," he said and carried Thomasin into her chamber, tossed back the coverlet that had replaced the one marked by her menses, and lowered her.

"Godspeed your journey," she said as he turned from her.

Wordlessly, he extinguished all but the candle on her bedside table and once more put the door between them.

As it should be, he assured himself. But not as he wanted it.

Hours later, dreams of the brigands' attack on Thomasin violently awakened him and moved his imaginings out of the false world into the real. Staring into the dark of his chamber, he saw again his wife's figure, black as ink but for crimson spreading from her center.

Hoping that whatever din had issued from him had not awakened her, he gripped his pillow and the sheet beneath him and listened for sounds from her chamber.

Naught.

Breathing deep to ease his heart's reckless flight, he rolled onto his back and untangled his legs from the sweat-dampened sheet. How long he denied himself further sleep, he did not know, but finally the new day which would see him away from Kelling began to turn back the night. Its dim light most fond of *The Betrayal* tapestry, it crawled up the threads and slowly revealed the figures woven of them.

How he resented that thing. But though he'd had no part in the betrayal of Foucault, and his father's betrayal had been justified, he could not rid himself of the tapestry—nor the guilt passed father to son. Thus, each morn he awoke to its abundance of red threads that boasted of blood upon the hands of Verdun, De Arell, and Boursier. And imagined tearing it off the wall and making a fire of it in the hearth.

Exhaustion tempting him toward sleep, he reminded himself he was to leave Kelling just after dawn. But as much as he detested unkept plans that would result in a rushed departure, he longed to defer to Thomasin, who would herself adjust her plans with little more than a shrug.

That was not who Magnus was, though in some measure he longed to be, but with the promise he would rest but a short while, he closed his eyes.

19

MAGNUS WAS GONE.

It did not surprise, since she had slept later than usual, fatigued not only by her menses but sounds that had awakened her during the night.

Whence had they come? The bailey outside her window? A chamber upon the corridor? The solar? She could not have said, nor was their nature known to her. Shouts? Curses? A struggle? Wolves crying at the moon too far out of reach? Perhaps only a dream mistaken for reality?

She would have investigated, but cramping and the ensuing silence had stayed her. And eventually, she had slept again.

Now, having dressed in the solar in Magnus's absence, loosely laced into her red gown that was nearly as reliable as the blue for concealing mishaps, she considered the bed in which her husband had passed the night. It was a mess—a corner of the coverlet clinging to its foot, the rest pooled on the floor, the sheet tangled, and the one pillow remaining on the bed bunched against the headboard. As if...

She curled her fingers into her skirts. Perhaps he had not slept alone. Perhaps taking his pleasure with other women was the reason he did not wish to share the solar. Of course, he would have shared it on the night past had she agreed.

Had her refusal to lie with him caused him to seek another—one of several young women who served within the castle? Had that which awakened her well before dawn sounded from the solar?

She scoffed at telling herself she did not care. She may not love Magnus, but her emotions moved in that direction. Surely, she would be wise to set them on another path? Perhaps, but the woman she wished to be in her husband's eyes would first educate herself about his appetites.

Thomasin exited the solar. Noting Rollo was absent outside Father Crispin's chamber, hoping it an indication the priest approached good health, she descended to the hall. She smiled at Sir Otto where he sat at the high table conversing with the steward, and inwardly groaned when the older man followed the knight's gaze and quickly descended the dais.

Though she had found more errors and questionable entries in the journals, thus far none was so blatant she believed monies had been misappropriated. Still, she was almost ashamed to scrutinize his figures without his knowledge. It made her feel like a spy.

"Harve," she acknowledged him, as always sufficed when they met.

He halted before her. "My lady"—his voice scraped his throat as if it resisted tumbling onto his tongue—"I have a matter I must discuss with you."

"Me?"

"As Baron Verdun is absent Kelling, I am given no choice."

Pity the poor man his sacrifice, she silently mocked. "Of what matter do you speak?"

"On the day past, your lord husband removed journals from my shelves, several of which I am now in need."

Moved by discomfort not a result of her menses, she said, "I know of what you speak. They are in the solar."

"With your permission, I shall retrieve them."

She hesitated. "If not for fear of incurring the displeasure of my husband who has arranged them in such a way it appears he makes a study of them, I would allow it."

Distress rearranged the furrows of his face. "I am sure he would not mind—"

"Alas, I am not sure. Fortunately, Baron Verdun will be gone but three days."

"Yes, fortunately," he muttered and turned away.

"Father Crispin and his man?" Thomasin called after him.

He paused. "After breaking their fast, the priest told they would go to the chapel for prayer."

"I thank you."

He inclined his head, and with the dragging steps of the aged and the disappointed, crossed the hall and turned onto the corridor down which lay his private chamber and the room where he kept the accounts.

She looked to Sir Otto, and finding his attention on his viands, continued to the kitchen. Mathilde and her help were caught up in preparations for the nooning meal, though with less urgency than usual, doubtless in light of the absence of their lord and the men who had accompanied him from Kelling. There would be fewer bellies to feed these next days.

"Lady Thomasin." Wiping her hands on her apron, Mathilde approached. "I began to worry over you." She looked to her lady's belly. "It gives you a fright of trouble, aye?"

Delivery of the stained items to the laundress on the day past had captured the attention of many, and memory of it made Thomasin's cheeks warm. "It does."

Mathilde leaned near. "All the more reason to see it filled with a babe."

Thomasin could not have hoped for a better excuse to ask of her what she must. "Can we speak—away from here?"

"I have herbs to pick. Come into the garden."

Thomasin followed her to the rear of the kitchen and out into mid-morning sunlight that was so beautifully warm she sighed.

"Of what do you wish to speak?" Mathilde eased her bulk onto her haunches amid chives, parsley, and sage, the latter reminding Thomasin of when she had breathed the scent of Magnus.

She lowered beside the cook. "Sage?" she asked, fairly certain one of the dishes on today's menu called for it.

"A small handful," Mathilde directed as she plucked sprigs of parsley. "Now speak. I have much to do this day."

Thomasin cleared her throat. "I know there is talk that my husband and I keep separate chambers."

"So there is," Mathilde readily admitted. But that was her, ever efficient in her use of time. "Though methinks not much more than there was with your husband's father who first held this demesne from Baron Foucault."

Thomasin looked up. "You are saying—"

"Aye, when I first took work at Kelling and mistakenly referred to the small bedchamber connected to the solar as the nursery, I was told it had been the bedchamber of Rand Verdun's wife ere she died. I thought it curious the lord and lady slept separate. And more curious when I learned neither did the baron's squires sleep in the solar—not even in the corridor outside, though most lords demand they be so well tended."

"What was the reason?"

Mathilde chuckled. "That is the question that much wants answering, even more so now the son follows suit."

"Then answer it."

Mathilde sat back on her heels. "There is only speculation that turns the tongue to gossip, which I would avoid. But be assured, if your husband has not told you, he has told none."

"He has told me, but…"Thomasin shook her head.

"You do not believe him."

"I cannot help wondering if he…"

"Entertains other women in his chamber?"

Thomasin's sigh was half relief, half affront. "Do you think his father did?"

"If so, the baron well chose his lovers, for during the years I served him before the son, never did I see evidence of it."

"Still, it seems likely he did and my husband—"

"My lady, the trysts of married men are oft revealed by their words and deeds, as well as those of their mistresses. Thus, it is more likely that the excuse your husband offered is true."

TAMARA LEIGH

Thomasin prayed so, but still her mind cast about for another explanation. "Was Rand Verdun's wife pleasing of face and figure?"

Mathilde tucked the sage Thomasin passed to her into an apron pocket. "I understand that though she was no beauty, she was pretty enough. More so than you, as that is what you ask, is it not? That you might know if what your husband does not tell is that he prefers not to awaken beside his plain bride?"

Thomasin nodded.

Mathilde slapped hands to her thighs and pushed upright. "Certes, Baron Verdun has his secrets, as did his father, but it would serve you best not to question your place in them. Regardless of the answer you seek, you are his wife, and as his father's wife before you, you will bear the lord's children. Then mayhap the menses with which you are afflicted will ease as oft happens following childbirth."

Thomasin stood. "I thank you. You have been——" Movement drew her regard to the kitchen door. One they had not heard enter the garden now retreated.

"Sir Otto!" she exclaimed.

When he turned in the doorway, his smile was apologetic. "Forgive me, my lady. Finding you gone from the kitchen, I sought reassurance of your safety."

"Fie on you, Sir Knight!" Mathilde snapped. "'Tis proper to announce one's self."

The cook's rebuke surprised. Not only had Thomasin become accustomed to Mathilde and Sir Otto bantering when he appeared in the kitchen, but regardless of the impropriety in not alerting her and the cook to their audience, Mathilde was yet a servant. And one did not speak so severely to a nobleman.

He narrowed his gaze on the woman. "Again, I ask for forgiveness," he said and added, "of the Lady of Emberly."

Certain he could not have heard much, having retreated upon discovering she was safe within the walls, Thomasin dipped her chin. "Forgiven, and I thank you for doing your duty to my father."

He bowed, stepped into the kitchen, and closed the door.

"I forgot my place," Mathilde said. "Such is the danger of becoming too friendly with one well above one's station."

It was true, as Thomasin had learned with little Joss. And yet, still she believed they had been friends of a sort. "Worry not. I am sure Sir Otto values your good humor too much to long be offended."

"And you? Did I not offend you by speaking in your stead?"

Thomasin laughed. "You did not. But then, I do not forget I am as common as I am noble, therefore not easily offended. And I am grateful for your defense of my person, Mathilde."

After a long moment, the cook said, "I would be honored did my lady call me Maddie."

Tears stung Thomasin's eyes. She did not know why she was so grateful for the woman's acceptance, but she was. "It would be my pleasure, Maddie."

The cook inclined her head. "Do you not like your sleeping arrangements, my lady, mayhap you ought to take them in hand."

As she had more than once entertained—and as many times rejected. But she would think on it more.

A quarter hour later, hunger subdued by the fine cuts of cheese Mathilde had spread before her, she started through the hall toward the stairs.

"My lady." Sir Otto stepped out of an alcove.

Noting his bunched brow, she halted. "As already told, you are forgiven."

"I would but assure you 'twas not my intent to listen in on a conversation that I too late realized was of a personal matter."

How much had he heard? Certes, enough to know he should not have. "I do not doubt you, though in future I ask that you sooner make your presence known."

It occurred to her that had Magnus not revealed himself to Sir Otto when they had followed her to the village, the knight might have witnessed the intimacy between husband and wife—at least, the kisses, for surely he would not have lingered beyond that. Unless he did not trust her husband.

"Under such circumstances, I shall," he said.

She thanked him and started past.

"One thing, my lady."

"Aye?"

"This day I shall send a missive to your father to assure him you are well. You are, are you not?"

Was his concern the result of what he had overheard in the garden? "I am well, Sir Otto."

"But?"

She frowned. "But?"

"Are you happy?" He made a sound of disgust. "Forgive me. I should not concern myself over that with which I have not been tasked. My only excuse is fondness for the girl I watched grow into a woman. I can see you are not miserable, but…" He blew out his breath. "I would see you more valued by your husband."

Her heart skittered, and as she stared at him, she once more experienced wonder that she occupied his thoughts to such a degree. And regret she had not done so sooner. Not that it would make a difference. She had been destined to wed another.

She nearly laughed. Concern for her happiness did not mean there could have been more to their relationship if not for the king's decree. Though Sir Otto had indicated she no longer reminded him of his sister, but was something more, she did not believe it.

But then he caught her hand and pressed his lips to her fingers. "How am I to stand by whilst Baron Verdun mistreats you?"

Glancing around to ensure they remained the only occupants of the hall, she gently pulled free. "He does not mistreat me. 'Tis simply not a love match. But how many marriages are?"

"Baron Boursier and Lady Elianor's, I understand."

As did she, and was happy their once adversarial relationship had turned to love. Such a blessing upon a forced marriage was surely too rare to happen again, and certainly not in Thomasin's case. But how she wished it for her father and Quintin Boursier.

"I thank you for your friendship and concern, Sir Otto. Inform my father I am well and content as the wife of Baron Verdun."

"I shall, my lady. But promise me that as long as I am at Castle Kelling, you will call upon me should things become…difficult between you and your husband. Whatever I can do, I shall, even if I must steal you back to Castle Mathe to keep you from harm."

"You are too kind." Questioning again why he had not sooner been so disposed toward her, Thomasin continued to the stairs. And the question persisted hours later when, hand cramped by the scratching of her quill, she pulled her tired gaze from the bed that should be as much hers as Magnus's and retreated to her chamber.

20

⸺

"As should not be news to you, he tracks too well to himself be easily tracked. Thus, I dared follow him only a short distance."

"Which direction?"

"He rode east, so likely——"

"Aye," Sir Otto said sharply, as does one who knows what follows and would not waste ear on it.

Thomasin pressed her lips tight. *Did* he know where Magnus had gone on the day past when, according to Kelling's man-at-arms who must be in Sir Otto's pay, his lord had ordered his men to continue to the next village without him?

"Though I daresay you could have done better, John," Sir Otto said, "'tis something."

So that was the name of the man who betrayed Magnus—surely in the interest of her father. Still, it did not sit well with her. Disloyalty, by way of heart or by way of greed, could be the ruin—possibly the death—of the betrayed.

The jangle of a purse. The clink of coins dropped into a palm.

"What is this?" John's voice pitched notches above what had been gruff.

"Gratitude, of course. Mayhap your woman would like some fine sweets. Or you, the best brew coin can buy."

John chuckled. "Be assured, my woman is well enough fed. Brew 'tis."

"Then make haste to the nearest tavern."

Footsteps sounded on the packed dirt floor, but as Thomasin pressed herself tighter against the wall, the scuff of hard soles ceased.

"What of the lady?" John asked. "When——?"

"Do not concern yourself. Be assured, I take seriously the charge given me."

Another chuckle. "She does have a fine figure, far better than my woman's." Now a heavy sigh. "Though once mine was fair lovely."

"Good eve, John."

The bulky man-at-arms exited the stall thirty feet from Thomasin who hid amid shadows just inside the stables where saddles, bridles, and blankets were stored. As he passed within five feet of her, she had her closest look at the one she had first seen conversing with Sir Otto weeks ago when she had assumed the knight sought to practice at arms. Perhaps not.

Though this sighting of the man-at-arms was limited to his profile, it was telling. From the center of a face two score aged jutted a long, distinctive nose, its end bulbous, its underside so flat the nostrils were barely visible.

Familiar, she mused. On whom had she seen such a face?

He opened the stable door, and as it closed behind him, Sir Otto strode from the stall. Chin down, he kneaded the back of his neck.

As he moved to follow John from the stables, Thomasin acknowledged the irony of doing unto Sir Otto as he had done unto her in the garden, though her eavesdropping was intentional.

When the man-at-arms and a knight had appeared at Kelling in advance of Magnus and his other men, tasked with ensuring the household was prepared to receive the returning party, she had started for the kitchen to instruct Mathilde to delay supper. But then she had seen Sir Otto move not after her but, rather, the man-at-arms.

Something had bid her follow them. And now she knew the length to which Sir Otto went to do his duty to her father.

Relaxing as the knight reached for the door, she shifted her thoughts to the conversation she had listened in on and regretted how quickly the hope of Magnus's pending return had soured with the possibility he had ridden off alone to——

Movement. Then a body slammed into hers, a keen edge stung her neck, and a cry she ought to have closed her mouth against sounded upon the air. But an instant later, her attacker lurched backward.

"Lady Thomasin!" Sir Otto dropped his dagger, bent forward, and braced his hands on his thighs. "God's mercy, I could have killed you!"

Trembling, she pushed off the wall. "Forgive me, I should not have…"

"I am the one who must be forgiven. Far sooner I should have known John and I were not alone. Almighty, I grow sloppy in the absence of your father's guidance!"

"Or I grow more stealthy," she attempted to lighten the moment.

He raised his gaze, smiled wryly. "I may have to demand that, in future, *you* make your presence known immediately."

As she had demanded of him in the garden.

He snatched the dagger from the ground, shoved it in its sheath, and straightened. "I am sorry you heard what you should not have, and I beg your forgiveness for any perceived trespass. But as you know, your father has entrusted me to keep you safe."

"Aye, but buying away the loyalty of my husband's man?"

"Not only does it serve your best interests, but eventually it will benefit Verdun to know who most readily betrays him."

Though Thomasin knew she should feel no sympathy for the man-at-arms, her chest tightened. Likely, John was but weak and knew not the extent to which the information he passed to another could endanger his lord. Fortunately, it was Sir Otto to whom he reported.

The knight stepped toward her. "I pray you will trust me by keeping silent on what you learned this day. At least, while I continue to seek your husband's true character."

She moistened her lips. "You think he——?"

"I think naught that I can reveal now, my lady, and would not accuse Baron Verdun of something as yet unproved. You will not speak of this, aye?"

"But when he——"

"Did you not promise your father you would take my counsel?"

"I did."

"Then keep your word so he may keep his peace of mind."

She hated this, but he had his orders. "I suppose I shall have to trust you in this."

He nodded at the door. "I am sure you have much to occupy yourself with in advance of your husband's return."

Much it would be difficult to set her mind to, but she would. And for a time, she did.

If it was not another woman within Castle Kelling, it must be one without——one who resided to the east.

That was nearly all Thomasin could think while seated beside Magnus during the evening meal, and now in the solar where she waited for him to finish conferring with his steward belowstairs.

She looked to the ledgers——one reason for eschewing her own chamber, but the least of two. Hearing again Mathilde's suggestion that the Lady of Emberly take it upon herself to resolve the matter of sleeping arrangements, Thomasin peered down her bodice. And snapped her chin up when the door opened.

Surprise flickered across Magnus's face. Sliding his gaze from her to the ledgers as he swung the door closed, he said, "I am weary. Whatever you have discovered can wait on a good's night rest."

TAMARA LEIGH

She would not argue it, for the longer the delay in revealing her second reason for being present in the solar, the lower her courage would slip.

As he halted before her, she turned her back to him. "Then, pray, undo my laces."

He spoke not a word, reached not a hand to her.

"Just my laces," she whispered, and closed her eyes when the warmth of his body drew close, slowed her breath when he gathered her hair, stopped breathing when his hand brushed her nape and shoulder, shivered when the tresses spilled over her breasts. Then the whisper of the bow's release and fingers tripping across her spine as they tugged at the laces' crossings.

"'Tis done," he said low.

"I thank you." She did not move, hoping he would proceed to do what was expected of a man long without the comfort of a woman.

"Good eve, Wife."

Then his appetites were recently satisfied? Or did he honor her refusal to lie with him until she claimed her place here? If that last, it was in her hands.

She turned to him, gripped her skirts, and drew them up.

"What do you, Thomasin?"

She held his gaze until she pulled the gown off over her head, recaptured it as she dropped the garment to the rug. "I make ready for bed. As should you."

Feeling a rise in the tension he seemed always to exude, she crossed the solar in her thin chemise, stepped out of her slippers, and turned back the coverlet on the right side of the bed.

As she settled against the propped pillow, the strain on Magnus's face was so pronounced he looked years older. He could not have made it more obvious he did not wish her here, and his continued rejection cut more deeply. But here she would remain.

She swept the coverlet over her lower body. "Like it or nay, this night and every night henceforth, I will sleep here. 'Tis up to you whether or not *you* keep a separate chamber."

Magnus did not know how to respond to one whose deep disquiet and anger he had felt upon his return despite smiles that made it no further than her lips. And now this, demanding her place as if she had more right to it than he. But to her credit, she did so in a way that did not make her seem a girl. This was a woman who regarded him as if scorned. Unfortunately, it surely seemed that way to her.

"You are upset with me, though not only because I did not allow you to accompany me around the demesne, aye?"

Candlelight sparkled in her eyes. Tears?

Her throat convulsed. Aye, tears.

"What has happened, Thomasin?"

She raised her chin higher. "Have you another? A woman with whom you..."

Inwardly, he startled. She could not know he had visited Eamon and Nanne on the day past. But why else would she ask this of him? Certes, if he smelled of a woman, it was of his own wife whose softly scented hair had tempted him to run his hands through it, pull her head back against his shoulder, and kiss her mouth with all the desire that had gnawed at him since that day in the rain. Had resentment over a promise not kept seeded suspicion? Or was this coincidence?

She gave a huff of laughter. "You do have someone. Tell me, do you bring her to our nuptial chamber? To our bed?"

Cursing himself for leaving her question unanswered, he strode forward. And paused when he nearly stepped on her discarded gown. Determinedly leaving it where it lay, he strode forward, tossed back the coverlet, and scooped her up.

"Nay!" She reached for something to hold her to the bed, and grasping only air as he settled her against his chest, gathered up fistfuls of his tunic.

"Hear me, Thomasin!"

"I will not be like your mother—will not sleep separate from my husband!"

"Who spoke to you of my parents?" he demanded.

TAMARA LEIGH

Regret unsettling her expression of outrage, she stilled. "'Twas not told freely, but in response to my inquiry into talk that you and I sleep separate. But fear not, the reason for the peculiar arrangement between your parents is as unknown to the one who spoke of it as is the reason it exists between you and me."

"I have told you the reason."

"And I think you lie. Regardless, I will not do as your mother did, nor will I share my place with another woman."

"There is no other woman. I have only you and, I vow, shall have only you until my last breath."

As she searched his face, he hoped she did not see the guilt he had no cause to feel. Nanne had long been a friend, but their continuing friendship was mostly contingent upon Eamon.

"Then where——?" She pressed her lips.

"Where?"

She looked to her hands gripping his tunic. "Where will you sleep? Here with me, or in the other chamber?"

Was that what she had meant to ask? Or had she nearly inquired further about the lover she feared? Since it had not occurred to him to instruct his men against speaking of his parting from them on the day past—something he'd had no need to do while unwed—she must have overheard talk at supper.

"Here with me?" she pressed.

He felt trapped. His mind was more at ease than usual, and he would likely pass the night in the company of benign dreams, but...

As much as he wished to spare Thomasin the horror of those other nights and himself the indignity, he supposed it would all come around. Like his mother before her, she would herself decide it was best to sleep separate. Better that than she believe he did not find her capable of holding his interest.

He turned.

"I will not leave!" She gripped his tunic tighter.

"So you will not." He strode around the bed to the left side. "This is your place, Wife." He lowered her and remained bent as she continued to hold to his tunic.

Finally, she opened her fingers and glanced at the space beside her. "You shall sleep there?"

"As is a husband's proper place nearest the door—if needs be, the easier to set hand to the sword fit to the underside of the mattress so he might defend his wife."

She blinked. "These things I did not know."

"Now you do." He raised her chin, pinning her with his gaze to impress upon her the importance of what he told. "Promise me that never, not even in my absence, will you sleep on that side which first an intruder approaches."

"But the sword—"

"Do you know how to use one, my lady?"

She shook her head.

"Then divulging its presence would prove of greater danger to you. Thus, I would have you keep a dagger beneath your pillow or on the bedside table."

"You so fear an attack?"

"Since I do not avail myself of the added protection of a squire inside the solar or outside my door, the extra precaution allows me to sleep better." When his dreams were not fueled by blood-soaked violence. "Now your word, Thomasin."

"I vow that never shall I sleep on my husband's side of the bed."

He released her chin and turned away. After extinguishing the candles around the chamber, he returned to the bed amid silvery moonlight, disrobed down to his braies, and slid beneath the covers. When he turned on his side and drew her into the curve of his body, her gasp evidenced she was as surprised by the show of husbandly affection as was he. But in his arms was where he wanted her, foolish though he was not to think through his wants before acting on them.

Wondering again how this small woman could undo years of rigid habit that had served him well, he felt the stiff go out of her as she sank against his chest, abdomen, and the legs he fit to the backs of hers.

"Is this what you wanted, Wife?" He moved his arm higher to just beneath her breasts and tucked his hand under her quickly rising and falling ribs.

"'Tis. Is it what you want?"

He kissed the side of her neck. "This and more. But…your menses?"

"Blessedly, near its end."

Near…The Church dictated that husband and wife relations be suspended during a woman's time, but it was not that which eased his body. It was memories of the blood bright upon her the day her womb had proved empty.

Knowing he would not soon sleep, he sought a change of topic. "You are no longer my wife in name only."

"Indeed, I am not." The smile in her voice made him smile.

"Then no longer have you an excuse to deny me tale of your life before Blackwood."

"Now?"

"Unless you would rather sleep."

He felt her disappointment, and he was stirred knowing she would prefer to be one with him. "I am not tired," she said, "but you are."

As told when he had entered, as much to gain his rest as to remove the temptation of her. "So I am, though more awake now that my wife has claimed her place beside me."

Thomasin liked his breath moving her hair and sweeping the curve of her ear, so much she wished he would first reveal his past so she might feel that stir of air again and again.

"I will tell my tale," she said, "though it will likely prove so tiresome it delivers you unto sleep." She slid her hand over his curled beneath her, fit her fingers in the grooves of his. "I grew up in the town before Waring Castle, raised by my mother who kept us fed by serving as laundress to the lord's lady and pouring drinks in a tavern. Of my first six years, I remember little, but…much I remember thereafter."

Feeling dark clouds move in her direction, those that loosed cold, hard rain, she reminded herself that the years were not all bad.

"Tell me, Thomasin."

"When I was seven, my mother met a man at the tavern—one of the sword who so desired her that he offered marriage. But with one condition."

Though the years had blurred memories of her mother's face, the one that drew level with hers was lovely—unlike the desperation in Alice's voice. *He is a good man in need of a wife,* she choked, *but alas, not a daughter.*

It had taken more than a year for the girl Thomasin had been to truly understand and accept what that meant, and only when the long wait for her mother's promised return was without reward.

"What condition?" Magnus asked.

"That she leave me behind."

"Did she?"

His disbelief nearly shamed her for what her mother had done. "Aye."

"She abandoned you."

"'Twas not as bad as that. She provided for me as best she could by giving me a piece of parchment folded and bound so tight I had only to close my fingers over it to conceal it in my palm. She said that if ever I found myself in danger, I should find someone to read it to me." The next breath she drew shuddered from her. "Then she gave me in service to the lady of Waring Castle with the promise she would return."

"She did not," her husband said, and not only with condemnation.

She gasped. "I do not want your pity, Magnus Verdun!"

He rose behind her and turned her onto her back. "Already you have it, and none would deny 'tis your due. You were a little girl."

Trying to subdue her anger, she told herself that at least he did not try to make pretty of his pity.

"But no matter how bad it was, Thomasin, you are here now. With me. That life will never be again."

Anger slipping, she laid a palm to his jaw that was rough from several days' growth of beard. "I thank God for that. Do you? Are you truly pleased I am here?"

Considering it was not by his invitation, she expected hesitation, but not of such short duration. "Against my better judgment." He drew her hand to his mouth, kissed her fingers. "I do not know what it is about you, but you scatter my darkness."

One moment her heart surged, the next it ebbed. "What darkness?" Though he had denied being not right of mind as her grandfather had warned, perhaps...

This time, his hesitation was notable. "You will see," he said softly, then lowered her hand to the mattress. "I am right that your mother did not return?"

Assuring herself she would gain his trust and he would share what he would not now, she said, "You are right. I...almost wished her dead so she would have good cause for not returning. And perhaps something terrible did happen that prevented her from keeping her promise. But I can never know."

"What duties had you at Waring Castle?"

Relieved to leave behind talk of her mother, she said, "I was given charge of my lady's four-year-old daughter. For six years, I served as her help and companion."

"How?"

"Joss's lower body was so misshapen and shriveled she could not walk. Thus, I cleaned and fed her, played with her, and carried her about. She was sweet and mostly kind, but she knew she was not wanted. Her mother tried to love her, but less and less she visited the upper floor where Joss and I lived out of sight of her father."

"He did not acknowledge her?"

"He did not, and I was told he had wished to set her out in the wood the night of her birth."

"I have heard of such means of ridding one of children born with defects. Was the lady kind to you?"

"Providing I kept Joss hidden and content enough to control her fits of frustration, I found favor enough with her." Though not in the early days when she had been so frightened and lonely, but that need not be told. The stinging slaps and bruising pinches had done no permanent damage. And once the lady had apologized.

Magnus propped his head on a hand. "You were educated alongside Joss?"

"She had a tutor, but I did not learn alongside her. The tutor did not like all the questions I asked, and Joss's mother warned that I could be replaced with one of a more quiet and obedient disposition. Thus, I was educated in back of Joss, with only her the wiser. Since her wandering mind often tempted her thoughts elsewhere, learning was difficult. So when we were alone, I helped her practice her letters and numbers and recitations so she would not disappoint her mother who wished her daughter to enter the Church."

"You said you were with the child six years, at the end of which she was given to the Church?"

Thomasin had known her tale would deliver them to the day she had done what she should not have. "Nay, she was not, and I am much to blame."

He closed his hand over hers that she had not realized gripped the bottom sheet. "For what?"

"You know I like the rain."

"In that we are compatible."

She sighed. "Joss napped often, sometimes for hours. When it rained, and if it was not chill, I would steal to the garden so I might feel it on my face and in my hair. But one day I was seen. Joss had fallen asleep on the window seat, and upon awakening, she saw me in the garden. When I returned abovestairs, she asked me to carry her outside and whirl her around in the rain as I had been doing. I objected, knowing the punishment would be severe were we caught." She shook her head. "But Joss would not relent. She threatened to tell her mother I had left her alone and she had fallen. I told myself I had no choice, but I did. I could have taken my punishment, whether I was beaten or cast out."

"That is no choice for a girl."

Thomasin turned toward Magnus, pressed her face to his chest. "Perhaps not. Still, I chose wrong. I took Joss to the garden and danced with her in the rain. She was so happy I realized she had never been truly happy before, and so we stayed until we were drenched."

"You gave her the gift of happiness. That is nothing to regret."

"Not at the time. Indeed, I was also happier than I had been since before my mother left, but it did not last. Hours after I settled Joss to bed, she began coughing. I tended her, and when her condition worsened, I sent for her mother and the physician. Only the latter came. Selfish though it was of me, I was grateful that by the time my lady entered the chamber the following day, Joss was no longer coherent enough to reveal I was responsible for her illness."

"You were not responsible." Magnus slid his fingers through her hair and turned her face up. "That is a lie you tell yourself."

"Nay, it was my duty to protect her. And to protect myself, I sacrificed her."

He lowered his face near hers. "Even grown men and women make such mistakes."

"That does not forgive me."

"Methinks God does, that He sees what you do not and does not hold you responsible."

"You think you know God's mind, Husband?"

"I know that just as He allows those He loves to be afflicted with great suffering, He forgives those who repent of their sins and shortcomings. Perhaps more so those who find themselves in a lion's den and are too frightened by being so near tooth and claw that they make choices that speak ill of them."

She frowned. "You have found yourself in a lion's den, have you not?"

His fingers tensed against her scalp. "I have been bloodied in it." He sighed. "Joss died?"

Though she longed to know more of his time in the lion's den, she said, "The next night, after much suffering. Her mother wept some, her father...He continued on as if he had lost naught of great value."

"What happened to you afterward?"

"I was put to work as a maid. It proved easier than caring for Joss, but it was tedious. Worse, it brought me to the notice of my lord's men and guests. I had to be watchful and clever to stay out of reach, but I was not always successful. Still, I was able to escape hands that sought curves I was growing into—until my lord's steward took an interest in me. He was harder to escape and came close to ravishing me. But when I approached my lady and beseeched her to intervene, she advised me to turn the situation to my advantage by demanding coins for my favors."

Magnus cursed, and not beneath his breath.

"You forget the letter my mother gave me ere she left."

"Aye?" he said warily.

"I knew its contents, having read it once my learning was sufficient."

"What did it say?"

"My mother told that I was the daughter of Griffin de Arell—that his father, the Baron of Blackwood, had sent her away when he learned she was with child. She warned that no welcome would I receive from my grandfather if he yet lived, but if ever I was in danger, it would be worth the risk of seeking the aid of my father who she did not believe was aware of my existence."

"Was he?"

She shook her head. "For that, there remains a great rift between him and my grandfather."

"So you traveled to Castle Mathe."

"Lest I lose my position at Waring Castle, I dared not. I wrote my father a letter beseeching his aid and wrapped it around my mother's." And still she remembered every word, having repeatedly practiced them in the dirt before inking them on her one piece of parchment—*Sir Griffin de Arell, You know me not. Fourteen years past, I was born to Alice of the village of Cross upon the barony of Blackwood. I have no proof you sired me, but if it is as my mother told in the missive herewith, I pray you will grant me a boon. My situation is dire where I have resided at Waring Castle since my mother gave me in service to its lord seven years past. If you would deliver me free and grant me a place upon your lands, I vow to ask no more of you. Your daughter, Thomasin*

"How did you get the letter to him?" Magnus asked.

"I paid a traveling merchant all the coin I had and prayed he would deliver it to my father as he vowed to do. But while I continued to evade the steward, a sennight passed, a fortnight, a month. Fearing my coin and proof of my parentage were lost, I lay awake at night imagining my letter tossed onto a fire, either by the merchant or my father."

"But Griffin de Arell came for you."

Thomasin recalled the fear of being summoned to the great hall, the sight of the tall, broad-shouldered man standing alongside her lord, his intense blue regard that made her feet drag, the doubling of fear at the thought he was another guest who wished more than an escort to his chamber, the scrambling of her mind for a way to evade the attentions of one of such size. And then dizzying joy when he caught up her hand and spoke his name.

She smiled. "He did, and took me away. I know there has been much ill between your family and mine, but my father is a good man, honorable where his father was not, and I love him for it."

"I saw that when he was here. But what of Ulric de Arell? How did he receive you?"

"He did not. By then he had passed the barony into my father's hands and was established in his apartment abovestairs."

"Passed? I heard rumor your father forced him to give up Blackwood and locked him away to ensure his succession."

She laughed. "My father did not. The other rumor that my grandfather relinquished the barony to his son after falling seriously ill is much nearer the truth."

Magnus stroked her hair, and she wondered if he knew he did it. More, did he know what his touch did to her insides?

"How serious an illness was it that he yet lives all these years?"

An illness kept hidden from all but family and trusted servants. But not from her husband who was now an ally. "A cruel, slow illness that eats away at one."

His hand upon her hair stilled. "Leprosy?"

"Aye."

"Then you have never laid eyes on him."

"Indeed, I have—many times. When I first came to Castle Mathe, I had not the courage to seek out the one who had banished my mother and me, but I am a curious one, and eventually curiosity made me daring. Without my father's knowledge, I stole into my grandfather's sanctuary. When I introduced myself, he cursed me, shortened my name to *Sin* to remind me of the circumstances of my birth, and said I was so much on the ugly side of plain I could not have De Arell blood in my veins."

Magnus growled, and she almost laughed with joy that he cared enough to be angered.

"But despite his hatred, he allowed me within his chamber time and again—and quite near him. But eventually, the heart went out of his cruelty, and he demanded I keep my distance."

"He had hoped to infect you in the beginning?"

"I fear so."

"Cur!"

"I thought that, too, but still I sought his company."

"Did your father never learn of your visits?"

"If he did, which is possible since it was long ere I discovered he had set Sir Otto and others on me when I stole from the castle, he never revealed it."

"Why did you persist in visiting the old baron?"

"He is my grandfather, and though I did not like him for what he did to my mother, I pitied him for being so isolated with only a dog for regular company—a state that worsened upon my father's receipt of my letter. Though I was told relations were not often good between Ulric and Griffin, what little was good became barely tolerable when my father learned the truth of my mother's disappearance."

"He cared for her, then."

"Aye. He told me he had wished to make her his wife, but when he approached his father, Ulric refused to allow him to wed a commoner. Alice disappeared shortly thereafter, and though my father suspected Ulric had sent her away, my grandfather vowed he had not and suggested she had run off with a man-at-arms who had recently left his service. At the time, my father was but ten and six—years from knighthood— and with little recourse. So eventually he wed the woman to whom he was betrothed. He told me that though he had cared for his wife and mourned her passing, the best part of their marriage was the birth of my half brother, Rhys."

"He is…eight years old?"

She was surprised he knew, but she supposed the long-standing feud gave their families cause to make note of momentous occasions such as the birth of a future enemy. "Aye, eight, and a handsome lad."

"You care for him?"

"Of course. I love him."

Magnus stroked her cheek. "You find it easy to love, do you not?"

His question surprised her. "I have never thought of the ease or dif- ficulty of loving another. It just happens. Sometimes of a sudden, other times with such stealth, I have to look back to see the crumbs that lead to the cake I find in my hand."

He laughed—and how she liked the rumble of his chest against hers! "Is it easy for you to love, Magnus?"

The rumbling ceased. "Nay."

That single word cast from her mouth the smile that had stretched it wide. If he did not love easily, and she was not easy to love—

He grunted. "I do not know why I asked that of you."

Though she knew she could hardly be seen in the dim, she returned the smile to her lips and teased, "Methinks you asked in the hope I would declare my love for you and number among...How many have loved you, Magnus? Too many to count?"

"Too few."

She scoffed. "I do not believe that. One is not given a face and body such as yours without women falling in love with you, and their own beauty and devotion causing you to love them in return."

"That is not love, Thomasin. At best, that is desire, wanting something only for how it catches and holds the eye and rouses the body."

He was right, though not entirely. "'Tis not love in the truest sense," she conceded, "but love could not have an easier beginning, could it? What the eye beholds, the body wants, thereby opening the path to one's heart."

"I appreciate beauty, as do most men and women, and 'tis true it is oft how one first comes to the notice of another, but it does not necessarily open one to love. And it certainly does not make love a given."

"What does?"

He was slow to speak. "As I told you when you gifted yourself to me in the wood, it is true beauty that ought to draw one person to another—seeking first the soul that has no chance of pleasing the eye. And upon finding it, longing to be as near another in the dark as in the light." After a long moment, he added, "If ever I could love and be loved in return, that is how I would love and wish to be loved."

If ever...

Determined not to linger on those words, Thomasin embraced the others that sounded as if spun from the pen of a poet. "If your words are not just pretty, Husband, I rejoice in knowing 'tis possible you may come to love my soul in lieu of beauty I have not. Indeed, 'tis likely you will know a greater longing to be near me in the dark than in the light—"

Of a sudden, she was on her back, Magnus's thighs straddling hers, his hand cupping her face. "I will hear no more from them, Thomasin. Henceforth, they will be silent."

Hardly able to breathe for fear here might be the man who was not right in the mind, she whispered, "Who will be silent?"

"Ulric de Arell and any other who makes you question your worth. I want the voice that speaks from you to be yours. Not theirs."

Not madness—anger. And in defense of her. Relieved, hoping to settle his mood, she said, "Ah, but why not save myself the effort since 'tis true that, whereas my mother was quite lovely, I am—"

"You ought not care what your mother was on the outside. In the end, God shall measure her for what she was on the inside. And, certes, that was not lovely. It was ugly."

She gasped. "Cease!" Though a part of her hated her mother for leaving her, it was too dark and dangerous to dwell on lest it infected her and did to her insides what leprosy had done to her grandfather's outside.

"She may have had a pretty face, Thomasin, but ugliness made her sacrifice her little girl to seek her own happiness. Were she not your mother, would you not think the same of a woman who abandoned her child?"

She moistened her lips. "I know it was wrong. Of course I do! But I will not live like that—ever brooding on the ill, especially now that I have so much to be thankful for."

"I do not ask you to brood on the ill. I but wish you to see and judge less with the eye and more with the heart. And not only others, but yourself. I would have you cease comparing yourself to those unworthy of standing ten feet behind you."

His words further muddled her, but in a different way. He spoke as if he cared much for her. But he could not, could he? If ever, certainly not yet. "I shall try, Husband."

The slow release of his breath warmed her brow. "Do you know what I see when I look at you, Thomasin?" He lowered his body until his hips touched hers, chest brushed her breasts, face drew so near it was entirely in shadow. "I see a winsome soul shining from a face I am selfishly relieved those who are blind think plain, that loves more easily than 'tis safe, that takes blame that ought to be bestowed elsewhere, that tempts my soul to speak where I did not believe it ever would."

Thomasin had never been as aware of the beat of her heart as she was with him. "Might your soul one day love mine?" she whispered.

He came nearer and against her lips said, "Do you think it capable of love?"

"I do, for surely one who knows what love requires—seeking first the soul and longing to be as near another in the dark as in the light—can love and be loved."

"If that is so, how does one prove one's love?"

She shook her head. "Prove?"

He drew his right hand down her jaw, traced a finger across her lower lip. "'Tis said love is patient."

As he had been with her, even when she had defied him by stealing out of the castle to visit the village. Had she been as patient with him?

He kissed the corner of her mouth. "It is not arrogant or rude."

Yet more aware of the blood moving through her heart, she dismissed arrogance as the reason he had refused to share the solar. But rude…Of that she was guilty, frustration having several times spilled proof of the commoner from her tongue.

As he moved his mouth up her cheek, the rasp of his unshaven jaw made her shiver. "Love seeks not its own and is not angry."

In that they had both failed, she reflected as his breath near her ear stole hers from her mouth.

"It rejoiceth in the truth."

Bible verses. And how she was glad he was unaware she only now realized it. As for love rejoicing in the truth…In that had he failed her when he had ridden east away from his men?

He pressed his lips beneath her ear, the corner of an eye, her brow. "It endureth every thing."

Could she endure if he had lain with another woman? And continued to do so?

His hand trailed her neck, her shoulder, traced her ribs from breast to waist. "It believeth every thing."

She pressed her body up against his, but despite wishing to be nearer him, still her mind worked. Dare she believe he had no other, would have only her until death?

His calloused fingers traveled the outside of her thigh, gathered up the hem of her chemise. "It hopeth all."

Dear Lord, she silently beseeched, *with all my hope, I would have him be true. Pray, if You will not bless me with his love, grant me his devotion.*

His lips were above hers again, and as he angled his head, he said, "It never fails," and kissed her mouth open with such hunger she could have believed him near death by way of starvation.

As was I, she thought well past the middling of night when she lay with her head on his bare shoulder, beneath her hand his chest slowly moving with sleep, beneath his hand the flat of her belly that, after this night, might not long remain flat.

How she hoped it would not.

21

IT HAD NOT bothered him last eve—rather, it had hardly bothered him.

He moved his gaze over the gown upon the rug and told himself to leave it. Then he swept it up, crossed to the bed, and draped it over the feet of his wife who lay on her belly beneath the sheet he had drawn over her. A sheet spotted with her menses.

This bothered him more, but less than expected. As yet, there were no crimson flashes to ward off, just as there had been none to disturb his dreams, which would have all the sooner caused Thomasin to concede they should sleep apart. Indeed, he could not remember the last time his rest had been so undisturbed that it seemed but a minute passed between closing his eyes against the dim and opening them upon the day.

Too much liking the warmth and sight of the bare body tucked against his side, he had not lingered abed lest he yielded to the temptation of disrupting his wife's sleep.

Now as he watched her dream dreams that did not crease her brow or quicken her breath, that so softened her face and relaxed the bow of her mouth he thought her not plain but simply lovely, his mind returned to the night past. After taking one unexpected turn after another, it had ended far distant from where it had begun. Though his desire for Thomasin had been dampened by tidings her menses were yet upon her, the longer she had lain beside him, the less of a deterrent it had been.

And when she had not tried to hide how much she wanted to be abed with him...

When he had surprised himself with the admission she scattered his darkness...

When in exposing her past, she had revealed more of her compassion and ability to easily love what others would deem unlovable...

When her determination to take responsibility for the ill suffered by others had made him rise up in her defense...

When she had seen him clearly enough to know his talk of finding one's self in a lion's den was from personal experience...

When she had shown such courage in seeking out her father—more, the repugnant Ulric de Arell...

Magnus looked down. Imaginings of the old baron's throat beneath his fingers had turned his hands into fists. Though disheartened by the importance Thomasin placed on external beauty—her mother's store of it and what she perceived to be her dearth of it—it was understandable considering she had been abandoned, mistreated, and told she was so on the ugly side of plain she could not be a De Arell. If ever he came face to face with her grandfather—

Thomasin drew a strident breath, opened her eyes on the empty place beside her, and slid a hand across the mattress. As she splayed her fingers over the impression he had left there, she sighed, the contentment of which caused his hands to relax.

"Methinks I am missed," he said.

She snapped her head up and around, and her lips parted with a mischievous smile. "Indeed, you are." Making no attempt to keep the sheet from slipping and exposing the tops of her breasts, she turned onto her back and lowered her gaze over his robe-clad body. "You could return to bed."

"I could, but the sun has climbed high, and much was neglected during my absence these past days." More, though, he had a promise that needed keeping.

"Pity, for I am of a peculiar mood to remain abed all day."

Fighting the temptation she presented, he crossed to the wardrobe. "The blue?" He lifted the gown's sleeve.

Her sharp breath brought his head around.

Clutching the sheet to her where she sat up, color brightening her face, she darted her eyes over evidence of her menses. "Oh, have mercy!" She glanced at him and quickly away.

He lifted the blue gown from its hook and carried it to her. "Worry not. The bedding is easily laundered."

"Nay, not easily. The blood has set."

Unsettled by her discomfort, Magnus said, "Mayhap you would prefer to perform your ablutions in the other chamber?"

She snatched the gown from him, pressed it to her, and scrambled off the bed.

But as she started for the door, he pulled her around. "Thomasin, there is no shame in it."

With palpable reluctance, she raised her eyes.

"'Tis natural," he said. And it was. The blood of her menses represented the promise of life, not the threat of death. A blessing, not a curse. He had but to remember that the same as she.

She swallowed. "But I have ruined——"

"Naught of consequence." He laid a hand on her cheek. "Were the day not so old and burdened, I would lie with you again. Now."

Lest her tentative smile tempted him to a kiss that could lead where it was best it did not at this time, he released her. "When you are done, return to me and we will discuss what you found in the ledgers."

Once she departed, he strode to the wardrobe and clothed himself. Then he summoned a chamber maid to change the bedding to save Thomasin further embarrassment.

"Though there are quite a few instances that make it appear money is missing, often it reappears elsewhere." Thomasin turned a half dozen pages and pointed to income from the sale of wool. "'Tis twice what my father earned for the same, the difference nearly equating to the excessive expenses of previous entries."

"Coincidence?"

"At first, I thought so, but as told, 'tis a fairly regular occurrence." She flipped several pages ahead. "In this case, the expense is too low, and later, the income is half what it should be."

"Then?"

She looked up at where Magnus leaned over her with one hand braced on the table. "I could be wrong, but methinks the only thing your steward cheats you of is the truth about his ability to keep your books day to day—at least of recent, since the inconsistencies have steadily increased these six months. Unfortunately, it follows that by the time he discovers past errors, they are impossible to alter without blatantly inking the pages with corrections. Thus, he adjusts his miscalculations by increasing or decreasing income and expenses where necessary."

Magnus straightened. "But you cannot be certain. And you did tell he was distressed upon discovering I had removed these ledgers from his keeping."

Thomasin frowned. "You do not trust him?"

"Just as he gave my father no cause to think our monies ill used, he has given me none, but I find it strange that once my niece is no longer present to oversee the accounting, he begins to lose his grasp of numbers."

"He is quite old." Despite Thomasin's aversion to the steward, she hated that an honest man who made mistakes might be wrongly accused of being a dishonest man who engaged in deceit.

Magnus straightened. "True. He was of middling years ere Emberly was awarded to my father, but now that we know Foucault supporters have infiltrated our families, we must look beyond excuses if we are to root out the traitors."

"You think your steward might support the Foucault cause?"

"I do not, and yet neither did I suspect Agatha—your Aude—who often dwelt here. 'Tis possible she was not the only betrayer amongst us."

"Will you confront your steward?"

"Even if I knew for certain he betrayed, I would not, for much knowledge is gained from an enemy who thinks he yet enjoys the status of an ally. But he will be watched, and I will ask you to serve our household as Elianor did." He nodded at the books. "You, dear wife, shall be my second set of eyes."

Dear wife. Her heart bounded. "I am honored to be so highly regarded."

"You have earned such regard. With little study, you saw errors I did not."

"I suppose Joss's tutor did his job well."

"Indeed. Now, I must see to business and prepare for another journey."

The happiness in which Thomasin swam began to drain. "You are leaving again."

"Father Crispin is ready to depart Emberly and has requested an escort. Thus, my men and I will accompany him and his man-at-arms to Castle Adderstone."

She did not even try to smile, certain the expression would fall so short of pretty it would make her look sickly. "It is necessary you go as well?"

"Did I not, I would be remiss in not remaining at my wife's side."

"I do not—" She gasped. "I am to join you?"

"If you wish."

She sprang off the chair and threw her arms around him. "I wish! And we shall ride the horses the king gifted us, aye? And stay at Castle Adderstone how many days and nights? And I will visit with Lady Elianor and Lady Quintin—"

Magnus laughed, a sound so singular she rose to her toes to offer her mouth.

"I thank you," she said as he brushed a kiss across her lips, then dropped back to her heels. "When do we depart?"

"Three days hence."

She wrinkled her nose. "I had hoped this day."

"First, demesne business, but you may begin packing—enough for two days upon Godsmere and two upon Blackwood."

Another gasp. "We go to Castle Mathe as well?"

"Ere our return to Emberly."

Thomasin longed to dance, but lest she appeared childish, clasped her hands before her. "You know not how happy you make me."

"I am pleased. And now to work."

Warmed by the knowledge that though she might never be loved by him, he seemed to want, value, and desire her, she stared after him until the door closed. Then, humming, she stacked the ledgers, settled them against her chest, and feeling light of foot despite the weight of the books, descended to the hall.

The great room was vacant but for servants setting it to rights in anticipation of the nooning meal and Sir Otto in a chair before the hearth, legs stretched before him, hands clasped behind his head.

"Good morn, Sir Otto."

His eyebrows rose. "My lady's happiness seems much improved from the night past when we sat at supper."

She halted before him. "Does it?" she said, though she knew she had failed at hiding how affected she was by what she had overheard him and the man-at-arms discussing.

"Aye. Most telling is the pastorela you were humming when you came off the stairs."

That halfway surprised her, but it was near enough in memory for her to know she had, indeed, hummed the song learned from Aude.

The knight leaned forward, set his elbows on his knees, and let his hands hang between them. "Many a time I have heard it from you, and usually when you appear most content. You are, aye?"

"Indeed I am."

"I am glad of it." Though, as ever, the curving of his mouth made him more handsome, she thought it curious that her heart did not flutter as enthusiastically as it had in the past. Of course, she was now a married woman in every sense, and she very much liked her husband—not only his looks, but his touch, words, and deeds.

She glanced at the ledgers. "I must return these to the steward."

Sir Otto inclined his head and she continued to the room off the far corridor where Harve sat with quill and parchment. "My husband has finished with these." She lowered the ledgers to the table before him.

"And?" he said.

"They appear to be in good order."

"Of course they are. I hope you are satisfied, my lady."

Then he suspected she had been poring over the entries? "My husband is satisfied, and that is what matters."

His glower speaking words he surely longed to thrust at her, she felt her mood darken as memories pulled her to another steward with whom she had also experienced poor relations. Blessedly, this was of a different sort.

Reminding herself that the darkness of her early life and whatever darkness Magnus had said she scattered were in the past—and would remain there—she withdrew.

22

⟨⟨⟨⟩⟩⟩

"Tale is, you and your husband now share a chamber."

Thomasin halted on the landing and turned to Sir Otto who, unbeknownst to her, had followed her abovestairs.

Where he stood three steps down, he raised a beseeching hand. "Forgive me. I know it seems inappropriate that I should comment on the circumstances of your marriage, especially regarding matters of intimacy, but rumors have roots, and the ones to which I am privy so firmly grip the soil I believe my concern is justified."

She stared, disturbed by the first words he had spoken to her in the two days since he had noted how happy she seemed. Though they had often been in each other's presence and she had felt his gaze—sometimes to the point of discomfort—he had remained distant. Until now.

"Though I appreciate your concern, Sir Otto, all is well."

"Is it?"

"It is. Now I must—"

Catching the voice of Father Crispin and the grunt of Rollo on the stairs below, Thomasin peered past the knight, who quickly ascended and took her elbow.

"My lady, may we speak in private? What I have to tell you is of great import."

"But—"

"Your father would wish it. Demand it, even."

She reluctantly nodded, and he pulled her into the solar and closed the door just as the priest and Rollo gaining the landing.

Thomasin freed her arm and crossed to the table where it seemed best to converse in the lord and lady's bedchamber. As she lowered into a chair, she gestured Sir Otto toward the seat opposite.

He started around the table, but slowed to take in the tapestry.

She saw what he saw, and as always, liked it not. "'Tis violent, all that blood. I prefer tapestries adorned with ladies, knights, and flowers. You, Sir Otto?"

He halted, and with his back to her, considered the wall hanging. "I noticed this on your wedding night and was surprised it was displayed in a bedchamber."

"As was I. Though I hope to convince my husband to replace it with one that is pleasing to the eye and heart, since his father commissioned this one and it has long hung here, that may prove difficult."

"It must be meaningful to the Verduns." He slid his fingers across threads whose over and under and back and forth journey had woven into the tapestry the Latin words by which it was named. "The Betrayal," he murmured and peered across his shoulder. "That by Foucault's vassals, aye?"

"As I was told."

He nodded. "And yet it seems not a celebration of that betrayal but a…"

"Reminder." She looked to the upper left corner that showed the bearded nobleman fallen on crimson ground. "A cautionary one."

"Mayhap even an admission of guilt." Sir Otto frowned. "From what I understand, Rand Verdun was initially opposed to betraying his liege."

"I have heard that as well, and that he was most concerned with the fate of Baron Foucault's children."

Sir Otto angled his face toward the two figures who prayed over their fallen husband and father. "The baron's wife," he said, "and here his daughter, Lady Maeve—the same whom Archard Boursier wed and is believed to have been murdered last Christmas."

"Aye."

"Foucault also had a son, did he not?"

"There in the lower right corner." She eyed the clean-shaven fig-ure. "Simon died in France ere he could contest his family's lands being divided amongst the Verduns, Boursiers, and De Arells."

"Do you think he was murdered?"

Thomasin jerked. "By the three families?"

Keeping his back to her, he shrugged. "His death was convenient, do you not think?"

"I suppose it is possible," she conceded what she preferred not to.

"Just as 'tis possible he did not truly die, this...Simon Foucault."

Thomasin blinked. "If he did not, where has he been these twenty-six years?"

The knight turned from the tapestry, pulled out a chair, and dropped into it. "You are right. To be silent so long, he must be dead. Still, 'tis an intriguing possibility he lives and is the one behind the attacks on the baronies—that he leads the Foucault uprising."

"I pray 'tis not so."

"Better him dead, aye?"

Thomasin grimaced. "It sounds terrible and self-serving, but a mind so long set on revenge is beyond frightening." Even more frightening than the men who had attacked her and whose bloodied corpses Sir Francis had gifted Magnus and her.

"But we are here to speak of other things," she said. "So these rumors with roots you spoke of, Sir Otto?"

His brow rumpled just long enough to evidence the tapestry had made him lose his place. "Gossip tosses my stomach, but not to follow the slippery string from one end to the other would leave my lady's back exposed and, quite possibly, cause me to fail your father. More, you."

She folded her hands atop the table. "Pray, what concerns you?"

He leaned toward her. "Though you and your husband appear to have come to an understanding—indeed, you seem amicable—I ask that what I tell you remains between you and me lest Baron Verdun is offended and makes it difficult, if not impossible, for me to protect you as is my duty."

She forced a smile. "If 'tis your intent to worry me, you have succeeded."

"It stays between us," he pressed.

She did not wish secrets between Magnus and her, but neither did she want Sir Otto to earn her father's wrath should Magnus eject the knight from Kelling. Too, what of those who spread the rumors—likely castle folk whose families could be devastated if their positions were lost due to idle tongues?

"Very well. It stays between you and me."

He inclined his head. "Rumor is that the peace-loving Rand Verdun could not keep peace with his wife, that though he disguised his afflic-tion, his mind was not right."

A chill swept Thomasin as she recalled what her grandfather had said of the Verduns. "How so?"

"At times, he turned violent, especially at night, possibly after much drink. Thus, his wife insisted on a separate chamber"—he glanced at the door between the two rooms—"and barred him from it. And just as he did not allow his squire to sleep in the solar or outside it, your hus-band does the same." An apologetic smile. "Of course, what is true of the father may not be true of the son. But I believe you should be aware of the possibility to better protect yourself."

Gaze drawn to the tapestry, Thomasin let her eyes roam its abun-dance of crimson thread. If Magnus's father had suffered a diseased mind, had the wall hanging before which he had fallen asleep, and to which he had awakened, contributed? Had guilt further twisted his mind?

"Aye," Sir Otto said, "perhaps that is further proof."

Hating that he knew her thoughts, she looked to him. "I thank you for your concern, but I assure you that, regardless of the state of Rand Verdun's mind, my lord husband is strong of mind."

His jaw shifted. "Providing he makes you happy, and you are as safe as your father and I wish you to be, I shall aspire to worry on it no further."

"He does make me happy. And I am quite safe." She thought of Magnus's insistence she sleep on the left side of the bed, of the sword beneath his side whose scabbard she had discovered was fastened horizontally to the taut ropes supporting the mattress. Certes, with Magnus she was safe.

Sir Otto stood. "I thank you for the audience. And now I must prepare for the morrow's ride to Castle Adderstone."

Of course he would join them, she told her surprised self. Where she went, her father's man went. But for some reason, she liked it less than before.

"Good day," she said and caught the flick of his gaze toward the tapestry as he bowed at the door.

"Am I being foolish?" she whispered when he had gone. "Does he see things I should and will later regret I did not?"

She made a sound of disgust. Whatever the truth of Rand Verdun, Magnus was not ill of mind. As a warrior he was violent when violence was needed, but he would not harm her. Never would they require separate chambers.

23

─ ⟨⟨⟩⟩ ─

"YOU NAMED HER well," Magnus said in as light a tone as he could summon when Thomasin came into his arms. "Certes, she is swift as a swallow."

His wife smiled, and when he set her to her feet, moved to the mare's head and stroked its jaw.

Using the opportunity to further study the flat, open wood through which the stream ran, grateful one had to be near to see the muscle moving at his mouth, Magnus casually glanced around. As expected, his men did not stray from the routine established when the brigands' attacks on the baronies had begun. Armored despite the added weight throughout the long ride, half remained astride while the other half watered their mounts. But for all that, most did not appear as alert as they ought to be, and that was good, for it meant the signal had been received and passed to those most trusted by their lord. They but appeared unprepared.

"Aye," Thomasin said. "Arundel is a fitting name for my lovely lady."

The horse nickered.

Magnus's wife laughed, then turned to him and jutted her chin at the massive destrier. "Still you have not decided on what to call your horse?"

Resisting the urge to turn his fingers around a hilt, he folded his sword hand into a fist. "I yet learn him as he learns me. When we better know each other, I shall name him."

She put her head to the side. "From what I have seen of the great beast, I have two names I believe a good fit. You would hear them?"

It was hard to affect ease in the absence of peace, harder yet amid anticipation of what was to come. But she could not know. Not yet.

She raised her eyebrows above wide eyes and grinned, an expression so impish there was some truth in the smile he forced. "I would hear them."

"I am thinking..." She looked to his mouth and frowned. "Something is amiss?"

"Naught." Through his smile, he drew a slow breath to keep the muscle at his eye from also jerking. "Tell me the names."

Though some of her frown dissolved, enough remained to evidence she knew him better than he wished her to. Still, she said, "Eton, meaning swift as an eagle, or Cerus, meaning——"

"Swifter than the wind." He nodded. "You may be right."

"I am."

"I will think on them." With a ring of the armor he had donned this morn in little expectation it would be put to use, he turned toward his squire who stood at the stream alongside two knights. Catching the young man's eye, he motioned him forward.

"Spotted south and east," the squire said low, then inclined his head when instructed to tend his lord's and lady's horses.

Magnus took Thomasin's arm and led her in the direction the sun would set, away from Kelling's party of eight knights, including Sir Otto, half as many men-at-arms, including Rollo, four squires, and Father Crispin.

"I need not relieve myself," she said as they neared the denser foliage.

He had not expected she would, it being less than two hours since they had departed the village halfway between Castle Kelling and Castle Adderstone, but it was a useful pretense.

"Thus, I hope you wish privacy in which to kiss me," she said with teasing he would have warmed to under different circumstances. But her suggestion was another useful pretense. He halted beneath an immense oak visible to those at the stream—and beyond—and drew her into his arms.

Her response was perfect for those yet unseen. She laughed, threw her arms around his neck, and leapt onto her toes.

Magnus bent his head and against her lips said, "We are soon to be attacked, Thomasin."

Her lowering lids sprang up. "What?"

He angled his head, and in lieu of a kiss said, "We have been followed since before our arrival at the village."

She stiffened. "Brigands?"

"Pray, look as if you enjoy this. Push your hands into my hair."

At her hesitation, he growled, "Now!"

As her fingers slid up his nape and over his scalp, she whispered, "If you knew this, why did we continue on?"

"Had we altered our course, our pursuers might have suspected they were detected and set themselves upon us in or near the village, using innocents as shields. There will be enough bloodshed this day without the people I am called to protect adding to that river." Not unexpectedly, speaking aloud the words increased the intensity of the crimson flashes his imagination had conjured since he had become aware the precautions in place for such an attack had served him well.

"Then?" Thomasin breathed as he moved his mouth to her ear.

"If they intend to attack, and 'tis likely, they will strike ere we reach Castle Adderstone. Therefore, I chose the place most advantageous to our numbers."

"What of their numbers?"

"Unknown, but two parties have been spotted. One from the south, the other the east."

"And you lead me opposite."

"Out of harm's way."

She swallowed. "What of you?"

"I fight alongside my men—providing we can draw out our pursuers where they would prefer not to engage."

"How?"

"By appearing to further lower our guard. When I lift you, laugh."

She nodded, and as he swept her against his armored chest, did as told.

Hoping she sounded more joyful to those farther out, Magnus carried her deeper into the wood, and once they were out of sight, returned her to her feet.

"They will think we go to the wood to make love," she said.

"Let us hope it makes them bold enough to attack." Magnus turned her north, away from where their pursuers would search them out. As he sought a path that would make tracking difficult, he silently cursed the loamy, moisture-laden earth. The impressions they left told what would not escape him were he the one in pursuit. Hopefully, the brigands were not as versed in tracking.

Shortly, he veered toward a massive outcropping, and upon reaching it, thrust aside vines and handed Thomasin into the space between a curtain of leaves and a wall of rock. It was not a cave like the quarry where they had made love, but it provided good cover.

"I want your word you will remain here until I come for you."

"But what——?"

"Your word!"

The reluctance of her nod making his gut tighten, he curled a hand around her arm, dragged her against him, and kissed her with an urgency that surprised him as much as it seemed to surprise her. He lifted his head. "Stay, love."

Her breath upon his face ceased, evidencing he had surprised her again—though no more than himself.

Wondering how *love* had found its way onto and off his tongue, he released her, dropped the vines, and swept his sword from its scabbard.

Praying the blood to be spilled would not be his or his men's, that he would soon return for his wife, he ran.

The brigands did not wish to attack. Not here where it was more open than they would have liked, thereby providing their prey time to order their defense. That was the most telling about their leader—that he was not rash. And he likely suspected all was not as it seemed, his blood and that of his men at great risk of spillage. But could he be tempted past caution? Were his numbers great enough to chance this place and time not of his choosing?

Where Magnus had worked his way around the wood to the far eastern side, he sat on his haunches with his sword across his knees and watched the six mounted riders who studied Kelling's men from cover of the wood. Did they await a signal?

He considered the second gathering of brigands. Though they were too distant for their exact number to be known, it appeared both parties were equally manned. Regardless, if their sum proved greater than Kelling's party, it would not be by many. Thus, the wait.

"Fight here or another day," Magnus muttered, and an instant later caught movement well in back of the brigands—there and gone. Likely, it was the one whose failure to appear in the village within half an hour of the arrival of Kelling's party had served to alert Magnus that he and his men were followed. And now his senior household knight, Sir George, was well positioned to bring down one or more brigands should they set themselves against those biding their time at the stream.

As Magnus waited for the brigands to decide, he readied himself for the blood that might soon spill. As often he did when given time to prepare for battle, he pulled out memories of the day a determined effort had been made to beat the devil out of an eight-year-old boy.

"I do not understand what plagues you," Rand Verdun said through teeth so tightly met their grind was heard as he cleaned blood from his son's arms, shoulders, and back. "But it is a great heartache to learn you suffer what I have long suffered. Thus, I would have you know that which took me years to accept."

"Father?" The voice was pitifully strained by an attempt to contain sobs.

Rand Verdun lightly gripped the back of his son's head and brought his face up and around. "What you see and feel"—his eyes were fierce—"what makes your stomach strive to retch its contents, will not make you less a man, Magnus. It will make you more a man."

A dry, loud swallow further shaming the boy, so much that bile moistened his throat, he croaked, "I do not understand."

The Baron of Emberly returned to his ministrations. "That with which you are afflicted will not allow you to indiscriminately shed blood as do cowards and those seeded with evil—who are more animals than men."

A gasp as a flap of skin was pressed back into place…a muffled whimper…a shudder…

"When there is a right reason to bleed another, that which your blade lets will be their due, no matter that you see it over and again and regret it was done by you."

Now the salve, one moment soothing, the next stinging, causing the boy to dig nails so deeply into his palms that salve would be required there as well. "I am your heir. What if I cannot swing a sword to protect my family?"

"You can and you will."

"How?"

"Three things you require which you already have and will possess in greater abundance as you grow into a man—anger over injustice, fear that if 'tis not their blood it will be yours, and prayer." Another layer of salve.

"Only those—?" A cry became a grunt as teeth and lips closed over it, and only after the bandages were placed did the question once more venture onto his tongue. "Only those three things?"

Vigorously rubbing a towel over his hands, his father came around to stand before him.

The boy averted his eyes from the crimson marking the towel, drew a deep breath that made him quake, and looked up at the one whom his mother had struck with her fists while screeching it was Rand Verdun's fault—that he was to blame for their son's weak constitution that would make him other men's puppet.

The boy's father looked to his hands, balled the towel, and flung it into the hearth. As flames sprang up over the blood-stained material, it opened like a flower in spring.

Returning his gaze to his son, spasms at eye and mouth warning of the anger inside, he said, "Those three things are the most important, but there is more."

"Aye?" The word was almost devoid of voice.

"You must become accustomed to blood—the look, feel, smell, even taste."

Bile once more singeing his throat, the boy choked it down. "T-taste?"

"In battle, blood does not simply flow. It flies. No matter how far the reach of your sword, that which your blade lets will fling itself at you, even rain upon you."

"How do I become accustomed to it?"

"As we have done with your knighthood training thus far, we will take it little by little, day by day." Rand Verdun nodded as if to himself. "And now there is a priest who has much to say to me." His smile was grim. "Though not as much as I have to say to him, hmm?"

Magnus returned to the body of the man he now was and the possibility that this day he would become yet more accustomed to blood. Narrowing his eyes on the brigands, he silently prayed for the Lord to stay his side should he meet them in battle, then repeated, "Fight here or another day. Choose!"

Whatever signal they awaited, finally it was given. Swaths of black fabric down around their shoulders were pulled up over their heads, the excess wrapped around their lower faces and secured at the neck. Then swords were drawn, spurs applied, and both gatherings of brigands shot from cover toward knights and men-at-arms who would soon prove they were far from oblivious.

As thought, the nearest party of brigands would pass close to Magnus. Better yet, their horses were ill matched, causing a gap to widen between four who rode abreast and two who trailed. Having sacrificed the advantage of having a horse to carry him into battle in order to lull the brigands into believing the ruse, Magnus smiled to find himself presented with an opportunity that would all the sooner see him fighting alongside his men.

He stood, exchanged his sword for his dagger, and calculated how far ahead of the last brigand he must hurl the blade for his quarry to become intimate with it. Moments later, the man took the dagger in his upper chest with such force he was thrust back, allowing his mount to ride out from under him.

Praying the brigands did not look around, Magnus ran toward the riderless horse as it slowed and swerved toward him, snatched hold of the saddle's pommel, and swung astride.

As he turned the horse back toward the attackers, a glance over his shoulder verified the movement he had seen beyond the brigands was Sir George who now spurred from the wood.

Magnus drew his sword, thrust it high to acknowledge his knight, then set the blade before him and dug in his heels. Falling in behind the brigand who had been ahead of the one who had yielded up his horse, Magnus watched Kelling's mounted men charge toward their attackers while those who had dismounted sprang into their saddles. The only ones to remain behind were the squires, Father Crispin, the big man-at-arms who stood sword-ready to defend his charge, and Sir Otto who remained alongside his destrier, doubtless struggling between joining Kelling's men and searching out the woman he was sworn to protect.

The thunder of hooves rolling across the ground, light flashing off blades and armor, Magnus urged his mount to greater speed and wondered if he had made the wrong decision not to inform De Arell's man they were followed. He could but hope Sir Otto chose to lend his sword to the battle.

A battle the brigands no longer wished, Magnus saw when their headlong flight slowed and they began to veer away. They sensed the iron teeth of the trap that sought to snap closed on them. But it proved too late for more than half, momentum carrying them too far forward.

Shouts and cries tore from throats. Steel met steel. Blood flowed and flew. And when Magnus entered the fray ahead of Sir George, his far-sweeping blade added to the crimson spray.

After severing the lives of two, he searched out his next opponent and caught sight of a brigand who had made it past Kelling's men. Bent low over a great destrier whose coat was smeared with mud—surely a means of concealing identifying marks—the man rode toward the stream. The leader of the brigands? With such a horse, it seemed likely.

Magnus swung his gaze to the one who stood the best chance of cutting short the brigand's ride. But Sir Otto was no longer at the stream, nor had he joined Kelling's men. He rode toward the trees in the direction Magnus had led Thomasin.

Magnus cursed him. If the knight was adept at tracking, he could lead the brigand following him to Thomasin.

Determining his men could finish the battle, Magnus turned his horse aside and into the path of a brigand whose head covering had fallen down around his shoulders. With a broken-toothed snarl, the man swept his sword high to deliver a blow that would fall across the Baron of Emberly's neck.

Magnus's sword arm being opposite and having too little time to bring it around, he blocked the swing with his left arm, causing the blade to slam into the chain mail sleeve covering the lower half of his arm.

As pain reverberated through muscle and bone, so wrenching Magnus could barely see straight to end this conversation of blades, he summoned more anger and fear and brought his sword around.

He was too near. But there was no other way.

His blade sank into the man's neck, and as shock leapt from the brigand's eyes in concert with the life fleeing them, crimson rained upon the victor.

The pound of Magnus's heart the only sound between his ears though steel continued to meet steel on all sides of him, he dragged himself back from the horror with a single utterance. "Thomasin!"

Then he spurred the horse toward his destrier whose strength and speed would more than compensate for the time lost in exchanging one beast for the other.

24

SHE WAS NOT accustomed to hiding. Evading—of course, as had been necessary at Waring Castle when men of an age to have been her father or grandfather had sought to take from her what she would not give. But hiding...

Though the sounds of battle were distant, they filled her head, making it ache...filled her throat, making it hard to breathe...filled her heart, making it shudder.

"Please, Lord," she prayed all she could think to pray.

Did Magnus yet fight? What of his men? Father Crispin? How much longer must she remain helpless and useless? She had made Magnus a promise, but if something happened to him that she might have been able to prevent...

The thought was ridiculous. Her teeth and nails were nothing against swords, daggers, and men's fists. Still, should she not try?

"You promised," she hissed.

But some promises had to be broken to keep other promises. And when Magnus and she had wed, she had vowed to be one with him—for worse as much as for better.

She squeezed her eyes closed. "Please, Lord."

"Lady Thomasin!"

She startled, peered through the leaves at the one whose voice she knew. Sir Otto appeared far to the right where he trotted his horse through the wood, his head turning side to side as he searched among the trees, lowering as he searched the ground.

He called again, but she hesitated over her promise that she would remain where Magnus had hidden her. But what if he could not come for her? What if he had fallen in battle? What if he had sent Sir Otto in his stead?

She held her breath, listened. The sounds of battle had lessened. Because Magnus and his men triumphed? Or failed?

"Lady Thomasin!"

The knight was turning east and would soon be out of sight.

"You promised," she whispered, and a moment later heard another approaching horse.

But it was not Magnus. Face swathed in black cloth, the brigand rode toward Sir Otto who showed no sign of realizing he was followed by one whose hand gripped a bow and sword bounced at his side.

Unless the knight who sought to protect his lord's daughter was alerted, he would be run through.

Thomasin thrust aside the vines. "Behind you!" She waved her arms, pointed.

Sir Otto's head came around, and he turned his horse toward her.

"Behind!" She pointed again at the brigand who was now near enough for her to see an arrow was fit to his bow's string. A bow he raised.

As Sir Otto continued forward, gaze fixed on her, she silently cursed him for not understanding what she could not make more clear. She had revealed herself to warn him, and now they might both die.

Having only a meat dagger on her person, no match for the brigand's weapons, she shouted another warning to the knight who was now near enough he had to hear her.

But the response she received was not his. "Thomasin!"

Destrier flying beneath him, Magnus appeared between the trees in pursuit of the brigand, just as the brigand pursued Sir Otto who finally glanced around.

The surprise on the knight's face when he looked back at Thomasin turned to horror as an arrow ceased its whistling flight and toppled him from his horse fifty feet distant from her.

She ran forward, and as she dropped to her knees alongside Sir Otto, heard Magnus shout her name again.

Hand gripping a place between neck and shoulder, blood running between his fingers, Sir Otto turned his head toward her. "I but wished to protect you—to do my duty, my lady."

With a glance at where Magnus and the brigand no longer were, her husband surely in pursuit of the one who fled, she said, "This I know," and slid an arm beneath his shoulders and tugged him onto her lap. She peered at his hand on the wound and the blood seeping over it onto her skirts. "Is it bad?"

"Nay, my lady. The arrow did not embed. Sliced the surface. Continued on."

Which accounted for its absence. "Show me."

He lifted his hand. The skin was torn, perhaps the muscle beneath, but it did not appear to be deep.

Moments later, the approach of a horse brought her head up, and as Magnus neared, she was jolted by the sight of so much blood on his face and armor.

Lord, let it not be his, she silently beseeched.

With a spray of soil and leaves, he reined in, dismounted, and yanked the knight up off her lap. "You failed her!" His saliva flew into the other man's face. "Sworn to protect her, you led him right to her!"

"I did not mean—"

"Had I not given chase, she would be as much a corpse as you."

Thomasin jumped up. "He is injured, Magnus!"

"But a flesh wound!" His gaze swept her face and dropped to her bloodied skirts. With a growl, he shoved the knight aside, and as the man stumbled to keep his feet under him, took one great stride that placed him before Thomasin. "And you!"

Her racing heart reached its legs longer as she stared into a face that, at worst, had only ever looked less attractive. Now the anger leaping off it was so dark, the smears and spatters of blood so bright, the baring of his teeth so wide, that his handsome countenance was nearly unsightly.

"You did not keep your promise!"

"I thought you had—"

"You thought wrong."

"But you could have been injured. You might have—"

"I was not. Did not. Instead, I left my men with one less warrior to aid in their fight against blood-thirsty miscreants so I might prevent this fool from endangering your life as I prayed you would not allow him to do." He moved nearer, so much taller and broader that he entirely cloaked her in shadow. "But you did, when all I asked of you was to await my return. That you keep your word to me—your husband!"

Frustration, resentment, anger, and more fear than she wished to acknowledge sprang from Thomasin's every corner. Despite her attempt to sweep them back into those dark places as she had promised the Lord she would do, they wrote themselves into words.

"Though I was terrible afeared for you, I kept me promise. And I woulda continued to, but I could not stand by and watch Sir Otto be killed."

"'Twas his place to protect you, not yours to protect him. Instead, he exposed you. Had not that arrow found his flesh, it could have found yours!"

She clenched hands tempted to stir the air with fists and palms as once they had done at Waring Castle when men of greater size and strength had loomed over her.

But this is Magnus, she told herself. *He will not harm you. His anger is out of fear for you.*

"I am sorry," she cried, "but I had to give warning."

His nostrils flared, shoulders rose and fell with great breaths. "What good did those warnings do?" He jerked his head toward Sir

Otto who stood unmoving, eyes shifting between them. "He was blind and deaf to them."

"I had to try!"

He thrust his face near hers. Still nearly unsightly. And frightening. "Nay, you had to keep your word to me."

An instant later, Thomasin's palm burned, and she could not have said why until Magnus turned his face back to her and beneath the blood drying on his cheek she saw flushed skin the size of her palm.

She slid her gaze to her hand that remained raised between them. It was also flushed, and upon it were traces of blood Magnus had worn before her. She shuddered out a breath, and on the last of it said, "Forgive me. I know you would not harm me, but..." She braved his stare, saw that though anger still shone from him, it emptied quickly like the finest wine from a pitcher.

Then he lowered his lids, and when he raised them, only fragments of that terrible emotion remained. Gently gripping her arms, he turned her so his back was to Sir Otto, shielding them both from sight. "Waring Castle haunts you still," he said.

Her heart surged with gratitude that he understood why she had struck him. "You were so close, so..."

"You felt threatened." He slid a hand up her shoulder. "Nay, I would not harm you, Thomasin. And the word *I* give, I keep."

As she should have done. "I *am* sorry."

His head descended, but as she tipped her face higher in anticipation of his kiss, Sir Otto said, "Baron Verdun is right, my lady. I failed you. And I shall answer to your father and willingly receive the punishment due me."

Magnus turned to the knight. "So you shall," he said, then drew Thomasin toward the destrier the king had gifted him. As he lifted her onto the saddle, he tossed over his shoulder, "Mount up, Sir Otto. If the battle is not yet done, mayhap you can find a measure of redemption in it."

While the knight retrieved his horse, Magnus swung up behind Thomasin.

"What of the brigand who shot Sir Otto?" she asked. "Did you fell him?"

"Had I trusted your safekeeping to your father's man, I would have, but I turned aside lest you remained in danger. Most unfortunate, for though the markings of the brigand's destrier were disguised with mud, such a fine animal likely belongs to the leader."

Meaning his death or capture could have ended the Foucault uprising. "I am sorry, Magnus."

"Worry not. There will be another day for us to meet over swords."

And she was not to worry over that? She was to believe beyond a doubt her husband would be the victor? "I was so afeared for you, Magnus. I—"

He held up a hand, narrowed his lids, and appeared to listen. "Methinks the battle is done, and unless all that Kelling's men gained whilst I fought amongst them was lost, we have won."

As he reined his horse around, she said, "It would seem the king's gift served us both well."

"Swifter than the wind. Cerus 'tis." Leaving Sir Otto to follow on his own, her husband urged the destrier to a gallop.

When they emerged from the trees, Magnus confirmed what he had believed of the battle's outcome. After handing Thomasin down to Rollo whose sword at his side evidenced he had severed the life of a nearby brigand, he rode to the bloodied body, with the tip of his sword peeled back the head covering, and did not recognize the man. Nor did he recognize the half dozen farther out, among them those he had himself laid down.

Thus, having lost one man-at-arms to the brigands and with two knights sustaining injuries that, the sooner stitched closed the better their chances of continuing to earn their living by the sword, they continued on to Castle Adderstone.

25

The BEAUTEOUS Lady Elianor was not round. Except for a slight bulge about the belly, she was as slender as when the Baron of Godsmere had forced her to accompany him to Castle Mathe in hopes of using her to gain his sister's release.

Thomasin recalled peering out from the battlements at The Boursier and the great number of retainers he had brought against her father. She had delighted in discovering that the woman at his side, whom he had wed in haste, had allowed him to believe she was Thomasin.

Griffin de Arell had seemed as delighted, for he had ridden out to meet his enemy as if better to witness the rare sight of that one's defeat. When Thomasin's father had called for her to show herself upon the wall, the shock and humiliation borne by The Boursier had been obvious.

Equal parts curiosity over the one who had impersonated her and pity that the woman would suffer the wrath of the man she had fooled, Thomasin had been surprised when her father allowed his enemy to enter Castle Mathe.

Though she had longed to become acquainted with the woman who was revealed to be Elianor of Emberly, Magnus's niece, there had been little time to do so. Once The Boursier had verified his sister was unharmed, he had wed Lady Elianor a second time to legitimize vows first spoken in the name of Thomasin. The next morn, the reluctant bride and her husband had departed Castle Mathe. And it was with much resentment The Boursier left behind his sister when Griffin refused to release the tempest who had attacked him with a dagger—and whom it fell to him to wed to join their families as decreed. But that marriage had yet to take place, Thomasin's father having returned Lady Quintin to her brother upon the death of her mother, and the king granting a stay of marriage to permit the lady time to mourn. That same lady who, this day, was not present among those assembled to welcome the Baron of Emberly.

The injured knights having been hastened into the keep to be tended by the physician, The Boursier offered what seemed a genuine greeting to Magnus before moving to Thomasin.

From his great height and breadth, out of a flinty but somewhat attractive face framed by auburn hair, he settled his singular gaze on her. "You are most welcome at Castle Adderstone, Lady Thomasin."

She glanced at the black patch covering his left eye that evidenced the least of the things he had lost years ago upon discovering Magnus's sister had made a cuckold of him. Rather, at the time the eye must have seemed the least of things. As Thomasin understood it, despite the deceit with which the fearsome Bayard Boursier's second marriage had begun, love had refined it.

So wondrous that I can feel it between them, she mused and glanced at Lady Elianor who had risen to her toes to embrace Magnus. Though two feet separated The Boursier from his wife, Thomasin imagined that if she reached out, her fingers would pluck the threads reaching from one's heart to the other.

Oh blessed, she sent heavenward, *if only Magnus could feel half as deeply for me.*

Alarmed by tears, she blinked. "It is good to see you again, Baron Boursier."

He leaned near. "Better circumstances than those under which we last met—and for which I am indebted to you."

It was in the wood they had met again, as she returned from a village. The Boursier had been bound for Castle Mathe to inform his sister of her mother's death when he caught sight of Thomasin—and Sir Otto who, unbeknownst to her, had been tasked by her father to follow her when she ventured outside the castle. That last had put her in a temper, during which she had unwittingly revealed to The Boursier the location of Aude's hovel. It was there he had found not only the woman Thomasin naively believed was her friend, but his wife who had been abducted in his absence and destined for death.

"I am glad to have been of use, Baron Boursier."

He drew back, and she saw a softening about his mouth. "More than of use, Lady Thomasin. Far more."

As her cheeks warmed, he stepped past her to greet Father Crispin and Rollo.

Then Lady Elianor surprised by drawing near and kissing Thomasin's cheek. "I am pleased my uncle brought his lovely bride to Adderstone." She laughed. "'Tis peculiar to think that now you are my aunt."

Thomasin had not considered that. It was even more peculiar than Magnus being uncle to a woman who was only seven years younger than he. But Constance and he had been born to their parents many years after the birth of their older sister. "It does not seem right," she agreed.

Lady Elianor looked closer upon her. "Either my memory serves me ill or you are much changed."

Thomasin blinked. "Am I?"

"Aye, but now you are more wife than daughter, hmm?"

Meaning the girl she must have seemed when they had first met was less apparent. Recalling yanking her skirts high, uncaring how much of her legs she revealed so she might more quickly reach the imposter and learn the tale of how and why she had taken the name of Griffin de Arell's daughter, Thomasin was pleased by the lady's observation. "Indeed, I am more wife."

"After all you have endured this day, I am sure you wish to rest."

Thomasin sighed so deeply her shoulders sank. "I am quite tired."

"Come." Lady Elianor took her arm and moved her toward the keep. "A chamber has been prepared for you and your husband."

For only one night, Thomasin silently bemoaned the change of plans wrought by the brigands. Rather than two days at Castle Adderstone and two days at Castle Mathe, Magnus had determined they must return to Kelling on the morrow to ensure the safety of his people.

When Thomasin entered the great hall alongside Lady Elianor, she saw it bustled with servants who readied it to accommodate guests for the evening meal. But amid the commotion, two caught her attention. Lady Quintin, a dark beauty to Lady Elianor's light, stood in profile alongside stairs that accessed the upper chambers. Before her was Sir Otto, who had entered the keep with Kelling's injured knights. Hand gripping his bloodied shoulder, head lowered, he said something to which Lady Quintin replied and punctuated with a short laugh.

Doubtless, had he truly felt attraction for Thomasin as alluded to, it was overshadowed by what he felt for the lady with whom he and so many others at Castle Mathe had been entranced. But Thomasin did not regret it as she had before wedding Magnus and spending nights in the arms of a man who seemed to like her there. Though that still baffled her despite Magnus's assurances that what lay beneath was more worthy of regard, she held to the hope of it.

"Lady Quintin," Lady Elianor called to her sister-in-law, "Lady Thomasin is here."

Sir Otto stepped back from the lady, offered Thomasin a nod, and ascended the stairs.

Lady Quintin turned to the two who halted before her. Eyes taking in Thomasin's skirts that were stained with Sir Otto's blood, as well as the blood of the knights she had helped bandage, she said, "I hope your stay at Castle Adderstone is more pleasant than was mine at Castle Mathe, Lady Thomasin."

Thomasin faltered over the bitter tone. Though the lady had been something of a prisoner, once The Boursier had departed Castle Mathe and it was fairly certain his sister would wed Griffin de Arell, the attraction between the two had become more obvious, their disagreements and arguments seemingly more a means of distracting them from what they really wanted—to be nearer each other. Then the death of Lady Quintin's mother had turned that tide. Though Griffin had agreed to allow the lady to return to Godsmere to bury and mourn her mother, Lady Quintin had heaped blame on him, stating that had she been a daughter rather than a prisoner, she might have prevented her mother's death.

Thomasin had seen guilt in her father's eyes and heard it in his words, but that was nearly six months ago. Surely by now Lady Quintin's misplaced anger should have found its proper place with the brigands.

Despite the longing to defend her father, Thomasin determined she would make him proud by being a lady and not returning barb for barb. "I am pleased to see you again," she said. And she truly wished to be, for she had taken a liking to the woman.

Something shifted in Lady Quintin's eyes. "And I you, Lady Thomasin."

Thinking she had moved her in a kinder direction, Thomasin said, "My father—your betrothed—is well."

Not a kinder direction, as evidenced by the narrowing of that lady's lids. "I am happy for you," Lady Quintin clipped and looked to her sister-in-law. "I know you would like to settle your guest, so I will leave you to it." She slipped past, pointing herself in the direction of her brother who stood with Magnus.

"My apologies," Lady Elianor said. "The death of Lady Maeve has been difficult for her."

"I understand. I just..." Thomasin shrugged. "My father is a good man and will make a good husband."

The lady took Thomasin's elbow and moved her toward the stairs. "I am sure they will come right in the end."

"As did your Boursier and you?"

A pretty blush wandered up Lady Elianor's face. "As did my Boursier and I. And as I hope my uncle and you shall come right if you have not already."

Thomasin started up the steps. "Magnus is good to me."

"Only good?"

Thomasin grinned. "He is more than that. I only hope——" She stilled her tongue, wondered what made her speak such things aloud.

"What do you hope?"

Thomasin sighed. "The same as you——that Magnus and I will be blessed with the strength of feelings that bind your husband and you."

"Surely wanting it is halfway to attaining it."

A lovely chill spread across Thomasin's limbs. "You are much in love, then——both of you?"

"Quite."

They reached the landing and, halfway down the corridor, Lady Elianor led her into a chamber. "Rest now. We shall speak more later."

"Lady Elianor!" Thomasin drew a deep breath. "Do you...I mean...I know I can, but do you think Magnus can?"

The lady's eyebrows rose. "Can——? Ah." She nodded. "You are not the only one who appears changed, Lady Thomasin. Though many who bother to seek beyond my uncle's handsome countenance would name him emotionless, that is only the surface of him. As an intensely private person, he allows few to delve what lies beneath, but I have glimpsed him, and saw even more of him this day. Thus, my answer to your question is that I do believe he can love. Mayhap already does." She flashed a smile and turned. "I shall see you at supper."

When the door closed behind her, Thomasin sat heavily on the bed and pondered the lady's words. Then her own. "Not only can I love," she whispered. "I do."

It had all the makings of a brutal night. A battle that time and again assaulted him with crimson flashes. Blood Thomasin had so carelessly worn he yet imagined it was her life seeping into the floor of the wood. Bone-deep fatigue that had caused him to resent the hours-long evening.

And now his wife tempting him to bed, the last place he ought to be with the day's events promising to make his dreams bleed.

Feeling trapped, Magnus once more dipped the towel in the basin of water and dragged the material down his face and neck that, before departing the stream in the wood, had been cleansed of all evidence of his sword's terrible swing.

"How did you know we were followed from Kelling?" Thomasin asked.

He hesitated over the longing to rewet the towel, folded it, and set it down. "I watch my back, and more this day with you at my side."

"I thank you that you care so much."

He looked around at where she sat propped on a pillow, bedcovers down around her waist revealing her chemise. Tempting him. "Of course I care. You are my wife."

She raised her eyebrows, smiled. Tempting him. "Pray, exactly how did you watch your back this day?"

He extinguished the candles about the chamber, and leaving only the one on the bedside table lit, approached his wife. But when she turned back the covers to invite him in, he moved to the nearby chair.

Noting her wavering smile, he said, "When I depart Kelling, I leave a man behind. If he does not appear at the appointed place within a half hour, his absence serves as warning that either he follows those who follow our party or ill has befallen him. Thus, my men and I are more diligent in watching for pursuers."

Thomasin's smile recovered. "That is clever."

"It has served us many times, but never as well as it did this day. And had not Sir Otto revealed your hiding place, it would have served us better."

The sparkle in her eyes fled. "I am sorry I did not keep my word."

"I do not require another apology, Thomasin. I but remind you of the importance of trusting me to keep you safe."

She nodded, then brightened. "Did you not notice I chose the right side of this bed?"

He had, and had hoped forgetfulness was not responsible.

"Though at Kelling I sleep on the left side, I saw that in this chamber the right is farthest from the door."

He sat forward, propped his elbows on his knees, and clasped his hands between them. "I am pleased."

Silence fell, and she moved her gaze to the empty place beside her. "The day has been long enough, do you not think?"

He struggled against stiffening. "It has. Unfortunately, my mind is awake." Too awake, he reflected, but not so his body that demanded its due as much as did the crimson flashes.

"Then you can hold me whilst *I* sleep." She fluttered her lashes. Tempting him.

He settled back in the chair. "I would not have my wakefulness disturb your rest."

This time his words turned her smile wrong side up, and she asked softly. "Is it the lion's den?"

The question was so direct and knowing he could not subdue his startle. "What say you?"

"Only that I believe it bothers you to spill the blood of others, especially if you must slay them."

"As it should bother me," he snapped, then chided himself for turning defensive.

Thomasin slid beneath the covers, turned on her side to face him, and bunched the pillow under her head. Candlelight flickering over her face, picking out her beguiling blue eyes, she said, "Aye, but whereas your men dwelt upon this day's battle mostly to celebrate their triumph and thank the Lord they live another day, you do not. You brood, and I think that is what keeps you awake though your body aches for rest."

Magnus stared at the one whom he had not long ago mistakenly regarded as more girl than woman. Thomasin saw him. But how much of what she saw—might see—would she tolerate?

The words to deny what she believed of him were in his throat, but they slid down. As he struggled between dragging them back up and leaving the lie where it lay, she reached across the mattress. "Come to bed, Husband."

He nearly refused as he should, but a calm settled over him, and that part of him that wanted to feel her curled against him prevailed once he assured himself he would not sleep, would only hold her until she drifted off.

Clothed but for the boots he had earlier removed, he lowered to the mattress and set his shoulders against the headboard.

"Should I be jealous?" Thomasin asked as he drew her up against his side.

"Of?"

"Lady Quintin as you are of Sir Otto. You seem much to enjoy her company and she seems to enjoy yours."

Magnus knew he should not be surprised, for he had felt the strain between his wife and Lady Quintin following the evening meal when he had joined the ladies at the hearth and Boursier's sister had engaged him in conversation.

"You have no cause to be jealous. Lady Quintin and I but talked. And, certes, I do not look at her as I have seen Sir Otto look at you."

"Then you are not attracted to her as I am—was—to Sir Otto?"

Was. He liked that. Though he wanted to deny what she asked of him to ease her worry, he would not lie, just as she had not when he had inquired after her father's knight. "She makes for interesting company, and 'tis true I was attracted to her when I made her acquaintance months past here at Adderstone, but as naught could come of it, naught did, and naught ever shall. I view her only as the woman who is sister-in-law to my niece."

He felt Thomasin relax. "I am glad."

Pleased she did not seek further assurance, he added, "It is peculiar to think she shall soon be stepmother to my wife."

"Unhappily so. Indeed, when she looks at me, 'tis as if she sees my father in me ere she sees the daughter."

"Then they were much at odds while your father held her at Castle Mathe."

"In the beginning—understandable since she drew a blade on him—but they were coming 'round. So much I thought it quite funny how often they did not kiss when they seemed both to want it."

Imagining the gruff Griffin de Arell and the tempestuous Lady Quintin dancing around desire, Magnus smiled.

"Most unfortunate," Thomasin continued, "it seems she continues to hold my father greatly responsible for her mother's passing."

"How so?"

"She believes had he allowed her to return to Castle Adderstone, she might have prevented her mother's death."

A possibility, Magnus considered. But as he was ever learning, just as one could not thrive in what might be, one could not happily live in what might have been.

Ruefully, for he liked Lady Quintin and thought he might also come to regard Thomasin's father kindly, he said, "That could make for a difficult marriage."

She tilted her face up, and he thought how lovely she was in candlelight that ran the curve of her mouth and nose and teased out bits of gray in the blue of her eyes. "More difficult than ours?" she asked.

He frowned.

She laughed. "You look stricken. Ah, but over that I should not tease." She rose up, and as she moved to kiss him, said, "Truly, I am most content with what I know of my Lord Husband."

What she knew…He received her kiss without adding to the temptation of it, and when she lifted her head, said, "Sleep, Wife."

She scooted back down and settled beneath his chin. "What of you?"

"When my mind tires, I will sleep." Though where, he did not know, for if this calm was short-lived, he risked proving Ulric de Arell's claim that the Verduns were ill of mind.

Curse the brigands! Curse—

"I am impressed you know your lands so well." Thomasin drew a hand up over the fabric stretched across his chest. "First the quarry where we sheltered from the rain, today the outcropping with its veil of vines."

"Like my father, I value Emberly such that I am acquainted with its most distant corners."

"My father knows Blackwood, but not so well that he was aware of Aude's hovel beside the lake. You never saw it?"

"From a distance." Magnus was acquainted with the heavily-wooded lake where the baronies converged, that body of water divided amongst the three. "But as 'twas upon Blackwood land and it appeared unoccupied when I passed near, I did not concern myself with it."

A pity, he thought. Had he known the one who occasionally inhabited it was the same Agatha who dwelt within his walls, he would have investigated.

"It was not for you to do." Thomasin trailed her hand up his collarbone and around his neck. Tempting him.

Knowing he would more easily yield to sleep were he intimate with her, he drew her hand back to his chest.

"You showed great courage in tending my knights following battle," he said.

"Blood does not much bother me, though it did at the beginning."

"What beginning?"

"When little Joss was given into my care. She had fits, mostly of frustration, and when I could not control her screaming and crying, her mother sent the physician for bloodletting. Sometimes I could distract her so it was more quickly done, but often I had to hold her down, and it was not unusual for there to be more blood on me than in the bowl."

"It weakened her sufficiently to quiet her," Magnus growled.

"Aye, but as she grew older, she gained control—at least, enough that when her emotions tipped too far in the wrong direction, most times I had only to remind her that she might be heard. I hated it, but it seemed the only way to keep the blade from her."Thomasin yawned. "She was terrified of blood."

Something the boy Magnus had been understood. Something the man he was, yet struggled against.

He stroked a hand down his wife's hair. "Sleep."

He felt her nod, and minutes later, all of her relaxed. Minutes after that, she breathed deep.

He stared across the shadowed chamber at the unadorned wall alongside the door, grateful he did not look upon *The Betrayal* tapestry that would add fuel to the flashes which, blessedly, had lessened considerably once Thomasin was in his arms.

Just a while longer, he promised, then he would seek a far stable, if need be, and gain whatever rest could be had.

26

—∞∞∞—

THE DEVIL WAS on Magnus's heels, or so it sounded as Thomasin was snatched from a dream both hopeful and frightening—rain bathing Magnus and her, his hand enfolding hers, running, glimpsing the dark figures of those in pursuit.

But the images scattered when a shout brought her head up from Magnus's perspiration-dampened tunic.

She peered at him in the dim of the expiring bedside candle. Though his features were indistinct, she saw his head snap to the side, beneath her hand felt a growl spring from his chest.

"Magnus?"

His body stiffened, then arched like a bridge over still water. She scrambled off before he collapsed back to the mattress as if the waters had turned violent and washed away the supports. He shuddered, his hands clawing at the sheets, and she imagined his planks being torn asunder, his nails ripping through the wood to drag across the river bottom.

"Nay!" he shouted hoarsely.

She touched his face. "Magnus."

He whipped his head toward her, scraping his teeth across her palm and naming her something foul.

Nay, not her—the devil that was after him.

She wavered, uncertain if she should let him find his way free of the dream or reach into its infested waters and pull him out.

Another growl, like that of a vicious dog. Then he thrashed and his arm struck her shoulder, knocking her onto her back.

Tears pricking, more for whatever horror he visited than the bruise blooming beneath her skin, she came up on her hands and knees and leaned in. "'Tis only a dream, Magnus."

His breath whipped across her face, saliva flecked her cheeks.

Taking hold of his shoulders, she lowered her head toward his. "I vow 'tis not real." She touched her lips to his. "But I am."

He groaned.

"Magnus, my love."

His body eased, and he mumbled something.

Lest he was yanked back from the surface toward which he rose, she put her face alongside his and said, "You are with me."

His long, slow breaths moved her hair, circled her ear. "Crimson." The word was so thickly spoken she was certain much of him remained in the dream. "Everywhere."

Further evidence this warrior of hers neither gloried in nor shrugged off the spilling of blood.

"Cannot...reach."

She frowned. "Reach what?"

"Her."

Thomasin pressed her teeth into her lower lip. Dare she believe she was the one he spoke of with such longing? That she had been in his dream as he had been in hers? Or was it another woman he could not reach?

She did not want to think where the conversation overheard between Sir Otto and the man-at-arms moved her, but there she was—once more questioning where Magnus had gone when he had sent his men ahead of him. And there was that which she had tried to ignore during supper. As cool as Lady Quintin was toward her, the woman had warmed considerably in Magnus's presence.

Cease, she told the seeds of jealousy seeking good soil in which to burrow.

"Blame," Magnus rasped, and between them she felt his anger surge anew. "'Tis upon me."

Desperate to keep his head above the surface he was slipping beneath, she rose up over him. "Awaken!"

Seeing a flash of bared teeth, feeling the bed shudder as he thrust his legs against it, she shook his shoulders. "Awaken!"

He cursed and his back began to arch again.

Before she raised a hand against him, she gave it a moment's thought. But unlike in the wood when it had happened without her consent, this time the sting of flesh striking flesh did not return Magnus to his senses.

He wrenched to the side, thrust her beneath him, and landed a hand high upon her neck.

She held in her scream, but there was no containing her trembling as she tested the strength of the hand at her throat and found that though breath did not come easily, fear was more responsible than the convulsing of his fingers.

Counseling calm while he breathed fast and shallow as if it had taken much effort to subdue her, she peered into his face and caught the glitter of his eyes. He was at the surface, but she did not think all of him was, not with him yet threatening her breath.

"'Tis me." She laid a hand on his jaw. "Your Thomasin."

The wall of the room that stood between Magnus and the one he was too late to save blurring, the crimson he could not remove from his hands dissolving, he drank in the sweet, warm notes of the voice that reached into him.

"Magnus love, I am here."

He blinked and found himself surrounded by blessed black, warm curves beneath his body, a pounding pulse against his fingers.

"Are you returned to me?" asked the one whose voice seemed to possess the power to gentle the devil he had been battling most of his remembered life.

Thomasin. Here with him. This side of the wall. Alive. Her throat beneath his hand.

"Almighty!" He released her and fell onto his back. As he pulled in air that did not taste of iron, he waited for her to spring from the bed. When she did not, he turned his head toward where she remained unmoving as if for fear he would be on her again if she too deeply drew breath.

"Forgive me," he said in a voice so graveled he knew he must have been trying to shout his way out of the bloody dream. "Did I harm you?"

She moved onto her side, and with a slight tremor in her words said, "You did not."

Silently, he thanked the Lord, then cursed himself for a fool who had known better than to lie with her so soon after the letting of blood. "A dark dream I had," he said, thinking no more need be told.

"Aye. 'Tis the blood that haunts you?"

Then he had spoken in his sleep. A chill traveling his perspiring limbs, he asked, "What did I say?"

"You spoke of crimson everywhere, that you could not reach someone, that you were to blame."

He ground his teeth. "What did I do?"

"Kicked, swung, cursed, shouted—though, it seems, not so loud you roused others from their beds."

"You are sure I did not harm you?"

Her laugh was humorless. "Methinks I did you more harm when I slapped you awake."

Only then feeling the prickle across his cheek, he guessed the hand she had raised to him had shaken him free of the dream—and made him retaliate. "*More* harm," he murmured. "I did hurt you, then."

"Your swing caught my arm, but I do not think it will bruise badly."

He thrust to sitting. "First I bruise you, then I near strangle you!" He swung his legs over the side of the bed, but before he could rise, she was at his back, wrapping her arms around him.

"I could breathe, Magnus. I was in no danger."

"So you think." He leaned forward to free himself.

She held tighter. "I know."

"Even if you are right—in *this* instance—still I frightened you."

"A little. More, I was frightened for you, for the terrible things in your dream."

Crimson on his hands. Rivulets streaking his armor. Pooling at his feet. Crimson on the other side of the wall. Seeping beneath an immovable door. Telling its tale of Thomasin—for whom he came too late.

Feeling a shiver beneath his skin, fearing it would make him quake as sometimes happened when his perspiring body cooled, he assured himself it had only been a dream and closed his eyes the better to feel his wife here with him—curves pressed to his back, arms holding him, hands clasped over his heart.

"I tell you true"—her lips brushed his ear—"you did me no harm."

He opened his eyes and stared into the dim. "My hand was at your throat—"

"Magnus, after what I have told of when I was at Waring Castle, you think I have never had a hand at my throat?"

The thought of that—her breath being stolen for what she refused to yield—made him ache to do far worse to her attacker. "I could have strangled you!"

She came around the side of him. "Could have, but did not." She put a leg over him and settled on his lap facing him. "Indeed, I do not think you would have touched me at all had I not asserted I had more right to you than a dream. But I could not leave you in it."

"Why?"

"'Twould be like watching one blindly approach a cliff and doing naught. And so I called you back to me." She touched her forehead to his. "Magnus, are such dreams the reason you did not wish to share the solar—why you do not keep a squire near at night to tend you?"

Shame tempted him to assure her this night was rare, but though crimson dreams were hardly an every night occurrence, he was certain his wife already knew much of his truth. And what she did not know would soon find its fit in questions already asked of him, specifically what her grandfather had warned her about. The Verduns—at least father and son—suffered what some would say evidenced they were mad. Though Rand Verdun had said it was not so, and neither did Magnus believe it—or did he just not wish to?—something was not right in his head.

He sighed. "I would not have you know me so well, Thomasin, but you are determined."

"As I should be. Not only am I your wife, but it would be wrong not to know well the man who shall father our children."

He tensed further. "What I am going to tell that I thought never to speak of again may change your mind about bearing children—for their sake."

"Their sake?"

"Your grandfather warned you Verduns are not right of mind."

"That does not make it so."

He nearly smiled that she so readily defended him. "Still, there is some truth in it. But 'twill be easier told without you on my lap." Far easier, for he would prefer to distract them both with lovemaking.

She started to rise, but he hooked an arm around her, dropped back onto the mattress, and rolled her onto her side.

A soft laugh escaping her where she lay facing him, she curved a hand around his neck. "What bedevils you, Magnus?"

Wishing it were the straw of a stable's loft he had shouted his dream into, he said, "I do not know that there is a name for it, for to speak of it to others is…" He shook his head. "If not dangerous for what might be believed of me, then disturbing enough I could find myself ostracized."

"I vow I will not think ill of you."

"You believe you will not."

"I will not."

Wanting it done, he said, "What I suffer my father suffered. The least of it is an ache for order and cleanliness, at times so persistent I am distracted from my purpose. The middling ground is dark imaginings—usually of blades and blood—that threaten to consume me. The worst of it is memories of blood I have spilled or seen spilled that haunt my waking hours, and when I can no longer keep my eyes open, turn dreams into nightmares. Nightmares so real that this eve I believed myself attacked and retaliated by attacking you."

"You did not attack me. You but prevented me from striking you again."

"I wish that so, but I do not trust it to be."

"You will see. Come the morrow, you will find no marks on my neck. But tell me, are these dark dreams the reason your father had your mother keep a separate chamber?"

Magnus nearly laughed. "Sleeping separate was my mother's idea. Rather, what she demanded."

"She feared your father would harm her?"

"That may have been some of it."

"Some?"

Very little, Magnus thought, remembering the woman who had hated what she perceived to be her husband's shortcomings, which was likely the reason there had been so many years between the birth of Elianor's mother and Magnus and Constance. Distaste over her husband's affliction and separate chambers had made for few intimacies. Indeed, if not for the need to provide at least one male heir, it was likely the two children born late to her would never have been.

"What else was it?" Thomasin pressed.

"My mother was an only daughter, born after four sons and before three more. Her father being known for his sword, he made certain his sons were as well. Thus, my mother measured a man's worth by the amount of blood on his hands. Though my father was beyond proficient at arms, he was not indiscriminate in shedding an opponent's blood and took great pains to avoid wearing it. My mother viewed his aversion as weakness and was repulsed." Would Thomasin be? He did not think so, and yet...

"I am sorry," she said.

"As was I for my father. He was a good man."

"Did your mother know you shared his affliction?"

"Before my father knew, though methinks he suspected. In my seventh year, when my mother pressed to have me fostered with her family to begin training toward knighthood, my father refused, causing a greater strain in their relationship that could be felt even when they were rooms apart. Thus, I began my training at Kelling. But as I progressed and my wooden sword was replaced with steel, blood began to flow, and not always from mere scratches. I was not bothered by my own as much as that of others. I tried not to think on it, but my mind seemed determined to revisit and enlarge those images, and when I sought to suppress them, I began to exhibit the same facial spasms for which my father was known."

"Then for that you look strange at me when I talk about getting all twitched."

"Aye, at first I thought you referred to what you saw upon my face, but then I realized it was but an expression."

"Most certainly," she assured him. "How did your mother react?"

"She was much disturbed and demanded I be sent to her family, who she believed were more capable of raising me into a man. But my father would not be moved. And so she waited."

"For what?"

"The opportunity to fix what she feared was broken. It came when the king summoned my father to London. Though she mostly devoted herself to instructing my sister, Constance, in the ways of a lady, during my father's absence she sought me out and engaged me as never she had. I was wary, having more experience with her being distant, argumentative, and demeaning, but one night I succumbed. While she put out candles in my chamber, I asked her to leave one lit. She agreed, providing I gave her good reason. I told her I had been having dreams so frightening they awakened me. She stroked my head as she had not done for years, and I confided that I suffered not only memories of blood, but during waking hours I was beset with visions conjured by the mere sight of a blade—that I had even imagined cutting Constance, and it frightened me more than the dreams."

Remembering how still his mother had become and the chill creeping over the fire-warmed chamber, Magnus felt ice course his limbs. "She believed I was ill of mind."

Thomasin sat up, and he thought now she would distance herself as his mother had done. Instead, she pulled the coverlet up, and as it settled over them, resumed her place beside him.

"I do not understand why you thought such things," she said, "but they were only thoughts. Not wishes. And certainly not deeds."

Magnus drew her nearer, and when her warm, pliant body came easily to him, the ice began to recede and his knotted insides to loosen. "That is as I told her, and I assured her that just as I did not wish my sister harm, never would I do her harm."

"Did she believe you?"

"She spoke no further word and snuffed the candle. The next morn…"

Thomasin swallowed. "Tell me."

"I awoke to find Emberly's priest in my chamber. He said my mother had told him of my visions and asked for aid in ridding me of them."

"Through prayer?"

"Aye. More, though, by way of a scourge. He placed one in my hand and said that if I wished to be free of the devil, I must beat him out of me."

"You flogged yourself?"

"At the beginning while he prayed over me. When my pain was too great, he did what I could not and I prayed—or tried to." How his mind had screamed, louder than the sounds escaping his mouth that he had tried to seal against them. Even now his mind protested the blood his eyes could not see but whose every path he had felt course his back.

"The lion's den," Thomasin whispered.

Where he had been bloodied.

Her chest jerked against his, and he touched her face and found tears pooled alongside her nose. "I did not mean for you to cry."

"How could I not? A man should not have to suffer that, and you were a child."

"It seems we both had to grow up too soon."

After a time, she asked, "What of your father? Did you tell him?"

"I would have had to, my injuries being so severe that were it truly possible to beat the devil out of a person, he would have fled me. But my father returned that day and discovered it himself. Never before had I seen him that angry, nor afterward. But ever disciplined, he controlled himself, and it was he who tended my injuries."

"And the priest?"

"He left Emberly and never returned."

"Is that why you have not a priest at Kelling? You do not like them?"

"As my father before me, I have much respect for men of God like Father Crispin. However, when one is called elsewhere or passes away, I replace him only when I have found one I believe can be trusted to faithfully lead my people and me."

"Then your father replaced the priest who did that to you?"

"Aye, though it took him a year."

"He must have been angry with your mother."

"He was a forgiving man, but it was months ere I heard him speak to her. And as distant as they were with each other before, they became more distant. I am sorry to say, but I do not believe my father mourned her when she passed away."

"Did you?"

"I did. I cannot say I missed her much, but I had been fond of her when I was young—while she was yet proud of me."

"She was wrong not to esteem you. You know that, do you not?"

"My father was of the same mind."

"The right mind. I am glad he and you were close."

"He understood me, helped me control as best as possible whatever 'tis he passed to me." He sighed. "So tell, Thomasin, do you still wish to share my bed?"

She snorted. "More so now I know 'tis not me you wanted to keep out."

"I told you it was not."

She nodded. "You truly did wish privacy. And now I understand the reason you left me on our wedding night, why you were so against displaying blood on the morning after sheets, and the sounds I awakened to the night ere you departed for your tour of the demesne."

"I feared you heard me."

"Not clear enough to be certain it was you. Had I known..."

"What would you have done?"

Thomasin did not need to give her answer any thought. "Not what your mother did." She put her hands to his shoulders, leaned up, and kissed the corner of his mouth. "This I would do." She wiggled higher and kissed the corner of his eye. "And this."

There was amusement in his voice when he said, "You would kiss away my twitches?"

"That is not all." She rose and pressed a hand to his shoulder, urging him onto his belly.

"What is this, Thomasin?"

"Your wife. For better, for worse."

As he settled face down, she pushed the coverlet to his waist and lifted his tunic. "In sickness, and in health."

"What are you——?"

"Shh." She set her hands to his back that was too shadowed to see the scars that likely evidenced the day Kelling's priest had put a scourge in his hand. But she felt them as she began to rub the muscles. Blessedly, they were thin and almost smooth beneath her fingers, so much she would have missed many were she unaware of what he had suffered. His child's skin had been forgiving.

He groaned, and she stilled her hands until he said, "Pray, continue. Your touch heals."

She kissed the back of his neck, and feeling him relax further, returned to stroking and kneading his muscles. And though her hands ached, she did not stop until he breathed the deep of sleep. Then she returned to his side, pillowed her head on his back, and considered all he had told her.

Though Sir Otto had imparted the rumor Rand Verdun could turn violent, for which his wife had insisted on a separate chamber, Thomasin did not believe it. True, this night his son had so quickly come up out of his crimson dream he had reacted to her slap by putting a hand to her throat, and it *had* frightened her, but Magnus had meant her no harm. More, he had done her none. Her husband's mind might have its dark places, but she did not think that made him mad.

As for his mother…

In a manner, the woman had rejected Magnus as surely as Thomasin's mother had rejected her little girl. For this had Magnus been so angered at Alice for abandoning Thomasin? Knowing himself how deep the hurt of losing a mother's love?

Thomasin sighed. No matter her husband's fear of passing on his affliction, she would bear him children—in their solar where she would pass every night regardless of his dreams. And like his father, and with her at his side, he would aid his children were the affliction visited upon them.

"I do love you," she whispered. "Oh, how I love you, Magnus."

27

ALL WAS QUIET. Magnus said too quiet, as if something held its breath.

Since their return to Castle Kelling four days past, he and his men had patrolled the demesne, ever returning weary and empty handed. But unlike Magnus, Thomasin was inclined to believe it meant the Foucault threat had ended en route to Castle Adderstone.

She closed the ledger the steward had, with slightly less grudging, delivered to her in the hall after supper. Though he did not like a *half-commoner* confirming his figures as once Lady Elianor had done, Thomasin was determined to gain his acceptance with the honey of kind and tolerant words despite being tempted to the vinegar of returning his muttered insults. And in quietly correcting his errors before they bled across other figures, she made progress.

Belly grumbling, she looked to the windows set high in the wall through which moonlight streamed. Magnus and his men had not returned in time for the evening meal, though she had delayed it an hour. But soon, she told herself, refusing to dwell on it being the latest he and his men had been out—and denying her imagination its sport of envisioning harm befalling them.

When her husband returned, she would curl around his back or he around hers. They would speak of great and small things and whisper themselves to sleep as they had done each night since she had learned his secret. Though he had yet to suffer another dream as deeply troubling as the one she had witnessed, his restlessness and low groans had awakened her their first night back at Kelling. With murmurings and caresses, she had awakened him, and he had called her *love* again, gathered her close, and fallen into a peaceful sleep. In the morn, she had opened her eyes to *his* murmurings and caresses. He had not spoken of the dream, but after making love to her had said he prayed she would be at his side every night.

Belly once more reminding her she had picked at her supper, she rose quietly from the chair so she would not disturb the castle folk who had settled on their pallets, snuffed the candle on the table, and by the light of dim torches picked her way across the hall to the kitchen.

The fire in the hearth within gave shape to the cavernous room and lit the way to the immense table upon which Mathilde had set out cheese and bread for Magnus's return.

Thomasin halted alongside it and broke off a piece of dark bread, for which the common side of her had a fondness despite most nobles' preference for more costly white bread. She topped it with soft white cheese and sighed into the bite.

"Have you forgiven me yet?" asked one who had gained his pallet in the hall a half hour earlier.

Nearly expelling her mouthful, she snapped her gaze to Sir Otto as he came alongside her. Quickly, she chewed and swallowed. "I did not hear you enter."

"Then my stealth improves." His mouth lifted, and it struck her this was the first genuine smile she had seen from him since before the attack in the wood.

"I am hardly a good measure of that. The day my husband and you followed me to the village, I thought myself quite alone."

"That day, aye. But many a day you have feigned ignorance, eh?"

She tried not to smile. "A day here, a day there."

He nodded. "So, am I forgiven for failing you on the journey to Castle Adderstone?"

"Of course."

"I am grateful, though still ashamed. It can hardly inspire confidence in my ability to keep you safe."

"You have kept me safe for years, Sir Otto. We all make mistakes— just as I did in answering your call though I promised my husband I would remain hidden until he came for me."

He grunted. "The baron wishes me to return to Castle Mathe— would see me dishonored."

"I do not believe that is his intent. Certes, he but wishes to take full responsibility for me as should a husband."

"Then you would have me leave you?"

She smiled apologetically. "As I am now settled at Kelling, it seems a good time for you to return to my father's service."

He stared, and his gaze became so intense, she felt herself blush. "I shall miss you, my lady."

"And I you, Sir Otto."

He lifted a hand and drew the backs of his fingers down her cheek. "You truly are a woman now."

She jumped to the side. "I know not why you persist in flirting with me, Sir Knight. Certes, 'tis not by order of my father."

He shrugged. "Ever the courtly knight wants more what he cannot have."

Hoping to lift the discomfiting mood, she snorted. "Methinks you have mistaken me for Lady Quintin."

"Lady Quintin?"

"I have eyes to see, Sir Otto. And from the way you looked at her during her stay at Castle Mathe and again at Castle Adderstone, I have no doubt where your true affection lies. Unfortunately for you, it lies on the path my father is to take."

He gave a crooked smile she had once found charming. Now she did not know how she found it. "A man can dream."

"Providing he does not dream *of* or *with* another man's wife," spoke another, evidencing that just as Sir Otto had entered the kitchen unheard, so had Kelling's lord.

Thomasin and the knight turned toward where her husband stood just inside the kitchen, hands in fists at his sides.

"Sir Otto," Magnus said, "you trespass where you ought not, and that puts you in grave danger."

Thomasin heard the knight at her side swallow, knew Magnus heard as well.

"You err, Baron Verdun. I hold your wife in high regard, and though 'tis true I seek her side, it is only to fulfill my duty to Baron de Arell."

"A duty of which you will soon be relieved."

"I am prepared to depart when my liege orders it."

"He shall. Very soon."

The knight looked to Thomasin. "My lady," he said and strode opposite. When Magnus did not move aside, he stepped wide around him.

With the closing of the door, Thomasin clasped her hands at her waist. "Tell me you do not believe I would cuckold you," she said, and in her voice heard anger seeded by anticipation he did believe it.

Hands splaying as if to release objects they had squeezed so tightly they had become embedded in his flesh, Magnus strode forward, and she told herself that no matter his answer, she would give him no cause to dismiss her feelings and words as belonging to those of a child—that she would keep her word to the Lord.

"I do not forget you professed attraction for that man," he said, halting before her. "But nay, Thomasin, I do not believe you would be unfaithful."

She had not realized her chest was so full of breath until she emptied it.

"But as Sir Otto himself told," Magnus continued, "he wants the forbidden. And you are that. You are mine."

That much of the conversation he had heard, then. She was glad, since he knew she had rejected the knight's flattery.

"As you are mine, Husband."

He pulled her into his arms, and she smiled beneath his chin. "All is well upon Emberly?" she asked.

"Too well—blessedly, I would like to believe." His breath warmed her scalp. "But did I, I might not see what lies in wait."

Praying nothing did, she said, "Come the morrow, linger abed with me."

"Would that I could. But whoever he is, I feel him out there. Watching."

She drew back and pushed hair off his brow that was darker than usual from too many days in the saddle that made sleep a priority over bathing. It was too late to call for a bath, but she would give him one as best she could with a basin of warm water scented with the sage and rosemary he liked.

Hearing the approach of booted feet belonging to the hungry men who had ridden with him, she nodded at the door. "Go abovestairs. I will bring your meal and water to bathe you."

"I would like that."

"And disrobe," she said as he withdrew from her, "all the way lest I cannot awaken you."

He paused at the door. "For that reason only?"

"You need rest, Magnus."

"Mayhap I *will* have to linger abed come morn." He opened the door, on the other side of which came his men, and looked around. "Sir Otto will depart Kelling, Thomasin."

"Aye, it is time."

"I will send your father a missive on the morrow."

"Of course, but…"

Despite the breadth of the room between them, she saw furrows dig into his brow. "Speak, Thomasin."

She glanced to his men, who had halted their advance. "His only crime being flirtation, I pray you will not be too harsh."

"No more than is required to assure that when my ally weds, he has not to worry on a young knight tempting his lady wife away from him."

At her hesitation, he said, "Your first concern ought to be for your father and peace in his marriage. With his betrothed already set against him, he does not need another trying to draw her away."

"I just…" She sighed. "You are right. Now go. I will follow shortly."

When she entered the solar bearing a tray that held a basin of scented water, viands, and a cup of wine, Magnus lay face down on the bed. Unclothed as requested.

28

That day. The one in the wood. Pray, come soon.

Cryptic, but not to Magnus who knew that day and what the one in the wood had done. And how could he not? He bore much of the responsibility.

He lifted his gaze from the inked words that, for all the care taken in forming the letters, were as if from the quill of a child. Nanne learned alongside Eamon, and at Magnus's insistence. But now, it seemed, the lessons had served her well.

Unfortunately, his promise to take Thomasin riding, now a sennight since their return to Kelling, would have to keep. He was almost grateful time was of such import that another would have to tell her.

"Squire," he called forth the young man who had delivered the missive to the stables after Magnus had sent his men to patrol Emberly.

The squire halted before him. "Aye, my lord?"

"Seek out my wife and inform her I have received tidings that require me to depart Kelling and that I shall return as soon as possible." And somewhere between now and then, find an excuse to explain his sudden departure.

Nay, a lie, his conscience challenged. And not for the first time, he acknowledged he would have to tell her of Eamon and Nanne. Perhaps this day—upon his return to Kelling.

"I shall tell her, my lord." The young man hastened from the stables.

Magnus retrieved his sword belt and mantle from the bench he had laid them on while readying his destrier and Thomasin's palfrey. As he strapped on his sword, he noted that though his garments were not fine, neither were they of the homespun cloth he wore to ride upon the barony of Orlinde. But there was nothing for it other than cover of the simple mantle he had chosen this morn.

Minutes later, having exchanged his destrier for a worthy horse that did not proclaim its rider a lord, he spurred away from Kelling.

"Not Foucault,"Thomasin whispered as she had done often since Magnus's squire had delivered the message hours past. Though she had asked the young man what had caused her husband to set aside plans to spend the day with her, he had said he knew only that his lord had departed after receiving a missive delivered by a passing merchant.

A merchant, meaning the tidings were likely from a commoner who, unlike a noble, might have a man-at-arms carry a message the better to ensure its arrival.

"Not Foucault," she said again, certain that were it so dire, Magnus would have taken men with him rather than ride out alone. But then, what was of such import he had to leave immediately?

She rose from before the altar where she had come to pray for her husband and their people after hours of trying to distract herself with needlework. Sliding her gaze over the cross mounted to the wall, she beseeched, "Return him safe to me. Pray, no bloodshed."

She stood silent, listening should the Lord whisper something into her as He sometimes did. Either this time He did not, else she did not attend well to His voice. Likely the latter, for she had been remiss in her prayers and, since her wedding, attended mass only the one time on the morn her husband and she had departed Castle Adderstone.

Certes, Castle Kelling was much in need of a priest, and when Magnus returned, she would offer to aid in the search for a man of God worthy of ministering to the people.

She turned and, as she walked the aisle, recalled the day she had done so with Magnus at her side. And stepping into their path had been the king's man whom she had pitied for the burns to his visage—until his taunting of her and Magnus and his gruesome wedding gifts had shown he was not only monstrous on the outside.

She exited the chapel. The sky that had been lightly hung with clouds when she had entered was clear and the palest blue of a day bright with sunshine.

And advancing toward her was Sir Otto who had yestereve received orders from her father to return to his service.

Surprised he had not yet departed, she raised her eyebrows. "I thought you would have left this morn."

"An opportunity arose that delayed my plans." He halted and looked over his shoulder at the lone figure alongside the inner gate-house—John, the man-at-arms in his pay. Where he stood facing the chapel with the sunlight full upon him, Thomasin saw him more clearly than before.

She frowned. In the stables with Sir Otto, something about him had been familiar, but he was more familiar yet.

"John is just returned from a task I set him," the knight said, "and he—What is it, my lady?"

She blinked. "He much resembles someone I knew." She had only seen him from a distance, but that face, especially set with such a nose, and even in the absence of a beard…"Nay, not knew," she corrected. "Someone I saw."

"Who?"

"You are going to think me silly when I tell you it is eleven years since I laid eyes on him, but his distinctive face much resembles that of the man for whom my mother left me."

"What was his name?"

She laughed. "Also John."

"A common name."

"Aye, but though he was bearded then, all else about him is familiar."

Sir Otto looked around. "As you say, his face is distinctive. But also as you say, you were a child."

She pulled her lower lip between her teeth. "If 'tis him, then my mother—"

"My lady, do not torment yourself over something that is hardly likely, especially as there is a matter of great import I must discuss with you. About your husband."

She pulled back from the edge she had nearly stepped over. "What of him?"

"Though I regret what I must tell you, I vowed to keep you safe. And I hope once you are past the pain, I will be redeemed in your eyes."

She stared at him, part of her wanting him to spill all, another part wanting to seal up the place from which it would spill. "You frighten me, Sir Otto."

"I wish I did not have to, but you ought to know the truth about the man you wed the better to protect yourself when I am gone."

Seal it up, Thomasin, that part entreated. *Hold to the man whose arms welcome you. That is the truth of Magnus. It has to be.*

The knight bent near. "John risked much to follow the baron this morn. And what he witnessed..." He shook his head. "I pray 'tis not as it appears, but one would have to be blind to overlook what was seen this day."

She swallowed. "What is that?"

"I am sorry, my lady, but your husband has a woman upon the barony of Orlinde, just over Emberly's border."

A chill went through her. It was upon Orlinde that Magnus had left the woman beaten by brigands in the care of one named Nanne. "Do you know the name of this woman?"

"John says your husband called her Nanne, and the two seemed intimate. Too, there was a boy who might...I should not speculate."

Thomasin was surprised she did not stumble back, so great was the feeling of being struck. Nanne had professed not to know the traveler who had delivered Thomasin's beaten body to her, just as Magnus had said the woman was a stranger. But if John had misinterpreted—

Not likely. Had Magnus not known well Nanne and her son, surely that woman's summons would not have caused him to abandon his plans to take his wife riding. He would not have ridden off alone, just as he had done weeks past when he had sent his men on ahead of him. And the man-at-arms had reported then it was in the direction of Orlinde he had gone.

Should she tell Sir Otto it was Magnus who had saved her from the brigands and given her into Nanne's care? Feeling very alone, she longed to have someone to confide in but held her tongue. Though the knight had delivered this news, he need know no more.

"Since speculation is a poor substitute for proof," Sir Otto continued, "I will ride to the village where this woman and her son dwell and see for myself what John reports." He set a hand on her arm, and she realized she swayed. "My lady, are you well?"

She pulled her arm free. "Well enough to accompany you."

His eyes sprang wide. "Not only would I not risk more of your husband's wrath, but it is possible brigands yet abound."

She put her chin up. "Then I will go on my own." If she was to believe such a thing, she must see it herself.

"Very well, I will take you. But we must be discreet since your husband's men will not allow me to leave Kelling with you."

"You have a plan?"

"In a half hour, I will ride as if for Castle Mathe. A quarter hour after, you will slip outside the walls in a commoner's cloak and meet me just beyond the edge of the wood. There I will have John tether a horse for you. You are sure you wish to do this?"

"I am."

He turned away.

As he crossed toward John, she moved opposite, her heart so heavy she almost feared it would fall through her and shatter at her feet.

"Dear Lord," she whispered, "let Magnus have a good reason for his lie if that is what it is. Let me not be a fool who begs the impossible of You."

29

———∞∞∞———

THE COTTAGE WAS known to her where it sat far back from the others in the village. Blessedly, what was not known was the horse outside. Though it appeared to be worthy, it was not a destrier as Magnus would have ridden.

Thomasin looked to Sir Otto who crouched beside her among the trees bordering the village. "That is not my husband's mount."

"It is the one upon which he departed this morn," he said low, then frowned. "Did I not tell you that the day he sent his men ahead, John told he traded his destrier for one of his men's horses?"

She nearly pressed a hand to her heart. "You did not."

"Methinks he hides his identity from Nanne and the villagers—does not wish her or any others to know he is a baron."

She did not want to think about that. What was important was what her husband did inside the cottage, and with each minute that passed, her imaginings increased the bile in her belly such that she had to swallow often to keep the burn from her throat.

A boy exited the cottage, called something over his shoulder, and closed the door. Eamon, the funny-faced lad.

"He does not look like a Verdun," she said.

"That is no proof your husband did not father him."

True. She herself had not grown into her mother's loveliness.

Eamon crossed to the horse, fed him what looked to be a slice of apple, and patted his neck.

Come out, Magnus, Thomasin silently beseeched. She could accept that before she had wed him he had made a child on Nanne, but not if he remained intimate with her.

As tears blurred the scene before her, the boy scooped up a stick. Returning to the front of the cottage, he dropped to his knees and began scratching in the dirt. He practiced his letters, just as she had done as a child when she could steal outside or happened upon dust accumulated on ledges and in corners.

The door opened, and Magnus stepped out, crushing her hope it was another to whom the horse belonged. He ruffled the boy's hair, lowered to his haunches beside him, and spoke in a voice that carried only enough to be heard.

Eamon laughed, and with sweeping gestures told something. Then Nanne appeared, came alongside Magnus, and set a hand on his shoulder.

Thomasin pressed her lips to hold inside the distress that wished to be outside her. Recalling Lady Elianor's comment that perhaps her uncle already loved, she rebuked herself for the hope that if ever he felt such, it would be for his wife.

"You wish you had not come again?" Sir Otto asked.

Again? The frown tightening her face tightened further. But he did not know—

"She is rather pretty," he said above a whisper that made her sweep her gaze to Magnus for fear he had heard. Fortunately, Eamon's chattering appeared to have provided cover for the knight's blunder.

"Heed your voice!" she hissed and moved her regard to Nanne. "Aye, she is pretty." *And I am not,* she silently added.

"Forgive me." Sir Otto squeezed her shoulder. "As you know me to be guilty of with Lady Quintin, a lovely face and figure draw a man, even those happily wed. Have heart, though. This arrangement may have been in place long ere the baron took you to wife and may remain so only because of the boy."

Might that be true? Magnus was here merely in the capacity of a father? He was not unfaithful as his sister, Constance, had been with Baron Boursier?

Nanne said something, and when Magnus motioned her nearer, sank down beside him. Even at a distance, her smile was lovely.

For some minutes, the three scratched in the dirt, then Eamon jumped up and, with a wave, ran to the road in the direction of the village. Magnus stood and pulled Nanne to her feet. He immediately released her hand, but then the two returned to the cottage.

"I am done here," Thomasin said.

"I am sorry," Sir Otto spoke the three words she wished never to hear again.

Careful to keep to the cover of the trees, she retreated. She did not care if the knight followed, wanting only to get away as quickly as possible. As they had tethered the horses at a good distance to more easily approach the cottage undetected, it took several minutes to reach them.

Emotions as much responsible for her labored breathing as exertion, she snatched up the bridle and pried at the knot securing her mount to a tree. As it came free, a hand settled on her back.

"I should not have allowed you to accompany me," the knight said.

She whipped her head around. "So I might remain blissfully oblivious? Nay, I had to see for myself."

His brow rumpled. "It hardly seems possible, but perhaps he has a good explanation."

"Or a good lie!" To her horror, she felt her face crumple.

"Thomasin, I am sorry." He pulled her into his arms.

Glad for the breadth of his chest, she pressed her face against it and held on.

She did not know what words he murmured, only that she was grateful for his soothing voice. She did not know why he stroked her head, only that she was glad he cared enough to offer solace. But when he caressed her ear and neck, she rose above her misery. And when he lifted her chin and set his mouth on hers, she shrieked and shoved her hands against his chest.

Stumbling backward, she came up against a tree. "You should not have done that!" She dragged the back of a hand across her mouth.

"Why?" He stepped toward her.

She pushed off the tree, but before she could sidestep, he pressed her back with his body. "Cease, Sir Otto!"

Staring down at her through half-lowered lids, he began drawing up her skirts.

"I said cease!"

His hand touched her knee. "'Tis no more than what he does with that trollop."

"I am no trollop." She pushed his hand away, strained to the side, gasped when her braid snagged on the bark and ripped strands from her scalp. "I will not play eye-for-an-eye with ye!"

As the commoner came off her tongue, her skirt fell, but he caught her arms and pinned them to her sides. "Then do not lie with me for revenge. Do it for pleasure."

"Pleasure! I do not—"

"Aye, you do. How often have I seen you look at me with longing?"

"Which I do no more now I am wed!"

"To a man who, at this moment, likely makes another babe on his mistress."

Heretofore, Thomasin had been ruled by shock and outrage. Now came fear. Never would she have believed her father's man capable of ravishment, but he seemed hardly different from the steward who had attempted to violate her. And though he did not beat her, he might prove the same as the brigands who had attacked her not too distant from here.

Sir Otto lowered his head and put in her ear, "You liked my kiss."

As his lips moved to her neck, she struggled to hold the primal scream Magnus was surely too distant to hear.

She shivered again, and determinedly used her revulsion to what she prayed was good effect by forcing a moan of pleasure and softening her body as if in passionate surrender.

"See"—he nipped her neck—"it has ever been me."

"Aye, ever."

His hands on her arms loosened, but not enough to greatly increase her chance of escape. "Kiss me again, Otto."

He released her arms, cupped her face in his hands, and pressed his mouth hard to hers.

As she tasted blood, her hand found his dagger's hilt. She pulled the blade from its sheath, snarled, "Get off me!" and pressed the blade to his side.

His head snapped up.

"Now! Else I will put ye through."

His lids narrowed. "I do not believe you capable, Thomasin, daughter of a harlot."

So this was Sir Otto. The one Magnus had good reason not to trust. And she had sought to protect him from the wrath of her husband and father.

"Until ye said that, I was not so sure meself." She applied pressure to the dagger.

From the flare of his nostrils and heightening of color, she had likely pricked his flesh.

"Shall we discover together how much more this commoner is capable of when she has little to lose?" She raised her eyebrows. "'Tis possible I will surprise ye as much as ye have me."

He drew back and raised empty hands in a show of surrender.

She followed, a glance down him confirming he bled through his pale blue tunic—and his sword was near at hand. Telling herself she could thrust the blade into his side if need be, she said, "Why, Sir Otto?"

His mouth convulsed. "I weary of playing the puppet."

"'Twas not for me ye set John on my husband, was it?"

"Aye, for you." As he took another step back, she took one forward. "It was no lie I care for you."

"So says one who sought to ravish me."

"'Tis not ravishment if both parties wish it."

"I do not wish—"

He jumped back and reached for his sword.

Once again, she followed, and having lost contact with his side, slashed upward and caught the edge of her blade on his jaw and up into his cheek.

As he lurched and tripped on a gnarled root thrusting up through the earth, Thomasin ran. She snatched the pommel of her horse's saddle, clambered astride, and reined the animal around.

"Thomasin!" the knight called as he gained his feet.

She did not look back. Every moment counted lest he followed, and she was certain he would and stood a good chance of running her to ground.

Only if he can find you, spoke a small voice that she questioned. Its answer was that once she was out of sight, she must flee opposite.

Unfortunately for her husband, she would have to inconvenience him.

He had failed. Again.

Otto closed his eyes and let his shoulders fall beneath the weight they seemed ever to carry. A short reprieve only, he promised the one to whom he would answer if he did not end the woman he cared for despite her commoner's blood.

He opened his eyes, dropped his head back, and laughed at the sky visible between the leaves. Nay, not *despite* her commoner's blood. Because of it. True, it was only of recent he was attracted to her, having heretofore regarded her as an impetuous, plain-faced girl. But since the day she had returned to Blackwood beaten by brigands, and he had taken her in his arms, feelings he ought to reserve for Lady Quintin had time and again made a fool of him.

He had told himself his flirtations were only a means of rendering her and Baron Verdun vulnerable, but he had not been entirely honest. It was his duty to be attracted to Lady Quintin, an easy thing that made the doing believable, but it was Thomasin with whom he felt a kinship. Forbidden kinship that interfered with what he was called to do.

There had been opportunities to deal with her as instructed, but ever he awaited a better time and place, just as he had done the day he had followed her to the village near Castle Kelling—and been beyond grateful for his hesitation, for he might have fallen to Magnus Verdun. The day Verdun's party had been attacked en route to Castle Adderstone, he had vowed to do his duty, and it had become all the more pressing when he had felt upon his neck the breath of one who had been there to ensure it was done. But once more, Verdun had saved his wife.

Otto gripped his bandaged shoulder that was slow to heal from the arrow put through it. Though the injury had been done him to allay suspicion, he did not doubt it also served as punishment for another failing. And now this one.

He considered the sheath Thomasin had emptied of its dagger. Instead of putting her up against a tree, he should have put the blade through her.

He moved his gaze to the blood on his tunic that evidenced he had been the one cut, then lifted his hand from his shoulder and fingered the slice that started beneath his jaw. Tracing its bloody seepage up to his cheekbone, he determined it was not deep. Thus, if it scarred, it should not be unsightly like...

He chuckled and wondered how it was possible to sound as aged as he did. "Tired," he rasped. But if he did not fulfill his role in this long charade, more punishment would be his.

He pushed up his sleeve, rode a finger over the scars, wished another—two, five, a dozen—was the worst of what awaited him. But berating would also be his.

He pressed his lips, denying himself the breath required to voice the anger, sorrow, and fear that wished to howl from him like an old woman grieving the loss of a lifelong love. Still, his chest convulsed, and he began to tremble from the effort to hold in what had not been tolerated since he had come down off his mother's hip.

His clenched teeth loosened, and he gulped air that sent a great sob around the wood. Then he was on his knees, gripping his head and pressing his face to his thighs to muffle cries that belonged to a woman. Again and again they sounded, wetting his face with tears, saliva, and mucus. But finally, he emptied enough to pant himself back to a semblance of a man, one who had no choice but to go after Thomasin. Fortunately, despite her lead, it should not be difficult to overtake her. And then...

He could not return to Castle Kelling or Castle Mathe. For a time, he would have to dwell in the shadows—even more so than the one who had cruelly marked the failures of a boy...a youth...a man. The same whose judgment would be all the more harsh if Thomasin escaped.

Telling himself he must think of Otto—only Otto—he breathed deep. And moaned, "I am sorry, Thomasin."

30

MAGNUS MADE NO attempt to hide his shock over his wife's appearance at the cottage, nor his dread of what would be believed of his presence here.

He strode from the doorway where he had halted upon seeing whose horse pounded up the road at such speed he had questioned if the animal could be reined in before reaching the cottage.

Breathing hard out of a face bright with color, Thomasin stared at him with eyes that had never been less blue.

"Magnus?" Nanne called.

He did not follow Thomasin's gaze to Eamon's mother, knowing it would waste the precious moment he had to grab his wife's reins should she decide to spur away.

Taking hold of the leather straps in one hand, he stepped near and laid his other hand on her leg, felt the quake of her small frame. "Thomasin, what——?"

"I require an escort," she whispered, as if her throat was too closed to give more, then shifted her regard from Nanne to him.

He had expected her to demand an explanation, but amid the accusation in her eyes was something like fear that made him look nearer upon her.

He had thought she wore her hair unbound, unusual though that was outside their bedchamber, but some of it was pulled back from her face, evidence of the braid he had watched her fashion this morn. It could be the result of a reckless ride, but what he glimpsed on her gown between the edges of her mantle told there was more to it.

He pushed aside her mantle and revealed flecks of crimson across her bodice and streaks at her waist where an unsheathed dagger rode beneath her girdle alongside her meat dagger. Her gown appearing intact, he did not think the blood was hers.

"What has happened?" he asked in as level a voice as he could command.

"What would not have happened had you spent the day with me as promised, rather than…" Her shoulders jerked with the replenishment of breath. "…her."

"I will explain all, Thomasin, but first I must know what befell you."

"All you need know is that though I hate asking it of you, interrupting your…" She looked to Nanne again. "…whatever this is, the only thing I require is an escort home. Rather, to Castle Kelling. Mayhap on the morrow I shall go home."

He wanted to curse this day for all that had been dealt those for whom he had a care. But on the matter of Thomasin, he had only himself to curse. He should have told her about Eamon and Nanne. Instead, she had learned on her own—

Nay, not on her own. He did not know that dagger, but he could guess to whom it belonged.

Feeling a jerk at his mouth, he asked, "Where is Sir Otto?"

"He lives. Now, if 'tis not too much inconvenience, would you return me to Kelling?"

She was lucid and angry enough that he did not believe she was in shock, but nearly so. "I will," he said gently, though he felt far from gentle knowing that knight was behind this and not knowing exactly how far behind. "First come inside and drink something to warm you."

"What is cold in me cannot be warmed by drink. I will wait here until you are done with her."

It was so dully spoken, and with less anger than moments earlier that he was tempted to pull her from the saddle and carry her writhing and biting into the cottage if need be.

Not trusting her to stay put, he looked to Nanne. When last he was here, he had told her the truth about the woman whose injuries she had tended. Thus, she knew exactly who Thomasin had been and now was, and he ached for the sorrow on her face. He had done his best all these years not to encourage her, but his wife's presence stung.

And I am to blame for both their hurts.

"Lead my horse near, Nanne," he said, and she did as asked.

Continuing to hold Thomasin's reins, he mounted and looked from his wife's downturned face to Nanne's questioning one. "Though I do not believe you have anything to worry about, keep Eamon near and send word if he is bothered again. And tell him I am sorry I could not stay for a proper parting."

She looked to his wife. "My lady?" When Thomasin's eyes flicked to her, she said, "Do not mistake what you see here for something it is not—even though I wish it so."

Magnus tensed, and Thomasin was unresponsive so long he did not think she would answer.

"I left ere thanking you for the care you provided me," she finally spoke. "I would have you know I intended to seek you out to express my gratitude." She lifted her chin. "Such circumstances I did not expect. But then, it was not intended I should." She returned her attention to Magnus. "You both lie well."

He set his teeth. "Come, I shall take you home, and you will tell me for what you left Kelling and what happened thereafter."

"Will I?" she said, but seemingly more to herself than out of defiance.

"Good day, Nanne." Magnus turned the horses toward the wood.

He did not attempt to converse again until they were out of sight of the village on a narrow path beaten into the floor of the wood by frequent travelers.

"How did you know to find me at Eamon and Nanne's cottage, Thomasin?"

Her hand convulsed on the saddle's pommel as if he had startled her back to the present. "Eamon," she said. "You had me believe you could not recall the boy's name, just as you claimed his mother was a stranger."

He sighed. "I am sorry I deceived you, and I shall explain, but first I must know how you came to be here."

"Funny that, for this morn I meant to ask if we could ride to the barony of Orlinde to thank that woman. Had you agreed—though of course you would not have—I would have found myself here with you as I do now." She looked down her front. "Only I would not have blood on me."

He halted their horses. "It is Sir Otto's blood, is it not? His dagger in your girdle?"

"Aye. And aye."

"What did he do?"

She frowned as if he asked of her something that had happened too far back, then said, "He told you had a woman on Orlinde, and when he revealed her name and that it was to her you had gone this day, I insisted he bring me so I could see with my own eyes." Her mouth tilted. "When I had, we left."

"But you came back. Alone."

"Had I not, he would have overtaken me."

He was tempted to shake her, but he held to what remained of his patience. "What did he do to you?"

"Comforted me. And I thought it very caring until…"

Feeling the pound of his heart, spasms at mouth and eye, Magnus longed for the cold steel of his sword.

She dragged a hand across her mouth. "I told him he should not have done that."

"What?" he barked. He knew there had been intimacy between them, but how much? And to what had she resorted to stop him? Was the blood on her from a minor injury? A dire one? Though she feared the knight pursued her, she might have dealt him a wound that this moment bled the life from him. A not unwelcome prospect.

She moistened her lips. "He thought to convince me I should retaliate in kind for my husband's unfaithfulness."

"But you did not," Magnus said, certain of it and grateful—providing the knave had not forced himself on her.

"I would not." She touched her blood-stained gown. "But it took effort to convince him of it. I cut his face."

"I shall kill him!"

She blinked rapidly, and he saw some of the Thomasin he knew return to her eyes. No matter the anger there, this one he much preferred over the numb one he did not know, nor wish to.

Her lids narrowed. "Surely I have more right to slay Nanne for what she has stolen from me than you have the right to slay one who stole but a kiss."

Only a kiss, he assured himself in an attempt to veer his thoughts from what else the knight would have taken had his wife not defended herself.

He turned his horse around and up against hers so they faced each other. "I know my deception gives you no cause to believe me, but I vow, never have Nanne and I been lovers. Eamon is not of my loins."

More of her returned to her eyes as she searched for the lie in his own, parted her lips as if to say something, and shook her head.

"Ask me anything," he said, fearing she would slip away again. "I will answer truthfully."

As last, anguished words spilled. "If you are not lovers, why did you abandon me for her?"

"I am responsible for Eamon."

"But if he is not your son, how can you be responsible?"

Magnus slid back eight years to when the pretty girl from the village, who had smiled often at him across the years, had tempted him to know his first woman, and secured from him a promise to meet her at the edge of the wood. He should not have agreed to what he knew to be a sin, but her kisses had been sweet and she had assured him it could not be wrong to lie together providing they loved. Magnus had liked her and been attracted to her, but that was all.

"As a squire," he said, "I declined to join my peers in the pursuit of women, and there was some talk of my lack of experience, but naught that a fist to the gut did not remedy. But once I was newly knighted and still had not been with a woman, the taunting was harder to quiet. Thus, when Nanne professed love for me and offered herself, I agreed to meet her. And we did meet after I had time to think on what I intended. Though I told her I had no deep feelings for her, she tried to convince me love would come. When I could argue it no further lest my body betrayed me, I told her to return home and left her crying in the wood." He shifted his jaw. "Had I seen her back to her village, she would not have been attacked, what she had wished to give me taken by one she had never seen and has not seen since. But who, it would seem, has returned."

Thomasin caught her breath, and he knew she remembered her own encounter in the wood.

"Eamon was conceived of that violation. When I learned Nanne's family had set her out upon discovering she was with child, I moved her and her unborn babe to the village on Orlinde so she could begin anew in the guise of a widow. Since, I have visited fairly often, ever discreet so those whose paths I cross know me as her brother and uncle to Eamon. Hence, the reason I eschew my destrier, and with the exception of this day when I had not time to change, I dress as a commoner."

Thomasin's eyes were all over his face, but she would find no lie there.

She frowned, reached up and touched the spasming at his eye, then the one at his mouth. Did she think them indicative of deceit?

She dropped her hand back to her lap. "Nanne saw her attacker this day?"

"Nay. While shopping in the village market on the day past, she sent Eamon for a candle, and when he returned, he said he had met a man who claimed to be his father. Thus, she sent a missive beseeching me to come. What took me from your side was not only worry for Eamon and her, but the hope I might finally lay hands on that miscreant." He touched her cheek. "Tell me you believe me."

Her lids started to lower and her mouth to turn into his hand, but she drew back. "You lied."

"I should have told you about Eamon and Nanne. I am sorry—"

"I weary of people saying they are sorry even as they make plans for which they will have to apologize again!" She laughed bitterly. "Sir Otto is good at that. I am sorry, but your husband has a woman. I am sorry, but though the boy does not resemble him, it does not mean he did not father him."

Sensing soon she would be weeping, Magnus gripped her shoulder. "That is enough."

She shrugged free. "I am sorry, I should not have allowed you to accompany me. I am sorry, but let me comfort you—and kiss you though you do not wish it, and touch you where you do not wish to be touched, and ravish you though 'tis not ravishment if both want it."

He was about to call to her again, but that last was said with finality, and so he waited.

She blew out a breath. "I need none to remind me I have also lied, as I did in telling my father it was upon Blackwood I was attacked, but this day has asked too much of me, and I have no more to give. So if you are truly sorry, return me to Kelling."

Recalling she had earlier made a distinction between Castle Kelling and Castle Mathe, and how it had cut that she regarded the latter as more her home, he reined his horse back around and said, "Then 'tis *home* to Kelling we go."

He set a moderate pace in consideration of her vulnerable state and to more closely watch for any who followed. Blessedly, the ride was uneventful, and as expected when they entered Kelling's walls, not only were the guard unsettled to discover Thomasin accompanied him, but it was confirmed Sir Otto had not returned.

Thomasin allowed him to lift her from her horse, and to lead her into the keep and up the stairway. But she pulled free before the solar and continued to the door of the chamber she had previously eschewed.

"Here is where you belong, Thomasin." He nodded at the solar.

"I thought so, too, but perhaps I do not. Though not because I fear your dreams might cause me bodily harm. Because my heart is hurt, and I would not have it hurt more."

He wanted to ask if she had feelings of love for him as he had begun to suspect, but the timing could not be worse. "I am sorry—and ashamed—that I hurt you, Thomasin. But this I vow, just as I told that you are mine and you told that I am yours, there has been no falseness in our marriage. Nanne may want more from me, but she has never had and will never have more than I now give. Thus, I am guilty only of waiting too long to reveal her existence that has all to do with Eamon. But know this, I would have."

She considered him, then lowered her gaze and murmured, "I am tired."

Though he longed to convince her of his innocence—to bring her back to him—he knew it would be wrong to push her in a direction she was not ready to go. "We will talk more of this later, then."

Without further word, she closed herself in the room.

The chamber Magnus stepped into had never felt so empty, and he wondered how he had so quickly moved from yearning for privacy to yearning for his wife to fill this space with her talk, laughter, mutterings over the accounts, and whispers in the night.

Assuring himself she but needed time to think on what he had revealed and forgive him his lie, he turned his thoughts to alerting Griffin de Arell to the serious trespasses of his knight. Not that he believed Sir Otto would return to Castle Mathe, but one must be prepared should the man prove exceedingly foolish.

31

THE DOOR OPENED so quietly it was no creak of wood or cry of hinge that alerted Thomasin to her night visitor. It was the light of the corridor sweeping into the chamber. But it could not be Magnus. He would have used the door between their chambers—providing he had returned to the solar following the evening meal as she knew he had not.

She did not move from where she lay on her belly with her face opposite the door, one of several positions by which she sought sleep that had not come all these hours since she had left Magnus in the corridor.

Though she knew she should probably be afeared since only her husband would seek her out in the night, after all that had gone this day, this one thing more seemed hardly notable.

"My lady?"

Thomasin rolled onto her back and peered at the cook where she stood on the threshold holding a lamp. "Maddie?"

"May I speak with you?"

Guessing it was a matter of import well beyond the planning of menus, Thomasin sat up and swung her legs over the side of the bed. "Come inside."

The woman closed the door, and by the light she brought within, crossed the chamber. "I worried on you when the serving women told you were not present with your husband during supper," she said and set the lamp on the bedside table.

Thomasin patted the mattress. "I am sure it has been a long day. Do sit."

The woman lowered and shifted her bulk around to face Thomasin. "You are ill, my lady?"

Ill of heart, Thomasin mused. "I am tired."

"After the day you yourself have had, 'tis to be expected."

What did the cook know of her day? Surmised from prattle of castle folk who had learned their lady had slipped away from Kelling and been returned by her husband? "What know you of that, Maddie?"

"Enough that I had to speak with you though night is upon us."

"I am listening."

"My man is worried."

Thomasin raised her eyebrows. "You have a husband?"

The woman's eyes lowered, and it discomfited Thomasin to see her less than her usual confident self. "We never spoke vows, though we meant to."

Feeling her shame, Thomasin laid a hand over the woman's clasped in her lap. "How can I help you?"

She breathed deep. "The matter on which I would speak has all to do with Sir Otto. Or mostly."

Having time and again snatched her thoughts away from the knight who had proved more of a danger to her than Magnus ever had—with the exception of her heart—Thomasin barely contained her startle. "What of him?"

"I thought kindly of him, my lady, and he gave me good cause, being so amiable, but after what my man has told me, methinks we may have been deceived."

Thomasin sighed. "You are not the only one to discover there is something dark about him."

"Did he work ill upon you when you met him in the wood?"

Thomasin gasped. "How know you of that?"

"My man is John."

The one to whom Sir Otto had given coin? Who had declared he would buy drink rather than sweets for his woman who was well enough fed and had once been lovely? Whose distinctive face had reminded her of the John who had stolen her mother from her? Could this woman be—?

"When you returned this afternoon with Baron Verdun," Mathilde continued, "John confessed all to me. He said Sir Otto enlisted him to keep watch for him and report odd behavior, and that this morn he followed your husband to a village where he keeps a mistress, and this noon left a horse in the wood for you to accompany Sir Otto to witness your husband's faithlessness."

As Thomasin looked nearer upon Mathilde—if that was truly her name—the woman turned her hands up and squeezed her lady's fingers. "I vow, all he did was to ensure your safety. At least, 'tis as Sir Otto convinced him."

Breathless over the possibility this woman was her mother, Thomasin delved the fleshy face in search of the lovely Alice she had not beheld for eleven years. She did not see her mother, but if it was her, how was Thomasin able to remember the man who had taken her mother from her but not the woman she had loved? Was it all the weight Mathilde now carried?

"My lady," she entreated, "I vow John did not mean you ill. If you tell your husband he aided Sir Otto—"

"I recognized John this day," Thomasin blurted. "Are you my mother?"

The woman's head jerked and eyes widened. And her sharp breath revealed more.

But what? Thomasin pondered. *What I wish it to reveal? Or what I do not?* She pulled her hand free. "Are you Alice?"

Mathilde's shoulders dropped, and she chuckled. "All these weeks, you did not see me, and I was glad of it. To think 'twas the man your child's eyes only glimpsed who revealed me."

In that moment, Thomasin almost wished for a warming fire. But as felt earlier with Magnus, her chill was more of the heart.

She shoved up off the bed. "Why did you give me away?"

"I am sorry, Daughter."

Thomasin nearly screamed at hearing those three words again. "You have no right to call me Daughter."

"Should I leave?"

It was what Thomasin wanted, and yet she did not. "Tell me how you could abandon me."

Mathilde pressed her hands between her knees. "You recall I met John in the tavern?"

"I do."

"He was a mercenary. He said he was weary of travel and intended to seek his living as a man-at-arms. Thinking he might make a good husband and father, I encouraged him to approach the lord of Waring Castle, but he wished to travel farther west. And he offered to take me. But only me."

"I have not forgotten, Mathilde," she said, unable to name her *mother*, or even *Alice*. "You told me he was a good man in need of a wife but not a daughter."

"He would not be moved, and in all my years at Waring Castle, it was the most any man had offered me. I was weary of being unhappy and unloved."

"I loved you."

Mathilde averted her gaze. "The love of a child is not the same as that of a man."

Eamon rose to mind, and Thomasin wondered if Nanne would have left her son had Magnus asked it. Not that he would have. A man who claimed responsibility for a boy not his own would never ask such.

"So you gave me to the lady of Waring Castle."

"As you were of an age to earn your keep, and she needed a companion for her girl, I gave you into her care."

"Her care? You have that quite turned around." Thomasin slapped a hand to her chest. "This seven-year-old was given care of the lady's daughter and made to tend her child's every need. Though I loved little Joss, it was hard work."

Mathilde raked her teeth over her lower lip. "But the lady was good to you, was she not?"

"Providing I kept my charge out of hearing and sight. And for years, I mostly succeeded. Then Joss died, and I was made a servant subject to the attentions of men who thought my common blood gave them the right to seek to violate me."

"Did they?" Mathilde asked softly.

"Nay, though had I remained at Waring Castle, they would have." Remembering the bit of writing her mother had pressed into her hand the day she left, she said, "But you did not entirely fail me. I did what you said I should if ever I was in danger. I appealed to my father."

The woman's mouth curved. "Such gratitude I felt when I heard he had claimed you."

Thomasin recalled the day Griffin de Arell had readied to depart Kelling and she had seen the cook watching them before quickly returning to the keep. How much had it hurt to see again the father of her child?

"You cannot have felt as much gratitude as I did," Thomasin said. "How did you come to be at Kelling, so near my father's demesne?"

"'Twas here John found work. I was wary since Ulric de Arell had threatened that if I came near Blackwood he would ensure I never did again. And that is why I called myself Mathilde. Though the feud was still going strong between the families then, I could not chance coming to the notice of the old baron or one of his people."

"What does John think of your past, that your daughter is a De Arell?"

"Never did I tell him I birthed Griffin de Arell's child, nor that I had once lived upon Blackwood. And still I would not have him know you are my daughter."

Thomasin nearly asked how she had explained her name change to John, but there was a more pressing question. "Then he did not send you to speak to me of his betrayal?"

"He did, but only because he knows I have the ear and respect of the Lady of Emberly."

Thomasin frowned. "Why do you not wish him to know I am your daughter?"

Mathilde sighed. "He is not the man I hoped I could make him. Too much he loves his drink, and he has a streak of greed that goes all the way through him. To feed both, he trades in secrets as he did with Sir Otto."

Then Mathilde feared he would try to make use of her relation to the Lady of Emberly?

"So you see, though I love him as much as he can be loved, in some measure I have been punished for choosing him over you."

Yet another question pressed itself upon Thomasin. "Does he hurt you?"

"As I knew the night I met him, he can be an ugly drunk. But there is much good about him."

"Good? He never wed you."

"Aye, but other than one indiscretion, he has been true to me." Mathilde's gaze settled heavily on Thomasin. "Agatha."

Thomasin blinked, recalled when she had been in the kitchen with Mathilde and Sir Otto, and the cook had named Agatha a snake. It surprised it was for infidelity Mathilde had not liked the other woman, for the Aude whom Thomasin had known had not been one to attract men.

"A kitchen lad saw him coming out of that one's hut," Mathilde said, "and after several nights of keeping watch, I saw it too. He vowed it would not happen again, and he has been true to me since."

Or so she believed.

"So, my lady, I ask a kind turn, though I deserve it not. As Baron Verdun has not retaliated against John, I know you have not revealed my man was in Sir Otto's pay. Thus, I beseech you to speak naught of it."

Thomasin stared. She did not wish to repay Magnus's deception with one of her own, and was that not what she would be doing if she withheld this truth? Surely he ought to be made aware that one of his men had broken fealty? Even Sir Otto had said that what he had done in buying away the man's loyalty would benefit Magnus, who would know who was not true to him.

"I give you my word that never again will John be disloyal," Mathilde prompted.

"What of his word?"

"He has given it to me."

But would a man who traded in secrets keep it? He had not kept the word he had surely given the Verduns upon entering their service.

Thomasin crossed to the window and opened the shutters. As she peered into the torchlit bailey, she recalled Sir Otto also asking her to withhold information from Magnus. The only hurt it had done her husband was to reveal his lie. The hurt it had done her—

Better I know the lie, she told herself and nearly laughed that John's greed had made it possible.

"If you cannot do this for me, my lady, give us time to depart ere your husband's wrath descends."

Thomasin looked at where Mathilde peered across her shoulder. "You would leave as well?"

The woman rose. "I sacrificed much to have John. I will not lose him now."

And once more Thomasin would be parted from her mother. But this time, it should not hurt much. Perhaps not at all. What would hurt was being parted from the one who had been kind to her and insisted Thomasin claim her place as Lady of Emberly, not only among the castle folk, but in Magnus's bed.

"I must think on this."

"If you decide your husband ought to know of John's betrayal, will you give us time to leave ere you tell him?"

Thomasin wanted to agree, certain Magnus would be fearfully angry over the betrayal, but she repeated, "I must think on it."

Mathilde inclined her head. "I thank you, my lady. Ere I leave, there is another matter. As I am a much better cook than a mother, methinks it best I remain only that, in your eyes as well as your husband's."

One more thing to keep from Magnus. How the secrets mounted! "Again, I will think on it."

Mathilde lifted the lamp from the table. "Good eve, my lady."

For the first time, it struck Thomasin as strange that this woman titled her such. "Mathilde?"

She turned at the door.

"The day you left me at Waring Castle, you promised you would return. Why did you not?"

She looked down. "It was easier to forget you than tear open that wound which would once more gape when I had to leave you again. But if I could have kept you with me, I would have."

"But you could have," Thomasin whispered. "You had only to choose me."

"Ah, but look at you—a lady, the wife of a baron. Had I not done what I did, likely we would both yet toil at Waring Castle. And never would you know the love of Magnus Verdun."

"Love! Your man told you where my husband was this day."

She nodded. "I do not understand that, and methinks you may not either, but I have been at Kelling since before Baron Verdun earned his spurs. Though he is not without sin and fault, as none of us are, the one I serve is a fair lord. Aye, he distances himself and gives good cause to think him unfeeling, but I have glimpsed his heart. And more so since your arrival at Kelling."

As Thomasin stared at the woman, her own heart aching all the more for the hurt inflicted on it this day, Mathilde continued, "He may not realize it, but he is coming to love you as you love him."

Thomasin almost denied her feelings were of the heart, but it would be a lie, and she would not add to those already told, nor those lies born of silence disguising themselves as truths.

"Good eve, Mathilde."

Moments later, she was once more alone. An hour beyond that, huddled beneath the covers, she heard Magnus enter the solar. When he ceased moving about, she wished he were sliding into bed alongside her, drawing her into his arms, and giving his dreams into her care. How would he sleep this night without her? Would he be troubled by Sir Otto's blood upon her gown?

She tossed back the covers, dropped to her knees beside the bed, and clasped her hands against her mouth. "Dear Lord, let my husband rest well, moving only through dreams memorable for their peace and hope. And my mother…Should I not give back to the woman who has given much to me these past weeks? But how without making the wrong between Magnus and me worse? Without betraying him?"

32

The struggle over whether or not to tell Magnus of John's betrayal resolved when Thomasin awakened in the morning determined to stay true to her husband even if he had not stayed true to her. And though she feared she might be a fool, she was inclined to believe what he had revealed of his relationship with Nanne and Eamon.

Still, when she descended to the hall and the steward revealed her husband had once more accompanied his men to patrol his lands, her thoughts flew to the cottage upon the barony of Orlinde. This moment he might be with Nanne, might—

I will not think on that, she told herself and pushed aside the almond milk and honey porridge a kitchen servant had brought her. Instead, she would think on how to approach Magnus in such a way he would grant her request of leniency for the man her mother would not be parted from. Alice, now Mathilde, may have proved a poor mother, but she had become a friend her daughter was loath to lose.

Thomasin glanced toward the kitchen, knew the woman awaited her answer.

"My lady?"

She turned toward the steward who sat three chairs down where he had been at his books upon her arrival in the hall.

"Harve?"

"If you do not intend to break your fast," his voice creaked, "I would discuss the changes you made to the accounts."

She sat straighter. "You disagree with them?"

"Would that I had cause to, but you persist in proving my mind is not as quick, nor eyes as clear as once they were."

"Then?"

He folded his hands atop the table. "Methinks I am done at Kelling, may even have been done whilst Lady Elianor oversaw my figures."

"You would leave my husband's employ?" Thomasin was strangely averse to losing the disagreeable man.

"I do not wish it, this having been my home all these years, but it is humiliatingly obvious I am of little use when one such as you must correct me."

She held her tongue with the reminder she had been called worse when she was years younger and her grandfather had expressed his own distaste for one such as she.

"Thus, though always I endeavor to go beyond paying for my keep, methinks my contribution to the household begins to weigh more heavily on the expense side of the accounts."

Deciding she would deal with him as she had done Ulric, Thomasin raised her chin. "If you leave Kelling, where will you go?"

His lids narrowed.

"I know you do not welcome the prying of one you think beneath you, but I fear it will prove difficult if not impossible for a man of such advanced years to gain employment elsewhere."

He snorted. "I have handed you what we both want, and yet you discourage me from leaving?"

She sat back. "Of course I do. My husband esteems you." She flicked her gaze at the ledgers. "And though I am proficient at verifying the entries and correcting the few that require it, I have not the time or inclination to be responsible for the accounting in its entirety. Too, I care for my husband's people who are now also mine and would not see your years of loyal service reduced to a pitiful existence."

His face, over which a multitude of sour emotions had marched while she spoke, settled into a deeply grooved frown. "You know I will never truly respect you, aye?"

She almost laughed for how much he sounded like her grandfather. "I respect your learning, Harve, but I doubt I will ever truly like you. Hence, as we are in accord, I see no reason why our current arrangement cannot stand. But if still you are determined to leave Kelling, I pray you will do my husband the courtesy of remaining until you have taught me all I need to know to replace you." Hopefully, the prospect of spending so much time in her company would discourage him from leaving.

She glimpsed a tug at the corner of his mouth before he turned back to the ledgers. "I will think on it," he grumbled.

She was not tempted to laugh, for his words were a reminder she owed Mathilde an answer. "Do," she said and stood and crossed to the kitchen.

As expected, the cook was within. What was not expected was John.

"Out!" Mathilde ordered the kitchen help.

They scurried, some through the door that gave onto the garden, others around Thomasin and into the great hall.

Wiping her hands on her apron, Mathilde nodded at the man-at-arms perched on a stool alongside one of the smaller tables, before him chunks of bread and a pot of what Thomasin guessed was butter. "My John."

Wishing he were less in shadow so she might better gauge his reaction to what she had come to say, she acknowledged him with a nod.

He dipped his head. "My lady."

"You have thought on it?" Mathilde asked.

Thomasin clasped her hands at her waist. "I would betray my husband if I did not reveal your man's arrangement with Sir Otto. Thus, I cannot do as you ask."

John grunted.

Though Mathilde remained standing, she slumped so greatly it seemed she stood a hand shorter. "Then we must leave."

"I do not think so." Thomasin stepped forward. "You said you believe my husband is coming to love me. If so, it is possible my appeal for leniency for John shall be granted."

With a creak of wood that protested the nails holding it captive, John rose from the stool. "'Tis obvious you do not well know your husband, my lady." He pinched a chunk of bread, dipped it in the pot, and licking the tips of his fingers gripping the bread, moved toward her. "Did you learn naught from what Sir Otto revealed of the baron's disregard for his new bride?"

"John!" Mathilde exclaimed.

"Be silent, Maddie!" As he neared, the light found his face and swept over his distinctive nose to reveal a bend halfway down its length that Thomasin did not recall. Sometime between her seven-year-old self and this self, he had broken it. Or someone had broken it for him.

He halted, and she struggled not to reveal her discomfort at him being so near, and her further discomfort when he tossed onto his tongue the bread that proved to be coated with honey. He chewed it open-mouthed, revealing front teeth she did not believe had been broken when she was a child.

He swallowed. "I think it best Maddie and I leave Kelling ere the baron returns this eve."

Reminding herself to be careful not to reveal his woman was far more than a friend, Thomasin looked to Mathilde. "Do you not think your lord will allow John to continue at Kelling if I ask it of him—and you as well, for I know he would not wish to lose you."

"It is possible, John," Mathilde said.

Thomasin returned her gaze to the man. "If he will not allow you to remain, I will insist he grant you safe passage away from Kelling."

His face puckered with thought.

"Thus, you have naught to lose in waiting for his judgment, and all to gain."

TAMARA LEIGH

"Methinks we ought to chance it," Mathilde entreated.

John looked around. "Then I suppose we will see if Lady Thomasin holds sway over her husband."

Mathilde's deep breath straightened her figure. "I thank you, John."

Her gratitude to a man who ought to be the one showing appreciation made Thomasin struggle to hold back a rebuke.

John glanced at her, nodded, and strode to the door. As it closed behind him, Thomasin said, "If my husband does not return too late, this eve I will speak to him on the matter."

Mathilde's smile was slight. "You do your mother proud, my lady."

Remembering how the cook had taken her new lady to task for shirking her duties, Thomasin said, "With much thanks to you, I am learning."

"Off with you." Mathilde waved a hand. "I have work to do."

"What of the new menu?"

"It will keep."

Because it would have to change were she not here? Thomasin pondered. Because no other was capable of preparing such flavorful meals?

Though tempted to sit down with her now to determine how best to feed Castle Kelling's occupants, Thomasin retreated, leaving the woman to her kitchen.

My mother, she thought as she traversed the hall. And forgave her some for leaving her behind.

Kelling needed a priest. Thus, he would set aside the excuse that the Foucault uprising precluded him from seeking a man of God and find one to minister to his people and him.

That vow and others lifted up, Magnus opened his eyes and considered the altar upon which burned the dozen candles always lit at dusk so those denied a priest in whom to confide could seek some solace following a long day.

Now, well into the night, the candles were not much more than glowing stubs, but they served, lighting the way to and from the altar.

"Merciful Lord, this I pray," he said and unclasped his hands. But as he started to rise from the kneeler, the chapel's door opened and *her* voice—the only one he wished to hear—came to him.

"Magnus?"

Silently, he thanked the Lord that the late hour did not see her ensconced in that chamber where she had retreated on the night past following the revelation of Eamon and Nanne.

"I have just finished my prayers," he said over his shoulder. "Come."

He heard the whisper of her slippers and rustle of her skirts as she once more walked the aisle, this time as his wife. And when she halted to his left, he caught the scent of violets.

"I am glad you are here," she said.

For a moment, he thought her gratitude was due to him seeking the Lord, but that was not likely with Nanne and Eamon yet between them. "You thought I might be upon Orlinde?"

"I…"

He looked around and only a little ways up from where he knelt, and it struck him how simply lovely she was with her day's-long braid loose about her face, a multitude of tendrils escaping it.

She sighed. "I am sorry, but when your men entered the hall without you, it did occur to me, but only that. And then your squire told you were here."

"You wished to make certain of it?"

"Nay, I knew he spoke true. I came because I would speak with you, and this seems a good place."

"It is." He reached a hand to her, and closing it around the fingers she set in his palm, drew her onto the kneeler beside him. "I am pleased you came."

"It has been a long day awaiting your return."

As his chest constricted with the hope she wished reconciliation, she glanced at the altar. "For what have you prayed?"

"Not only for what, but for what is—that there have been no further attacks upon Emberly and the ill seeking you has failed."

"What else?"

He looked into her upturned face. "Our marriage. Your forgiveness and trust."

She dropped her chin.

"You are not ready?" he asked gruffly.

"That is not it. It is that I have also been hours at prayer."

"For what?"

"Our marriage. Your forgiveness and mercy."

"Forgiveness and mercy for what?"

"I fear I have betrayed you as I thought you had betrayed me."

He willed her to return her gaze to his. When she did not, he angled his body toward her and lifted her chin.

"I speak not of cuckoldry, Magnus," the words rushed from her. "In that, I have been as true to you as you have been to me."

His relief was short-lived. "In *that?* How have you not been true? For what do you require forgiveness and mercy?"

She moistened her lips. "Forgiveness for me, mercy for one of your men."

He narrowed his lids, but before he could demand she spit out what was stuck to her tongue, she began to tell of the night she had followed Sir Otto and a man-at-arms to the stables. And as she revealed what she had overheard of their conversation, he struggled to keep his rising anger under control.

"So your father's knight set one of my own men upon me." Magnus felt the muscle at his mouth jerk. "And you kept this from me."

"When Sir Otto discovered me in the stables, he said I must not tell what I had heard. I protested, but he reminded me of the promise I made my father."

"What promise?"

"That I take counsel from the one set to watch over me." She laid a hand on his arm. "Sir Otto assured me all he did was for my safety and my father's peace of mind. He said no matter the outcome, it would benefit you to learn who, among your men, so readily betrayed."

"This man-at-arms is the same who followed me on the day past to Eamon and Nanne?"

"Aye."

"Who is he?"

Her throat convulsed. "'Twas Sir Otto's coin that turned him."

He removed his hand from her, lowered it to his side, and pressed his fingers hard into his palm. "You think that lessens the severity of his transgression? It makes him ripe for worse, Thomasin. Indeed, he might even be tempted to aid the Foucault supporters, and I will not have another Agatha within my walls. So I ask again—who is he?"

"My mother's man. For that, I beseech your mercy upon him."

Magnus startled so hard, he nearly cursed aloud his lack of bodily control, a state to which he was not accustomed after years of train-ing that had mostly reduced such expressions to less visible spasms and tightening of muscles. "Your mother? She who abandoned you? Whom you have not seen all these years?"

"I saw her last eve—rather, she made herself known to me."

Calm, he counseled. *Thomasin is no child, but neither is she beyond the gullibility of one of few years.*

He settled his hands to her shoulders. "How did this woman who claims to be your mother enter Kelling to speak to you last eve? And which of my men betrayed me?"

She drew a deep breath. "Your cook, Mathilde."

Magnus's body would have jerked again had he not steeled himself for further revelation.

"And her man is—"

"John," he spat, well aware of his relationship with the cook. The two had been together at least since Magnus's knighting eight years past, possibly as far back as when Mathilde served as a chambermaid.

Magnus frowned. "Was it not eleven years past your mother left you at Waring Castle?"

"Aye."

Though all within him turned restless, like men on the front line of battle who awaited the order to charge, he said as gently as he could, "Though you may want Mathilde to be your mother, she is not."

Thomasin blinked. "But she knows all. And I recognized John on the day past. Certes, he is the man who took my mother from me."

"Then that is how Mathilde knows all—from John."

"But—"

"Thomasin, I was taken to bed with grave sickness at ten and seven, and it was Mathilde—a chambermaid then—who daily changed my bedding. More than twelve years past."

She stared at him, then her shoulders eased so suddenly that had he not been holding to her, she would have sunk against him. "Then what became of my mother?"

As much as he longed to comfort her, something was afoot and gaining ground. "This stinks of Foucault, Thomasin."

"Foucault? I—" Her eyes widened.

"What?"

Aye, what? Thomasin concurred, staring through Magnus as she returned to the night past when Mathilde had defended John. "Aude," she whispered.

"What of her?"

"Mathilde told she had seen John steal into Aude's hut, and that when she confronted him, he admitted to having been unfaithful. But perhaps not. Perhaps he was..."

"He was and is," Magnus said with finality. "And methinks it no coincidence Sir Otto chose him. Why risk turning the loyalties of an unknown when already a betrayer is in place and has been for years?"

As pieces began to fit in a picture Thomasin should have seen sooner, shame moved through her. "The one time I saw Aude at Castle Mathe, she must have been there for Otto. And when I was attacked upon Emberly..."

"The rare day that knight did not follow you. Perhaps not only to avoid blame for your death but because he was among your attackers—the one who remained astride."

Thomasin longed to argue that her father's man would not have sat watching while the brigands sought to ravish her, but neither would she have believed he would betray as it seemed likely he had been doing for years the same as her husband's man-at-arms.

"The arrow he took to the shoulder was fairly harmless," Magnus said. "But it proved effective in throwing suspicion off him. Thus, it was made to seem his only crime was being a fool for leading the brigand to you."

"He meant to kill me?"

"If not him, then his fellow Foucault avenger."

"And on the day past..." She returned to that place, recalled what had bothered her before Sir Otto hastily noted how pretty Nanne was. "He asked if I wished I had not come again to Nanne and Eamon's, so he had to know it was there you delivered me after the attack." She swallowed the lump in her throat. "And he did not fear I would reveal his attempt to force himself on me because I was not to survive it." She dropped her chin. "I am a fool—angered to be called a child, though that is what I have been in not seeing what I did not wish to see."

Magnus's silence hurt, but even had he assured her she was not a fool, it would be meaningless. As were so many lies.

He propped up her chin, and his bit of a smile gave her hope of forgiveness. "Aye, my little fool, but you are not alone. Your father, The Boursier, and I stand with you. All of us prey to those who seek to undo us."

Tears sprang to her eyes. "Is this forgiveness?"

"It is, but there will be no mercy for John. As for Mathilde...She may prove as dangerous as Sir Otto and John."

Despite the woman's lie, it was hard to believe. Desperate was what the cook seemed, not of ill bent. But Thomasin would not risk defending her. "What do we do?"

Magnus raised her to standing. "The only thing you will do when I return you to the keep is go directly to the solar and remain there until I come for you."

"What of you?"

"I will root out John. If he is not in the barracks, he will be with Mathilde at her cottage in town. God willing, this night we end this, Thomasin, and be all the nearer to putting the Foucault uprising to rest." He retrieved his sword belt from the seat of a pew, girded it and adjusted his sword, then took her hand and drew her from the chapel. Not until they stood in torchlight before the doors to the great hall, beneath the watch of those on the walls, did they speak again.

"I fear for you," she said. "Promise you will return to me this eve."

He kissed her brow. "I shall. Will I find you in our bed?"

"This night and every night."

He released her, opened the door, and nodded her inside. "I will come to you in the solar as soon as my men and I have dealt with John."

Thomasin nodded and slipped inside.

As expected, it was dim in the hall and quiet but for the shifting of bodies on benches and pallets, the breath and mutterings of deep sleep, and the whistle and rumble of snores.

Grateful for a clear path to the stairs, she ascended the steps and paused outside the solar to consider the door to the chamber where she would no longer sleep. Instead, there she would make a place for the children she hoped God would gift Magnus and her. There their babes would grow and be loved, the wrongs done their mother and father never visited upon them.

"Oh, Maddie," she whispered, "I wish you had been true." She entered the solar to the light of a fire burning bright in the hearth and a large candle on the table. Though grateful Magnus's squire had seen to such comforts, the fire was not necessary. Night had cooled the day, but the slight chill on the chamber was easily shed beneath the bed's covers where this eve she would be with her husband.

Hoping he would come soon, she closed the door and started toward the bed. But candlelight drew her regard to the table and that which it illuminated before *The Betrayal* tapestry.

Curious, she altered her course and halted before the table to consider the large piece of engraved leather whose top and lower edges were curled as if the piece had recently been unrolled. It was a map, representing the barony of Kilbourne and illustrating how it had been carved into three pieces to award the Verduns, De Arells, and Boursiers. Thomasin had seen the like before, though her father's was penned on parchment.

She reached to trace the blue line marking the boundaries of Emberly. And was snatched back by the arm that wound around her waist and slammed her against a firm chest.

33

Her yelp a pitiful thing, Thomasin drew breath to scream, but closed her mouth when she felt a sharp edge against her throat.

"Shh, shh, shh," someone hissed, and further impressed upon her the need for silence by lightly drawing the blade across her neck.

Slowly, she raised her hands in surrender. "John?"

"Nay," a familiar voice warmed her ear, "but 'twas he who let me in. Did you not, John?"

The tapestry moved, and out from behind it stepped the man-at-arms.

"Sir Otto!" Thomasin gasped, holding her gaze to John to keep herself from sudden movement that could see her blood stain the rug. "What do you?"

"I finish what is too long begun. Regrettably, it was not your husband who came through the door, for then I might have spared you—for a while."

"Otto." Purposely, she dropped his knight's title for the familiarity that might benefit her and turned her head toward his.

"Do not!" he snapped. "You fool me only once, so unless you wish me to return the favor of letting blood, be still." When she complied, he said, "Now what to do with you whilst we await the baron?"

Praying Magnus's inability to locate John would long delay his arrival, during which she might find a way to escape, she returned her gaze to John.

The man-at-arms appeared almost ill at ease where he stood looking between Sir Otto and her, and she wondered if he might not be a Foucault supporter as Magnus surmised, that what he found himself in the midst of went beyond how much he had meant to betray.

"I do not think we have long to wait," Otto said, "but we ought to make ourselves comfortable."

Hopefully, meaning whatever he intended for her would wait as well.

"I am going to release you, Thomasin, and you will do as told, aye?"

If he wished to believe that…"I shall."

"And I will not have to gag you. Do you know why?"

"Why?"

"Should you scream, my men in the hall will begin cutting the throats of those innocents who gained their pallets in the expectation they shall arise come the morrow."

As she caught her breath, she glimpsed on John's face the beginning of a frown. Then it was gone. Was it a lie that Sir Otto had men below-stairs? Or was the man simply uninformed?

"We are of an agreement, Thomasin?"

As if she had a choice. "I will not scream."

He eased his hold, and when he came alongside, she looked up and saw what her blade had done on the day past. Hardly disfiguring, but there would likely be a thin scar from jaw to cheekbone.

"See, I am not vengeful," he said, tempting her to point out that as one who supported the Foucault's claim to the baronies, he could not be otherwise. But as she was learning in her quest to control her tongue, it would benefit her nothing to speak and could be of further detriment were she to reveal what Magnus had concluded about this knight who may never have truly been her father's man.

"I am grateful," she said, struck by the absence of a wicked glint in eyes of darkest brown that, for the first time, she noticed were ringed by a fine line of gold. Of greater note was the dull sheen of what seemed apathy, as if he were resolved to do what he must and no more.

He swept his dagger in the direction of the bed. "There, where your husband will find his welcoming wife the moment he enters—not a bad way to die."

Thomasin turned and, as she moved across the solar, shifted her gaze from her side of the bed to Magnus's where she was never to sleep. It was the latter she came around and settled to with her back against the pillows. Here she would come quickly to her husband's regard and, hopefully, serve as a warning that all was not as it appeared.

Sir Otto skirted the table, and facing her with his back to the tapestry, leaned in and set his hands wide on the table. "You have seen this?" He jutted his chin at the leather map.

"Not ere this night."

"You know what it is?"

"A map of what was Kilbourne."

"And will be Kilbourne again, Thomasin. These blue, green, and red lines will disappear, as will the families whose colors they represent."

She feigned surprise. "You are party to the Foucault uprising?"

"I am."

Making a pretense of adjusting Magnus's pillow at her back, she slid a hand beneath her own pillow and touched the dagger her husband had instructed her to keep there. Unfortunately, were she able to retrieve the sword fastened to the underside of the bed, Magnus was right—it would likely prove of more detriment to her than that of her attacker.

"For how long have you been an enemy?" she asked.

"Ever. And wearisome it has been."

She met her hands in her lap. "Then you never truly cared about me. It was pretense."

"It should have been, but I spoke true that I have become fond of you."

"More so as I grew into my woman's body."

He straightened. "Aye, thus it has not been easy to do what I am called to do—and failed at time and again." He rubbed a hand up his arm and down again, and she saw what appeared to be blood on his sleeve.

"You are hurt?" she asked.

He glanced at his arm. "For you."

"I do not understand."

He looked to John. "Stoke the fire."

As if 'tis not well enough warm, she reflected, more closely feeling the embrace of her garments.

As the man-at-arms moved to do as bid, Otto strode to the bed and halted beside her. "You would see?" He touched the cuff of his sleeve and, at her nod, pushed it up to reveal a long row of horizontal scars. And just above his elbow was a livid cut recently stitched closed and twice as wide as the others.

"What were you called to do?" she asked, not only to understand why they were here now, but to distract him sufficiently so that if Magnus came abovestairs, the knight would have little time to prepare for her husband's entrance.

"That which the brigands who attacked you upon Emberly failed to do."

Then he was the one who had remained astride? "You had a hand in that."

"I did, and for it made myself unavailable to follow you that day. I could not have your father blame me for your death, could I? One that would have happened between the village of Cross and Castle Mathe had you not ridden upon Emberly." He dropped into the chair beside the bed and thrust out his legs. "That should have been a boon, making it appear Verdun was responsible for the death of one he did not wish to wed, but he saved you. When I learned that, I thought God must be on your side."

"When you learned it? You were not there, then, when those men tried to..."

"Nay. I had to be visible to your father so no suspicion fell on me when he received word of the attack. Instead, shortly ere I happened upon you returning to Mathe, it was I who received word that Verdun had rescued you."

How grateful she had been it was his arms carrying her home. The arms of her enemy.

He clasped his hands over his abdomen. "When your father informed his men it was upon Blackwood you were attacked, I nearly corrected him." He smiled. "You did not wish him to know you had been even more of a fool, eh?"

The light in the room leapt, and as she glanced at John who prodded logs added to the fire, she said, "I was ashamed."

The knight considered her. "I was not pleased your father chose me to remain with you at Kelling, lest it fell to me to do this. And so it did. The morn of your wedding, as I listened to Verdun's conversation with your father in which he revealed the truth of your attack—that he had been your savior—I determined I would do what needed to be done. And yet I failed." He gripped his scarred arm and went silent.

Too silent. Enough silence in which to hear boots on the stairs should Magnus approach.

"When we paused en route to Castle Adderstone," Thomasin said, "you knew we were to be attacked."

"And there I failed again."

"To kill me."

His nostrils flared. "It was required of me."

"So had I not stopped you on the day past, you would have slain me in the wood."

More silence.

"Was I meant to hear your conversation with John in the stables?"

"Only the one I turned it to when I realized you were within."

"You sought to set me against my husband."

He shrugged. "He provided the means to do so."

"Was it you who incited him to ride to Orlinde?"

He raised his eyebrows. "You have a keen mind for being common."

"How did you do it?"

"I caught young Eamon alone at the market and told him I was his father. As hoped, his mother sent word to Verdun."

She gasped, looked nearer upon him. "You are his father?"

He scoffed. "You would like that, all the easier to believe whatever tale your husband told."

"Are you Eamon's father," she pressed, "the one who violated Nanne?"

His face darkened. "I am no ravisher."

It was her turn to scoff. "You cannot truly believe I wished the attentions you forced on me."

"I vow it was not me who sowed that boy. You must look to your husband for that."

"I will not."

He sat forward. "Then you refuse to believe the truth of him."

"That is not the truth of him. He is not like you."

His gaze wavered, and he looked away. "I know you will not believe me, but this is not who I wish to be."

"Then do not."

He drew his shoulders up to his ears, dropped them. "Never was I given a choice."

"A choice? For what must you rely on others to offer choices, especially those you find repugnant? You ought to make your own way!"

"You make it sound simple."

"'Tis not. But still I, of common blood you believe is inferior to your own, made my own way out of a life I did not wish. And I was but ten and four."

He laughed. "You once asked after my mother. Would you truly like to know about her?"

Anything to keep the silence from settling too long. "I would."

He nodded, then frowned, and she followed his gaze to the man-at-arms who watched from alongside the hearth. "Go belowstairs and ensure all is quiet, John."

If true he had men in the hall, would they not alert him of trouble? Thomasin wondered. Perhaps there were no others. Of course, there could be and this was but a means of gaining privacy in which to tell his tale to one he did not believe would have the opportunity to repeat it.

The man-at-arms opened the door, letting in air so much cooler than that within that Thomasin sighed with momentary relief. Then the door closed and Otto once more reclined and began tapping the flat of his dagger atop his thigh.

"I cannot say with any certainty I loved my mother." Perspiration was visible on his forehead. "Can one truly say that of so hard and twisted a soul? Methinks it better said I did not love her. Indeed, there were times when merely being in her presence, I feared for my soul."

Sympathy tugged at Thomasin. Alice may have abandoned her, but never had she been as Otto described the woman who had birthed him. And Thomasin *had* loved her mother.

"Still, it was as much her blood that gave me life, and so I learned to respect it though my father did not."

Was it possible he was not fully noble?

"Just as I learned to respect my place in the plan so I might right the wrongs done my family."

His family…Could it be? "Otto?"

He blinked as if surprised to discover his tale was not told only to himself.

She tugged at her clinging bodice, asked, "Are you a Foucault?"

More laughter. "Let none say your common blood makes you dim-witted, as neither does it make me."

"Then you are noble *and* common?"

He briefly lowered his lids. "Aye, baseborn, but worthier of Kilbourne than the families who stole it, Thomasin de Arell."

"Verdun," she corrected.

The tapping of his dagger ceased. "Most unfortunate, you will be a De Arell much longer than a Verdun. Now let me think on a clue to help you guess who birthed me."

She glanced at his dagger, wished he would return it to its scabbard so she might chance bringing to hand the one beneath her pillow.

He swept the blade up, tapped the heated air. "Ah! The pastorela of which you are so fond, the same I oft heard as a child."

She startled. "Aude's?"

"That is the one."

She shook her head. "Surely you are not saying Aude was your mother?"

"As much as she could be a mother."

Thomasin felt as if a fist had landed to her belly, and yet it made sense. And confirmed that when Aude had come to Castle Mathe, it had been for Otto. Dry mouthed, she whispered, "And your noble father?"

"You have already guessed 'tis a Foucault. There are not many it could be, Thomasin."

"I did not know there were any living."

"Because you believe lies." He pushed up out of the chair, and she tensed in anticipation he meant to harm her. But he crossed to the tapestry, and with his back to her, considered it—while she eased the dagger from beneath the pillow and slid it under her thigh.

"I think it almost noble the guilt the Verduns have shouldered these years," he said. "So much, methinks were it in my hands, I would spare them." He glanced over his shoulder. "And you."

"Whose hands is it in if not yours?"

"That is not for me to tell." He turned to the side. "As for my father…" He touched a figure woven into the tapestry—that of the fallen Simon Foucault.

"Surely not!" Thomasin exclaimed.

"Shocking, hmm?"

Recalling when last the knight was in the solar and had slyly mused it was possible Denis Foucault's heir had survived, she said, "Then he did not die in France."

He hesitated. "Most assuredly, Simon Foucault, beloved son of Denis Foucault, died."

Though not before getting Aude with child. However, if Simon Foucault was not the one responsible for the attacks on the baronies, and now Aude was dead, in whose hands was the fate of the three families if not Otto's?

"You have siblings?" she asked. It was possible that in all the years his father served in France, other children had been sown.

At Otto's look of disbelief, she said, "You told me I reminded you of your sister. You have one, aye?"

He snorted. "Likely somewhere. As you know, my mother was hardly lovely, not even in her younger years, though I am told she did have a fair figure."

"So another lie told."

"What is one more?" He gestured at the tapestry. "Now the betrayal...This is truth."

Footsteps. On the stairs.

"Stay!" Otto shoved his dagger in its scabbard and drew his sword. "If it is Verdun and you open your mouth, I will sound the alarm and my men will turn the floors in the hall red." Eyes fastened on her, he set himself on the other side of the door where its opening would conceal him as it had done when she had entered. "Aye, Thomasin?"

She jerked her chin in assent, her only hope that the warning she provided Magnus when he saw her on this side of the bed would be sufficient to keep him from Otto's blade.

Dear Lord, she silently prayed, *let Magnus see this for what it is. Let him prevail.*

A light tap sounded, and a voice rasped, "'Tis John." Slowly, the door opened, more slowly the man-at-arms entered.

Otto stepped forward and closed the door. "All is quiet?"

"In the hall, but I heard voices and peered outside. The baron was in the inner bailey and spoke my name to the captain of the guard. He searches for me."

"Then he will be here soon." Otto looked to Thomasin. "I am sorry."

"Another lie," she said. "Were you truly sorry, you would not do this."

He thrust his unsheathed sword in the direction of the tapestry. "Were the Verduns truly sorry, they would have righted the wrong."

"It was not known Simon Foucault had a son. Had it been—"

"Still your families would hold tight to these lands, even kill me to ensure never could I do to them what they did to my grandfather."

"Otto—"

"Quiet!"

"But—"

"There are other ways to silence you without making it a request, Thomasin."

"Be it now or later," she snapped, "you will do so."

He took a step toward her. "Do not forget I have only to alert my men, and the deaths of those in the hall are upon both our consciences."

Strangely, she believed his conscience would suffer as well. But though it gave her hope he would not call for the deaths of innocents, she could not risk their lives even to save Magnus who had a better chance of saving himself than did sleeping men and woman. "I will speak naught."

"Lie down facing away from the door. I cannot have you telling with your eyes what your lips do not."

What misfortune that he anticipated such! Keeping tight to the edge of the bed so there would be no mistake she had claimed the place forbidden her, she turned onto her side, closed her eyes, and prayed Magnus would not come.

34

Something felt wrong, though it seemed only the air was out of place.

Hand on hilt, Magnus reached with his senses for those things that wished to remain hidden. Though nothing tripped his eye as he moved through the hall, nor upon the stairs, he caught a scent and a sound as the landing came into sight.

It was not unusual, but neither was it expected on a night as mild as this. Breathing in burning wood and sweet sap, listening nearer upon the crackle, he halted three steps down.

Had Thomasin taken a chill and laid a fire? Such might be beyond most ladies who never attended the hearth, but not his wife. And it pleased him. He had imagined that if ever he wed, mostly it would be for ornamental purpose, but that was not Thomasin. She was more—water for a soul he had not known was so dry.

Pushing aside such fanciful thoughts, he returned to John, who was not to be found, Mathilde, whom he had ordered his men to escort to a cell, and the feeling something was awry.

He drew his sword. Mindful of the scrape of his boots on the steps, he ascended to the landing that glowed with firelight streaming beneath the solar's door—a good amount, but not of smoke to indicate the fire was no longer confined to the hearth.

The feeling was stronger here. If he had to chance his life on it, he would say Thomasin was not alone.

Cursing himself for not seeing her abovestairs, he moved to the next chamber. If any lay in wait for him in the solar, they would less likely expect him to enter through the adjoining room.

Slowly, he opened the door. It was dark inside except for the light from the torchlit corridor and that radiating beneath the door between the rooms. Grateful the fire's crackle masked his footfalls over the rushes, he crossed to the door and listened for sounds on the other side. Was it a waiting silence or merely one of Thomasin at rest?

Praying for the latter, he positioned his sword and eased open the door. The hinges did not betray him, and at a hand's width, firelight revealed his wife lay on the bed with her back to him. The wrong side of the bed. Either someone had placed her there, or his clever Thomasin defied him with good purpose. Blessedly, breath moved her shoulders.

He looked to the left. And was surprised it was not John who waited to gut him. Sir Otto held his sword close to his chest where he stood alongside the corridor door so that when it opened, he would be shielded from sight long enough to gain the coward's advantage of attacking an opponent from behind. Doubtless, the man-at-arms had admitted the one whose pay he was in. But where was John? Not near the hearth, nor the table upon which the leather map lay as it should not, its place the chest whose lock must have been broken. If the man-at-arms was inside, he lurked where firelight did not.

Knowing it was time to discover the truth of the roles Otto and John played in the Foucault uprising and exact payment for the former's attempt to ravish Thomasin, Magnus girded himself with his father's words: *Three things you require...anger over injustice, fear that if 'tis not their blood it will be yours, and prayer.*

"Lord be with me," he rasped and wrenched open the door.

The knight snapped his head around, and his shock gave Magnus time to cross the space between them and easily meet his sword against his opponent's. As he noted with satisfaction the cut Thomasin had dealt Sir Otto on the day past, the knight cursed, slid his sword off Magnus's, and lunged to the side. He swung again to strike his opponent's back, but

Magnus was not present to receive the blow, having distanced himself to gain more time to react to swings and thrusts and ensure blood more likely flung itself on the floor than on him. Of greatest importance, he had placed himself between Sir Otto and his wife, the latter having come to life.

"Get out, Thomasin!" he barked as Sir Otto advanced.

"He has men in the hall," she cried. "If they hear what goes, they will begin killing the castle folk."

Magnus sliced upward to deflect a downward swing, caught it mid-blade, and slid his blade off the knight's. Then he arced his sword low and opened up Sir Otto's chausses below the knee.

The knight shouted, evidencing blood had been let and would soon stain the garment.

"Magnus, cease! They will kill—"

"My men are below," he snarled as Sir Otto came at him again, the injury done his leg slowing him sufficiently so that when John thrust aside the tapestry and ran toward Thomasin, Magnus had the moment needed to assess his wife's situation. Having risen to her knees at the center of the bed, she held a dagger—a blade lacking in the reach needed to fend off a sword.

"Go, Thomasin!"

"Stay!" Sir Otto spat, and lurched to the side to block her exit from the right of the bed while John approached the left.

Had Magnus not put so much space between himself and his opponent, it would have been possible to deal with the man-at-arms, as well as Sir Otto, who had nowhere to retreat with the wall at his back. Now the only way to better the knight was to sacrifice Thomasin.

Knowing he risked much in exposing his back to Sir Otto, hoping the man's leg injury continued to impede him, Magnus ran at John.

The man-at-arms veered toward the hearth, opening up the way for Thomasin to reach the door providing she made haste.

With John momentarily distanced, Magnus swept around. But instead of coming off the left side of the bed, Thomasin scrambled to its foot and sprang into Sir Otto's path.

"Thomasin!" Magnus ran toward her.

It was too late. Or would have been had the knight chosen to run her through. Surprisingly, he turned his sword aside and thrust his shoulder into her, sending her weapon flying and her sprawling on the rug.

A second was all Magnus needed to reach her first, but that second was gifted to the knight who snatched hold of her braid and dragged her upright. "Now," he panted through the grim smile he flashed at Magnus, who had halted lest the blade against Thomasin's neck was drawn across it, "we are back to where we need to be." He glanced past Magnus. "John, relieve your lord of his sword that is only of use to him if he does not value his wife. Which is possible, hmm?"

Magnus beheld the fear and anger in Thomasin's eyes that, as he knew well, made strange but dangerous bedfellows. Dangerous to her if she acted when she should not. Dangerous to her captor were she given a chance to act where she should.

"She is but a commoner fitted up in pretty clothes," Sir Otto continued. "Of course, you like commoners, Baron Verdun. And making children on them."

The sword in Magnus's hand quivered, but he had no thought of turning it on John while Thomasin remained under threat.

The man laid a hand on Magnus's that gripped the hilt. "Give over nice like."

"Do not!" Thomasin cried. "Still they will—" She gasped as the knight's blade moved just enough to coax a thin line of blood from beneath her jaw.

"Nice like now." Sir Otto nodded at Magnus's sword.

Magnus let his sword—that guarantor of life—be taken from him as he would never have before.

"Honorable," Sir Otto said as John crossed to the table and laid the sword there. "It seems all may not be as it appears with Nanne and that boy, Thomasin, that your husband does have a care for you. And as much as you long for his kind regard, methinks you regret it now."

"This is not who you are," she said. "Do you make your own choices, you will see this is not one of them."

"Regrettably, I am in no position to do so. Thus, I do what must be done. As your husband must do what I say must be done if he wishes this to be as painless as possible for you." He nodded at the bed. "Settle yourself, Baron Verdun."

Thomasin's eyes widened, and Magnus knew she was thinking the same as he—here was hope.

Magnus moved toward the bed.

"Hold!" Sir Otto called, then to John, "Lady Thomasin found a dagger in that bed. Be certain there are no more."

Once again, her eyes went wide. But after tossing about the pillows and covers, the man-at-arms said, "None, Sir Otto."

"Settle yourself, Baron Verdun."

Though the sword was beneath the right side, Magnus knew that to move in that direction could give rise to suspicion with the left side so much nearer. Thus, he strode past John, and as he positioned himself back against the headboard, determined it would cost a second to lunge to the opposite side to retrieve the sword. God willing, it would not be the one second required to save his wife.

"You would know why I do what I do?" Sir Otto asked as he drew Thomasin toward the table.

"You are of Foucault," Magnus said.

The knight's eyebrows rose. "I suppose it follows after this."

"Before this."

Sir Otto canted his head. "Tell."

Magnus saw no reason to enlighten him, especially as the man seemed willing to do the enlightening, and the more time he took, the greater the chance of delivering Thomasin.

"Regardless," the knight said when Magnus denied him answer, "you cannot know as much as your wife now does." He pulled out a chair, pushed her onto it, and motioned the man-at-arms forward.

John returned his own sword to its scabbard, and when given charge of Thomasin, placed a dagger to her throat.

Sir Otto moved to the center of the table and propped his sword against its edge. He wiped a hand across his perspiring brow, slid it to his injured shoulder, then bent and felt down his leg to where his chausses were stained with blood. He grunted as if pained. But if he thought he hurt now...

Straightening, he met Magnus's gaze and lifted the map. "This is who I am. Not merely of Foucault. *A* Foucault."

It surprised, but not overly much. The fit was good. Magnus considered the tapestry, first the figure of Denis Foucault, then the fallen son. "You are of Simon."

Sir Otto's laugh was joyless. "My dear, departed sire."

Then Simon Foucault *had* died, but not before fathering a son.

"Thus, I have no choice but to restore what must be restored," Otto continued. "'Tis most unfortunate your families have made this so difficult."

Magnus looked to Thomasin, and he saw she eyed his sword on the table. He knew what she was thinking, but it would see her dead. Willing her gaze to his, he gave a slight shake of the head, then returned his regard to the knight. "You think you are due an apology?"

"An apology..." Sir Otto dropped the map to the table, turned sideways, and slapped the back of a hand against the tapestry. "This admission of guilt and regret is a beginning for the Verduns. But the rest of what you owe my family will be paid this eve."

"In blood."

"Sadly, it must come to that."

Magnus was more inclined to believe the man's regret was mockery, but strangely, there seemed some truth to it. "What was the plan?" he asked.

Sir Otto scoffed. "A painfully long one—setting Verduns against De Arells against Boursiers. First this way, then that. And when the king decided to join your families through marriage, it was decided the best way to destroy you was to end those marriages, and in such a way suspicion fell on the survivors. Thus, if not through escalation of the feud, then by the king's wrath you would be torn asunder."

"Cowards who set themselves at women," Magnus pronounced.

Sir Otto shrugged. "Why travel a debris-strewn road when a cleared one can more comfortably and quickly deliver you to your destination? Of course, such was not the case with your lady wife who likes to keep angels around her to summon you to her side, nor Lady Elianor who survived the frozen lake unlike…" He narrowed his gaze. "…my mother."

Magnus contained his surprise that Aude, known as Agatha, had birthed the miscreant. "And so it begins to come together," he murmured.

The knight set to rolling the map. "As told, it has been painfully long, like watching a wet piece of wood try to catch fire. But after much smoking and sputtering, and amid days of joy followed by weeks…months… years of disappointment, eventually the flame is embraced." He wrapped the leather thong around the map. "Most unfortunate, it takes twenty or more years to grow a babe into a man and endless trials to ensure he is worthy to lord a barony the size of Kilbourne. But that is my lot."

"You think to put the old barony back together?"

"As its rightful heir, that is my purpose."

"At which you have thus far failed."

Sir Otto laid the map alongside Magnus's sword. "Your deaths will move us nearer what we seek." He nodded at the tapestry. "And this will be made right."

Magnus did not think he had ever seen Thomasin so still for so long. But a blade at one's neck was good incentive, just as it kept Magnus from the sword beneath the bed.

A great tearing of cloth returned his attention to Sir Otto who had wrenched the tapestry from its hooks.

"What do you?" Thomasin gasped.

He swept the wall hanging onto the table. Amid billowing dust, he coughed, cleared this throat, and once more gripped his shoulder. "There is one who will be most interested in seeing this. Too, it and the map will make good family heirlooms—a grand tale of caution." With effort that evidenced his injuries plagued him, he began folding the tapestry.

Magnus eyed his sword on the table. "My blade as well?"

"One of three I must gain." Sir Otto coughed again, as did the man-at-arms whose jerking torso brought his blade nearer Thomasin's throat.

Lord, preserve her, Magnus silently prayed, then asked, "How are we to die?"

The knight nodded at the hearth. "By fire you will perish—one too many logs that rolled free and set your rugs aflame—but I am not so cruel as I am called to be. I would have neither of you suffer that."

Then their throats would be cut first?

The knight pushed the folded tapestry toward the map, rubbed his nose.

"Tell, Sir Otto, if you are truly heir to Kilbourne, who has the right to call you to be so cruel?"

As John coughed again, the knight glanced at Thomasin, who sniffed and blinked as the dust of years settled around her. "The one who has brought me this far would see you meet your end by fire."

Something bothered the back of Magnus's mind, but before he could drag it forward, Thomasin choked, "You speak of the one who cuts you?"

Whatever she referred to was obviously that much more she had learned of Sir Otto's involvement in the Foucault uprising.

"Aye, your greatest enemy."

"And yours," she challenged, and at his hesitation, continued, "You know 'tis so, that he sets you tasks your soul protests."

"They are done to secure my future."

"Are you sure 'tis done for you? Mayhap all that has been done in the name of Foucault has been for that who orders you. Mayhap you are merely a pawn."

He seemed to consider it, as did John whose glistening brow furrowed, but he said, "'Tis I who shall wed Lady Quintin, she who will sit my side whilst I lord all of Kilbourne."

35

"Lady Quintin?" Thomasin exclaimed and winced as if the blade nicked her.

"Aye, a Foucault herself. Despite the taint of also being a Boursier, she is the prize."

"But she is your cousin. You cannot wed—"

"None will know our blood was drawn from the same stream. That knowledge dies with you."

In this, Magnus saw opportunity. Whether or not it was intended that the knowledge also die with the man-at-arms, he said, "It seems you are to join us in death, John. I hope you well spoke your farewell to Mathilde."

The man-at-arms looked to Sir Otto. "You did not send me from the chamber this time."

Magnus was too distant to see what was in the knight's eyes, but his alarm was on the air.

"There was no need. When earlier I had you go belowstairs, it was only to ensure all was quiet. I trust you with my secrets."

"I am not sure you do." The man's hand moved, blessedly putting space between his blade and Thomasin's throat. Though not nearly enough to give Magnus time to retrieve the sword and make it across the chamber, there was promise in it. Then John stepped to the side, reducing Thomasin to a shield, and glanced at Sir Otto's sword propped against the table's edge. "Mayhap you no longer have need of me."

"Of course I do. There are many days ahead of us, my friend."

"It sounds a lie to me," Magnus said. "Regardless, you will not be missed at Kelling, John. Perhaps not even by Mathilde, have you even a care for her."

The man at arms shot him a glower. "Certes, she has helped pass the time."

"Then you have long been party to the Foucault uprising."

"Ere I arrived here eleven years past"—he jutted his chin at Sir Otto—"whilst this one was yet a lad." His words seemed directed at the knight, as if to remind him of how long he had been loyal.

"John," Sir Otto said, "Verdun seeks to set you against me, but you know him for the traitor he is to my family. Just as you know I will be the one to reward you for your years of service."

Magnus saw the question in Thomasin's gaze, noted the blade was nearer her shoulder. But more space was needed. "Pretty sentiments, Sir Otto," he pressed, all of him coiling should the rift between the two men crack wide open. "And yet your hand seeks your sword."

It was no lie, and as hoped, the man-at-arms jumped back and reached for his own sword.

Thomasin did not need to be told to move. Like a rag doll, she slid down her chair and onto the floor beneath the table as Magnus threw himself to the side and drew his weapon from the sheath strapped beneath the bed. Then he was running across the chamber toward his wife, who scrambled toward him.

"See what he does!" Sir Otto cried and raised his sword. "We must stand as one."

Magnus gripped Thomasin's arm and swept her up off her hands and knees. The door accessing the corridor blocked by their attackers, he spun her toward the one adjoining the chambers. "Lock yourself in!"

"I will go for help—"

"You will not!" For nothing would he risk her passing the solar lest one of these men intercepted her. Too, though aid might come too late, the commotion abovestairs would deliver it before she could. "You will stay there!"

How he prayed she would! But the answer to that prayer was not to be known, a wild-eyed John choosing the knight's side by lunging toward Thomasin. And Otto, with a break in his stride and blood glistening through the tear in his chausses, came for Magnus.

Magnus snatched his wife back and flung her behind him as John's sword sliced the air where she had been. With little thought of avoiding the spill of blood, Magnus attacked the man-at-arms with the full force of his body and one eye on the knight coming behind him.

Blades met. And parted when Magnus thrust off, putting his shoulder into it to send John into Sir Otto's path. Both men nearly toppled. Not surprisingly, considering the knight's injuries, it was the man-at-arms who recovered first and came again at the one to whom he had been falsely loyal. Knowing that to keep Otto from Thomasin, John must first be put down, Magnus lunged again.

Their swords clashed, and Magnus once more used the weight of his body to knock his opponent into the knight's path. And succeeded—until the knight started toward the hearth where Thomasin had retreated.

This time Magnus was near enough to deal with both men. Fear. Anger. Prayer. All he needed to fight the good fight and protect the woman he loved.

Aye, loved.

He took another step forward, swung his blade up from the floor, and opened up John's tunic hip to neck. Though he did not wait to see the man-at-arms fall, he heard the anguished shout as he gave chase to Sir Otto who sought Thomasin where she stood alongside the raised hearth wielding an iron poker.

"Otto!" Magnus called, at the end of which he caught the sound of boots on the stairs.

TAMARA LEIGH

The knight turned before the hearth. Had he continued, he might have reached Thomasin unhindered, but she was not unarmed. No longer easy prey.

Now Sir Otto of the Foucaults was prey. And Magnus was ready to bring the hunt to its conclusion. He swung his sword from on high, and his opponent countered with the ferocity of one who knows the only possibility of survival is to risk all. But it would not be enough to preserve his life—had Magnus wished to take it. He did not, for here was surely the means to bring the Foucault uprising to an end. And so he shouted back his men who rushed into the solar, and with quick crossings of blades, maneuvered the knight away from the hearth toward the corner between wall and garderobe.

Sir Otto became less predictable—and desperate, so much that his face reflected surprise when a wild swing sent the edge of his blade tearing through Magnus's tunic to bleed his ribs.

And there was the great anger needed to end the contest. Magnus swept his sword down, landing his against Sir Otto's with such force the knight lost his grip. As the man's sword dropped, Magnus drove him into the corner, slammed the flat of his blade across the knight's chest, and closed a hand over the one that turned around a dagger's hilt.

Face inches from Sir Otto's, whose furrowed brow ran with perspiration, he said, "Do you wish to live, albeit a miserable existence, you will tell me the name of the one to whom you answer."

Panting, the knight raised his gaze. "You think such a threat will gain you what you seek?" He coughed. "If you do not end me, the one I cannot reveal will—else make me wish it more than I do now."

"Tell me!"

Sir Otto dropped his head back against the wall. "Lord, I am tired."

"Speak the name!"

The knight slid his gaze to the side. "Lady Thomasin—"

"You will not address my wife."

"Tell your husband to finish me or get off."

Thomasin stared, and only then realized how closely her garments adhered every place they touched her skin. Lowering the fire poker, she glanced at Magnus's knights and men-at-arms. They stood over John, who whimpered and groaned as he held his gut.

Feeling lightheaded and very aware of the pound of her heart, she dropped the poker and gripped the mantel to steady herself.

"Thomasin?" Magnus asked.

She blinked at him. "I am unharmed. 'Tis just so warm and…"

"Sir George, escort my wife to the adjoining chamber."

As the knight strode forward, Magnus took the dagger from Sir Otto, tossed it aside, and wrenched him off the wall.

Thomasin hated appearing so faint-hearted, but she was grateful when Magnus's knight took her arm. "'Tis done, my lady. Come."

At a more sedate pace than that to which Magnus subjected Sir Otto, whom he dragged toward the door, she was led across the solar. But unlike Magnus and his captive, she could not ignore the dying man in their midst—he who would pass from this life with the answers she lacked.

She pulled free of Sir George, and as the knight reached to recapture her, sank down beside John.

"My lord!" Sir George called.

Magnus halted at the door. "Thomasin!"

She met her husband's gaze. "I must speak with him."

He looked ready to argue, but summoned his men-at-arms and commanded them to deliver his prisoner to the farthest cell.

When he came alongside Thomasin, she reached a hand to him and he folded it into his. "Make haste," he urged, "he is soon to trade heaven for hell."

She touched the man's shoulder. "John?"

He opened his eyes. "*Lady* Thomasin," he drew out her title as if testing it for authenticity.

She leaned nearer. "You are Alice's John?"

A smile flickered across his lips. "Aye, but first a soldier who...did what was told him to do. Though not where you were concerned."

"I do not understand."

"Mathilde knows not that I know who you are." He drew a rattling breath. "But I have long known. And you are here this day because eleven years past I could not make a corpse of you as I was ordered to do."

Thomasin glanced at Magnus, was certain her face reflected as much puzzlement as his. "You were to have killed me?"

He chuckled, a sound that became pained, and it was some moments before he proved he was not yet where the living crossed over to the dead. "The one who would see Kilbourne restored sent me to gut your mother and you, but she was so pretty and..." He moaned and wrapped his arms around his middle as if to hold his insides together. "It would have been hard to put a blade to her—nearly as difficult as putting one to a child—so I convinced her to leave with me and told my liege that by the time I rooted out De Arell's whore, she and her daughter had been taken by fever. Ironic, I have ever thought, that not a year after Alice and I arrived at Kelling, she died of fever, and with her our unborn babe."

Holding tight to her husband's hand, Thomasin sank back on her heels. She ought to have been prepared for such tidings, but she was not. Thus, she was moved to grief until John coughed, flecking his tunic with blood that told he had little time remaining.

She drew a deep breath, said, "But surely you were found out when my father claimed me four years past."

"Aye, and though I told I had been misinformed about your death, still I was punished." He shifted his gaze to Magnus. "I did not lie when I reported I was set upon by brigands during my patrol. I but neglected to reveal they were known to me."

"What of Mathilde?" Thomasin asked.

His eyebrows rose and fell. "A poor substitute for your mother. It was from her I let a room for Alice in the town, and the two became good friends. Too good, for your mother took Mathilde into her confidence, though I did not learn it until Alice was delirious with fever. When she passed, it seemed best to seek comfort in the arms of Mathilde, and after a time, she proved willing."

"You do not love her as she loves you."

"Only Alice I have loved."

Thomasin's heart hurt for Mathilde. The only good of the woman's loss was that it did not appear she was a party to the uprising—that she had allowed Thomasin to believe she was Alice in the hope of saving John.

Magnus lowered to his haunches beside Thomasin. "If 'tis not Sir Otto who leads the uprising, who?"

The man-at-arms moved his dull gaze to his lord. "Aude and her man."

"What man?"

He gave a grunt, almost a laugh. "You would not know his face."

"I but require a name."

John exhaled on a wheezing breath, and at its end, said, "*That* you would know." Then he looked to Thomasin and his eyes jittered and lids lowered.

Magnus dropped his head between his shoulders, muttered something, then drew Thomasin to her feet.

"How badly are you hurt?" she asked, peering at his rent tunic.

He lifted her chin and examined the cut beneath it. "More than you, thank the Lord, but naught that will not heal." He motioned his squire forward. "My wife and I will pass the night in the adjoining chamber. See 'tis lit, then clear the solar of this night's ill."

"Aye, my lord."

As the young man hastened away, Magnus turned Thomasin from the corpse. And hesitated.

She followed his gaze to the folded tapestry, then the wall absent the scenes of betrayal. "Magnus, can we not—?"

"Squire!"

The young man snapped around. "My lord?"

Magnus stared at the blessedly barren wall. He no more wished the tapestry returned there than did his wife—detested the thought of beginning another day with it being the first thing he looked upon. As it never should have been. Even had his father cause to feel guilty over the overthrow of Denis Foucault, Magnus did not.

He nodded at the table. "Burn that."

The squire's eyes widened and Thomasin caught her breath.

"But first, light the chamber." Magnus guided his wife toward it.

A torch was brought from the corridor and fixed in a sconce, and when Magnus was alone with Thomasin, she said, "Come, I will tend your injury."

"It can wait." There was something he wanted far more than the blood upon him washed away. He gathered his wife close, pressed his face between her neck and shoulder, and breathed in her scent. "Answered prayers," he rasped, then said, "I am sorry for the loss of your mother."

Her chest expanded against his. "'Tis an old loss. Though it saddens me to know its ending, it gladdens me to think it possible she would have returned as promised."

Would she have? Despite Alice's pursuit of happiness at the expense of her child, had she loved her daughter enough to come back for her?

Thomasin moved her mouth to his ear. "That is the past. This is the present. And in this present, I have something to give you. Have you something to give me?"

He lifted his head and peered into her wide blue eyes. "Only what I know to be true." But dare he speak it first? "Tell me, what do *you* know to be true?"

She raised her eyebrows. "You fear naming it."

And hated that he felt like an awkward youth trying to catch a pretty girl's attention—and that the muscle beside his eye betrayed how anxious it made him. "I do fear it, but I will name it." Recalling what he had spoken the night she had refused to be denied her place in the solar and he had told her what he believed of love, he said, "I sought first your soul, and having found it, would be as near you in the dark as in the light. That is love, Thomasin—how I love you and would be loved in return."

He had not known her eyes could be more blue, but in that moment, they seemed capable of lighting the darkest place. "Truly? You love me?"

"How could I not?"

She slid her hands around his neck, urged his face nearer, and kissed the corner of his mouth. "I have found your soul, Magnus." She rose to her toes and pressed her lips alongside his eye. "And would be as near you in the dark as in the light. That is how I love you."

Feeling as if something inside him that had never known ease suddenly did, that with her he had found a place of peace and rest where he had only to be Magnus, he pulled her closer. "Stay with me, this night and always."

She smiled, and he did not think he had ever looked upon so great a beauty. "Always, Magnus. Nights and days without end."

EPILOGUE

———✥———

"For what do you think the king associates with such a man?" Thomasin asked.

Standing with her on the gatehouse roof, Magnus stared at the leader of the five men who rode from Kelling with a prisoner between them. Magnus's prisoner, now King Edward's.

For nigh on a month, Sir Otto had languished in a cell, refusing to reveal more of his secrets. But all had changed with the arrival of the king's dog.

The missive Sir Francis had brandished crackled in Magnus's fist as he recalled the words inked there—orders that Sir Otto be given into the mercenary's custody for delivery to the king's prison for questioning.

Unbeknownst until this day, the young knight had years past been a ward of King Edward's father, and was years later knighted by the son who now claimed right and responsibility for discovering the extent of his crimes against the three barons.

What form would that discovery take? Though Sir Otto had mostly kept his bearded face lowered when brought before Sir Francis, his usually apathetic person had radiated fear.

"Magnus?"

He moved his gaze to his wife whose smile was taut with concern. And as ever, he was grateful she was at his side, her presence having aided in keeping the telltale spasmings under control when the mercenary and his tidings were received.

"You are angry with The Boursier," she said.

"And myself. I should not have allowed him to convince me to send word of Sir Otto's treachery to the king—certainly not until I myself had answers from the miscreant."

She pressed her lips, and he knew she held her tongue behind them. She had not wished him to alert King Edward, having disapproved of Baron Boursier's reason for doing so. As Sir Otto's perfidy further evidenced much of the feuding between the families had been reactions to acts perpetrated by Foucault supporters, the Baron of Godsmere had requested that his sister, who had no wish to marry, be released from her betrothal to Thomasin's father.

Thomasin had not liked that, certain from what she had seen of Griffin de Arell's relationship with Lady Quintin that both could be as happily wed as Magnus and she.

Straightening her shoulders, she said, "You could not know the king would take a personal interest in my father's knight."

"He oversteps, and then to send that mercenary…" Magnus looked around and ground his teeth when the last of Sir Francis and his men went from sight. As he returned his regard to Thomasin, he paused on Kelling's cook who chose vegetables from a villager's cart on this side of the town's walls. And hoped he had made the right determination. His wife was convinced Mathilde had not known of John's dealings with the Foucaults, and he was inclined to believe it as well. Still, he and others kept a watch on the woman.

"Though still she grieves," Thomasin said, having followed his gaze, "methinks she is on the mend."

Would she have been sooner had the whole truth of the man-at-arms been told—that not only had he been an instrument of the Foucault uprising, originally sent to murder Alice and Thomasin, he had regarded Mathilde as a poor substitute for his affections? Despite the urge to reveal all should the cook harbor ill against the one who had laid down her lover, Thomasin had assured Magnus it need not be told.

"I hope you are right about her," he murmured.

"I am." She laid a hand on his arm. "You have not given answer as to why the king associates with Sir Francis."

A thing pondered time and again. "'Tis said the mercenary is one who dwelt in the shadows that he might aid young Edward in securing his crown, which he did by participating in the demise of Edward's mother's lover."

"Mortimer." She nodded. "And so King Edward is indebted to Sir Francis."

"Too—and possibly of greater import—having no mind for his soul, he is unconcerned with trespassing upon God and Church."

"That is a dangerous man."

"Thus, I pray this is the last we see of him, though I expect the king will send him again to ensure the final alliance is made between our families."

"Of course, if King Edward grants The Boursier's request to excuse Lady Quintin from wedding my father..." She trailed off.

"Methinks that a false hope, that he will see his decree to its end."

His wife shrugged. "You know my mind on that."

"I do, and I would not wish your father denied the happiness I have with you, but if Lady Quintin remains opposed to marriage, more I would not wish such unhappiness on your father."

"She will come around." It was said with certainty. "Now tell, what answer did Nanne give?"

Returned to the conversation he had been forced to abandon following his return from the barony of Orlinde when word was brought of the arrival of the king's men, Magnus said, "She is not pleased, but she understands that if the brigands do believe Eamon is mine, her death and her son's could be sought as was yours and your mother's. Thus, she will accept the position at Castle Mathe."

"I am glad. It should be as safe for her there as it would be for her here."

The latter having been suggested by Thomasin as a means of protecting Nanne and her son. Though Magnus loved his wife all the more for her willingness to welcome into their home the woman and boy she had felt threatened by, he had rejected the idea. Not only would it be uncomfortable for all, considering Nanne's feelings for Magnus, but he would not have her son and her suffer knowing looks and whisperings from those of Emberly who would recall she had been set out of her home when it was learned she was pregnant. At Castle Mathe, she could maintain she was a widow and her son was fatherless as a result of her husband's passing.

"I am grateful your father has made a place for her in his home," Magnus said.

She laughed. "One good thing to come of being wed to his daughter."

"One of many," he said and felt the weight of Sir Francis's appearance at Kelling lighten.

"But not yet a child." Thomasin glanced at her belly.

Magnus hesitated over talk of children, though not as long as he had done weeks earlier. He yet feared he would pass to sons, perhaps even daughters, what had been passed to him. But Thomasin was convinced that just as they embraced their blessings, together they could embrace and overcome their every trial.

"'Tis early days yet," he said. "And until the Lord unfolds his plans, I shall be content to have you to myself." He drew her into his arms.

"Sage," she breathed. "How I love its scent upon you."

He tilted her chin up. "How I love you, Thomasin."

Her smile was teasing. "Why me?"

Words. Always women wanted words. "Because you are water."

Her eyebrows shot up. "Surely you could liken me to a flower. Water is so plain…tasteless."

He brushed a thumb across her lower lip. "Not this water. It is bright and clear and life-giving. And I would drink from it all the days of my life."

Her eyes widened further. "Oh, that is lovely."

"As are you." He touched his mouth to hers. "My Thomasin."

Excerpt

BARON OF BLACKWOOD

—⊸∞∞⊶—

The Feud: Book Three

1

Barony of Blackwood, Northern England
December 12, 1333

"Have a care, my lady. . You are within range of their arrows."

So she was. But she did not fear them. Only a man not a man would order a bolt loosed upon the defenseless woman come unto his well-defended walls. True, the Baron of Blackwood was surely torn from the same foul cloth as his sire, but no word had she ever heard spoken against his gallantry and few against his valor. Indeed, though it was much exaggeration, some said he was as formidable a warrior as her brother, The Boursier.

As for being a defenseless woman, that was also exaggeration. Quintin Boursier was no fainting flower. She had not been trained up in arms—her mother would not have tolerated it—but she could wield a dagger beyond the capacity to reduce tough boar's meat to edible bites. After all, many were the idle hours in a lady's day.

"Pray, come away," entreated her brother's senior household knight where he had halted his mount alongside hers. "Baron Boursier would not—"

"Nay, he would not, but he is not here, is he?" She narrowed her lids at the immense stone fortress whose crisply white walls evidenced they had been white-washed months earlier. "At least, he is not on this side of the wall."

Sir Victor went silent, but before she could relax into having won the argument, he said, "Tell me what you wish told, and I will ride forth and deliver your words."

Beneath cover of her fur-lined mantle, she squeezed her arms against her sides lest the shiver inside ventured outside, making her appear weak beside the knight seemingly unaffected by the late morning chill though he wore fewer layers of clothes than she.

"I thank you, Sir Victor, but I will myself deliver my demand to the Baron of Blackwood."

His cheeks puffed, breath blew from him, and he shrugged a shoulder. And she knew he was reminded of that of which her departed father had teasingly bemoaned—she would have fared better born a man.

She did not concur, liking very much having been born a woman. Still, at times the limitations of wearing skirts rather than chausses could chafe. And this was one of those times.

She shifted her gaze to Castle Mathe's gatehouse, then the battlements left and right, the openings of which were filled with archers whose nocked arrows were trained on the score of knights and thirty men-at-arms who had reluctantly accompanied their lord's sister to retrieve Bayard Boursier.

Her brother was here. She was certain of it—that the Baron of Blackwood had captured and imprisoned his daughter's betrothed to prevent the wedding two days hence. Thus, for defying the king's decree that the three neighboring families be united through marriage to end their twenty-five-year feud, the lands held by the Boursiers would be declared forfeit.

But that Quintin could not allow. Somehow, she would bring her brother out of Castle Mathe.

She moved a hand from the pommel of her saddle to the pommel at her waist. No meat dagger this. And no ordinary misericorde. She gripped it hard, knowing that were she to draw forth her hand as she had done several times during the chill ride, the impression in her palm would be that of the cross of crucifixion, pressed there by the jewels forming it.

This dagger should not be upon her person, but before the departure from Castle Adderstone this morn, she had gone looking for courage in the form of something better than a meat dagger. From the bottom of her brother's chest, she had drawn forth that which had belonged to their father.

Having received his knighthood training from the Wulfriths of Wulfen Castle, a fortress centuries-renowned for training boys into men, Archard Boursier had been awarded a coveted Wulfrith dagger. And Quintin could not recall a day he had not proudly worn it on his belt. Now she wore it on her girdle.

Sacrilege? Likely. But were her father yet alive, he would forgive her this as he had forgiven her all things.

"Better born a man," she whispered and tapped her heels to her horse's sides.

Sir Victor shouted over his shoulder, commanding the men of the barony of Godsmere to hold, then he followed.

Knowing she could not dissuade him from accompanying her, and not certain she wished to, Quintin picked her gaze embrasure to embrasure in search of the Baron of Blackwood who must surely be upon Castle Mathe's outer wall. As told her, he would be taller and broader than most men. As did not need to be told her, he would not be one of those whose bow was fit with a flesh-and-bone-piercing arrow. Griffin de Arell was a man of the sword.

Without warning shots or shouts, the garrison allowed Sir Victor and her to advance amid the sound of armored men shifting their weight, the breeze whispering of snowfall as it whistled through the brittle grass at the base of the wall, the flapping of the flag that bore high the green and black colors of De Arell, and the piercing cry of a falcon gliding above all.

Not surprisingly, the drawbridge did not let out its chains.

If only Griffin de Arell were a fool, Quintin silently bemoaned. Of course, were he the one she was to wed to end the feud, that would not do. It would be hard enough joined for life to an enemy without also suffering a dullard until death released her from one she could not respect.

Recalling the argument with her brother the day before his disappearance, she grimaced. She had tried to convince him it was better she wed De Arell who already had an heir, but Bayard's choice of the man's daughter for a wife meant Quintin would be bound to a different enemy within the next few months—Magnus Verdun, the Baron of Emberly, also not a fool, but likely full up on himself for as handsome as he was said to be.

Her long sigh misted the air. Her sharply indrawn breath cleared it when Sir Victor snatched hold of her reins and jerked her mount to a halt.

"Near enough, my lady. Far too near."

He was right. They were less than twenty feet from where the upper edge of the drawbridge would settle to the ground were it lowered. And it would be lowered.

Fingers stiff from the cold though her gloves were thick, she tugged to free her reins from the knight's grip.

He held on, raised his eyebrows.

"Aye," she conceded, "near enough."

When he returned control of her mount to her, she raised her gaze up the drawbridge to the roof of the gatehouse and looked from one archer-filled embrasure to the next. Just off center, she stopped on the one she sought. It was no highly-polished armor that revealed him, and certainly no bearing of self importance where he leaned forward as if to look out upon a day that held no challenge though fifty of his enemy were outside his walls. It was instinct that told her here was the Baron of Blackwood. And his eyes that captured hers. And his mouth that, when finally it delivered its expression, presented as a smirk.

Though the hairs across her limbs prickled, she did not avert her gaze, for that was no way to preface demands.

Slowly filling her lungs in hopes he would not notice she sought to breathe in courage the Wulfrith dagger did not sufficiently impart, she drew a hand from beneath her mantle, freed the ties that had cinched the hood about her face during the ride, and pushed the covering down around her shoulders.

Something nearer a true smile, albeit crooked, moved Griffin de Arell's mouth as her jaw-skimming hair celebrated its liberation by dancing in the breeze before her face—the same breeze that moved the baron's dark blond hair back off his face.

For but a moment wishing she did not eschew troublesomely long tresses that would have remained tucked beneath the neck of her mantle, she squelched the impulse to drag the hood back over her head and called, "I am Lady Quintin of the house of Boursier, of the Barony of Godsmere, sister of Baron Boursier."

"Of course you are," the voice of her family's enemy rumbled across the chill air. "Though you are not the one I expected."

It was Bayard who should have ridden on Castle Mathe this day to collect his De Arell bride, but the young woman's father surely knew that was impossible. He but played at ignorance. And not very well, for he had greeted Quintin's entourage with a raised drawbridge and archers ready to loose killing arrows. Hardly the way to welcome the man who was to be his son-in-law. Griffin de Arell was found out and prepared for Boursier wrath to descend.

Returning his skewed smile, she said, "Come now, Baron. Though I be the fairer sex, I am no more fond of silly women's games than you, a warrior, should be."

She could not be certain at this distance, but she thought his smile wavered. And in the next instant determined she could be certain, for she questioned his prowess before all.

"Ho!" he said as if with sudden understanding, though it was surely further mockery. "Your brother has chosen to wed Elianor of Emberly instead of my daughter. And you are the bearer of those tidings that, I confess, could not please me more."

Quintin dug her nails into her palms. "That is not why I am here."

He flashed white teeth. "Then since there must be a marriage between the De Arells and the Boursiers, you deliver yourself. A most eager bride."

Amid the sniggers of his men and the anger rolling between her ears, Sir Victor rasped, "Lady Quintin," his urgent voice prying at the emotion warming her insides as no wood-fed fire could do.

She held her gaze to the man she had told Bayard it was better she wed, and not only because the Baron of Blackwood already had an heir. Because she had wished to spare her brother marriage into the family of his most hated enemy, Bayard having been made a cuckold by Griffin's brother. Of course, Elianor of Emberly was nearly as unsavory, for she was the niece of Bayard's first wife, whom he had found abed with Serle de Arell.

I assure you, Quintin's brother had said, *one Verdun wife was enough to last me unto death.*

She stuck her chin higher, called, "I would put myself through with a blade ere delivering myself unto one such as you."

He lost his smile, gained a frown. Yet she sensed he was more amused than dismayed. "Then difficult as 'tis to believe of the mighty Boursier, one must conclude he has determined it is better to forfeit his lands than wed a wee De Arell lass."

Now, before all, he questioned Bayard's prowess.

Quintin did not realize how quickly her breath came and went until Sir Victor leaned near. "Pray, my lady, let us withdraw so we might discuss the best course."

"This is the only course," she hissed and once more raised her voice up Castle Mathe's walls. "Release my brother, Baron de Arell, else not only will you forfeit your lands when the king learns of your treachery, but your life."

He gave a short laugh. "Then your brother *has* fled."

"He has not. As well you know, he was stolen from his bed. Now release him!"

To her amazement, he lifted toward his mouth what looked to be an apple, paused, and called out, "Forgive me, but your arrival interrupted my dinner." He took a bite.

Realizing how far her jaw had descended, Quintin snapped it up.

Griffin de Arell chewed, nodded. "Were it true I held your brother, Lady Quintin, I might seriously consider releasing him—for you. But, alas, he is not inside my walls."

Ignoring what was only made to sound like flattery, she said, "I would see for myself."

"My word I give you."

Something in his tone tempted her to believe him. But that would require she accept what she dare not—that Bayard might be dead, whether by De Arell's hand or another's.

"Your word I do not trust." Her voice was half choked with fear.

He had raised the apple to take another bite, but he lowered it. "Methinks this bears closer discussion. I shall come out to you, Lady Quintin."

She blinked. Why? Because her voice had revealed vulnerability from which he hoped to benefit? Before she could think how to respond, he went from sight.

"I do not like this, my lady."

She looked around. "We are nearer to retrieving my brother, Sir Victor."

"I am not as certain as you that Baron de Arell holds him."

"All the more reason why we must enter." She pushed her chin in the direction of the drawbridge. "Even if I have to be a woman to his man, I will make a way in." In spite of her less than desirable short hair and, when riled, an inclination to speak as she wished to speak, she knew how to work her wiles. Providing she could hide from Griffin de Arell how much he repulsed her, she would tie a knot in him, loosening it only when he yielded what she sought.

Or so I pray, she sent heavenward, and wished she had not said she would rather put herself through than deliver herself as his bride.

At the sound of her entourage advancing, she snapped her chin around. Realizing Sir Victor had signaled them forward, she said, "Send them back." Not only might they turn De Arell from coming outside his walls, but they could prove too tempting a target for the archers.

Sir Victor shook his head. "Ere long, I may once more answer to your brother, and that day I fear more than this."

"But—"

The drawbridge chains let out, and she caught her breath in anticipation of the great planked beast grinding to a halt before returning to its upright position.

It did not, though Godsmere's knights and men-at-arms drew rein directly behind her.

The top of the portcullis came into view, and beyond its crossed iron bars she saw the buildings in the outer bailey, next the garrison. But it was the blond head and broad shoulders of the man striding—not riding—past the others that captured her regard.

Surely he did not intend to leave the protection of his walls on foot? But as the drawbridge so heavily thumped to the ground she felt it through her horse, Griffin de Arell halted before the portcullis and it began to rise. When it was at waist level, he did not duck beneath it so it might sooner lower and secure the castle entrance. And even when it was high enough that his head easily cleared and he strode forward, it did not drop.

He was that confident. But then, his archers still had Godsmere's men sighted down their arrows.

As the baron advanced, his eyes—were they the same intense blue as his brother's?—moved over Quintin's entourage, and she knew he measured Godsmere's men against the risk he took.

If he wore chain mail, and surely he must, she could not detect the metallic ring, nor the flash of silver links as she moved her gaze down his black mantle that parted with each stride. All she glimpsed was a dark green tunic above black boots.

He was a bigger man than his brother, Serle, but not of fat—of large bones and thick muscles like Bayard. And the nearer he came, the more she begrudged the appeal of his face, though its weathered skin and several day's growth of beard made him appear older than the thirty and four years she understood him to be. Too rough-hewn to be called handsome, but still attractive, this man whose half-noble daughter, Thomasin, was to have been Bayard's wife.

"Is to be," she whispered as her heart lurched over the terrible slip of the mind. Bayard was at Castle Mathe and would wed before the deadline to preserve his family's lands.

Lord, let him be here and hale, she silently pleaded.

The Baron of Blackwood halted before the drawbridge's threshold, less than twenty feet from his uninvited guests, and it was then she saw he still held the apple. And it looked to be more than half eaten, as if his crossing from the gatehouse roof to the drawbridge had been but a leisurely stroll.

But if that was so, it was no more. He stared hard at Sir Victor out of eyes that were, indeed, blue. Then he moved them to her.

She held steady, noting that the miserly sunlight reaching through the sparse gaps in the clouds ran its fingers through the hair at his crown that was lighter than that below, a sure sign he was often out of doors.

"You may approach, Lady Quintin," he startled her out of her reverie.

Resenting the warmth flushing her cold cheeks, hoping it was not as visible as it was felt, she urged her mount forward and Sir Victor followed.

One side of Griffin de Arell's mouth lifted, and he said dryly, "And you as well, Sir...Victor, is it not?"

Quintin was taken aback that he was familiar with the knight, but since Bayard knew the names of De Arell's and Verdun's most esteemed warriors, it followed this man knew those of Godsmere.

"It is," Sir Victor said, and at five feet from the drawbridge halted his mount.

Quintin did the same, glad to be no nearer her enemy, his regard intense enough. Further glad that just as he did not mirror his brother's slighter figure, neither did his features—excepting the color of his eyes, a remarkable blue that dragged her back years to when she had hurtled herself between Serle de Arell and Bayard.

"So you believe I hold your brother, that I seek to deny him my daughter and, thereby, cause him to forfeit," Griffin de Arell jolted her back to the present where she found the hand beneath her mantle turned into a fist she pressed to her lower abdomen.

Swallowing bile, she returned her hand to the Wulfrith dagger and breathed deep. "I do. Unfortunately, as evidenced by the history between our families, the word you give holds no meaning for the Boursiers."

"I grant that."

He did? She moistened her lips, and his gaze flicked to them—as expected. "Thus, I require proof. I would enter your walls to myself determine if you hold the Baron of Godsmere."

His lids narrowed, brow grooved—hopefully, signs he seriously considered what she asked of him.

"If 'tis true you do not hold him," she pressed, "you can have no objection, Baron de Arell."

"I can. And I do. However…" He looked to Sir Victor. "That I might prove your lord is not within my walls, and afterward invite your lady to my table, you would entrust her to me?"

"I would not!" It was barked with more indignation than Quintin could remember having heard from the self-possessed knight. "Where she goes, I go, accompanied by a sufficient number of Godsmere men to defend her if need be."

"It need not be. Should I honor Lady Quintin's request and she observes the rules, she will depart Castle Mathe the same as she entered it."

The rules? Quintin pondered.

"As my lady has clearly expressed, your word carries no weight with the Boursiers—or those who serve them."

The baron exhaled a misted breath that drifted toward Quintin and dissipated. "For your sake, I did try, my lady. But it appears we are at a place from which neither party can be moved."

"We are not." She urged her mount forward, heard Sir Victor curse beneath his breath, felt his arm brush hers. But too late he caught her reins. Her horse's muzzle was now but a step from Baron de Arell, and the man did not look at all concerned.

"A dozen escort," she asked for more than was needed to allow for negotiation that would return to him the control such men required. "Allow me a dozen, and we can move from this place."

He peered up at her, and she nearly winced at the perceived advantage she had over him that could not possibly sit well. But then he stepped forward. And out of the corner of her eye, she saw the knight at her side close his hand around his sword hilt. And knew those behind did the same.

"Do not, Sir Victor," Baron de Arell growled, once more causing the hairs across her limbs to stand to attention, then he glanced at his archers on the wall. "At such close range, those arrows easily pierce armor."

And she was to fault for that. When her brother's knight slid his gaze to her, she shook her head. He did not draw his sword, but neither did he remove his hand from it.

The Baron of Blackwood raised his own hands to show they were empty save for the half-eaten apple, then he parted his mantle to reveal he wore no chain mail beneath his tunic. There was, however, a great sword on his belt. "Precaution only," he said. "No harm do I intend your lady." Then he let the mantle resettle around him and gripped the bridle of Quintin's horse.

Dry-mouthed, she stared at the man whose size made her mount seem almost diminutive.

"A fine horse." Eyes that had been flint-hard once more gleamed with amusement. "Though methinks too tame for a Boursier."

She agreed, having pressed Bayard for a steed, and for a moment felt kindly toward the baron.

Fool, she silently rebuked. Were she the one to wed into the De Arells, this man would not gift her a worthy mount. As his wife, a mare would remain her lot. He simply baited her.

He fed the remains of his apple to her horse, patted the animal's jaw, and said, "Six men."

Though certain that would be enough, he must be made to feel she wanted more so his win would seem all the sweeter. "Ten, Baron de Arell."

"Six."

"Eight."

He released her mare's bridle and turned.

"Six!" she blurted, much to her disgust.

"My lady!"

Ignoring Sir Victor's protest that was answered by other Godsmere knights and men-at-arms, she met Griffin de Arell's gaze when he came back around.

"Choose whomever you wish," he said.

Quintin looked to her brother's knight. "I leave it to you."

His mouth crimped, but after raising his eyes heavenward, he summoned five of Godsmere's best men to join him in accompanying her.

Wishing her personal guard was among them—Rollo, who had been called home to tend his ailing mother—she gripped the Wulfrith dagger harder. If Sir Victor and the other knights could not keep her safe, she would see to it herself.

She guided her horse onto the drawbridge alongside Sir Victor, and when she drew even with the Baron of Blackwood, he turned and walked beside her.

"Methinks we are both pleased with our compromise," he said, and when she shot her gaze to him, he added, "though I would have allowed you a dozen men if required to assuage your fear."

"Fear?" she scoffed, and wished she had not, her distaste doing nothing to further the wiles she sought to work upon him.

As they neared the portcullis, she looked up at the archers. "For one who expected his future son-in-law, you make an unconvincing show of welcome."

"None was intended."

She frowned.

"I knew it was not Baron Boursier who rode on Castle Mathe, my lady."

"How did you so soon come by that?"

He did not answer until they entered the outer bailey. "I would think that obvious. Just as I am easily picked from among my men, so is your brother who is not only identified by his size but his red hair. Too, though I would have Baron Boursier so fear me that he would deem it necessary to bring such a great number of armed men to his wedding, he does not."

It *was* obvious, and she blamed a near sleepless night for a mind usually more clever.

Once her men were inside the outer bailey, the portcullis was lowered, cutting them off from the greater body of Godsmere men.

"You will leave your mounts here," Griffin de Arell announced to his *guests,* then reached up and closed a hand over Quintin's reins—and her gloved fingers that held them.

Though it was not flesh to flesh contact, a peculiar sensation moved through her, so warm...so languorous...so deep she did not attempt to correct his trespass, though she knew she should. And she met his gaze though she knew she should not.

"I thought so," he said low, eyes a darker blue than they had appeared outside the walls.

And still she could not bring herself to spurn his touch, though he in no way prevented her from doing so.

Drawing a thumb across her knuckles, he said, "Yet another reason I would not have my daughter wed your brother."

She stopped her breath. Did he infer the marriage between the houses of De Arell and Boursier be made, instead, through himself and her? Had her wiles worked that quickly? That well? Or was she the one who had fallen victim to them?

That last freeing her from whatever hold he had on her, she jerked her fingers from beneath his, twisted opposite, and dismounted from the wrong side. The mare did not like it, whinnying and sidestepping so sharply that had Baron de Arell not swiftly brought the horse under control, she might have trod upon her mistress.

But Quintin would not thank Griffin de Arell who was the cause of her unseemly dismount.

As she tugged her mantle into place, ignoring the curious looks angled at her by the men of Godsmere as well as Blackwood, the baron came around the mare.

"It seems I overestimated your ability to handle a horse," he said. "Indeed, this one may not be tame enough."

Closing her hands into fists, she said, "I await proof my brother is not at Castle Mathe."

He passed the mare into the care of a lad who stepped forward, then ran his gaze down Quintin. "And so you shall have it, my lady. Let us begin here."

For new releases and special promotions, subscribe to
Tamara Leigh's mailing list: www.tamaraleigh.com

ABOUT THE AUTHOR

Tamara Leigh holds a Master's Degree in Speech and Language Pathology. In 1993, she signed a 4-book contract with Bantam Books. Her first medieval romance, *Warrior Bride*, was released in 1994. Continuing to write for the general market, three more novels were published with HarperCollins and Dorchester and earned awards and spots on national bestseller lists.

In 2006, Tamara's first inspirational contemporary romance, *Stealing Adda*, was released. In 2008, *Perfecting Kate* was optioned for a movie and *Splitting Harriet* won an ACFW "Book of the Year" award. The following year, *Faking Grace* was nominated for a RITA award. In 2011, Tamara wrapped up her "Southern Discomfort" series with the release of *Restless in Carolina*.

When not in the middle of being a wife, mother, and cookbook fiend, Tamara buries her nose in a good book—and her writer's pen in ink. In 2012, she returned to the historical romance genre with *Dreamspell*, a medieval time travel romance. Shortly thereafter, she once more invited readers to join her in the middle ages with the *Age of Faith* series: *The Unveiling, The Yielding, The Redeeming, The Kindling,* and *The Longing*. Tamara's #1 Bestsellers—*Lady at Arms, Lady Of Eve, Lady Of Fire,* and *Lady Of Conquest*—are the first of her medieval romances to be rewritten as "clean reads." Look for *Baron Of Blackwood,* the third book in *The Feud* series, in 2016.

Tamara lives near Nashville with her husband, sons, a Doberman that bares its teeth not only to threaten the UPS man but to smile, and a feisty Morkie that keeps her company during long writing stints.

Connect with Tamara at her website www.tamaraleigh.com, her blog The Kitchen Novelist, her email tamaraleightenn@gmail.com, Facebook, and Twitter.

For new releases and special promotions, subscribe to Tamara Leigh's mailing list: www.tamaraleigh.com

Made in the USA
Columbia, SC
12 January 2018